A WORLD TO WIN I.

TIMELINE

World's End	1913 - 1919
Between Two Worlds	1919 - 1929
Dragon's Teeth	1929 - 1934
Wide is the Gate	1934 - 1937
Presidential Agent	1937 - 1938
Dragon Harvest	1938 - 1940
A World to Win	1940 - 1942
Presidential Mission	1942 - 1943
One Clear Call	1943 - 1944
O Shepherd, Speak!	1943 - 1946
The Return of Lanny Budd	1946 - 1949

Each book is published in two parts: I and II.

A WORLD TO WIN I.

Upton Sinclair

Simon Publications

2001

LCCN: 46003965

ISBN: 1-931313-07-5

Distributed by Ingram Book Com pany

Printed by Light ning Source Inc., LaVergne, TN

Pub lished by Si mon Pub li ca tions, P.O. Box 321 Safety Har bor, FL

An Author's Program

From a 1943 article by Upton Sinclair.

When I say "historian," I have a meaning of my own. I portray world events in story form, because that form is the one I have been trained in. I have supported myself by writing fiction since the age of sixteen, which means for forty-nine years.

... Now I realize that this one was the one job for which I had been born: to put the period of world wars and revolutions into a great long novel. ...

I can not say when it will end, because I don't know exactly what the characters will do. They lead a semi-independent life, being more real to me than any of the people I know, with the single exception of my wife. ... Some of my characters are people who lived, and whom I had opportunity to know and watch. Others are imaginary—or rather, they are complexes of many people whom I have known and watched. Lanny Budd and his mother and father and their various relatives and friends have come in the course of the past four years to be my daily and nightly companions. I have come to know them so intimately that I need only to ask them what they would do in a given set of circumstances and they start to enact their roles. ... I chose what seems to me the most revealing of them and of their world.

How long will this go on? I can not tell. It depends in great part upon two public figures, Hitler and Mussolini. What are they going to do to mankind and what is mankind will do to them? It seems to me hardly likely that either will die a peaceful death. I am hoping to outlive them; and whatever happens Lanny Budd will be somewhere in the neighborhood, he will be "in at the death," according to the fox-hunting phrase.

These two foxes are my quarry, and I hope to hang their brushes over my mantel.

Author's Notes

In the course of this novel a number of well-known persons make their appearance, some of them living, some dead; they appear under their own names, and what is said about them is factually correct.

There are other characters which are fictitious, and in these cases the author has gone out of his way to avoid seeming to point at real persons. He has given them unlikely names, and hopes that no person bearing such names exist. But it is impossible to make sure; therefore the writer states that, if any such coincidence occurs, it is accidental. This is not the customary "hedge clause" which the author of a *roman à clef* publishes for legal protection; it means what it says and it is intended to be so taken.

Various European concerns engaged in the manufacture of munitions have been named in the story, and what has been said about them is also according to the records. There is one American firm, and that, with all its affairs, is imaginary. The writer has done his best to avoid seeming to indicate any actual American firm or family.

...Of course there will be slips, as I know from experience; but *World's End* is meant to be a history as well as fiction, and I am sure there are no mistakes of importance. I have my own point of view, but I have tried to play fair in this book. There is a varied cast of characters and they say as they think. ...

The Peace Conference of Paris [*for example*], which is the scene of the last third of *World's End*, is of course one of the greatest events of all time. A friend on mine asked an authority on modern fiction a question: "Has anybody ever used the Peace Conference in a novel?" And the reply was: "Could anybody?" Well, I thought somebody could, and now I think somebody has. The reader will ask, and I state explicitly that so far as concerns historic characters and events my picture is correct in all details. This part of the manuscript, 374 pages, was read and checked by eight or ten gentlemen who were on the American staff at the Conference. Several of these hold important positions in the world of troubled international affairs; others are college presidents and professors, and I promised them all that their letters will be confidential. Suffice it to say that the errors they pointed out were corrected, and where they disagreed, both sides have a word in the book.

Contents:

BOOK ONE

The Pelting of This Pitiless Storm

———————————— o ————————————

1. The Hurt That Honor Feels

I

LANNY kept thinking: This must be the only man in France who can smile. At least it was the only one Lanny had met, and Lanny had done some traveling in this time of agony and grief. The man whose name spelled backward the same as forward, and who all his life had taken this as an omen of good luck—this man was in power again; he was overcoming all his enemies, thousands of them, yes, even millions. He sat at his desk by the window of what had once been a luxurious hotel suite, and beamed upon his visitor, reminding him: "It has happened just about as I told you, M. Budd." Lanny said it was so, and thought that the death of something like a hundred and twenty-five thousand Frenchmen, and the captivity of ten or twelve times as many, signified less to Pierre Laval than the ability to say: "*C'est moi qui avait raison!*"

It was midsummer of the year 1940, and a hot wind was blowing from the deserts of Africa over the plains of Central France. The French are never prone to open windows, and the Vice-Premier was shut tightly in his overdecorated office. He made no concession to summer fashions, but wore his customary black suit and the white bow tie which had become his trademark in French politics. He mopped his swarthy forehead as he talked, and now and then passed the damp handkerchief around his neck; elegance had never been his role, and the fact that he had amassed one or two hundred million francs made no difference. Now and then he chewed on his thick black mustache, and when he smoked his cigarette too low, Lanny feared that the fire might reach this adornment. Laval had odd slanting eyes, and his enemies called him *le fripon mongol;* the "rascal" part of this was undoubtedly true, and the other half might have been—who could say?

Ordinarily he was a free talker, but now he chose to listen, for his caller had just come down from Paris, and had talked there with the Führer of the conquering Germans. Laval was in touch with Paris, getting his orders, more or less politely disguised; also, there were German representatives here in Vichy, making no secret of their authority. But one who knew the Nazi leaders personally, and chatted with them socially, might pick up hints that could be got in no other way. An American was supposed to be a neutral, a friend of both sides; so the Mongolian rascal put one question after another and listened attentively. What were Hitler's real intentions toward *la patrie?* What would they be when Britain had quit? To what extent would he leave the control of French business in French hands? And what would be his attitude toward the Fleet? Delicate questions, which a statesman did not ask except from one he trusted.

And Britain? Lanny had been there just before Dunkirk, less than two months ago. What did the true friends of France in that country think about the present deplorable situation? What chance did they have to advocate their cause? Pierre Laval hated England with a bitterness which had now become a sort of mania, but he would be careful about giving voice to his feelings in the presence of an Anglo-Saxon. He would listen while Lanny talked about his "appeaser" friends, the extreme difficulties they now faced, and the work they were doing, quietly and yet effectively, to bring this blind meaningless struggle to an end.

"I don't suppose there is any more need for secrecy," said the friend of all good Europeans. "I carried a message from the Maréchal to Lord Wickthorpe; but I found that it was too late."

"Have you seen the Maréchal here?" inquired the other.

"No, *cher Maître.* It was Baron Schneider's suggestion that I should consult you first." *Cher Maître* is the way you address a French lawyer when you are a colleague or an important client; from Lanny Budd it was a delicate reminder of their last meeting, in the home of Denis de Bruyne, an old-time fellow-conspirator of Laval's. It meant that Lanny had lived in France and understood nuances, a word invented by a people who live by them. The butcher's son who had once been head of the nation would know that this was the son of a great airplane manufacturer, and the former husband of one of the richest women in America. Lanny Budd, a friend of the great, knew how to deal with them, flattering them, teasing them now and then, above all never failing to entertain them.

Presently the Vice-Premier inquired: "Where are you staying?"

"I haven't looked up a place," was the reply. "I checked my bags at the *gare*."

"You may have trouble, because this town is packed to the last attic and cellar."

"So I have been told; but I thought more of France than of my own comfort. You know, your country has been my home since I was a babe in arms."

"Perhaps you had better come out and spend the night at my place. In the morning I will see what can be done for you."

"You are very kind, *cher Maître*."

"Not at all; I want more talk with you." But Lanny knew that an honor was being done him, for the French rarely open their homes to strangers—and especially not when a million or two have come staggering into your peaceful province, and your gates are besieged by a horde of people, starving and many of them wounded, craving no more than to share the shelter you give to your horses and cattle; and convinced that they have some claim upon you because you are a friend of the people, and they have attended your public meetings, joined your party, voted for you, and worked for your election to the *Chambre*.

II

It was the Bourbonnais province, almost in the geographical center of France. Fourteen miles from Vichy lies the village of Châteldon, where Pierre Laval had been born. His father had been the village butcher, tavernkeeper, and postmaster—which of these you heard mentioned depended upon whether it was an enemy or a dependent of the great man who spoke. The lad had been put to work early, driving to the railroad to fetch the mail; apparently it was not locked up, for while the old nag jogged along, the driver read the newspapers, and so learned about politics in his native land and what the great Napoleon had called "the career open to talents."

Little Pierre had had talents, and had convinced his father and got an education. He had become the most rascally lawyer in France, and had come back a multimillionaire and bought the ancient castle which dominated the place of his birth. Also the mineral springs, whose water Madame de Sévigné had held superior to the water of Vichy. Pierre had known how to exploit that fact, and how to get the water on sale in the restaurant cars of his country's railroads. One of his fortunes had come from it; and sitting at cushioned ease in his shiny black Mercedes he forgot his country's troubles for a while and told funny stories about those early days—stories not always to his credit, but he didn't mind, provided that he had come out ahead on the deal.

The village has two rivers flowing through it, and high mountains surrounding it. The medieval castle has a round tower and a square tower, and the cottages and smaller houses are gathered close around it for protection, like chicks about a mother hen. The visitor's first impression was that it was neither very elegant nor very sanitary; but then, he reflected, neither was its owner.

The residence was the manor house, and when Lanny went inside he perceived that this had been remodeled to fit it for a great gentleman's residence. Before dinner he was taken in his role of art expert to see the murals in the castle. Over the immense mantelpiece in the dining-room hung a painting representing the defeat of the English troops in the battle of Auvergne during the Hundred Years' War. It was by a painter of the so-called Fontainebleau School; Lanny had never heard his name, but naturally he wasn't going to say this to the proud *propriétaire*. He praised the school, saying that its contribution to the art of historical representation was coming to be more and more appreciated. This pleased Pierre greatly; he said that whenever he found himself discouraged by the present international situation he came into this old banquet hall and read the inscription beneath the mass of charging horses and men-at-arms. It was in Gothic lettering, and told the lord of Châteldon that "Here the English were so well received that they never returned."

"God damn that bastard Churchill!" exclaimed Pierre Laval; and Lanny Budd politely agreed that he was a curmudgeonly character.

III

Madame Laval had been the daughter of the village doctor, and had risen as high as possible in her land. Like a sensible Frenchwoman she had stuck by her man in spite of his many forms of misconduct. They had had a daughter, with the black hair, olive skin, and slanting eyes of her father. He had been wont to exhibit her in the law courts and the Palais Bourbon, to show his fellow-deputies what a devoted family man he was. In due course it had become necessary to find her a husband, and Pierre had selected René, Comte de Chambrun, son of a French general and lineal descendant of the Marquis de Lafayette. One does not get a son-in-law like that without paying, and Pierre had put up a *dot* which was written in eight figures and had been whispered with awe all over the land. If anyone forgot it, Pierre would whisper it again.

They sat at the family dinner table. René was an international lawyer and his father-in-law's faithful errand boy; Lanny thought: He looks like a jumping jockey. José—pronounced French fashion, with a soft "j" and the "s" as "z"—was the most elegant lady in smart society. Both of them had met the son of Budd-Erling, and found him acceptable. His tropical worsted suit had been cut by the best tailor and everything about him was in harmony. He was to be forty in about three months, but his wavy brown hair showed no trace of gray. His neatly clipped little mustache looked like a movie star's, and his amiable smile suggested to the ladies that he was a person of kindness, and without guile. This last, unfortunately, was not entirely true.

The ladies questioned him eagerly about what had become of this person and that—one's friends were so scattered in these dreadful days, and it was all but impossible to communicate with them, on account of censors and submarines. But all the members of this snug little family were certain that the storm would blow over soon, and Europe would settle down to the longest period of peace it had ever known. The British would realize the futility of further resistance—and what more could they ask than the assurance that Hitler held out to them, that he had no slightest desire to interfere with or threaten the British Empire? .

They wanted to know what their guest thought; and Lanny spoke according to his role of art expert who did not meddle in politics, and who so far had been able to travel where he wished. Naturally his friends told him what they thought, and what they wished to have reported, and he reported it, though without guaranteeing it. What he reported concerning England was that Churchill's position was strong at present, but there was quiet opposition growing among influential persons, and perhaps after London had been bombed a few times they would be able to make headway.

The *père de famille* said that it had been the prime task of French statesmanship to keep Paris from sharing the fate of Warsaw and Rotterdam, and in that, at least, they had been victorious. Madame added, piously: *"Grâce à dieu!"*—and then added her opinion as to the source of all the trouble, that there were too many foreigners in her country, and especially Jews. Lanny agreed politely, in his secret heart recalling that one of the ladies with whom her husband's name had been connected through the years had been of Gypsy descent, while another had been a daughter of the wealthy family named Goldsky.

But it was Jewish men they were thinking about now: Blum and Mandel, that accursed pair who had been fighting Pierre Laval ever since he had deserted the working-class movement that had elected him to the Chamber of Deputies. They it was who had forced the ruinous alliance with Russia, which had made friendship with Germany impossible; they it was who had almost succeeded in dragging France to aid the Reds in seizing Spain. They were a traitor pair, and Pierre declared that every power he possessed would be used to have them tried and hanged by the neck. The cords in his own thick neck stood out as he denounced them, and his swarthy face turned crimson. So many enemies he had, and once he had been able to laugh at them and even with them; but now rage was coming to possess him more and more. It spoiled his dinner, and made his conversation repulsive.

Alone in his study with the visitor, he made it evident that he did not give much credence to Lanny's role as a non-political friend of man. He knew that Lanny had traveled to England on a mission—how could one travel otherwise in these days? Marshal Pétain had sent him, and Madame de Portes, mistress of the then Premier, Paul Reynaud. She had recently been killed in a motor accident, so Pierre couldn't find out from her. Lanny assured his host it was no longer especially important—just one more effort to persuade the British to join with the French in making peace; their position would obviously have been much stronger if they had stood together. Even now it would be stronger, for France had as yet no peace, only an armistice, and it was costing her four hundred million francs per day for the upkeep of the German Army which would have to stay so long as Britain fought. The Germans were using a great part of this sum to buy their way into the key industries of the country, and that would ruin any nation, lamented this lover of money. Lanny agreed, and tactfully refrained from hinting what he had been told by some of his Nazi friends in Paris, that Pierre Laval was handling some of these deals and taking a generous "cut."

And then the old Maréchal. No serpent ever slipped into its hole more silently than Pierre Laval trying to slip into the mind of Lanny Budd and find out why he wanted to see the head of the French State and what he was going to say to that venerable warrior. Lanny was all innocence; the Maréchal was a friend, Lanny's father had known him since World War I and before that, and as salesman for Budd Gunmakers had tried to persuade him that America had a better light machine gun than France. Now the Maréchal had asked Lanny to try to bring Britain into the armistice, and Lanny had failed, and wanted to tell the old gentleman how sorry he was.

Tactfully the host imparted the fact that when a man is eighty-four years of age his mind is not so active, he tires easily, his memory fails, and he needs guidance. The Maréchal had around him a horde of self-seekers, all trying to pull him in different directions. They played upon his pride in France and his memories of French glory; it was hard for him to face the fact that France was beaten, and that her future was in German hands, and nowhere else. "We cannot have it two ways," declared this black serpent with a white necktie. "If we are going to be friends we have to mean it and act accordingly." When the visitor said, "I agree with you wholeheartedly," Pierre went on to suggest that Lanny Budd should advise his aged friend to declare war upon Britain, and to turn over to the Germans the remainder of that French Fleet which the British had just attacked with shameless treachery in the ports of North Africa.

Lanny said: "*Cher Maître*, I do not imagine that the chief of your government will ask the advice of an art expert as to state policy; but if he does I will surely tell him that I am a lover of peace and order, and that I think Herr Hitler has discovered the formula by which the spread of Bolshevism over Europe can be checked."

"I perceive that you are a man both wise and tactful, M. Budd," replied the host. "You may do me a favor if you will visit Châteldon again and tell me whatever you can about your interview with the old gentleman. Let me add that I know your social position, and respect it, but at the same time I know what the world is, and that one has to live in it, and if there is any reward within my gift you have only to call upon me."

Lanny smiled. "Herr Hitler has several times made me the same tactful offer, and so has Reichsmarschall Göring. I tell them all that my profession of art expert has always provided for me. I don't need large sums."

"Money is not to be treated lightly," countered the master of Châteldon. "It is like toilet paper, when you need it you need it bad."

I V

Lanny slept well, and in the morning breakfasted on coffee and eggs and marmalade, all of them luxuries in wartime France. Driving back to town, he answered more questions of his host, and did not mind, because he could learn from a man's questions what the man wanted to know, what he hoped and what he feared and what tricks he was up to. When the two parted, Lanny knew of a certainty that Pierre Laval hated the venerable old soldier who was his chief, was counting the weeks or months that he might be expected to live, and was busily intriguing with the Nazis to be permitted to take his place.

The trouble was that the Nazis needed Pétain, or thought they did, to keep the French people quiet. Pétain was the hero of Verdun, whose picture was in every peasant's hut, whereas it was hard to find anyone who would trust Laval around the corner. Laval was all for doing whatever the Nazis demanded; he argued vehemently to Lanny that when you had once chosen sides you could no longer remain on both sides—as the ancient figurehead was trying to do. Pétain wouldn't let the Nazis have the French Fleet, or the air force in Africa, or the troops in Syria; he clung to these things as the last pawns in a lost game; he promised this and that, and then delayed to keep the promise, and argued over petty details in his stubborn dotard's way, and not even the shrewd Vice-Premier could be sure whether it was stupidity or malice.

Laval had arranged for the American to have a room in one of the cheaper hotels, the better ones having been taken over by the different government departments. It meant that somebody was turned out, but Lanny wasn't told who and didn't inquire. He deposited his bags and then went for a stroll, to take in the sights of this small resort city which had become overnight a sort of left-handed world capital. It lies in the broad valley of the river Allier, and its warm baths and mineral waters have been famous since the days of the ancient Romans. They were full of bubbling gases which made them seem alive, and whether this helped your stomach or not, you believed that it did, and that could help you immensely.

In modern days the wealthy had flocked here, and there had been built for them the magnificent Hotel du Parc, surrounded with plane trees; its five stories and broad tower were now crowded by offices of the new government. There were baths all over the place; one of them, the Thermal Établissement, covering seven acres, could take care of thirty-five hundred persons per day; you could float over red marble, or green marble, or mosaic tiles, and later you could stroll in palm-shaded porticoes and chat with your fashionable friends. There was every kind of luxury to be had for a price; the poor clamored for a hunk of tasteless gray bread, but for the wealthy there were still the dainty little brown cubes and the *croissants* to which they were accustomed. The jewelry shops did a land-office business, both buying and selling; for jewels are the most easily hidden and transported form of wealth—in an extreme emergency they can even be swallowed.

Lanny Budd was an art expert, and wherever he went he renewed his acquaintance with the dealers, and made inquiries concerning private collections. This was not merely the way he earned his living, it was also his camouflage; he had always in his suitcase a file of correspondence, and when it was opened and inspected in his absence—something which happened now in every country of Europe—the most suspicious police spy would be satisfied that the visitor was really the friend of American millionaires and the possible means of bringing real dollars into the poverty-stricken land.

You could never know in what part of France you might find an art treasure. In the dingy ancient mansions which were scattered about this countryside there might be some old work whose value the owner did not realize; or there might be some modern master who had fled from the Nazi tanks and bombing planes, and now was glad to exchange a painting for a loaf of the adulterated gray bread. Lanny strolled into the fashionable dealers' shops and introduced himself, and looked at what they had to show him and listened to their sales talks. His mind was a card catalog of personalities in "The States" to whom these sights and sounds might or might not appeal, and now and then he would ask a price and shake his head and say that it was much too high.

V

In one of the sidewalk cafés the visitor ordered an omelet and a salad, and while waiting he watched the few rich and the many poor who thronged the sidewalk. There were several million refugees in Vichy France, and as many discharged soldiers who had no place to go and nothing to do; many had no shelter but the trees in the park, and no food but what they could beg or steal. The son of Budd-Erling had been born into the leisure class, and had had to learn to eat his food and digest it, in spite of knowing that there were swarms of people about him who had poor food or none at all. He had been taught that it was their own fault; and anyhow, it had been that way through the ages and would be for ages to come and there was nothing you could do about it. Lanny no longer held that idea, and was trying to do something, after a fashion peculiar to himself.

Now and then he looked at his wristwatch; and presently, having paid his *addition*, he arose and strolled on. In Paris he had received a letter signed Bruges, telling him of an excellent collection of Daumier drawings which were for sale in Vichy, and adding that the writer of the letter could be seen at the Santé baths at two o'clock any afternoon. Lanny approached the place, but did not go inside; he strolled on the other side of the street at the hour named, and presently he saw, passing the baths, a dark-haired slender man wearing the dungarees and blouse of a peasant of this district. Lanny made sure that the man had seen him, and then he strolled on; out of town, along the banks of the blue Allier which flows through this fertile land, northward until it joins the Loire. Under the shadow of a willow tree he stopped, and the other man joined him and they clasped hands. "*Eh, bien*, Lanny!" and "*Eh, bien*, Raoul! How did you manage to get a letter through to Paris?"

"We have our ways," smiled the younger man, a Spaniard who had lived a full half of his life in France. He had delicately carved features and an ascetic face, as if he had not had a real meal for a long time; but when he met Lanny Budd he was so happy that the blood returned to his cheeks and he flashed a fine set of nature's own white teeth.

"I was worried about you," Lanny said. "Can you be safe in this nest of intrigue?"

"I have papers; they aren't genuine, but I'm all right unless the police should take my fingerprints, and I'll do my best not to get in their way."

"You know the terms of the armistice, Raoul. The French must surrender on demand anyone whom the Nazis want, and so long as Laval holds power they will do it."

"I know; but I have a job with a family who can be trusted. You won't want me to talk about it."

"Of course not. Your letter said Daumier, and I suppose that means leftwing politics. What have you to tell me?"

"We have a small center of activity here, and I think it will spread. I need a little money, but mostly I want your advice, what our line should be. Everybody is bewildered, and the main task is to keep them from despair."

"I know, Raoul, it's awful. I have a hard time myself."

"What hope can I hold out to anybody?"

"Britain is going to go on fighting; that I am sure of. The appeasers there have all had to crawl into their holes."

"But how long can Britain hold out against the entire Continent?"

"Hitler has told me that he means to invade, and I think he means it. But I think the Fleet will stop him."

"But the air, Lanny! He will bomb all the cities to rubble."

"He will if he can. Nobody can guess how it will turn out. But this I am sure of, Britain will not quit."

"And America?"

"We will send what help we can without getting into the war. That is the plan at present. How we'd behave if we saw Britain on the ropes I don't know. Public opinion over there is changing fast, but whether it will be fast enough, who can say?"

"And what can the French workers do, Lanny?"

"First, you have to give up the class struggle; forget it absolutely. There's only one enemy now, and that is Hitler. Churchill has to be your friend, no matter how little you like him."

"That's pretty hard doctrine for my comrades, Lanny."

"I know; but it's the fact, and every one of us has to face it."

"After what the British did to our Fleet!"

"What else could they do? They gave the French the choice, to be interned, or to go to America, or else to be knocked out."

"I know; but to the average Frenchman it seemed like a massacre."

"We can't appeal to the average Frenchman; we have to reach the exceptional ones, who understand what the enemy is and how many tricks he has. The Nazis want us to hate the British, because Britain is the last bulwark against them; and that tells us what to do. If Hitler can get the use of what is left of the French Fleet he can control the

Mediterranean, and take the Suez Canal and the oil of Mesopotamia. That is where the fight is going, and where we have to help."

"You would advise me to go to Toulon?"

"If you can get any contacts with the sailors, or with the workers in the dockyards and the arsenal—yes."

Raoul Palma, for nearly two decades the director of a workers' school in Cannes, could think of one-time students in almost every corner of the Midi. Many had been taken into the army, and their fate was unknown to him. Some had turned Communist, and were now describing this as "an imperialist war." Some had prospered, and were no longer keen about the cause of the dispossessed. Their ex-teacher sat beneath the grateful shade of a willow tree and wrinkled his brow in thought; presently he said: "I suppose I could manage it, Lanny. Toulon will be a carefully guarded place, and I'll have to go slow."

"Do what you can, and remember this: the Nazis may have the power to seize the Fleet, but they haven't the personnel to operate it. They would need a year or two to train Germans to use all that complicated machinery, and it is there that our hope lies. Right now the struggle in Vichy is between Laval's gang, who want to go all out with Hitler, and Pétain and his friends, who want to keep a partially independent France. I spent last night in Laval's home, so I can give you the straight dope; but you understand, you can't give any hint how you got it."

"I'll suggest a servant as my source."

"That would go all right. The situation is well known here, and will probably come to a head before long. Either the Nazis will oust Pétain and put in Laval, or Pétain will grow sick of intrigue and treachery and bounce the rascal out on his ear. I have been interested to observe that defeat hasn't changed the French politicians in the slightest; they are still pulling wires and wrangling; it is still every man against all the rest, and very little of friendship or even party loyalty."

VI

This was no new role that Lanny Budd was playing. Ever since he had met this young Spanish refugee working in a shoestore in Cannes, and had helped to set him up as director of the workers' school in an abandoned warehouse with a leaky roof, Lanny had been serving as an unsalaried secret agent, watching the activities of his own class, and bringing items of political and financial information which Raoul would put into unsigned articles for the Socialist and labor press of France. Lanny had been doing the same for his friend Rick, the leftwing journalist in England, and through the years he had had the satisfaction of seeing the workers' movements coming to an ever clearer understanding of the strategy and tactics of their opponents. Of late years he had been meeting his two friends only in strict secrecy, telling them less about how he got his information and asking less about what they did with it. The Nazis had made that necessary, by the grim efficiency of their Gestapo and its deadly cruelty.

"Where is Julie?" Lanny inquired, and Raoul answered that she had stayed in Paris, having contacts there. That was all; Lanny could guess that Raoul's wife had been the means whereby Raoul had got a letter to Lanny in Paris. The Germans had cut off all contact between Occupied and Unoccupied France; at least they had in theory. Postal communication was limited to official printed cards containing statements which you could underline or cross out—nothing else. But the boundary between the two sections, curving all the way from the Spanish border on the west to the Mediterranean on the east, extended for a thousand kilometers, and it would have required an army to keep it sealed day and night; all the Germans could do was to shoot persons who were found in the section they didn't belong in.

These problems the two conspirators discussed in detail. Lanny said: "You can write me from Vichy or Toulon in care of my mother; but don't expect an early reply. I have to go to London, and from there to New York; then, my guess is, I'll come back to Vichy, and if there are letters at Bienvenu I'll get them. But of course nothing except about paintings."

"I understand," replied the other. "You must know that I never mention your name. If one of the old-timers asks about you I shake my head sadly and say that I am afraid you are no longer interested in anything except selling paintings."

"And in my father's fighter planes. Don't forget that I'm a merchant of death! I find it convenient in England, for the British need nothing in the world so much as Budd-Erlings, and when it comes to travel permits and plane accommodations, I rank almost with royalty."

The conference lasted a long time, for they could not meet often, and Raoul wanted to know everything that Lanny could tell about the world situation; the secret purposes of the rulers and exploiters of the different lands, which he would explain to little groups of key workers in the immense dockyards and arsenal of France's great naval port. Some explaining it would take, if they were to learn to love Winston Churchill, arch Tory imperialist whose battleships had just assaulted and blasted half a dozen of France's proudest warships in the harbors of Oran and Dakar. But Winnie's voice was the one that was bellowing defiance to the Nah-zies, as he called them, and the Nah-zies were the number one enemies of everything the workers of the world cherished.

At last Lanny said: "I have to go now; I have an appointment." He walked back to town alone, for no one must see him in the company of a man in dungarees and blouse, a man who was carrying forged papers, and whose fingerprints would reveal that he was a Spanish Red who had recently been in jail in Toulouse for attempting to protest against the treatment of Spanish refugees in French concentration camps. No, indeed; and least of all if you were on the way to visit the revered personage who until recently had been the French Ambassador to the Madrid Government, and had returned to become head of the newly created État Français, newborn successor to the Troisième République, which Pétain in his youth had learned to refer to as *la salope*, the slut.

VII

The aged Maréchal was established in the Pavillon Sévigné, once home of the lively French lady whose letters were read all over the world. Here he had both home and office, a convenience for one whose powers had waned. It was a large drafty place, all right for the summer, but the old man dreaded to think how it would be when the north winds swept over these broad plains. So he remarked to his visitor, and added, plaintively: "But perhaps I shall not be here then; there are many who would be glad to attend my obsequies." He knew what a cruel world it was—he, the hero of Verdun, who had lived too long for his own good. His secretaries warned all callers that their stay must be brief, and that they must not say anything to irritate or excite the venerable soldier-statesman.

His hair was snow-white and so was his trim little mustache; his features were wrinkled and his expression tired. He had put off his uniform with seven stars on the sleeve, and also the cap with the three tiers of golden oak leaves; he wore a plain black business suit with a black tie. He was a little, dry, formal man, a martinet accustomed to command, rigid, jealous, self-righteous, and set in medieval ideas. His powers were near their ebb; if your speech was too long you would see his eyelids droop and his head nod. But when you stopped he would lift his cold blue eyes to yours, and would repeat in his quavering voice what he longed to tell all the world: that he had no thought but the welfare of France; a France restored and reformed, a Catholic, God-fearing France, a France obedient and moral, a France purged of all traces of the wicked revolution of a hundred and fifty years ago.

He remembered this good-looking and respectful Franco-American, who had so won his heart that he had addressed him as *"mon fils."* "Yes, yes, I met you at Madame de Portes', *que le bon dieu la bénisse!* She was a well-meaning woman, wiser than most of her associates."

When Lanny told the result of his mission, which had been precisely zero, the old gentleman remarked: "No one could have done more." When Lanny said that he had recently talked with Herr Hitler in Paris, Pétain responded quickly: "I have had to trust him, M. Budd; I had no other course. I appealed to him as one front-line soldier to another; but now and then I wonder whether he has the same sense of honor that we guardians of France have been taught. What do you think, *mon fils?*"

This was a question which many Frenchmen asked of Lanny Budd, and his reply had become stereotyped. He said that Herr Hitler was a man of moods, and was swayed by those who advised him. Some of these were narrow-minded racists and nationalists; others wanted much the same thing that conservative Frenchmen wanted, a Europe purged of Red agitators and labor demagogues. "No soup is eaten as hot as it is cooked, *mon Maréchal*, and I have the idea that Herr Hitler's world will turn out to be much the same as you yourself desire."

"France was happiest when it was a land of peasants," declared Henri Philippe Benoni Omer Joseph Pétain. It was one of his favorite themes, and Lanny could assure him that this would be entirely satisfactory to the Führer of the Germans, who wanted to have all the machines in his part of Europe.

A pathetic figure, yearning back to a far-departed age, and buffeted by forces of which he had but the feeblest comprehension. He wanted to use this elegant and cultured American to take his ideas to the New World, and call it to the rescue of the Old. He told about what he called his "National Revolution"; its motto was: "Labor, family, country." He preached this agitated sermon until his voice gave out and he had a coughing spell. When he tried to talk about the Fleet, and the infamy which the British had committed, his hands shook and he broke down, and one of his military aides had to come to the rescue. "I will never give up the Fleet, either to the British or Germans!" And then: "Go and see Darlan; he will tell you." To the aide he added: "Take him to the Admiral."

VIII

The Ministry of Marine was quartered in the Hotel Belgique, and here next morning the son of Budd-Erling presented himself, having received an appointment by telephone. In these offices there were no crowds and confusion, as in most of the others, for the man at the head was competent and by no means superannuated. He was of Breton descent, Catholic and Royalist, conservative, stubborn, and proud; not so different from one of the English ruling class, who had been his allies until a few weeks ago, and now were . . . what Lanny Budd had come to find out.

Jean Louis Xavier François Darlan was his name, and four-fifths of it was saintly, but he was surely no saintly character, on the contrary a seadog, famous for the amount of Pernod Fils brandy he could consume, and for cussing and general devilment. He was a man of medium height, broad-shouldered and vigorous, a fighter born and trained. His life had been devoted to building up the French Fleet according to his own ideas; outwitting the politicians and driving out the grafters, what he called "the golden bellies of the republic." He spoke of it as "my Fleet," and ruled it with a rod of iron.

To the caller he said: "I have met your father; a very competent man."

"You have also met my mother," was the reply, "though probably you do not remember it. You had tea at our home on the Cap d'Antibes not long after the Great War, when you came to Cannes for the graduation of your son at the Collège Stanislas."

"Oh, so *that* Madame Budd is your mother! A most beautiful woman!"

"I have always thought so," smiled Lanny. "I am pleased to have the confirmation of an authority."

So he discovered that there was another Frenchman who could smile. The Admiral was haggard and careworn, but willing to set his problems aside and talk about old times with a caller who was so evidently a man of parts. Said the caller: "I was close to you at another time, without your knowing it. I am a family friend of the de Bruynes, and was interested in the movement which you and they and the Maréchal were promoting several years ago, to get rid of the political riffraff that was ruining France. Doubtless you know that Denis had built a regular pillbox on his estate and had it stocked with machine guns and ammunition."

"Yes, I once had the pleasure of inspecting it."

"There is a story which might amuse you. One morning about three years ago the wife of Denis *fils* called me on the telephone, in a state of great agitation. The police had raided the château and arrested the father and were looking for the sons. I was to warn the sons, and also to take charge of some incriminating papers. I did my best; I put the papers in my suitcase, and tried to think where they would be safe from the Deuxième Bureau. It happens that I knew Graf Herzenberg of the German Embassy rather well, and had discussed with him and his associates the best way to promote a reconciliation between his country and yours. I drove out to his home, the Château de Belcour, and demanded his protection. He was greatly distressed—for of course it would have been more than embarrassing if he had been found assisting a conspiracy to overthrow the French Republic. But he couldn't quite bear to turn me out, and I stayed overnight. Next day, after I had read the newspapers, I decided that the scandal would blow over quickly—the politicians of *la salope* had too many crimes on their own consciences to prosecute our friends."

"You diagnosed the situation correctly," replied the Admiral. "If we had succeeded at that time, the history of Europe would have been far different."

"There is one report which I have often wondered about, *Monsieur l'Amiral:* that you had planned to put those officers of the Fleet who supported the corrupt regime on board the *Jean Bart* and take her out to sea and sink her."

"I meant it, absolutely. We could have spared that old battleship, and that kennel full of Red dogs would never have been missed by my service."

"I perceive that you are a commander who knows his own mind," commented the art expert genially.

IX

It was a great day for a collector of inside stories. The Admiral of the Fleet produced his large bottle of Pernod Fils and poured himself a swig, which lighted up his piercing dark blue eyes. His visitor took a smaller swig, enough for sociability, and listened while the half-Breton, half-Gascon, told how he had proposed to march an army over the Pyrénées and put an end to the Spanish civil war before it had got fairly started. How different history would have been if that simple and straightforward action had been taken! But *les cochons rouges* had forbidden it; and the same when Russia had begun her attack upon Finland. Darlan had been concentrating upon the building of light units for his Fleet, and had proposed using them to sink or capture all Red merchant ships at sea, and thus force the Kremlin criminals to give up their raid. He had wanted to save Norway by an all-out attack upon the German Fleet and transports on their way to the invasion. He wasn't surprised by it, he said: he had had full information; but in that tragic hour he had been under the command of the British Admiralty, which was one of the reasons he hated them so heartily and used so much fancy profanity when he mentioned them.

The visitor said: "*Monsieur l'Amiral,* my father is deeply concerned as to his course in this crisis, and many of his friends have to make up their minds what attitude to take. I am returning to the States very soon, and influential persons will be asking me: 'What is the program of the Vichy authorities, and how can we help?' What am I to tell them?"

"Say that I am trying to save France, M. Budd. I am in the position of a driver of an automobile who has his two front wheels hanging over an abyss. My first care is to keep the rear wheels from following, and my second is to get the front wheels back."

"A vivid simile, *Monsieur l'Amiral!*" It was no time for a smile, and Lanny said it gravely.

"I have the Fleet in my keeping, and I intend to guard it. I have been well warned, having seen the dastardly treachery of which my supposed allies are capable, and they will not catch me off guard again. Next time, our sailors will not fire into the air, as they did at Mers-el-Khébir. Also, we serve notice to our false friends that France is not going to be starved. We intend to protect our right to trade; we shall bring food from North Africa, and phosphates, and shall sell them to the Germans, because we have to in order to survive. Our duty is to France, and not to any other nation, or to either side in this war. *La patrie* is going to be restored."

"That is the hope of every right-minded man, *mon Amiral.*"

"It will be a different France, I promise you. The Maréchal and I are of one mind on the subject—you have seen that we have buried the so-called republic; both the chamber and the senate have abdicated their power and we are now the French State. That does not mean dictatorship—on the contrary we welcome the aid of every patriotic and Christian Frenchman; but we intend to purge the traitors and the Red dogs—*les cochons rouges*—the men who got us into the vile Russian alliance, a treasonable piece of statecraft which led directly to this war. I assure you that if I can have my way they will pay to the last scoundrel—and I won't waste even one battleship on them; I'll hang them from every limb of the plane trees that shade this hotel."

The visitor gave the assurance: "That reply will be satisfactory to my father and to all his friends."

X

The rumor had spread on wings of magic that there was an American millionaire in town, wishing to purchase old masters. In times of anguish such as this many persons were in need of cash, and some who had what they thought were valuable paintings wrote letters or came to call. Lanny went on inspection trips to ancient manor houses, damp and moldy even in midsummer, with narrow windows whose heavy curtains were rarely drawn back. He was a fastidious judge, and wanted only the best. Most of the time a glance would suffice and he would say: "I am sorry, that wouldn't do. Have you anything else to show me?" Rarely he would say: "What do you ask for that?" When the reply was: "What would you be willing to pay?" he would counter: "It is for you to say what you think the painting is worth. If I agree, I will pay it. I never bargain."

In one of the depressing mansions in which he was glad not to have to live he came unexpectedly upon a Boucher, a characteristic work of that gay and fashionable painter, an artificial-pastoral love scene out of the eighteenth century. His friend and client, Harlan Winstead, had been desiring such a work for years, and in this disturbed time he had authorized Lanny to use his own discretion. Lanny examined the painting carefully, and verified the signature; then he asked: "What is the price?" The reply was: "A million francs," which sounded enormous, until you translated it into ten thousand American dollars. Lanny said: "I am sorry, but that is out of the question." The elderly black-clad lady with the gentle voice and feeble chin looked depressed, and asked for an offer, to which Lanny replied that he feared her ideas were hopelessly out of line with his.

Between looking at other paintings he went to a bank in Vichy and identified himself. In his bank in Cannes he kept a large account for just such emergencies, and this he explained to the Vichy banker. In France people like to see real money, and checks are rarely taken; but from Americans anything can be expected, and for a small commission the banker agreed to make the inquiry by telephone and hand to this elegant and plausible stranger a package containing sixty of those new and crisp ten-thousand-franc notes which the Vichy Government was printing—mostly, alas, for the German conquerors!

With these in a pocket over his heart Lanny returned to the lady in the ancient ivy-grown mansion. It was something he had done probably a hundred times before, in France and elsewhere on the Continent, and rarely had his psychology proved to be at fault. The sight of actual cash was far more effective than talk about it or printed figures in a letter. Lanny said that he had inquired of his American client what he would be willing to pay—and this was literally the truth, even though the inquiring had been done several years ago. Lanny added that his was a generous offer, considering the uncertainties of the time, and that there were no strings attached to it, and no uncertainties; here was the cash, fresh from the bank in the lady's home town, and she might easily call the banker on the telephone and make sure it was real money.

He did not tell her the total, but proceeded to count it out before her eyes. Like a fascinated rabbit's, the eyes followed his hands from one pile to the other; and when he had come to the grand total, six hundred thousand francs, he added as a climax: "And you may keep the frame, which, unfortunately, I have no way to transport." That might seem absurd, but it wasn't; the frame was very good, and it was here, and much bigger than the painting. It was a sort of *lagniappe,* as the storekeepers in New Orleans call it, and while Vichy France did not have this custom, it had the same understanding of human nature.

The lady was so worried that the tears came into her eyes; she had to phone first to her brother, and then to the banker. In the end she accepted the offer, and signed the bill of sale which Lanny laid before her. He took the painting out of the frame and rolled it up; it was not too large to be carried comfortably, and he would get an oilcloth cover to keep it safe. He drank a cup of the lady's coffee and listened politely to her stories of the ill behavior of the refugees who swarmed about her place; then he drove off in his taxi, comfortable in the knowledge that his ten per cent commission would pay all the expenses of this journey. He sent a cablegram to Harlan Lawrence Winstead, Tuxedo Park, New York, telling what he had; and this was meant not only for the client but for censors and police spies as well.

XI

Gone, perhaps forever, were the happy days when the grandson of Budd Gunmakers and son of Budd-Erling had his fancy sport car, and when *essence* could be bought at any roadside filling station. Lanny had left his car in England, for Rick to turn over to the army; and now every move was a problem—the transporting of a hundred and sixty pounds of man, and perhaps fifty pounds of suitcases, plus a portable typewriter and an old master wrapped in oilcloth. Train travel was a nightmare, for there were literally millions of people who wanted to be somewhere else, and the Germans had taken most of the locomotives and cars of every sort. A bicycle had become the fashionable mode of conveyance, but wouldn't carry Lanny's load. A peasant cart, yes—but it would have taken a week from Vichy to the Cap d'Antibes.

What you did under the circumstances was to consult your hotel porter, whose business it was to know "somebody." "*Oui, oui, Monsieur, c'est possible; mais ça sera très difficile—et très coûteux.*" Lanny replied, "*Oui, je comprends, mon bonhomme; mais il me le faut absolument.*" So presently the functionary reported that he had found a man who had a car, and could get the necessary permit to buy government *essence*—but at a price fearful to mention. Wherever there are government restrictions, there begins to develop at once a "black market"—because the rich must have what they want, and cannot imagine a world in which money has lost its power. So it was with Lanny Budd; he agreed cheerfully that he would pay seven francs per kilometer for the rental of the car and driver, coming and going; that he would pay one hundred and fifty francs per liter for the bootleg *essence*, both coming and going; also for the driver and *pourboires*. He would pay part of all this in advance to a man for whom the porter vouched.

So in the early morning there drew up before the door a Daimler which had been an excellent car in the year 1923. The driver was one of those homicidal maniacs whom Lanny had seen racing taxicabs about the streets of Paris. How he had got this car he didn't say, and Lanny didn't ask; he listened to horror stories about the flight from *les boches*, and the panic of massed civilians on the roads of France being bombed from the air. Once the man was satisfied that this wealthy American was a friendly listener he proclaimed himself *un enfant de la révolution*, and talked so freely that Lanny wondered if he might not be a member of the leftwing group of which Raoul had spoken.

They rolled southward across the central plateau, past many of those strange round hills called *puys*, which are extinct volcanoes, often with small lakes on top; and presently they turned toward the east, and came into the wide valley of the river Rhône, familiar to Lanny from earliest childhood. It has been the highway for invading armies since the days of the ancient Romans at least, and if Lanny had had any of those powers of prevision which he so eagerly investigated in others, he might have seen the army of one or two hundred thousand "G.I. Joes" who would be marching up this *route nationale* within four years and as many weeks. But no, Lanny told his chauffeur that he could make no guess whether "Uncle Shylock" would come again to the rescue of Marianne; the majority of Americans had adopted as their political motto "never again"; and anyhow, it would take them a long, long time to match the Wehrmacht.

They rolled down the slowly descending valley, and had a late lunch at an *auberge* near Avignon. Lanny discovered that his companion had never heard the names of Abélard and Héloïse, and he told the sad story of the priest who had been castrated for making love to a prelate's niece. The *enfant de la révolution* replied: "*Merde!* They should do it to them all!" Lanny decided that it would be no use telling his companion about religious art works in that ancient city.

They took the highway eastward, away from the river, and in due course were on the Riviera, winding through the red Estérel mountains, plainly visible from Lanny's home. He had listened to the story of a Paris street gamin, hating the *flics* and dodging them while committing every petty crime on the police calendar. In return he told about the life of a little boy who played with the fishermen's children on the beach at Juan, and had everything in the world that his heart could have desired. The contrast was glaring enough to require no comment, and Lanny made none, for he was surely not going to reveal his point of view to a man who would go back to Vichy and repeat every word this unusual traveler had spoken.

Instead, he figured up the account he owed and had an understanding about it. In the falling twilight they drove through the blacked-out city of Cannes and along the familiar boulevard leading to the Cap. Here were the gates of Bienvenu, and the dogs rushing out barking wildly. Here came José, the lame butler from Spain, and Lanny's mother in the doorway, waiting. He counted out the money, with a bonus for cheerful conversation. Meantime the butler collected the luggage, including the roll of oilcloth, a familiar sight. Lanny got out, and the car chugged away, and that was the end of Lanny's first bootleg journey—by no means the last on this war-torn Continent!

2. *Though Every Prospect Pleases*

I

FOUR days before the French signed the armistice with Germany, the armies of Il Duce had advanced into the French Riviera and all along the boundary running to the north. Perhaps that was all Hitler would let him have; perhaps the Führer was expressing his contempt for his brother-in-arms, and setting a value upon his services. Or could it be that Mussolini had been afraid of the French Armies, still unrouted in this region? To put it more exactly, was he afraid to reveal to the world how little the common man of Italy was interested in fighting the common man of France, so much like himself?

Anyhow, Il Duce had got only as far as the edge of Monaco, a matter of a few miles; he held that wide strip of French mountains known as the Alpes Maritimes, and could amuse himself building fortifications in them, or perhaps coming to shoot capercaillie—only he had grown too fat for any sport. Lanny had vivid memories of this district, and of the grouse as big as turkeys which lived in the forests. He had been driven there in boyhood, when his mother had come to visit Marcel Detaze in the army, at the beginning of World War I.

Cannes and the Cap were safe, at least for the present; they weren't going to be Italian and they weren't going to be German, and everybody was pleased. Beauty Budd was one of the few who had refused to worry, for she said that the Italians were very good dancers, and the Germans spoke both French and English, and always they had mutual friends in Berlin and Munich. Really, did it matter very much, so long as people behaved correctly? Mr. Dingle, her husband, said that God was everywhere; and Mr. Armitage, husband of the Baroness de la Tourette, said that the trains would soon be running on time again, and prices would become normal when the discharged soldiers got back to work.

There had never been such crowds in the history of the Riviera. People had come by train and bus and motor car, bicycle and horse and donkey; tens of thousands had walked all the way from Northern France, having but one thought in the world, to get as far away from bombs and shells as possible; they had come until the Mediterranean stopped them. They were sleeping on the ground, on the beaches, in the parks; when it rained they would crawl under any shelter that was near. It was hard indeed to own a beautiful estate like Bienvenu, and keep on saying "No" to those whom you called "nice" people, those with whom you had dined and danced and played bridge and baccarat.

Beauty Budd, who had a kind heart, couldn't do it; and the result was that Bienvenu had become a village all by itself; guests would come and prove to be permanent—for where else could they go? Both the Lodge and the Cottage were crowded. A scion of one of the "two hundred families" was living with his bride in the studio which Beauty had built long years ago for Kurt Meissner and his piano; the instrument had been spoiled by sea air and was now used for a table and general catch-all. An elderly Belgian diplomat and his wife were camping in the rear part of Lanny's studio, the storeroom which had held the Detaze paintings; these, thank God, were safe in a bank vault in Baltimore, insured for half a million dollars.

All these people had to have food; and poor Beauty would decide that they weren't getting enough, and would invite them to a meal at her own residence, called the Villa. Fortunately she would never lack food, having been *la dame* of this estate for almost forty years. Leese, the peasant woman who had been her cook most of these years, had more grandnieces and grandnephews than you could keep count of, and they all knew where to get the highest prices for the best of their produce. What else could you do with money these days? Beauty had the best money in the world—American dollars—coming to her all the time, because every once in a while Lanny would sell another Detaze painting, and mention casually in a letter that he had deposited one-third of the amount to her account in a New York bank. Smart people had a saying: it was nice work if you could get it; all Beauty had had to do was to find a painter of genius and marry him, and to take care of him until the Germans killed him.

II

She was afraid that Lanny would be disturbed by all this uproar in the home which had always been his; but he told her he couldn't have stayed in any case, he had to go to London, and then to New York; the war wasn't going to make any difference to him, so far as traveling was concerned. It was difficult to explain this, for it made a difference to everybody else; he had to tell her that he was getting important information for his father, who was engaged in the greatest gamble of his life. You couldn't make planes without materials, and if you bought great quantities, and then the war ended suddenly, you would be sunk. The mother exclaimed: "Tell me, for God's sake!— how long is it going on?"

He had to say: "From all that I can make out, a long time."

"Lanny, I said I couldn't stand to live through another war!"

"I know, darling; but you chose a bad time to be born, and a bad time for your son."

"You're not going to get into it, Lanny!"

"No, I have no heart for it. They will fight to a stalemate, and nobody will gain." That was his role; it was what he told his rich and important friends, including his mother; he was the art expert and merchant of death, never the politician or the tool of such.

"Travel is so dangerous now!" she exclaimed. She was always pleading with him to stay at home and play—surely he had earned the right. It was her dream to find him a wife, and have him settle down in this spot, as lovely as any upon earth, and provide her with more grandchildren, some that would be hers to supervise and to spoil. Surely they had money enough for all! No sooner did Lanny arrive than there would appear at the family luncheon table, or at tea or dinner, some lovely damsel whose family was of social importance somewhere in the world; Beauty would drop hints about it, and Lanny would be his gracious self to the visitor, but afterwards he would say: "You are wasting your time, old dear! What I need to meet are the people who can tell me things that Robbie will be asking when I see him."

Up in the fashionable hills above Cannes was the estate of Lanny's near-godmother, Emily Chattersworth. Her health was failing, so she had an excuse for not crowding up her place with refugees as Beauty had done; but she had admitted a few carefully chosen friends, and these were persons who, if you got them off in a corner, might tell you the secret clauses of the armistice with Germany, or that with Italy. If her kind and much-loved Lanny were to ask the favor, she would invite some diplomat on vacation or some member of a royal house, who would reveal to him what Spain was up to in Tangier, or how the Fascist intrigue was succeeding in Iraq. Or it might be some great industrialist who knew the status of negotiations with Hitler over the postwar disposition of Lorraine iron ore. It was upon such matters that the peace terms would really depend, and the son of Budd-Erling would say, tactfully and cautiously: "My father is deeply interested in international affairs, as you know; but apart from that, I am a personal friend of the Führer and of Reichsmarschall Göring, and it may be that the next time I see them I can put in a word for your point of view." The important person would know about this art expert's wide acquaintance, for it had been talked about up and down the Coast of Pleasure, and no doubt the wise Emily would have reminded the important person over the telephone when she invited him to call.

III

The poet Heber had written: "Though every prospect pleases, and only man is vile . . ." Lanny looked about him at this landscape, so familiar, so bound up with the memories of all his days. The blue-green water of the Golfe Juan, varying in the shallows and with every change of the weather; the bright blue sky, with billowing white clouds; the red Estérels in the distance, with the sun going down behind them; the gray rocky points with straggly cedars and pine trees growing precariously; the flower-covered fields of the Cap—yes, one might be glad to spend several lifetimes amid this scenery.

But the people! Lanny tried to be charitable, but every time he saw them they seemed worse to him. People who had got money by hook or by crook, and had come here to enjoy their pleasures, at no matter what cost to others and to the human society; the wasters of all Europe, ravenous for their animal satisfactions, for gobbling costly foods and guzzling rare wines, for copulating on silken couches, for covering their flesh with delicate fabrics and decorating themselves with the furs of animals, the feathers of birds, and gems from the bowels of the earth. If they had been mere animals one would not have been so distressed by them, any more than by the sight of birds picking up bugs or hogs rooting for truffles in the forests; what made them revolting was that it was all the appurtenances of civilization, the symbols of culture they were debasing to their animal purposes. They called themselves elegant, smart, the salt of the earth; they had a score of fancy French phrases for themselves, they were *chic*, *très snob*, the *crême de la crême*; they were the *haut monde*, the *grand monde*, the *monde d'élite*.

They had the means to gratify every fancy; they had the stuff, the mazuma, the long green, the spondulix; in every one of the dozen languages you might hear on this Côte d'Azur they had intimate names for the deity they worshiped, the thing by which they lived, the foundation upon which their culture was built. If you had inherited it from your father and a long line of ancestors, so much the better; but anyhow, you had got it, and you hadn't been caught, so now you could have whatever you wanted, the world was your oyster. You were surrounded by people who were trying to get it away from you, but you knew how to take care of yourself and make them earn what they got. They danced attendance, they bowed before you, they flattered you and licked your boots; they spread out their wares and sang the praises thereof—whether it was food or raiment, music or poetry or painting. Men or women, young or old, black or white, if they did not have the money they were your inferiors and did what you told them, and learned to smile and like it, according to the American slang.

To Lanny Budd, the sociologist, it had been apparent from youth that this was one more case of the decay of a civilization. He had read Volney's *Ruins of Empire,* and knew that this had been going on since the dawn of history, that in truth history had been nothing but that: vast human societies arising and flaunting their glory, certain of their permanence and the favor of their gods, then slowly falling to pieces, like a great tree in a forest, which is attacked by rot, by fungus and parasites and borers, until at last it can no longer sustain its own weight. Was it a doom of nature or of God? Or were there causes of this evil which could be studied and remedies which could be applied?

To Lanny it seemed clear that the trouble lay in the social system; in exploitation and speculation which bred great fortunes, and in inheritance which made parasitism and perpetuated it. Every empire of the past had been based upon the private ownership of land and other privileges; men enjoyed wealth which they had not earned and power which they were no longer competent to wield; luxury on the one hand and penury on the other bred class strife which tore the society to pieces and exposed it to its foes.

Here it was, history repeating itself; and the extraordinary thing, how few people understood or cared about it. These refugees from a score of lands, including the sweet land of liberty overseas, talked politics and war incessantly, but when you listened you discovered that what they were thinking about was their own comfort, the preservation of the system which made their own lives so easy. What was going to happen to the "market"?—by which they meant the stocks and bonds from which their incomes were derived. If the Nazis won—and nine people out of ten were sure they had already won—what sort of government would they set up in France and how soon would it be before things got back to normal?—by which was meant labor getting back to work and dividends flowing in. Thank God, there would be no more unions and strikes, no more *front populaire* and Red newspapers! And would Hitler wait for a breathing space, or would he go after Russia at once? Such was the conversation of smart society on the French Riviera through this summer of the year 1940.

IV

There are many schools of sociology, also of philosophy; and difference of opinion, which makes horse races, also made discussions in the drawing-rooms of Bienvenu. Here was Beauty Budd's son, who believed that human society had to be reconstructed; and here was Beauty Budd's husband, who was equally sure that nothing could be done to reconstruct society until the individuals which compose it had been improved—or rather, until they had improved themselves. Parsifal Dingle was his unusual name, and he was an Iowa real-estate dealer who had accumulated a modest amount of money and come to live abroad because he wanted to think his own thoughts and couldn't do it in a small town where all the people knew him and were intrusively sociable. Beauty had married him, but had refused to marry his name; she had kept her own, which was really a professional name, she having been what was called a "professional beauty"—and no pun about it.

Parsifal, the man of God, had a rosy cherubic face and hair which had become snow-white since Lanny had known him. He was what was called a "New Thoughter," though he gave himself no label; he was interested in everything that went on inside the human mind, or soul, or whatever you chose to call it. He had discovered many strange things about it, and was sure it was as truly infinite in extent and content as was the universe of the body, to which astronomers can find no limits at one extreme, nor the investigators of physics and electronics at the other. Parsifal believed there was a spirit inside us, something which maintained us, or, as he preferred to say, perpetually created us; he called it God, but would add, "not God with a beard."

This force was in every person, in everything, indeed it *was* everything; and we could use it if we took the trouble; we could find out about this creative mental force in the same way that we had found out about electricity—by trying out experiments and seeing what happened. Parsifal was tireless in experimenting, and as a result had made himself into a kind of saint, a kind entirely new on the Coast of Pleasure, not approved by the church authorities who had taken sanctity as their private domain. Parsifal had found that by laying his hands upon people and concentrating his mind upon the certainty of their healing, he could help them to be healed. He did this, so he claimed, by the power of love, and made it his business to love everybody, regardless of whether they deserved it or not, and whether they wanted it or not. Sooner or later, said this man of God, everybody discovers the need of love, and it can be spread by example, just as evil is. Parsifal never argued with people, or forced his ideas upon them; he kept his kindness and serenity, and waited for people to ask him questions, which sooner or later they did.

During the great panic of 1929 in New York, while men were throwing themselves out of windows of their office buildings because they had lost everything, Parsifal Dingle had been experimenting with spiritualist mediums, and had discovered an old Polish woman whose spirits had told him things about his own life which she had had no normal way of finding out. They had brought this woman to Bienvenu and she was now one of the family pensioners; every now and then the healer would have a séance with her, and had many notebooks full of the things which her "spirit controls" had told him. Whenever Lanny visited his boyhood home, he would sit down with his stepfather and go over these notes and discuss them. Lanny's own experiments had been many, and if the pair had seen fit to constitute themselves the Juan Society for Psychical Research, they might have made quite an impression in the metaphysical world.

V

At the present time it was hard to get the necessary quiet in Bienvenu. Lanny waited until the elderly couple who were camping out in back of his studio had gone off to a reception—borrowing one of Beauty's cars. Then he escorted the Polish medium to the studio and placed her in the armchair to which she was accustomed; she sat back and closed her eyes, moaned lightly for a minute or two, and then was still. There came from her lips a deep man's voice, proclaiming that it came from Tecumseh, Amerindian chieftain long-since dead; he announced that Sir Basil Zaharoff was there—"the old gentleman with the guns going off all round him." Lanny sighed inwardly, for the munitions king who had been Robbie Budd's partner had become the greatest bore of Lanny's psychic life; he came uninvited and talked at length, and it had been several years since he had had anything of significance to say. He was a great worrier and prophet of calamity; just now he was insisting that Lanny should pay a thousand pounds which Sir Basil had owed to a man in Monte Carlo; but when Lanny asked how he was to get the money, the Knight Commander became vague and faded out.

Then there was announced Lanny's grandfather, Samuel Budd, one-time President of Budd Gunmakers in Connecticut. It had been some time since this stern old Puritan had bothered with his left-handed grandson, who had been shown the light in a Sunday-school Bible class but had refused to follow it. Whenever Grandfather came, it was to issue some rebuke, and now he wanted to know when Lanny was going to give up his idler's way of life and marry again and stay married. The good-for-nothing answered evasively, and in his secret heart was pleased to learn that the old gentleman thought as he did. Lanny surely didn't want any rumors going about in the spirit world that he was a secret agent of Franklin D. Roosevelt, posing as a Nazi-Fascist sympathizer and turning in reports about the doings of the Axis schemers!

The aged merchant of death faded out on a Bible text—nearly always the Hebrew Old Testament, which is full of fighting men and their weapons and war cries. There followed a long silence, and then a gentle old lady's voice with a trace of southern accent: the grandmother of Lanny's friend Laurel Creston. The old lady had been cross with the Budd scion for being what she called a bad influence in Laurel's life; very few seemed to approve of Lanny in the spirit world, and Tecumseh, the "control," was crossest of all. Now, however, Mrs. Marjorie Kennan, one-time resident of the Eastern Shore of Maryland, revealed that her granddaughter was in New York, and also that this granddaughter was a medium, and could be communicated with directly. The refined and well-mannered "spirit" was fair enough to acknowledge that Lanny had been responsible for this discovery, and she thanked him. Lanny asked how Laurel was getting along, and Mrs. Kennan reported that she was well, and that she was writing all the time but wouldn't tell what she was writing about; the grandmother tried slyly to find out if Lanny knew, but Lanny could only guess and didn't do that out loud. Instead, he asked how spirits were able to fly from Juan to New York and back again without airplane fares; the answer was that there was no such thing as space in the spirit world. When he asked to have that elucidated, he was told that he would understand it when he himself had "passed over." It was a favorite alibi of that other world.

There was nothing evidential in this séance; but Lanny wrote it out, as he had promised his stepfather, because Parsifal insisted that many things which didn't seem evidential at the time might turn out to be so in the light of later developments. Parsifal himself never questioned the reality of the spirits; they fitted in perfectly with his theory that fundamentally all minds were one, and that time and space were illusions of our senses. Thus he encouraged the spirits, and got along in brotherly love with the Iroquois chieftain who shepherded them and interpreted for them with perfect *savoir-faire*. But Lanny could never give up the notion that these communications might be products of the subconscious mind of himself and others. He would argue: "I knew that Laurel was in New York and I knew that she was writing; and

Laurel knows all about her grandmother." All the same, it would be interesting to tell Laurel about this séance, and find out if her grandmother's spirit had as yet made an appearance in New York!

VI

These developments were dutifully reported to Lanny's mother, and her reactions had nothing to do with metaphysics. Said Beauty Budd: "Are you corresponding with Laurel Creston?"

"I wrote her a note, to tell her that I expected to be in New York."

"Has she written to you?"

"Mails are uncertain nowadays, and there may be something waiting for me in London."

This was an obvious evasion, and Beauty Budd had been in the world longer than her son, and was not to be fooled by any of his tricks. "Have you had any letter from her at all?"

"Just a brief note, darling, telling me that she was settled and at work. She thanked me for our hospitality, and said that she was writing the same to you."

"I received that note. She is an intelligent woman, and just your sort, I suppose. How much are you interested in her?"

"I am deeply interested in her, both as a writer and a trance medium; but I'm not in love with her, if that is what you mean." He knew perfectly well that that was what she always meant.

"Lanny, I can't understand you. You are keeping things from your mother, and what is the reason for it?"

"Bless your heart, old dear—you can't understand because you don't want to. I am interested in my work, and not interested in getting married. I tried it once, and discovered that it's all right for those who like it, but not for me."

Beauty had said every possible word there was to say on this subject, but that didn't keep her from saying it all again. Lanny kissed her on her well-rounded cheek and tickled her gently under the ample chin which distressed her when she looked into the mirror. "Why should I want a wife," he demanded, "when I have a mother to tell me everything I need to know?"

Of course no woman is going to let herself be diverted by devices so transparent. "Tell me," persisted Beauty, "are you corresponding with Lizbeth Holdenhurst?"

"I wrote her a sort of bread-and-butter letter, and I've written to her father several times. I've had to, in connection with the handling of the Detaze paintings. I tell him news from Europe that I think will interest him."

"Why don't you write to Lizbeth?"

"Because I don't want to encourage ideas in her mind. I'm not in love with her and I'm not going to be, and she has to understand it and find herself some proper swain in Baltimore."

"Have you ever told Laurel that her cousin is in love with you?"

"Of course not. In the first place, Lizbeth has never told me that she's in love with me—"

"Her father has told you!"

"Yes, but fathers can be mistaken, and anyhow that is their secret. If they want to tell Laurel, it's up to them."

"Does Laurel go to Baltimore, do you know?"

"She didn't mention it. I told her when she was here that I had never mentioned to Lizbeth or her family that I had met Laurel in Germany."

"Why on earth didn't you do that?"

"I was never quite sure what terms the two families were on. Laurel is a sort of poor relation, you know, and the Holdenhursts are very conscious of their wealth and their importance. Laurel's ideas are different from theirs—antagonistic in many ways."

"You mean they would quarrel with her about that?"

"I don't know exactly. Lizbeth Holdenhurst is only a child, but she is a child who has always had her own way, and rightly or wrongly, I've an idea that she'd be upset because I didn't pop the question in Baltimore. I thought: If she hears that I've been meeting her cousin in Germany and here in Juan, which she thought such a delightful place, she might have the same idea that my own mother has, that I can't try psychic experiments with a woman, or read her stories in the magazines, without falling in love with her. She might be upset and perhaps spiteful."

"She's not at all that sort of girl, Lanny."

"I've learned that girls sometimes surprise you; and anyhow, it wasn't my business. I had the idea that Laurel was in Germany more or less clandestinely, and I wasn't sure that she had told her relatives. She doesn't like the Nazis, and may be writing a book to say so. I had to be careful where I met her for that reason. My general impulse is to let other people manage their own affairs in their own way."

"What a strange secretive person you are coming to be, Lanny! I am worried by the idea that you are up to something dangerous, and are hiding your affairs from me."

"Forget it, old dear!" he smiled. He had thought now and then of taking this shrewd mother at least partly into his confidence; but what good could it do? She did not share his ideas, and would have had a lot of anxiety which it would have been hard for her to conceal from others. Now he said: "I am watching the world, and liking it less and less the more I know it. I am keeping aloof and not making the mistake you are making, of getting involved with people who call themselves my friends and really haven't any idea but to get out of me all they can."

VII

If Lanny had been free to consult his own preferences, he would seldom have gone off the Bienvenu estate. He would have continued his experiments with Madame Zyszynski, and read some of the books in the well-chosen library which had been bequeathed to him. He would have had his piano tuned, limbered up his fingers, and played over again a rich treasury of sound. He would have taken up once more what he playfully called the subject of child study; in the enclosed court of the villa was a charming specimen, eager to be investigated—Marceline's son and Beauty's grandson whom they had named after the painter, Marcel Detaze.

He was half Italian, a quarter French, and a quarter American. His mother was in Berlin, dancing in a night club, and presumably happy with her Junker lover; but tiny Marcel knew nothing about that, and did not miss her. His divorced father, the Capitano, was a Fascist braggart, but the baby didn't know that either, and Lanny could hope that with wise training and example he might turn out better than his inheritance. He was just two, a delightful age; he raced here and there about the court, stumbling over half a dozen puppies and filling the place with sounds of merriment. Lanny would bring out the small phonograph and put on a record and teach him dancing steps—exactly as he had done for the little one's mother. Just twenty-one years ago that had been, when Lanny had come down from Paris after the Peace Conference which had undertaken to make the world safe for Democracy and instead had made it safe for Nazi-Fascism.

As a result of that, Lanny couldn't stay at home and read old-time philosophers and poets, and play the piano and give dancing lessons. He had to go out into a world of treacheries and corruptions, and make himself the playmate and pal of persons whose ideas and tastes he despised. He had to spend his money upon affording them hospitality. He had to listen to their conversation and cultivate the art of guiding it into channels he desired. He had to be sly as the serpent and watchful as the tiger on the hunt; every word had to be studied, every gesture, every facial expression, and many a time he had known that his life depended upon his shrewdness. For these persons were killers and the hirers of killers—and not merely in Germany and Italy and Spain, their own lands, but here in France, and even before the war had broken out. To turn traitor and menace them could mean not merely death but cruel torture preceding it.

And when, after these fashionable forays, Lanny would come back to the family nest, even then he was not free; even then Duty, stern daughter of the voice of God, controlled his life. Instead of reading Emerson and Plato, instead of playing Chopin and Liszt, he had to shut himself up in his studio and sit staring with blank eyes, going over in his mind exactly what he had heard and making sure that it was fixed in his memory. It had to be right or it was no good at all; and never once in the course of three years as presidential agent had he set down one single memorandum; never had there been on his person or in his luggage or even in his home anything that the Gestapo and the Italian OVRA were not free to peruse and to photostat.

VIII

Just across the Cap, a pleasant walking distance, lived Sophie Timmons, once Baroness de la Tourette and now Mrs. Rodney Armitage. She had a jolly disposition, a loud voice, henna hair which she would not permit to become gray, and most important of all, oodles and oodles of money. It was the Timmons Hardware Company of Cincinnati, whose advertisements you have seen in the magazines. Sophie's brothers and nephews ran it, and sometimes they came visiting, and when Lanny went to Cincinnati they bought Detazes and other paintings from him. They deposited Sophie's dividend checks in their home bank, and Sophie drew on the account for what she wanted, and it was a lot—for what was the use of having money if you didn't get any fun out of it?

She had been Beauty's friend in Paris before Lanny was born, and she and Emily Chattersworth had kept secret the fact that Beauty had never been married to Robbie and so had never divorced him. They had done it because Robbie had asked them to, and they had been pleased to thwart even partly the old Puritan father in Connecticut who had threatened to disinherit his son if he married an artist's model. So Beauty owed a lot to these older women friends—not so much older, Sophie would insist with a wry face. Lanny couldn't recall the time when her laughter and sharply cynical wit hadn't been a part of his world. Years had passed before he realized that she wasn't the most refined of persons, but even so, he found her good company; and useful, too, for all the world came to her parties, and Nazis and Fascists and Spanish Falangists were not particular whose food they ate and whose wine they drank.

Among Sophie's grandnieces was one named Adele Timmons. She had come on a yachting tour with friends, and had stopped off to visit her great-aunt and been caught by the war. They might have shipped her home on one of the liners, but she liked the Riviera, and shared

Sophie's belief that the Italians who had drunk her wine would never be impolite to any of the family. Perhaps also she had listened to stories about the wonderful Lanny Budd who sometimes came visiting at Bienvenu. She was just sixteen, but precocious for her age, a brunette with lovely large dark eyes and a soft, well-rounded figure; she was of a gentle, trusting disposition, and just ready to fall into some man's arms. At any rate, the ladies had that idea, and nothing would have pleased them more than for Lanny Budd to provide the arms.

A month or so previously Adele had stayed too long in the Riviera sun. It is right overhead in midsummer and not to be fooled with; the peasants, who have lived there all their lives, gaze with astonishment at visitors who lie out in it almost naked, broiling themselves to the color of an overdone steak. Adele had got a case of sunstroke, with high fever and almost coma. Sophie, in panic, phoned for a doctor, and also to Parsifal Dingle, and Parsifal stepped into a little runabout and got there first. According to his custom he put his hand on the girl's forehead and sat there, saying his prayers or whatever he called them, and it happened as it had in a hundred other cases, the girl opened her eyes and smiled, and in half an hour or so was all right.

That was before the doctor got there, and he would have had to be more than human if he hadn't resented it. Unfair competition—the same idea as the priests had. Parsifal did it in the name of God, but he never took money for it, and so there didn't seem to be anything the objectors could do; the law could hardly forbid an elderly cherub to lay his hand on a girl's forehead—while the girl's great-aunt was in the room watching, with two hands clasped together in terror. If this exemplar of divine love had been willing to accept a fee he could have had anything he asked; but his only desire was that great-aunt and great-niece should learn the lesson that love is the most priceless of God's gifts, and is free to all His children, and that their duty is to practice it and teach it to others who may be ready to learn.

In spite of all that skeptics and cynics can say it is a fact that this attitude is as "catching" as any disease. Adele Timmons came out of that experience convinced that she had met the most wonderful man who had ever lived; her vocabulary being limited, she repeated the statement many times. She gazed at him with awe-stricken eyes, she drank in every word he spoke and remembered it; she resolved fervently that she was going to live that kind of life, and love everybody —the worse they were the better, for that would be a test of faith. She read diligently all the "New Thought" literature he gave her. She came on every occasion to visit at Bienvenu and watch Parsifal give "treatments" to other persons, and now and then receive one herself.

There was nothing unusual about all that; it had been happening to this kindly man of God ever since he had appeared on the Riviera.

With him, exactly as with the apostle Paul, "some of them believed
. . . and of the chief women not a few."

IX

Such was the situation when Lanny arrived. Even before he had met
Adele, as soon as he heard her name mentioned he knew what the two
elderly ladies would be planning; he was to be the lucky man who
would marry her, and Sophie would give her a generous *dot* and will
her a block of Timmons Hardware stock. Many years ago Emily Chattersworth had had the same plan for one of her nieces, and it was
devilish awkward, for Lanny had been a ladies' man from boyhood—
and these were the ladies! He resolved to be very busy with picture
deals, and to have urgent engagements in London and New York, regardless of war. When he went to lunch at Sophie's, he treated Adele
as a child, which, according to etiquette, she was, not having made her
debut. He directed his fascinating conversation to the great-aunt, telling about mutual friends whom he had met on his tour. Kurt Meissner,
who had lived for seven years at Bienvenu and knew Sophie well, had
composed a *Führer Marsch* which the German Army had played on its
entrance into Paris; Kurt had taken Lanny to meet Hitler in the Hotel
Crillon, and later to the ceremony of Hitler's visit to the tomb of Napoleon in the Invalides. Nobody could fail to be interested in such a story
—not even a sixteen-year-old miss who had just acquired a religion.

Thus the much pursued and gun-shy Lanny Budd. He knew the
ladies would be disappointed, but they would have to bear it; he was
determined not to let them get him into another mess as they had done
in the case of Lizbeth Holdenhurst, who had got her cap set at him so
firmly that she had caused her father to come and make a proposal.
Lanny clenched his hands and resolved that he wasn't even going to
look at this girl; he wasn't going to be left alone with her, either outside in the moonlight or inside in any cosy nook; he wasn't going to
dance with her, or even go swimming unless others went along.

He was relieved to observe that the girl seemed to fall in with his
program. She flashed him no signals, no downcast eyes or sidelong
glances; she behaved as a child, and not as a romantic-minded miss.
Beauty, too, behaved better than he had expected; she didn't try to lure
him over to Sophie's and she didn't sing the praises of this "catch"; instead she talked some more about Lizbeth. Lanny sensed that there was
something peculiar in the situation, but he didn't try to find out; he
was glad enough to keep out of it, and his thoughts were concentrated
upon finding out the details of the headlong preparations which the
Germans were making for the invasion of England.

There was nothing especially secret about that program, for the

Führer himself had announced it to Lanny in Paris, and Lanny had got off a message to President Roosevelt through the American Embassy. Here in Cannes he went to take *eine Tasse Kaffee* at the home of Kurt's aunt, the Frau Hofrat von und zu Nebenaltenburg, an aged *Dame* who had refused to stir from her apartment at the outbreak of war, declaring her certainty that the Wehrmacht would arrive before long. The French had apparently not thought her worth bothering about, and now that the Germans were free to come to the Riviera for their holidays, her home had become a social center for various dignitaries and their wives. They all knew about Lanny Budd, who had been a visitor at Schloss Stubendorf, to say nothing of Berchtesgaden and Karinhall. He would tell them about the rapid spreading of sympathy for Germany in America, and how that man Roosevelt was grabbing rope to hang himself; in return they would discuss the tremendous preparations being rushed in the Fatherland, how landing craft were being built, and barges assembled from all the canals, and motorboats from the inland lakes and rivers. September was the month—*wir segeln gegen England!*—and meantime the Luftwaffe was engaged in knocking the British out of the skies. How confident they all were, and full of gloating! *Der Tag* was every day.

X

Only little by little Lanny came to the realization that his mother was distressed about something. She was unusually silent, she avoided her son, and when he got close to her he discovered that her eyes were red from weeping. He knew her too well to be in any doubt; and after a few days of it he went to her room, shut the door behind him, sat down on the side of the bed, and exclaimed: "Look here, old darling— what is the matter with you?"

He was fully prepared to have her declare that she was unhappy because her firstborn and only son wouldn't do his duty to posterity by settling down in Bienvenu and raising a family. He wasn't sure if it would be Lizbeth or Laurel Creston, or possibly Adele; Beauty might have been trying the experiment of letting him entirely alone, on the theory that in previous cases she had irritated him by pushing too hard. But no, it wasn't anything like that; it was something she didn't want to talk about, and Lanny became suddenly worried, for this was just the way his *amie* Marie de Bruyne had behaved before she had admitted that she had a cancer.

He asked if it was Beauty's health. No, it wasn't that; it was something too terrible to be voiced; she began to weep, and he wondered, in sudden horror, if it could be that she had fallen in love with some man other than her husband—she, at an age which she would never speak, but which was getting close to sixty, and with a son who would be forty next November!

"Look, dear," he pleaded, "it's much better to spit it out and get it over with. I've got to know it sooner or later. I've always trusted you and you have trusted me; and did I ever break faith?"

"No, Lanny, but I'm too humiliated! It's so utterly degrading!"

"Yes, darling, but that's all the more reason for telling me. I've got to leave pretty soon, and I surely can't go while you are in serious trouble. Imagine what my thoughts would be!"

"They couldn't be as bad as the reality, Lanny!"

"Maybe not, but they could be pretty bad, and I simply have to know. I'm going to sit here and not move till you tell me."

"Lanny, you'll swear to me you won't say anything or do anything without my consent?"

"Darling, of course. You are a grown-up person, and in the final showdown you're the one who has to decide your fate."

At last she blurted it out. It was indeed terrible, and beyond any man's guessing; a woman's possibly—one of the ideas that tormented her was that the shrewd-eyed Sophie might have got some hint of her humiliation. It was the fact that Parsifal was receiving visits from that girl, and that he prayed with her, and Beauty had seen him with his hand upon her forehead!

"But good Lord, Beauty, he does that to everybody!"

"I know, but not to young girls!"

"Male or female, old or young! Don't you remember he treated Leese's niece?"

"A peasant girl, Lanny; that's not the same as a social equal."

"Darling, everybody is Parsifal's social equal. Don't you remember how he helped a Senegalese soldier, and how the poor devil stank?"

"There's no use trying to fool me, Lanny; this girl smells of the highest-priced perfume she can buy."

"You are tormenting yourself with a fantasy. Parsifal doesn't know that any woman but you exists."

"I thought so, Lanny. But I know men; the old ones especially fall for the young things, and do they make perfect fools of themselves! I have seen it happen to one after another."

"You never knew anyone like Parsifal before, and you are doing your own self a wrong when you suspect him."

"I'm not really suspecting him, Lanny; I would despise him if I did. It's a sudden hatred of all men—and of all empty-headed women. I was empty-headed once, I know. So I hate myself, too. But I never stole another woman's man!"

"Do you think Adele wants to steal Parsifal? She is too young to think of him that way. She probably thinks even I am too old for romance—at any rate she has never made eyes at me."

"That's the most suspicious thing of all! Why shouldn't she be interested in you? It's her business to be looking for a marriageable man, and not for my old one. It's pure vanity—she wants to show me!"

"Darling, you are missing the point, I am sure. Adele thinks she has found a religion."

"Religion, fudge! What girl at her time of life is not looking for romance? For adventure, even for the thrill of showing a once famous beauty that her day is done!"

"You're surely off in that idea; ask the Catholic Church! They know that Adele's age is just the time to catch them for spiritual devotion. The neophytes have religious ecstasies, they become the brides of Christ, and spend the rest of their lives telling their beads and scrubbing floors in the service of a Heavenly Bridegroom."

Beauty found comfort in those words. She stared at her son and exclaimed: "Lanny, do you really think he is teaching her to be good?"

"I'm sure he is trying to," he replied, "and you ought to know how effective he is; didn't he make a saint of you? Now forget this foolishness, darling, and think of good old Parsifal—how hurt he would be if he had any idea of your suspicions."

"Oh, Lanny, he mustn't know. I must manage to get myself together. I must think up some other trouble, if he asks me why my eyes are red! Don't think me too foolish, Lanny—try to realize my plight! What chance has a woman with wrinkles against a young girl with dimples?"

XI

Lanny went off and thought it over. Surely this was one of the oddest human entanglements he had come upon in a life among odd people. He thought about both parties in the suspected intrigue. He had spoken with vigorous certainty for his dear mother's benefit, but in the secrecy of his heart he wondered: could it conceivably be that Parsifal Dingle, a man in the sere and yellow leaf, was being lured by the dream of budding youth and blossoming beauty, things which he had missed in his own early days in a small unlovely village of the Middle West? Parsifal didn't say much about those days, but Lanny had gathered that they had been barren. All life was barren without God, the healer said, and Lanny could agree with that; but men sometimes find difficulty in making sure what is God and what is Satan.

As for that "young thing with dimples," anything might be true. Sex was written all over her, but that wasn't her fault, it was her time of life. Lanny knew all about it, because Rosemary, now Countess of Sandhaven, had been at just that age when she had taken Lanny into camp, and under her particular tent, so to speak. She had told him all about it, every thrill and shiver, being an unusually matter-of-fact creature, and under the influence of what had then been called the feminist movement, which made it a matter of principle to talk about everything, and in many cases not about anything else. Adele, so far as Lanny knew, had never heard of such ideas; but she was like a tinderbox, ready to catch fire at the smallest spark. Who could guess what might happen when a divine hand was laid upon her forehead and a divine voice murmured words about universal and all-possessing Love?

Yes, it was a situation to think about. If Beauty should prove to be right in her suspicions, what could she do? Certainly not anything to affront Sophie Timmons or her great-niece; and certainly not anything to wound her husband's feelings. What would probably result would be a flare-up of wifeishness on Beauty's part, a wild impulse to hold her man; but she would be too shrewd to find much hope in this strategy. She would know that if Parsifal could once become "like some other old men," he would find plenty of Adeles to fall for. From now on until the end of her life Beauty would be watching every tiniest sign; and she had the eyes of a hawk when it came to other people's secret thoughts. Her life would become a tragedy—the tragedy of a woman too old to charm a new mate, and too genuinely devoted to her husband ever to want another.

XII

Lanny worried; and a day or two later, passing his mother's door, he heard what he thought was suppressed sobbing. It was mid-morning, and Parsifal was out in the court, reading one of his devotional books. Lanny tapped several times, and more imperiously; finally his mother opened the door and let him in. There she was, with tears streaming down her cheeks, in spite of dabbing with a wet handkerchief. He knew it must be serious this time, and said: "What the devil?"

"Oh, Lanny, the most awful thing!" Then, somewhat contradictorily: "Oh, I am such a fool! You will think I have gone crazy."

"I can't think anything till you tell me what it's all about, dear."

"Oh, Lanny, I had a dream! The most awful dream in all my life!"

"A dream!" he exclaimed, lost in wonder. "You mean you are in this state about a *dream?*"

"But it was so vivid, and so utterly horrible. I can't realize that I am awake. I can't believe that it isn't symbolic, that it isn't a warning. You have told me many times that dreams are sometimes that."

"What was the dream?"

"I found Parsifal in Adele's arms; and Parsifal told me he no longer loved me. Then Adele defied me; she said: 'Don't you know that you are an old woman? You are *through*, and he is mine! Mine, *mine!*' She screamed it at me—oh, the little vixen, the viper! I could have strangled her!"

"I hope you didn't hurt her," said Lanny gravely.

"I woke up before I could do anything to her. I lay there perfectly rigid, numb with horror. I couldn't bring myself to believe that it hadn't happened. It was so real, so paralyzing. It was early in the morning, but I didn't dare go to sleep again, for fear of falling into the clutches of that nightmare. Even now, when I tell you about it, I am certain that it happened, that it is a warning; I know that it's real, and that I have been a fool, that I should have acted long ago to stop it—and now it's too late!"

The tears were still flowing; and Lanny thought: "It is becoming an obsession. I've got to tell Parsifal. He is the only cure." There was that modern saint, sitting out in the court thinking Love, with a capital L, and the Power of the Mind over the Body. He really believed in this power, and Lanny did, too. But after you had become convinced, what a bore to keep on repeating it! That was what these New Thoughters did, that was what you had to do if you wanted to make the thing work inside you. You had to keep on thinking it. "Stand porter at the door of thought," Mother Eddy had commanded, and over and over again she had insisted that the mind must hold continuously to the one thought, of God as Love, Life, All. Call it autosuggestion, or self-hypnosis; but they were only names for a power of the mind. Some called it God, and it worked better that way. Lanny could not find any answer to one question: "If God meant me to say prayers all day, why did He give me such an intense curiosity about the outside world?"

Anyhow, there was Parsifal in a shady corner of the court, as contented as the bees and the butterflies fulfilling their routine and never bored by it; and here was his beloved wife shut up in her room, tormenting herself with a dream! "Look here, old dear," said the son, "you've got to snap out of this! You're really driving yourself crazy."

"I know it, Lanny; but I can't get over the idea that this awful thing has happened, or is on the verge of happening."

"It's perfectly obvious that you have simply made a dramatization of your own suspicions. You've got to use your reason and convince yourself that it has no basis in reality."

"That's so easy to say, Lanny; but it only shows you don't know what is in the hearts of women—all women."

"You mean that all women think their husbands are going to be unfaithful to them?"

"When a woman gets to be my age, she discovers something horrible—she finds that men love only youth!"

"I don't agree with you that all men are satyrs; and I think there is such a thing as growing old gracefully. When you were young, you saw other women doing it; you must have realized that your turn would come."

"I suppose I knew it, as a matter of theory; but I never actually faced the idea that I might grow too stout, and then if I reduced I'd be full of wrinkles!"

"You've never been a merely beautiful body. You're nobody's fool, darling, and it's time you used your brains and admitted that you're going to be sixty, and that's different from sixteen. Age has its comforts, too, and its dignities. You can learn things and understand life, as you couldn't hope to do then."

"That's all true, Lanny, and I argue it with myself. But when I face the thought that some younger woman is going to grab the man I love, and leave my home and heart empty, then it seems to me that my life has come to an end. And when I have these horrible dreams—what on earth am I going to do?"

XIII

Lanny didn't really know what to suggest. It helped her to confide in someone she loved, and he was glad he could help her that much. When she exclaimed that it was her own freedom in love that was bringing a harvest of dragon's teeth, he could comfort her by saying that she had never broken up another woman's home. Four men in a period of more than forty years wasn't such a bad record—when it was in Paris and on the Coast of Pleasure. She had had only one of those men at a time, and had loyally served and helped each of them to the best of her understanding. She might have married Robbie Budd if she had been more cold-blooded; but she had known that his family and the family institution of Budd Gunmakers were his ordained life, and if he had been cast off and disinherited he would never have been a happy man and might have gone entirely to pieces.

Then, after some years, when Robbie had decided that it was his duty to marry and raise a family in Connecticut, Beauty had consoled herself with a French painter for whom she had posed. That he had been a man of genius had been a bit of luck, but that he was a wise and kind man, and had loved her truly, was no accident, nor even merely her physical charms, but also her good sense and devoted attention. That was a matter of ten years or so, and when Marcel had been defaced in the war, she had married him and stuck by him until he died. It hadn't been easy, but she had stood the trial.

A year or two later she had fallen in love with Kurt Meissner, Lanny's friend and boyhood hero. That had been a scandal, because she was so much older than Kurt; but it had been real love, or so they had thought, and Beauty's son thought so too. The facts stood that she had saved Kurt's life, and taken care of him while he became a famous *Komponist*, and that his best work had been done during the seven years he had lived in Bienvenu. Then his country had called him, and he had become a friend of Hitler, and a devotee of the Nazis. That hadn't meant much to Beauty, who did not have a political mind; but he had told her the same thing that Robbie had told her, two decades earlier, that his parents wanted him to marry a young wife and raise a family, and that he felt it his duty to oblige them.

Finally she had chosen this odd marriage, to a man of God whom all her friends had considered to be slightly cracked. But thirteen years had passed, and they had been compelled to love him, willy-nilly—for how can you hate anybody who refuses to hate you? Beauty, after her fashion, had tried to be of use to him, and to accommodate her ways to his. When she had been married to a merchant of death, she had done her best to sell death; when she had loved a painter, she had listened to talk about art and tried to learn what the strange words meant; when she had been the wife of a *Komponist* she had listened to his compositions and praised them in the German language. So now she read New Thought literature, and was sure that she was becoming spiritual, and said that she was no longer concerned to be fashionably dressed, and to meet smart people and play cards for high stakes; but of course she only partly meant it, and couldn't practice it too strenuously—because that would have hurt the feelings of her smart friends!

XIV

Lanny went off thinking about dreams. What an extraordinary phenomenon, that we should abandon control of our minds, and that they should go tearing off like an automobile without a driver, like the screws of a steamship "racing" when a wave passes and they come out into the air. Someone has remarked that we are all insane for one-third of our lives; and here was the subconscious mind of Beauty Budd, taking her imagined troubles and weaving them into an elaborate web of fiction which might bring her close to real insanity.

In Lanny's own mind something hardly less freakish had been going on; he had manufactured for himself a recurrent dream—a dream about China, everything in China, camel trains with bells, pagodas with gongs, city streets with rickshaws and crowds shuffling along in straw sandals and padded cotton garments. Lanny had seen pictures of such scenes, both in books and on the screen, but he had no special interest in that remote land, and no thought of going there. But several years ago in Munich an astrologer had cast his horoscope and told him that he was fated to die in Hongkong. Lanny had no particle of belief in astrology, nor in the integrity of this sharp-witted young Rumanian; but something in his subconscious mind had picked up this theme and proceeded to make up stories about it. As a result, one interesting method of tapping the subconscious mind had been quite spoiled for Lanny; he no longer amused himself looking into a crystal ball, because all he saw there was a Cook's tour of the land of Cathay.

What was to be done about Beauty's dream life? The son thought that it would be an interesting case for a hypnotist; put her into a trance and tell her that she would never again believe any evil about her husband! But it isn't so easy to hypnotize a person who knows you as well as your mother does; and Parsifal of course was out of the question to perform his service.

A couple of days passed, and fear was still written on Beauty's usually placid face; her smiles when her husband was present were so forced that to Lanny they seemed like grimaces. Then one morning the phone rang, and Lanny, in the living-room, heard his mother answering in the hall. "Oh, hello, Sophie," and then a silence, and: "Oh, dear me! Is there anything we can do?" Then: "Well, tell her good-by for us. She is a lovely child."

The wife of Parsifal Dingle came into the room with a face of rapture: the expression of the man who coughed up the alligator. "Lanny! Adele is going home!"

"What for?" The thought flashed over him: had Beauty appealed to Sophie in her distress?

But no! "Her father has cabled. The mother has been hurt in an automobile accident. Adele is to take a plane from Marseilles by way of the Azores. Her father has made the arrangements."

Tears of delight, of utter bliss on the features of Beauty Budd! "Oh, Lanny, nobody can ever tell me that God doesn't answer prayers!"

Lanny couldn't restrain a burst of merriment. "Tell that to Adele's mother, old dear!"

3. *This Sceptered Isle*

I

LANNY BUDD was an American, and therefore a neutral, a privileged position in this war. He wanted to travel to England, and the route lay through Spain and Portugal. From Lisbon it would be easy.

because as the son of Budd-Erling he was important to the British; but he could hardly expect that to help him with the Vichy French or their Nazi overlords. He could have got help from Laval or Pétain, but that would probably have come to the attention of the British and wouldn't have sat so well with them. Better to put his trust in that universal world power which knows no boundaries and no sympathies; "bright and yellow, hard and cold—gold! gold! gold! gold!"

Lanny called upon his friend Jerry Pendleton; good old Jerry who had been his tutor a quarter of a century ago and his tennis partner ever since; a lieutenant from World War I, and now the owner of a travel bureau in Cannes. There wasn't much travel nowadays, but Jerry's little French wife owned half a *pension*, and that enabled the family to eat. For a matter of two decades Jerry had had an excuse to go fishing with Lanny Budd—they were providing food for the boarders. One of these had been Parsifal Dingle, so that Lanny had been fattening his future stepfather and psychic collaborator without having any idea of it.

Now he had only to say: "I want to fly to Madrid, and it's worth whatever it costs." Jerry would charge only the regular commission, and would know the right *douceur*—sweetener—to pay to clerks and officials who were on fixed salaries while the cost of living went up day after day. So it would come about that persons who had been clamoring for bookings would go on clamoring, while Lanny Budd would get a place on the next plane from Cannes to Marseilles, and from there, with only a few hours' delay, on a plane to Madrid. By an extra payment he could take not merely himself but his suitcases and his portable typewriter and his precious roll of painting.

He had visited Madrid during the previous winter, the period of the so-called *Sitzkrieg*, the "phony war." Marshal Pétain had at that time been the French Ambassador to Spain, and the Nazi agents had been bamboozling him with talk of gentlemen's agreements, precisely as they had bamboozled Prime Minister Chamberlain in Munich a little more than a year earlier. To Lanny Madrid had seemed the most desolate of capitals. The Nazis, with all their crimes, were at least efficient and put up a fine show; whereas Franco was nothing but a little whole-sale murderer in the cause of his medieval Church. He didn't even know how to repair the buildings he had smashed in the course of three years of civil war, and they stood there, gaping wrecks open to the sky. The Germans, who wanted his iron ore and copper, had to come and supervise the getting of it, the only means of collecting the huge debt due them for having set the Caudillo on his throne. He had two or three million of his people in prisons and concentration camps; shootings went on night after night, and famine stalked the streets of the great metropolis. On the stairs of the subway swarms of miserable, half-starved child bandits clamored to sell you lottery tickets and filthy postcards.

The landlords and the ecclesiastics—often the same persons—had won their war, and were prosperous and fat as always through the centuries. Lanny did not need to enter their palaces and ask questions, because he had got it all in Vichy and Cannes. He knew that Hitler had Franco's written permission to march through Spain whenever he felt strong enough to take Gibraltar; he knew about the arrangements for Il Duce to send the bombing planes, and about the submarine refueling system from Spanish ports.

II

By train through the desolate countryside, part of it barren, part wrecked by war, and on to Lisbon, which had become the spy center of Western Europe. The dictator who ruled this little country couldn't be sure which side was going to win, and he shrewdly played each against the other and raked in the cash. In his capital was the same contrast of riches with bitter poverty; you could buy costly perfumes stolen from the shops of Paris, and you could see barefooted women carrying huge loads of farm produce upon their heads. Nowhere could you escape the sight of German "tourists" wearing golf costumes, and if you talked in any café on the swanky Avenida da Liberdade, you might discover several persons trying to overhear what you said. Uniforms were everywhere, and of all colors; it must be that the officers of Portugal's small army designed their own, and so gaudy that you could imagine yourself on the stage of an operetta.

Lanny wasn't interested in talking to anybody in Lisbon, for in neutral countries he was a neutral and not desirous of attracting attention. There were great transport planes flying regularly to London, and others to Berlin from the same airport; this was a convenience to both sides, and as a rule they were not attacked. Reservations were beyond price; but Lanny was Budd-Erling, and his father had spoken for him; all he had to do was to send a cablegram to his father's solicitors in London, and three days later he boarded a plane at the crowded airport.

The start was at dawn, and the journey was supposed to take six hours; the passengers sat in their seats and dozed if they could. When their watches told them the time was longer, and a strange leaning in their seats told them that the plane was circling, they became anxious, and were informed that the Croydon airport had just been bombed and repairs were being made. It was impossible to see anything, because the windows of the plane had been covered with boards, held in place by suction cups—presumably so that no one might observe the elaborate defenses being constructed all along the coasts of this sceptered isle, this England.

When at last they touched the ground it was daylight, and there was a badly wrecked hangar still burning, and a landing field spotted with craters. No chance to see more; they were loaded into a bus and hurried off to London, a journey interrupted by road blocks and tank traps every mile or so. This time the windows were not blacked, and you could see how the fields of Southern England had trenches dug across them, and logs, carts, cast-off motor cars, and other obstructions to make trouble for planes and gliders that might drop down in the night. Lanny was astonished to see how much of such defense work had been done since his last visit; also by the number of bomb craters, even in the open fields. Homeguardsmen were active everywhere.

III

He had got a reservation at the Dorchester, which was fortunate, for so many people had been bombed out that the hotels were crowded. He ordered toast and coffee, orange juice, and eggs—the rich could still have these luxuries. He arranged to have his clothes pressed—one of the primary duties of a gentleman of elegance. Clad only in his shorts on a hot morning, he set up his little portable and set to work on his report.

It went fast, because he had been over and over it in his mind, week after week; everything that he had learned in Vichy and on the Riviera: the French Fleet, and the armies in French Africa and Syria; Franco and what he was doing and planning; the German preparations for invasion, and the activities of their agents in unoccupied France. Lanny used as few words as possible, for he had always in mind the stack of documents and reports he had seen on the reading table of his Chief at every visit; but he had been told to cover everything, and he did not spare even the American agents who were in Vichy, and whose trail he had been interested to follow. Mr. Robert Murphy, tall, partly bald career diplomat, was in Vichy presumably because he was a Catholic, and so could speak the language of Holy Mother Church, which claimed in the name of Almighty God the exclusive right to dominate the souls of men and women, to educate their children, and to be in all ways superior to the temporal state. The Holy Mother had got what she wanted in Franco Spain and now in Vichy France; and what was a free American to make of it?

Lanny made no carbon copy of his report. He sealed it in an envelope which bore no marks, and addressed it: "Personal to the President. Zaharoff." That was the code name which F.D.R. had assigned to him;

a name pretty well forgotten now, and borne by no one else, so far as Lanny knew. The aristocratic Spanish lady who had inherited the bulk of the munitions king's fortune had seventeen other names and didn't need his.

Lanny put the sealed envelope in another and larger one, and addressed this to "The Hon. Joseph Kennedy, U.S.A. Embassy, Grosvenor Square," and marked it "strictly personal." The Hon. Joe had instructions that the inner envelope was to be forwarded by diplomatic pouch, which, of course, always went by air. Since Lanny could never tell when a pouch might be leaving, he went out and found a taxicab, and watched from the window while the driver delivered the missive at the Embassy door. The passenger did not ride back to the hotel, but paid off the taxi and walked. By such elaborate precautions he had in the course of three years managed to send close to a hundred reports, and without slip-up so far as he knew.

IV

Next Lanny went to the police station. You had to register now and explain your business, just as on the Continent. They gave him a "food book," but he never once had to use it, because he ate at restaurants or with friends. The first of these he sought was Eric Vivian Pomeroy-Nielson, leftwing playwright and journalist, Lanny's contact with the anti-Fascist world in Britain. They had last parted amid the confusion of Dunkirk, and had not seen or heard from each other since. Now Lanny called the home, which was in Bucks, and asked for Rick's wife; he did not give his name but said: "This is Bienvenu," and the reply was: "Rick is in town; he has taken a job on the *Daily Clarion*." No more than that, for since Lanny had pretended to join the camp of the near-Fascists, he had never visited The Reaches, and his meetings with Rick and Nina were a carefully guarded secret. Lanny called the *Clarion* office and said: "Bienvenu"—nothing more. Rick answered: "I'll come."

They had agreed upon an obscure hotel where neither was known. Lanny went there and got a room, and his friend came. And what a time they had, swapping stories and news! Lanny was free to tell everything, except the single fact that he was a presidential agent; whatever Rick could use without pointing to Lanny as the source was all to the good from the point of view of both Lanny and his Boss. Rick had joined the staff of a labor paper because he couldn't stay at home in this crisis; he wanted the workers of his country to know what the war meant to them, and what would be their plight if the "appeasers" could manage to have their way one more time.

To Rick it was one conspiracy throughout the world. The holders of privilege had hired gangsters to protect themselves against social revolution, and that was the meaning of Fascism, National Socialism, Falangism, and all the different "shirts," black, brown, green, white, gold, silver. Always the clubs and daggers and revolvers had been purchased with the money of the great landlords, the owners of mines and mills, the holders of patents and paper titles which enabled them to levy tribute upon the toil of nations and empires. Rick's mind was a catalog of these people and the corporations and cartels they had set up; because he knew their economic motives, the sources of their income, he could foretell what they were going to do, and when they had done it he could explain why. He held them guilty of ten million murders, and this World War II was but one episode in their struggle to buttress their power.

Lanny told how he had met the German Army in Dunkirk, and had got through to meet Hitler and Göring, Kurt Meissner and Otto Abetz, and the rest of his Nazi friends; he told how Schneider and De Bruyne and Duchemin and François de Wendel and others in Paris were making their peace with the Nazis. In Vichy it was somewhat different—the leaders there hoped to preserve their Catholic culture, and to have a Church Fascism like Franco's; but at Nazi command they were having to persecute the Jews, and were hunting out the refugees, the Reds and the Pinks of every shade, the liberals and democrats, everybody of whom the Nazis had ever heard, and who might by any chance speak a word against them. "You can't imagine how it feels to live in Vichy France," Lanny said. "You can't find out anything but what the regime wants you to know; you can't even find out what the laws are—there are so many new decrees, and not paper enough to print them. You have to stand on a street corner and read the *affiches* in order to know what you're forbidden to do."

V

Were the Germans going to try an invasion of Britain? That was the question everybody talked about, not merely on this island but all over the world. Lanny told what Hitler had said, that he was coming as soon as he was ready. But did he mean it? Would he have said it if he had meant it? "He is a strange semi-lunatic," Lanny opined; "cunning wars with vanity in his soul, and it would be hard for him to forego the glory of announcing what he was going to do. He will come if his generals do not oppose it too strenuously."

Lanny was one who had a right to be informed, and his best and dearest friend withheld nothing from him. England for twenty miles back from the coast had been declared a military zone, and day and night labor was turning it into one vast fortification. Every beach was mined, and covered with a tangle of tightly strung barbed wire; there was hidden artillery of all sizes, and no end of pillboxes with machine guns, carefully camouflaged. There were great railway guns which could be rushed from place to place. Most important of all, the period of the *Sitzkrieg* had been utilized to devise and install a series of pipes extending out under the sea, connected with oil tanks and heavy pumps. In case of an invasion attempt, oil would be poured out in floods; it would rise to the surface, and there was a magnesium device to ignite it, so that the invaders would find themselves caught in an inferno of flame. And even when they came to the shore, they would find the beaches ablaze, and flamethrowers concealed behind garden hedges.

Rick told about the situation he had discovered on his return from Dunkirk. Tanks, artillery, trucks, machine guns, all the costly equipment of an army of two or three hundred thousand men had been lost in Flanders; the Germans had it, and the British had only one fully equipped brigade to defend their shores; troops guarding the beaches had to be armed with shotguns, sporting rifles, even muskets out of museums. "Your President saved us," declared the baronet's son. "Have you heard what he did?"

"I didn't see an American or British paper till I got to Lisbon."

"This hasn't been published yet, that I know of. You had a million World War I rifles in your arsenals, and Roosevelt had them loaded onto fast steamers and sent over to us. They are out-of-date, but they saved us once and might have done it again. He's been letting us buy some torpedo boats and other small stuff that your navy can spare. They are sold to private dealers who resell them to us; that's according to your laws, it appears."

"It wouldn't appear so well during an election year," was the reply.

"I know, I know," said Rick. "You have about a hundred over-age destroyers, left from the last war. We need them the worst way in the world, to keep our convoys on top of the water. We're trying our best to buy them, so the Pater tells me. Put in a word for us, if you meet anybody with influence."

"I'll do that, you may be sure. But tell me this, old man—what are you going to do if the Germans do succeed in breaking down the door?"

"We'll fight inside the house, of course; we'll fight to the last man."

"I know, but that won't help much; civilians can't fight a modern army. I'm going home, and my father will ask me questions; some of his friends are influential, and their decisions may make a lot of difference to you. Suppose these islands are conquered—what will the Fleet do? Will the Germans get it, or will it come to Canada as Churchill promised?"

"The Pater has talked with members of the Cabinet about it, and they say there has been a formal vote. We'll do another Dunkirk—put our fighting men on board every sort of ship we can get together, and the Fleet will escort them to Canada. We'll fight from there, and come back home some day. My understanding is, we have already given that promise to Roosevelt in writing; and we've taken the first step by shipping every ounce of gold in the Bank of England's vaults to New York and Montreal and other places of safety. That was quite an adventure, believe me—and it's strictly hush-hush!"

"It's the best news I've heard in a long while," declared Lanny. "My father will sleep better when he gets it."

"What I want you to send me back," replied the Englishman, "is the dope regarding Roosevelt's chances of re-election. What do you know about this fellow Willkie?"

"I never heard his name until I read a three-line dispatch in *l'Éclaireur de Nice* saying that the Republicans had nominated him. The Continent isn't allowed to know about American political affairs. Even the Swiss papers are not allowed into Vichy France any more."

VI

Lanny inquired about the family, whose home he had visited so often in youth and early manhood. Sir Alfred had taken a desk job in the Local Defense Volunteers; he was old, but so long as his strength held out he would set free some younger man. Nina, Rick's wife, was running the home, and the women of the neighborhood came to roll bandages in their spare hours. The two girls were training to be nurses, as their mother had been in the previous war. Young Rick, the younger son, whom Lanny remembered as a long-legged schoolboy, was training with the Air Force, following in the footsteps of his adored older brother. Alfy, lieutenant in the R.A.F., was down near Dover, the hottest spot this side of hell, his father said. "We haven't seen him for a couple of months."

"I suppose they're on call day and night," the other remarked.

"You can't imagine the tension, Lanny. They sleep with their boots on, and when the siren sounds they leap into their flying suits and dash to the planes. There are so few, and everything depends upon them."

"You said they would prove to be better than the Germans. How is it working out?"

"Well, they're outnumbered six or eight to one, and they have to get several of the enemy for every one they lose. The figures aren't given out, of course; but Alfy says they are holding their own."

"My heart goes out to Nina," remarked the visitor gravely.

"It's rugged, but not so much so as you might think. There comes a point where you can't suffer any more, and you stop. Alfy is credited with five Luftwaffe planes and so far he hasn't been hit, but that can't go on forever; nobody has an unlimited drawing account in the bank of luck. Some day there'll come a telegram. Alfy is married, by the way."

"You don't tell me!"

"Right after he came back from the Dunkirk circus; to Lily Strawbridge, the family just down the river from us; you may remember them."

"Very well indeed."

"A fine girl; and she has just learned that she is pregnant. So Nina will transfer her affections. That's the way it goes in wartime. This generation has to be written off; at any rate the airmen."

Lanny thought for a moment, then said: "I think I should have a talk with Alfy before I leave. Do you know if he has had anything to do with the Budd-Erling?"

"He has tried one out."

"Well, my father will have a hundred questions to ask. Nothing can take the place of actual battle test."

"I'll see what can be done about it. You're going to Wickthorpe, I suppose."

"That is my plan. How are they?"

"I don't see that family any more. They wouldn't relish my conversation. I've heard a rumor—it may or may not be true—that his lordship is thinking of resigning from the Foreign Office."

"Good grief!" exclaimed the American. "What would that mean?"

"I rather fancy he's been a fish out of water for a long time, and he can't have been entirely happy."

"Irma will tell me about it, I imagine."

"Don't you tell *me;* I'll get the story myself and be free to publish it—unless you prefer that I didn't."

Lanny thought for a space. "It might be better if you left that particular scoop to somebody else, Rick. Everybody thinks of me as Irma's former husband, and many of them have not forgotten that I used to be your friend. After all, it's not an important story—not so much so as some of the things I can get if I keep my appeaser sympathies untouched by suspicion."

"Righto!" said the playwright. "I'll spare the mother of your child, and you find out for me how much truth there is in the report that Hitler is making another peace offer through Eire, and that he's holding off the invasion to give us time to think it over."

"What I've heard," replied Lanny, "is that Sam Hoare is negotiating in Spain. Both may be true. God help us!"

VII

Lanny telephoned to Wickthorpe Castle, as courtesy required, to ask whether it would be convenient for him to pay a visit to his little daughter. Irma answered: "Certainly; but, Lanny, there are so many people wanting to get out of London, I had to let some friends have your cottage. Would you mind using Mother's spare room?"

"Of course not," he replied. "I can't stay very long, and I'd be ashamed to keep a whole cottage empty in times like these."

He took the train, and a pony-cart from the Castle met him at the station. His lovely little daughter was in it, some three months older and perhaps half an inch taller than when he had seen her last; eager to greet him and to ply him with questions, and to tell him about her own adventures. War might be hell for a flying man, but it had its compensations for a child: so many things going on, so many changes in routine, so much news. The poor little rich girl named Frances Barnes Budd was ten years old, and more things had been crowded into her life in the past year than in all the previous nine. And now came this handsome and delightful father who had been in Paris and seen the conquering German army, and met the dreadful wicked Führer—Frances had to be taught that he was wicked because everybody else on the estate and in the village believed it, and she had to be a patriotic little English girl, even though her father and mother were both Americans. Lanny, skilled at playing roles, had to play two at the same time in this ancient remodeled castle.

After the little one had gone reluctantly to bed, he was shut up in the privacy of the library with his former wife and the wife's new husband; a strictly modern situation, never before heard of or imagined in these ancestral halls. Irma's divorce had been got in Reno, Nevada; and within a half-century an English earl had been sentenced by his peers to six months' imprisonment for putting his trust in that variety of escape mechanism. But this time it was the woman who had got the unshackling; and here she was now, living in what her Church called adulterous relationship; but all the same, the rector came to tea and the curate played bowls with his lordship on the green.

"We mustn't quarrel," Irma had said, "if only for Frances' sake," —and Lanny had agreed with her. Some of their friends thought they couldn't have been very much in love, or they wouldn't have taken their parting so easily. Apparently their friends would have thought it a sign of true love if they had thrown the dishes at each other's heads, or made a scandal in the newspapers; perhaps even if Lanny had strangled Irma, or if she had put poison into his coffee. That had been the old-fashioned way; among the portraits in this ancient castle was one of a black-whiskered military earl who had hurled his unfaithful wife down the great stairway and broken her neck. At least, that was the way tradition had it; he had said it was an accident, and there was no law that could contradict him. That kind of marital solution made tremendous Elizabethan drama, but it didn't appear so well suited to everyday use.

Irma was now a countess, and that was what she wanted; that was the way she got something for her money. As the wife of Lanny Budd she had got little, because Lanny didn't respect money, indeed flouted it openly; he couldn't see that it was any fun to spend great sums entertaining a swarm of people who didn't care a hang about you and would have snubbed you on the street if you had gone broke. But now as Lady Wickthorpe, Irma had a whole community in awe of her and treating her with ceremony. A handsome brunette woman of thirty, quiet and dignified in manner, she went about with the blue-eyed rosy-cheeked lordship at her side, knowing that everything was exactly right. If now and then she found him slightly dull, she wouldn't admit it even to herself. She had borne him two sons, and thus had settled her obligation to the British peerage; the fact that she had a child by a previous marriage and that the father of this child came visiting was taken by the Wickthorpe villagers as an Americanism.

VIII

What Lord and Lady Wickthorpe were doing now was trying to save civilization; their own phrase, and they were in deadly earnest about it. Lanny had known "Ceddy" since boyhood, when he had been a viscount; he had always been serious-minded, and talked a lot about duty to the "Empah." Now he said: "This war is the most tragic blunder in our hist'ry." His wife's usually so placid face wore an expression of pain as she added: "The most cruel and wicked thing!" A woman thought more about the human side of it: the young men going out and not coming back, the homes being blown into rubble, the women and children buried beneath them.

"We must find a way to stop it," continued his lordship. "We are simply throwing away our heritage; we are turning all Europe over to a band of Asiatic barbarians."

That was the point of view of a large group of British aristocrats, industrialists, men of affairs; even after Dunkirk there were many who felt sure in their hearts that nobody could benefit from this war except Stalin. They pictured him in their imaginations, the Caucasian despot, gloating over the blunder his capitalistic foes were committing; he sitting back watching, getting ready to leap in at the end, when the other nations had completely exhausted themselves. "There are two great civilizations in the world, the Anglo-Saxon and the German," declared Ceddy; "and these two are going to destroy each other's cultures and leave the world to the lesser breeds. Surely Hitler must see that as well as we!"

"He does see it," responded Lanny. "He has set it forth in practically the same words. The problem is, how to get the two sides together."

This couple knew no one else who was in position to meet the top-flight Nazis at the present time; so now they proceeded to cross-question him and to drink in every word. Numbers One, Two, and Three—Hitler, Göring, and Hess—they had come to Paris for the victory parade and Lanny had talked with them. They were all in agreement, they had no quarrel with Britain, no claims against the British Empire; they wanted nothing but a free hand in Eastern and Central Europe, a part of the world in which the British had no proper interest and no right to interfere.

Hitler had said it over and over in his speeches; he had assured Lanny that he was willing to get out of France—except perhaps Alsace-Lorraine; he was willing to help restore Belgium and Holland and Norway, which he had been compelled to take, partly by the accident of geography and partly by British intrigue. Hitler was sure that he could invade Britain, but he didn't want to, and couldn't understand why the British ruling classes failed to appreciate the service he had done them in putting down the Reds throughout the greater part of Europe—to say nothing of his offer to invade the vulture's nest in the east and smash it once for all. Hitler had said: "Poland? *Um Gottes Willen*, how did we come to get into a war over Poland? Poland is a pigsty; Poland stinks! You British tell the Americans that you believe in democracy; you don't, of course, but even if you did, what has that to do with Poland, a dictatorship of landlords and colonels? Poland is the breeding-place of the typhus-carrying louse!"

It all seemed so simple to the Wickthorpes and their little coterie. They weren't pacifists, but they wanted to fight the right war, and when they knew they were fighting the wrong one, they begrudged every drop of British blood, every dead Tommy or officer, every home that was bombed, every factory and shipyard and oiltank and whatnot. They grieved for the Germans almost as much as for themselves; they were quite sure that if the Nazis had been treated with tolerance and consideration they would have developed the same conservatism as British statesmen. "You know we were pretty rough ourselves in the old days," remarked Ceddy, who liked to read hist'ry. "Building an empah is never a milk-and-water proposition. Take Clive, for instance—or, for that matter, Cecil Rhodes." He was talking to an old friend, and could speak frankly.

Lanny reported on Pétain and his regime. A humiliating position they were in, but they had got into it by their own bad judgment, declared the noble earl. There was no need for England to do the same; nothing of the sort was desired by Hitler, and to say otherwise was merely the trickery of demagogues, of Reds open or camouflaged. Britain and Germany should be friends; they should define their separate interests and recognize each other's right to live and grow; the world was big enough, but not big enough to support war. There should be an armistice at once, then a frank discussion and settlement. Churchill, of course, would have to resign. After Lanny had told all he had learned about efforts being made to this end, Ceddy went into detail about Hitler's proposals through his agents in Eire and Sir Samuel Hoare in Spain. Something was surely coming out of these dickerings, declared his lordship.

IX

Lanny waited for the couple to bring up the delicate subject which Rick had mentioned; and sure enough, Irma remarked: "Ceddy is thinking of resigning, and we both of us wonder what you will think about it."

"You surprise me," responded the secretive one. "Won't you be sacrificing a lot of influence?"

"We don't think so, Lanny. It is impossible for us to function under the present Cabinet."

"I know that permanent officials aren't supposed to have anything to do with policy, but I have always felt certain that Ceddy was finding ways to make his influence felt."

"That used to be so, but the time appears to have passed. Churchill dominates everything, and no one dares lift a voice in opposition. He really believes that he can win this war; he means to try, even if he wrecks all Europe."

"A man who is prey to his hatreds, I fear. But as to Ceddy, I am troubled to see him giving up the career that has meant so much to him. Won't you miss your daily routine, old man?"

"I was happy in it so long as I thought I was accomplishing something; but I no longer feel that, and it irks me to take the orders of wrong-headed men."

"But take the long view, Ceddy! Times will surely change."

"My reading of our hist'ry convinces me that in the long run an Englishman does not suffer politically from following his conscience."

"Take the case of Ramsay MacDonald," put in Irma. "He stood out against the last war, but after it was over he became Prime Minister." Irma was too young to remember those events, but she, too, had been reading hist'ry—or at any rate listening to it in her drawing-room.

Lanny might have replied that the Scotch idealist had resigned because he stood to the Left, whereas the Earl of Wickthorpe stood to the Right, and that made all the difference in the political world. But it wasn't Lanny's role to suggest ideas of that sort. Instead he remarked: "I shall miss the inside view of things which you have given me."

"I don't think it will make much difference in that respect. There are others who share my point of view, even though they don't feel free to act upon it. They will keep me informed."

"What does Gerald think about it?" That was Gerald Albany, a colleague in the Foreign Office whom Lanny had often met at Wickthorpe and in London.

"He agrees that it's all right for me, but for various reasons he doesn't care to join me. I am in a peculiar position, as you know, on account of my rank. I had no business to be a civil servant."

Said Lanny: "I've always appreciated your devotion to the public welfare. Are you going to make a personal issue of your resignation?"

"Irma and I are in agreement that it isn't the time for that. My resignation will speak for itself. I'll retire to this place and become a country squire for a while—Britain will need food as much as guns."

"But you won't give up your activity on behalf of peace!" exclaimed Lanny anxiously.

"We shall do what we can in a quiet way to spread an understanding of the situation and to counter the intrigues of the wild men. We count upon you to bring us news from America, and from the Continent, if you are able to travel there."

The wife put in, anxiously: "Do you think the decision is wise, Lanny?"

"On the whole I believe I do. After all, a Foreign Office job is a routine one, and there are many men who can fill it. It is a humiliating job for a man of Ceddy's station and ability; his friends have known that for a long time—I have heard several say it. As a member of the House of Lords his words and example will count for more than he realizes. He might be the man to name the Prime Minister and determine the policies of the Government."

Really, it was a shame to play with Irma that way. Lanny knew her so well, it was like tempting a child with candy. From earliest childhood she had been taught that she was a person of tremendous importance, because of the fortune of J. Paramount Barnes, utilities magnate who had killed himself gaining it. Quite literally, Lanny doubted if Irma had ever even heard of the idea that her money didn't constitute her a privileged person, until she had found herself married to Lanny Budd. Now the vision of herself as wife of the man who was really dominating the Government of the British Empire—well, it swelled her up visibly, and that wasn't so good, because maternity and good living had already done their work with her, and she was worried about *embonpoint*, just like Beauty Budd, and living on a diet of mutton chops and salads, which were supposed to be "reducing."

X

Not far from here was the estate of Rosemary, Countess of Sandhaven, Lanny's old flame. She was a year older than he, still blooming, and a lovely person to look at, with gentle regular features and two great ropes of straw-colored hair which she had refused to cut off in spite of fashion. Her husband was in the diplomatic service and just now in Brazil; he had given his word not to get into any more scandals, but he had never promised to live within his income. Sandhaven Manor was in debt, and any time Lanny came to England, all he had to do was to call up Rosemary, and have tea with her and stroll in the long gallery where her husband's ancestors and their ladies were portrayed. He would remark: "I think I might interest somebody in that Romney." Rosemary would reply: "What do you suppose it would bring?" and they would go through a routine of his refusing to set prices, she saying what a nuisance it was, she had nobody else to advise her and why couldn't he be sensible?

The way it would end, he would say: "Well, if it was mine, I would think that five thousand pounds was a good price." She would answer: "All right, if you can get that, I'll put it up to Bertie." Lanny would send cablegrams, and in a few days would have the money; then Rosemary would cable her husband and he would authorize the sale. Lanny would get ten per cent from his client and Rosemary would take ten per cent of what Bertie got—and in addition would make him agree to use part of the balance to pay off this and that creditor who was worrying her. Half the British aristocracy was in debt, Lanny judged from their conversation.

Such a picture deal would mean that Lanny would pay at least two visits to Sandhaven Manor, and drink two cups of hot tea per visit, and nibble as many cookies. Also he had to sit and look at a very lovely blonde, who for two considerable periods had been his sweetheart and teacher in the arts of love. She was a product of the feminist movement of the nineteen-teens; she had once smuggled a hatchet into the National Gallery so that an older woman could smash a picture in the cause of votes for women. She had learned to assert her right to do everything that men did and a little more of it. Both she and her husband enjoyed the privilege of taking love where they found it; and Rosemary had never found more with any man than with the grandson of Budd Gunmakers.

She was completely free-spoken; she had as much right to make the proposition as a man had, and she never failed to talk about these matters, inquiring as to Lanny's love life, and why they couldn't be happy now as they had been in their teens and again in their twenties. Lanny had made up his mind that he wanted an exclusive love, if any, but he couldn't tell Rosemary that without seeming a prig, and incidentally hurting the feelings of a good friend. It wouldn't help any to say that he was in love with some other woman, for Rosemary wouldn't have seen why that should make any difference. It was a problem how to deal with this situation, and Lanny had taken refuge in the idea of being a queer fellow who had been so much hurt by love that he had sworn off it for the rest of his days.

He would divert the conversation to Rosemary's two sons, who were both in the army, one a German prisoner, and the other having escaped by the beaches of Dunkirk. Lanny said nothing about it, but he thought: Perhaps young Bertie had been one of those many men whom he and Rick had helped to lift out of the water. There had been so many of them, and the work of getting them onto the ships had gone on by night as well as by day; many had been too exhausted to speak, and Lanny hadn't seen their faces or even their uniforms. It was the toughest ordeal that he had ever undergone, but now, looking back upon it, he felt proud of himself.

XI

A seat on one of the Clippers crossing the Atlantic these days went not by price but by favor, and you had to be very important. But few could be more so than a man who was making airplanes to help in the salvation of Britain, and when such a man said that his son was bringing him data which might be the means of improving the plane, the authorities had to take his word. Robbie's London solicitor, Mr. Stafforth, said he would arrange it as soon as possible; and apparently he knew the ropes, for two days later the laconic gentleman called up to report that arrangements had been made for the following Friday.

Also there came a call from Rick, saying: "Our friend will call on Thursday afternoon." So Lanny bade farewell to his family at Wickthorpe and went up to the huge sprawling city under the silvery barrage balloons. He always went to the Dorchester, because there, in the super-luxury lounge, he would find the sort of people whose talk was important to a P.A. "People with Munich faces," Rick had called them; and sure enough, Lanny could have found a dozen in an hour who would say that we had already lost the war and what was the use of making so much fuss about it? People to whom the war meant nothing but personal inconvenience, and who meant to have as little of that as they could contrive!

Lanny lunched with an exquisitely corrupt youth whose father had got him exempted on grounds of his being indispensable to a banking business. Now with a pretty little doll who called herself a chorus lady but didn't work at it, he outlined to the son of Budd-Erling—whom he imagined to be immensely wealthy—a scheme for making a fortune out of speculations in French electrical shares; they were down to a quarter of their value, and this tipster had information as to which concerns had made their deals with the Nazis and would stand to come out on top when peace had come—which would be before the leaves fell, his father was sure.

Expecting Alfy's visit, Lanny went to the obscure hotel where he had met Rick. It was a cheap place and a drab room, but had the advantage that nobody knew you or concerned himself about what you were doing. Lanny was lying on the bed reading back copies of New York newspapers when the Royal Air Force man tapped on his door.

The Hon. Alfred Pomeroy-Nielson, twenty-three, would become a baronet if he could manage to live long enough, which seemed far from likely at the moment. He had been Lanny's friend since his nursery days, and was one of the few who shared the secret that Lanny was an enemy of the Fascists posing as their friend. Alfy knew that his father had got important information through this American, and he assumed that someone overseas must be doing the same. Four years ago he had been flying for the Spanish Republican government, and Lanny had been the means of helping him out of a Franco dungeon. For that he owed his life, and was ready to pay the debt if ever the opportunity came. Just now what Lanny asked was to learn all he could about the air war now coming to its climax around and above the coasts of Britain. So Alfy would set aside the rule of silence which his group had laid upon him.

He was a tall, slender fellow, with his mother's fair hair and his father's thin features and alert expression. He was very much of a "Red," more so than either of the elders; he saw this war as a deliberate assault of the German cartels—steel, coal, power, and munitions—upon the labor movements of the rest of the world. Hitler was a puppet of these interests; they had bought him the guns, without which he would have remained a street-corner rabble-rouser. The end of the war must be the overthrow of those giant exploiters, not merely in Germany but all over the world; otherwise it would be a "defeat in the victory," as Lanny's friend Herron had written after the last war—and what a prophet he had proved to be!

For the moment Alfy's job was hunting the Hun, and he had been at it day and night. He was thinner and paler than ever before; obviously he was living on his nerves, and his friend would have liked first of all to buy him a square meal and then put him to bed. But no, he had only a few hours' leave and they must talk "shop." This was a war for survival, as Churchill had said; the balance was swinging one way and then the other, hour by hour, and the little push that you could give today might determine which way it would swing for keeps.

Alfy explained that the Hun flyers were trying to counter the British blockade. They had their bases close to the coast of France; indeed they had them all along the coast of Europe, from Narvik in Northern Norway all the way to the Spanish border. They were trying to establish command of the Channel and block off the British ports; they were coming in flights of five hundred at a time; bombing ships and shipping, docks and harbor installations, oil depots, and everything of military value. For the most part they came at night, because their daytime losses had been too heavy. But night bombing wasn't accurate; and now the British had a wonderful new night-fighter with a device for seeing in the dark so ultra-secret that even Alfy didn't know what it was. He revealed also that the British had constructed great numbers of imitation air bases to fool the Germans; they were so good that the Germans were dropping more bombs on them than on the real ones; so good that the British flyers had trouble in remembering not to land on them.

XII

Alfy talked about the new Budd-Erling known as the Tycoon. He spoke plainly; no use shirking the facts. It was good, but not good enough; nowhere near so good as the newest British fighter, the Supermarine Spitfire, shortened to "Subspit." Alfy went into technicalities, and Lanny made careful notes, for it was all right for him to have data on this subject, especially since he was leaving on the morrow. These new terrors had eight machine guns, four in each wing, and they made a terrific cone of fire; but .303 caliber wouldn't do, they had to be fifty. That added to the weight, of course; there was a tendency for the fighters to become heavier; more speed meant larger engines, and there was a call for armor over this vital part and that.

Like the century-old duel between gun and armor on battleships was the duel between safety and maneuverability on pursuit planes. Alfy pointed out that there was such a thing as having too much

maneuverability; more than the human organism could make use of
If you turned at a speed of more than two hundred miles, you were
pretty sure to black out, and you might not come to until you had
hit the ground, or until the enemy had drilled you through. The
Englishman drew an extraordinary picture of what it meant to be
carrying on an air duel four or five miles above the ground, breathing
from an oxygen tank, pursuing an enemy who was ducking and
dodging at the terrific speeds these planes could now attain. The Hun
was swerving; you almost had him in your sights, and if you could
swerve a tiny fraction more you would have him; but there came,
as it were, a yellowish-gray curtain before your eyes, the first warning
of the blackout; you had to know exactly how far you could go
toward unconsciousness, and you might have to make that decision
a dozen times in the course of a prolonged duel of wits with your
opponent—he facing exactly the same problem. If you straightened out,
you would lose your man; also, you might discover another enemy
plane on your tail, one who might get you in *his* sights.

This greatly dreaded blackout was caused by centrifugal force
driving the blood from your head. There were ways to counter it
partially; you contracted your abdomen, and held an extra amount
of air in your lungs; that took a powerful man, which Alfy wasn't.
Leaning forward helped a little, because it lowered the head and made
the task of the heart easier. The flyer said: "If it wasn't for that
yellowish-gray curtain, I could have got five times as many of the
bastards."

Lanny replied: "I will tell you something important. Robbie tells
me that our scientists are working on the problem of a flying suit that
will prevent the blackout. It will have inflatable rubber pockets over
certain parts of the body that will restrict the flow of blood to the
extremities and so tend to keep it in the head. The thing will be
automatic; when the centrifugal force reaches a certain point, the
clamps will be instantly applied. It won't feel so comfortable, but
it may enable you to get the enemy in your sights."

"You can tell Robbie if he gets that, he can forget about armor and
concentrate on maneuverability and firepower."

"Don't say anything about it, even to your superiors," Lanny cautioned. "It's a rather obvious idea, but the Nazis may not have hit
on it. If we get it, you can be sure we'll send it to Britain."

XIII

When these two had last discussed the prospects of the air war, the
baronet's grandson had said: "Our men are better." Now Lanny
wanted to know how it was working out, and the answer was: "We

are holding our own; and nobody could ask more, considering the handicaps. The Hun is on the offensive, and that means we are always outnumbered; sometimes we fight ten or twenty to one, and have to manage to survive until help arrives."

The basic handicap was that of geography. The Germans had bases close to England, and could be dropping bombs on British cities a few minutes after they were discovered; but if the British wanted to bomb German cities they had to fly for an hour or two, exposed to flak all the way; the enemy had time to assemble great fleets of fighters—in short he had everything in his favor, both going and coming. "When one of our men catches a Hun by himself, the Hun ducks for the nearest cloud and has no shame about it. That tells the story of who is the better."

Alfy talked about the men with whom he flew. They were a sober lot, far more so than those of the last war, by Rick's account. They had put the future out of their minds; they lived in the moment and its dangers. They were saving England, or trying to, but they seldom talked about that; they talked about the enemy and his tricks, and the critical tenth of a second in which they had got him. Always something new to learn, some new formation, some device of teamwork. While resting, they read mystery stories, or talked about girls. Most of them were young, and the newcomers still younger.

The Royal Air Force had been a volunteer organization, and the pilots were mostly of the upper class. Alfy said: "I hate to admit it, but it's the old school tie that is doing the job, because there's nobody else. But that won't be true for long; we're having to take qualified men wherever we can find them now. And that's all to the good; if we don't break down England's caste system, we'll find this war was hardly worth fighting."

Lanny agreed with all that; but he wanted to shake his head sadly when the flyer went on to say: "There will be a different England after this war. Our people will never be content with the old life, after the sacrifices they have made." Lanny had heard exactly the same words from Alfy's father during World War I, before this youngster had been born. However, there was no use saying anything to discourage a man who belonged to death.

"First we have to win," Lanny said, a proposition beyond dispute. Alfy wanted to know what help could be expected from overseas, and how it was possible for the people there to be so blind to the meaning of Nazi victory for themselves. Were the "isolationists" in America the same as the "appeasers" in Britain, persons who thought more of their class than of their country?

"It's not quite the same," Lanny explained. "It's what I call the peasant mind. The peasant is interested only in his own fields and doesn't see beyond them, except, perhaps, for a small strip that he would like to add to his own. Americans have been safe behind their three thousand miles of ocean, and it's hard indeed for them to realize that that ocean has dried up. A few men of vision understand the situation, and have to awaken the others. Fortunately Roosevelt is such a man."

"Many of us over here think he's the greatest statesman in the world, Lanny."

"He is a lot better than the American people deserved, or would have accepted if they had known what they were getting."

"Do you think they'll re-elect him?"

"I'll be able to judge better when I'm back there. I've been reading the New York papers." Lanny picked up a copy of the *Times*. "You see this headline: 'Willkie Says President Courts War.' That seems to be the level on which the campaign is being conducted."

They talked about American politics for a while, and Lanny explained as well as he could the curious practice by which the party out of power is compelled to attack the policies of the party in power, regardless of its own historic principles. So now the Republicans were the party of isolationism, even of pacifism, whereas for half a century they had been the party of imperialism; more fantastic yet, they were the party of states' rights, which surely must make the body of Abraham Lincoln turn over in his Springfield tomb. "Anything to beat Roosevelt" was now the one Republican principle.

"Have you ever met him?" Alfy asked, and Lanny hated to lie outright to one whom he loved. "I have met him casually. He is one of the hardest-worked men in the world, I imagine. What we load onto him is enough to break the back of an elephant."

XIV

They went out to dinner, in a small restaurant where nobody would know them. The great city was full of men in uniform, and no one paid special attention to an officer with wings on his sleeve. They talked about their two families, home news which would be of no interest to enemy ears; everyone was on the alert just then, because more than fifty empty parachutes had been found in various open places in England and Scotland—which meant that enemy spies had come down during the night. These spies would undoubtedly be English-looking and English-speaking men and perhaps women, so the newspapers warned; they would be saboteurs, equipped with explosives and incendiary materials; or they would carry suitcases containing radio transmitting sets, powerful enough to reach the French coast or submarines lying close to shore.

There came the scream of sirens. People had had a year to get used to them; some leaped up and ran for the nearest shelter, others sat quiet and finished their dinner; it was a matter of temperament. The sound of guns was heard in the distance, and then nearer; the ack-ack made quick sharp sounds like the barking of a dog but much faster; they spread all around, an all-pervading clatter. Then another sound, a dull boom, which people had agreed to describe by the word "crump." Alfy, familiar with all sounds of war, exclaimed: "By Jove! They have broken through! The first time they have done it by daylight!" Lanny didn't need to ask; he knew the sounds of bombs from many scenes of war.

They had finished their dinner; Lanny paid the bill and they strolled out with carefully preserved dignity to the street. There were people looking up; there were always people willing to risk their lives to see a show, and this was a free country. It was after sunset, but there was still enough light to see that the air was full of planes, high up, darting in every direction, for all the world like a swarm of midges in the springtime. Hundreds of them, perhaps a thousand, and you couldn't tell which was which, you couldn't pick out any particular "dog-fight." But now a great swarm of larger planes came sailing straight across, more slowly, out of a mass of cumulus clouds. You knew that these were the bombers; these were what the others were fighting about. They were so close together that it seemed to be a solid web. The bursts of firing mingled into a vast whirring, filling all the sky; and if this pair of diners gazing upward hadn't been so afraid of showing the least sign of concern, they might have admitted that many millions of bullets being released in the sky had to come down somewhere on London streets and roofs.

"When you see a show like that," remarked Alfy, "you have only one thought, you want to be up there."

"You can't do everything," was his friend's reply. "This is your day of rest."

"This is damn serious," replied the unresting airman. "If they can break through like this, it means we're losing. It's what they haven't dared before."

They went on discussing air-war strategy and statistics, until there came a terrific mechanical scream and then a deafening explosion, and a house about half a block away went up in a blast of flame and smoke and flying debris. The air compression hit them like a sort of universal blow, sparing no part of them, inside or out, and almost toppling them over. Showers of rubble fell about them, and it was at least a minute before they could speak, and longer before they could hear. Meantime there came more explosions, near and far, behind and before them.

"Shall we go and help?" shouted Alfy; but Lanny caught him by the arm. "Leave it to the wardens, old man; you have your own job."

<h2 style="text-align:center">XV</h2>

So they condescended to seek shelter. Near by was an entrance to the underground railway, to Englishmen "the tube." They walked, rapidly but not running, to this goal. Many other people had been seized by the same idea and were not under the necessity of preserving their dignity; they got there first, and it was some time before the two gentlemen could crowd themselves in. The place was packed almost to suffocation, and the conditions were not pleasing to persons of refined sensibilities. There was public clamor for Government to "do something about it," but Government had a lot of other things on their hands at the moment. It seemed more important to use steel for guns and ammunition than for the building of an underground city for seven million Londoners, to say nothing of the inhabitants of Portsmouth and Southampton and Sheffield and Birmingham and all the rest.

There were many, especially women and old people, who had taken up the tube as their dwelling place; they brought a pallet or a blanket to sleep on, they brought baskets of food, and refused to be driven out into the open. The sanitary arrangements were inadequate and the filth shocking. At first the police had tried to force people out, but as the danger increased and more homes were wrecked and people buried under them, the authorities had to give up and allow this subterranean way of life to become general. Was there going to develop an underground race of creatures, pale and spindling, unable to bear the sunlight, as predicted long ago in the stories of H. G. Wells? The son of Budd-Erling, squeezed like a sardine in a can and jarred to the marrow of his bones by blast after blast of the bombs, would have had to be superhuman if he had not thought with a certain amount of relief about a ticket for tomorrow's Clipper reposing safely in a pocket over his heart!

He groped his way through the blackout to his hotel, and spent the night without sleep, listening to the uproar of that infernal battle. He had made the mistake of choosing a hotel which was just across the street from Hyde Park, and all London parks were full of anti-aircraft guns. Every time one of these went off the blast of air shot the window curtains straight out into the room and tried to lift the covers off Lanny's bed. The walls shook as in an earthquake, and small objects on bureau and tables jumped and rattled. Lanny decided that it was folly to risk staying in bed, and put on his clothes and went down into a crowded shelter. His knees were shaking and his teeth chattering—not merely for himself but for England. He knew this was the real blitz, this was the supreme effort, which both Hitler and Göring had told him was coming. Up there in black sky the night-fighter pilots were racing at a speed of four hundred miles an hour, hunting the murderers, trying to save England, trying to save the democratic world. Lanny's prayers went up for them, and his thoughts were those that Winston Churchill was soon to put into immortal words: that never in history had so many owed so much to so few.

BOOK TWO

Comes the Moment to Decide

———————————— o ————————————

4. Hands across the Sea

I

FROM the smooth water of a little port on the coast of Ireland
the magical Clipper transported Lanny Budd to the smooth water of
a larger port near the end of Long Island: a safe and comfortable
journey, but slightly monotonous, for in the calm weather in early
September one part of the Atlantic looked exactly like another part,
and you could only wonder why the Lord had taken the trouble to
make such immense quantities of water. Lanny entertained himself
with magazines which he had brought along, and in one of them he
read an article about a huge plant on the coast of Texas which was
busily extracting magnesium from ocean water and turning it into
airplane parts, and also incendiary bombs to be dropped from the
planes. So he turned his thoughts from the works of God to those of
man, and found one as incomprehensible as the other.

At the airport he put his painting in storage with the customs
authorities, and went straight to the nearest telephone. In his mind he
carried the number of a little brick house in his national capital, and
now he called it and asked for a man named Baker. He had never
been told this man's first name, or what he did; the man meant just
one thing, the way to Franklin D. Roosevelt's bedroom, whether at
the White House or at Hyde Park, New York. At this hot season of
the year it would have been the great man's pleasure to be at his
country home; but in this hottest of war seasons he was chained to
the sweltering capital.

Lanny spoke: "Is this Baker?"—and then: "Zaharoff One-oh-three."

The reply was: "Call me in three hours"—that being, presumably, the time it took to get to the White House and arrange an appointment. Lanny wondered: Were there really a hundred and three presidential agents, or had some of them died or quit? And were the same precautions taken with all who were still working? He would never ask these questions.

He went in to New York, got himself a hotel room, and telephoned to his father. He bathed and shaved and fed himself, and read the latest newspapers; in times like these the history of the world might be changed between the three-star edition and the four. It was hard for Lanny Budd to think about anything but that sky battle over London—it was going on while a P.A. was bathing, shaving, eating, or whatever it might be. Alfy would be in it, and perhaps at that very instant was blacked out, or shot, and plunging headlong from a height of several miles.

Promptly on the minute Lanny put in his call and was told: "There is a reservation for you on the 7 p.m. plane from La Guardia Field. Meet me at the usual corner at 10 p.m." He replied: "O.K.," and that was all. He could tell from the promptness of the appointment that the Big Chief was eager for his report. The Chief knew, even better than Lanny, about the sky battle and its meaning in the history of mankind.

Lanny's ticket was paid for and he had only to board the plane and sit and make note of the familiar sounds and feelings while it was airborne. Never would he cease to marvel at this happening; he was old enough to have heard of its first beginnings, and now it was in process of reducing the size of the world, making the nations one and compelling the formation of an international government. So, at any rate, Lanny had come to believe, and the only question was who was to run that government. Hitler or Roosevelt? So the issue presented itself, not merely to the son of Budd-Erling, but to those two heads of states: two masterful men, each of whom knew what he wanted, and knew that he could get it only by thwarting the other.

Lanny used the hour of this flight to go over in his mind exactly what he wanted to say. In these rare interviews—he had had nine of them in three years—he felt that he was helping to change the world, which needed it so greatly. He couldn't get in everything he planned, for F.D. also liked to talk, and was used to having the right of way. But before Lanny left he could always say: "There is one matter that I ought to speak of, Governor," and the "Governor" would answer: "Shoot!" If it was something that surprised him he would exclaim: "Great guns!"—or perhaps: "You don't tell me!" Lanny had found himself taking up these phrases, as he had taken up many of the ideas and points of view of this great leader whom he loved.

II

At ten o'clock on a hot September evening the P.A. strolled idly by a Washington street corner, and a car drew up at the curb and he stepped in. There were two men in the car, and while one of them drove, the other flashed a torchlight into the passenger's face. "Zaharoff," Lanny said, and the other replied with the indispensable "O.K." In the old days they had searched him, but now they knew him, and if the Chief wanted to see him, that was all there was to it.

The front door of the White House, under the tall white pillars, is known as the "social door," and serves the purpose of a back door, since it is rarely used. Lanny had always been taken there, and usually no word had been spoken. But now it was wartime and there were two soldiers on duty. One of them said to Baker: "You know this party?" and then: "The President is expecting him?" So they were passed in, and went up by the side stairway. The President's Negro valet sat dozing in a chair just outside the bedroom door, ready to give help to a crippled man whenever the buzzer sounded. Baker tapped, and Lanny heard the warm voice which all the world knew over the radio: "Come in."

He entered that high-ceilinged bedroom with the old prints on the wall and the big mahogany bed with the blue counterpane. Sitting propped up with pillows was the man with the big head and massive shoulders, covered by a pajama coat of blue-and-white-striped pongee. He held out a large hand, and his features wore the usual welcoming smile; he spoke first to Baker, saying: "All right, and thanks." The man went out, closing the door behind him, and only then did F.D. address Lanny. "Welcome to our city! Take a seat, and tell me all about Europe!" Never would this genial soul begin an interview in any but a playful mood. But in spite of that, Lanny thought that he was paler, and his face lined with care.

"You got my reports?" the visitor asked.

"Every one, according to number." He pointed to a stack on his reading table. "I got them out in your honor. They have been invaluable."

"That is what I need to hear. I have just come from London, where I saw the bombing of the night before last. It has been going on continuously ever since, as I read in the papers."

"It has been going on tonight, so Churchill told me a couple of hours ago. I could hear some of the racket over the phone."

"I take it to mean that Hitler has made up his mind there's no chance of the collaborationists having their way. One item I have just learned: Lord Wickthorpe is resigning from the Foreign Office, and that means the same thing—he is hopeless as to making progress at the moment."

"Will that restrict your access to information?"

"I think it may have the opposite effect. He will feel more free to talk when he is not bound by his official conscience."

"Such people won't count for much in England now, I imagine."

"They will bide their time and wait for the world to come their way. I have been on their errands to Madrid and Paris and Vichy, and it's curious to note how they are the same crowd, whatever their nationality. It is one type of mind all over Europe—and America, too, I gather. The cookie-pushers whom our State Department sends to Vichy might be Marshal Pétain's own sons, or grandsons."

"But we *have* to send that type, Lanny! If I sent a Pink like you, the old gentleman would decide that I must be Stalin's brother-in-law. Nobody can talk to those people but a Catholic."

"I suppose not; but the trouble is, they talk so much like Pétain that he thinks it's his own voice."

"We have some liberal Catholics, Lanny."

"I have heard it said, and it may be so. All I can tell you is that the only way a Catholic can be liberal is by being ignorant of the fundamental doctrines of his Church."

"Well, what they don't know won't hurt them," chuckled the President. "My job is to try to keep the French Fleet out of the hands of the Nazis. I have a good old Irish Catholic admiral here in Washington, and I'm thinking of sending him over to pray with the Marshal day and night."

III

The Chief Executive had on his reading table a report from Lanny Budd giving the essential facts as to the situation in Unoccupied France. But the Chief was more than a filing cabinet full of facts, he was a human being with personal curiosities, a boy who loved adventure stories. He wanted to see these persons and hear their voices; he plied his agent with questions about the aged Marshal and his entourage; about Darlan the Admiral of the Fleet and Weygand the General of the North African Armies, and especially about the evil Pierre Laval and his wretched family. "I envy you, Lanny," said F.D., and not altogether jokingly. "You can travel and see the world, while I—look at what I have to read and sign!"—pointing to the stack of papers on the bed beside him. "By golly, if I'd known what they were wishing onto me, I'd have remained the Squire of Krum Elbow and Senior Warden of St. James's Episcopal Church in Hyde Park."

But this man of great affairs had put his hand to the plow, and had to go to the end of the furrow. Different from most plowmen, he was working in the dark and couldn't see what lay ahead. Many boulders, many stumps, and perhaps—who could say?—enemy-planted mines! Just now a national election lay ahead; and how many blunders a free-spoken political manipulator might commit! One careless sentence might be enough to turn an election, and bring to naught the labors of eight years!

After hearing about Vichy France, he wanted to know about Paris and the masters of that country—the Comité des Forges, the cartel owners, and the deals they were making with the military conquerors to save their possessions and power. What was Schneider doing, and was Le Creusot going all out for German munitions production? Lanny said: "He is greatly humiliated, because the Germans have reported that his works are out-of-date and they can't make much use of them."

"And what about the British? Will they bomb these and other plants, or will there be a gentlemen's agreement, as before?" Lanny replied: "This time they will go all out. This isn't going to be a gentlemen's war."

And then the Nazi leaders! Hitler, Göring, Hess, Abetz—the President of the United States would never have the pleasure of meeting any of these extraordinary characters, but wanted to see them with his mind's eye. Lanny said: "Unless the British should capture them, and send them over and exhibit them in cages." This brought one of F.D.'s hearty laughs. He listened, fascinated, while Lanny described the Führer of the Germans doing a little jig in front of the motion-picture cameras after the astonishing armistice had been signed, and then brooding in front of the tomb of Napoleon, whom he greatly admired and meant to supplant on the pedestal of Europe's history.

"He doesn't want to fight Britain," Lanny explained. "He really means that with all his heart; he considers it a painful necessity which has been forced upon him by vicious politicians, and the pluto-democratic-Jewish press, which he calls irresponsible, meaning that the press lords publish what they please, instead of being told by the government."

"This air war is the real beginning, I take it?" queried the other.

"I should guess so. There were rumors when I left London that an attempt had been made to embark an invasion army from Belgium. I didn't have time to find out if it was true."

"I can tell you about it, if you won't pass it on."

"I never pass anything on, Governor—except what you have told me to."

"It was a rehearsal; the Germans were practicing embarkation, but the British didn't see any reason for sparing them on that account. The bombers dropped large tanks of oil with devices to ignite them.

From my accounts there were thousands of enemy troops consumed in the holocaust."

"They will try it again," the agent opined. "Hitler has a million men whom he considers expendable, because he expected to lose them in France and didn't. But first he has to knock out the R.A.F."

"What do you hear about the chances?"

Lanny described his interview with the baronet's grandson, who had worn the "old school tie" but didn't love it, at least not as much as he loved the work shirt. Lanny told what he had seen of the bombing and of the air-raid shelter in the tube. He did not spare the Budd-Erling plane, but told what Alfy had said about its weaknesses. "I thought it was the best in the world," remarked F.D., and Lanny replied: "It was, a year ago; but these days a year's improvements are crowded into a month. As Alfy said: 'Your father is making planes for money, but we are making them for our lives.'"

"Your father will be catching up, I hope."

"I asked him over the telephone if he had a new model on the drawing boards, and he said: 'We have it in production.' You can be sure he's getting full reports."

IV

They talked for a while about this battle of the skies, upon which everything else depended. Tennyson had predicted it a hundred years earlier, but he had probably not foreseen that it would be over his own village. "It is touch and go," declared the President. "Britain has never been in such peril—not even from the Spanish Armada."

Said the visitor: "For God's sake, do everything you can to help."

"I have emptied our arsenals into Britain. They weren't so very full, alas!"

"May I ask you a question, Governor?"

"Sure thing."

"I heard some talk about our over-age destroyers that the British are hoping to get. I didn't know what to answer—and you know it helps me to get information if I am able to give some."

"It's a curious situation, which can't be talked about because it would be taken as putting blame on Churchill. We've been reconditioning fifty of those old four-stackers and have them practically ready—torpedoes in the tubes, oil in the tanks, food in the storerooms—they could be in Halifax in a few days. But you see, it was my idea to exchange these ships for the bases we must have in British territory on this side of the water. I want to call it a trade, and it seems a fair one, considering the fact that we have to build the bases and that they will be as important for British defense as for ours."

"And Churchill can't see it?"

"Darned if I can make out what is in his mind. Apparently it's something ancestral, perhaps racial. He is a Tory imperialist—or is that a redundant phrase?"

"I suppose one could think of an imperialist who isn't a Tory. Cecil Rhodes might be an example. Does Churchill think you want to get possession of his islands?"

"I have sworn to him that he couldn't give them to me if he tried. Believe me, they have been my fishing ground, and I know them. They would be nothing but headaches, and we have enough already in Porto Rico and the Virgins. They are economic vacuums; worse yet, their populations are mostly Negro, and we have enough race problems already. Imagine me having to administer the affairs of colored people who have been brought up in the British fashion, to sit in their local councils and be received as social equals! Imagine what our Southern congressmen would say, and what our Harlem population would answer!"

"Churchill can't see that?"

"I don't think he doubts my word, but apparently he doesn't trust the future. He has some queer idea of prestige; he thinks it would be more noble and dignified to make us a present of the concessions, and then we'd make him a present of the fifty destroyers. But I tell him our people wouldn't see it that way. Every Yankee knows what a horse trade is; but a gift, that is something else, and it would raise a hullabaloo, it might cost me the election. There's a grave question whether the deal will be constitutional anyhow; Jackson, my attorney general, has been tearing the law books to pieces trying to find some justification. But I can't get Churchill to see it my way; I think he has the idea that if he makes us a free and generous gift, some President ninety-nine years from now may be less tempted to hold onto the lease!"

"And you mean that he's letting the U-boats sink his shiploads of munitions because of a point of prestige?"

"He's been doing precisely that for a couple of months."

"May I make a suggestion, Governor?"

"I've said that if anybody can solve this problem for me I'll give him all the plastic elephants on my office desk!"

"Tell me what the bases are that we're to get."

"Two up in Newfoundland, and then Bermuda, and half a dozen spots on the islands from the Bahamas to Trinidad. It's really a tremendously important thing, because it means that British sea and air power is being replaced by ours in the Western Atlantic. Empires don't give up so easily as a rule."

"This occurs to me: have you offered to split the difference with him? Let him make you a present of the bases he considers most important, say those in the north and Bermuda; and make your horse trade for those in the Caribbean, which he knows have less value as land, or for tourists, or whatever."

The President sat lost in thought. "By golly, that might do the trick! At any rate, it can't do any harm to try." He pressed a button, and spoke into a transmitter by his bed. "Get me Secretary Hull." And then to Lanny: "Hull and Lothian have been arguing about this till they're both ready to drop dead."

A buzzer sounded and he took the telephone. "Hello, Cordell? I have an idea about the four-stackers." Lanny was amused to note that he didn't say: "Somebody has suggested an idea." Nor did he say: "I have thought of an idea," for that wouldn't have been quite true. He outlined the plan, and apparently the elderly secretary was pleased by it, for his Chief beamed and said: "O.K.—go after him right away. If they won't take that there's something really wrong." Then to his visitor: "If the deal goes through, the elephants are your commission!"

V

Lanny always made it a point to offer to leave. The stack of papers over which the great man worked in bed always seemed like a hint, and never once had it been necessary for him to terminate an interview with this agent. But now he wanted to talk. "I don't see you very often," he said. "Are you finding it difficult to get about in wartime?"

"My father's business is a sufficient pretext so far as Britain is concerned; and as for Vichy, I rather think that Wickthorpe will be wanting me to go there, and will find some way to arrange it."

"Are you planning to visit Germany again?"

"I'm not sure. They know all about my father's help to Britain, and the destroyer deal will make Americans still less popular. I'll probably go into Switzerland and get word to Hess; he might come to see me there, or invite me into Germany to see the Führer. I have a strong tie with Rudi, because of our interest in psychic matters."

"You really take those things seriously?"

"I take them very seriously, though I don't claim to know what they mean. I can only say that I have had experiences which nobody can explain. I won't start telling you about them, because we might talk all night, and your tomorrow's schedule would be knocked out."

"That would be nothing new to my secretaries," remarked F.D. with one of his grins. He took a sort of impish pleasure in breaking out of harness. But not so often in these tragic days. Lanny thought: Poor soul! and would have liked to stay and try to help; but he knew what the President's answer would be: "Nobody else can do what you are doing abroad."

"At this moment," continued the Chief, "the important question is whether Hitler can get a toehold on the British Isles. Bill Donovan, whose business it is to find out, tells me that the Germans haven't enough landing craft, and can't build them in time; the British navy will smash them—unless they can win complete control of the air. We ought to know about that in the next couple of months. How long before you plan to return?"

"I have some picture business to attend to. It will take a couple of weeks, unless you need me sooner."

"I may have to break away for a bit of rest. My doctor is making a fuss because I am run down, and when that happens I get a cold, even in midsummer."

"I agree with your doctor," Lanny said, smiling in turn. "I'll wait until you come back, and then call for instructions."

"Do, please," was the reply. "I always think of things that you might do for me."

He held out a cordial hand, and Lanny wrung it. "Take care of yourself, Governor. The whole world needs you."

"The same to you," was the reply. "I won't say the whole world, but *I* need you, and that's no applesauce."

VI

The great port and manufacturing center of Baltimore, which calls itself the Monumental City, and is known to the world as the city of the orioles, both the birds and the baseball team, lies a half hundred miles north of Washington. It was the home of Lanny's friends, the Holdenhursts, and he had a standing invitation to visit them when passing. It was somewhat embarrassing, because Lizbeth, the family darling, still had the notion to marry him, and Lanny had had to explain frankly to the father that he wasn't a marrying man. If he had consulted his own preferences, he would have stayed away from tempting and being tempted; but the situation was complicated by the fact that Reverdy Johnson Holdenhurst was one of the heaviest Budd-Erling stockholders, and a source of new capital, much needed in this crisis when the airplane industry was expanding at a rate never equaled.

The President had publicly called for fifty thousand planes. It sounded like a joke, or a bit of braggadocio, to most of the world; but the insiders discovered that it was seriously meant, and if they didn't get busy on an adequate scale, the Army and Navy and a lot of officials kept calling up and raising cain. If for any reason you weren't moving fast enough they would start buying your best men away from you—for the "know-how" was the all-important thing, which neither you nor they could get along without. They literally tried to force money upon you—millions, tens of millions. But Robbie was afraid of public money, and of the bureaucrats who handled it; they always tied strings to it, and every day they would have a tighter hold on the business, telling him what he could do and what not. He preferred private money, because he believed in private business and the sort of people who were satisfied with dividends and had no interest in control.

Robbie had said over the phone: "Reverdy has asked for another block of stock. Do stop by and say hello to him." When Lanny showed up, his father would ask: "Did you see the Holdenhursts, and how are they?" There was subtle scheming behind this, for both Robbie and his wife were convinced that Lizbeth would make the right sort of wife for Lanny, and they hadn't given up the hope that he would change his mind.

Then, too, Reverdy had developed a sudden interest in old masters. He hadn't had it when he and his daughter had first arrived at Cannes less than two years ago; and it was hard to believe that a man would take to spending money in large quantities just in the hope of getting a not-too-eligible art expert for a son-in-law. Lanny thought this might be the first time in the life of the sweet and gentle Lizbeth that she had wanted something very much and had not been able to get it. Lanny had lived his life among the children of privilege, and was familiar with the demands they made—and the fuss when their desires were thwarted. Compared with some of the affairs he had seen and heard of on the Riviera, this Holdenhurst intrigue was naïve and touching, something out of an Elsie Dinsmore story.

Reverdy had told Lanny the sort of paintings he wanted, and Lanny had been on the lookout for them, and had accumulated a list of half a dozen. It wasn't the sort of thing that could be attended to by mail; you had to answer questions. So next morning, after telephoning and ascertaining that a visit would be agreeable, he took the first train to Baltimore, and the Holdenhurst chauffeur met him at the station. This being a democratic land, the chauffeur told him the latest news about the city, and asked the latest about the old Continent, the source of all troubles. Lanny was democratic, too, but couldn't show it; when he met strangers he was always the lover of the arts, *au-dessus de la mêlée*. But he was free to tell how it felt to be bombed and how the London people were taking it. Everywhere in America he could be sure of an absorbed audience for conversation on that subject.

VII

Here was Greenbriar, this elegant country estate, with gracious and cultivated people ready to welcome him. Here was every form of recreation at his disposal; he could play tennis or the piano, or he could sit by the best of radio sets and listen to voices from this or other lands. The weather was hot, but there were shaded porches and electric fans, and there would be mint juleps with cracked ice, or lemon squashes, with or without a "stick" in them. Soft-shell crabs were in season, and bluefish; if you didn't mind the sunburn you could take a trip to the bay and catch fish of varied hues. You could motor on fine roads, still called "turnpikes." In the evening there were dances at the Country Club—in short, there was everything you could think of for comfort and pleasure, and if some of the women were drinking too much, and the girls running about without chaperons, you could say that it was the disturbed state of the world, the New Deal, the war, the general license. You could go on in the comfortable certainty that "Bawlamaw" was the finest city in the world, "Bawlamaw" women the most beautiful, and "Bawlamaw" food and cookery the envy of all mankind.

Lanny told his friend about the paintings he had come upon, and delivered one of his learned discourses about them. Reverdy didn't really know much about art; the examples he possessed, except for the Detazes, were commonplace; but he was graciously willing to learn, and it wouldn't be long before he would be passing these opinions on to others—including Lanny. Such an experience every art expert has now and then with his clients, and it is his part to listen gravely and to agree heartily.

And then Lizbeth. She was lovelier every time he saw her, the visitor thought. She was twenty now, and no longer a child; she appeared more thoughtful, and Lanny had the idea that perhaps not having her own way had been good for her. She had spent a winter at home with her mother, not taking the customary yachting cruise with her father. Doubtless it had been the mother's idea to give the eligible men of the Monumental City an opportunity to lay their gifts at her feet. Had any one of them succeeded in impressing her? Lanny asked no questions; his manner was that of a kindly uncle, which he was old enough to be.

He told her about Bienvenu and the people there—but of course not saying anything about Beauty's bad dreams. He told about Mrs. Chattersworth, and the guests who came there, and about life on the Riviera under war conditions, with everything growing scarcer day by day. He told about London under the bombs. He tried to have others present while he talked, but the others had a way of excusing themselves, which was rather pointed, and at least made it plain that Lizbeth hadn't yet centered her thoughts upon any other man. She drove him to the Country Club, and they played tennis and then swam; the bathing suits had been contrived so that a man who was contemplating matrimony wouldn't be left in any doubt as to what he was getting. But Lanny wasn't contemplating anything except to guard his grim wartime secret, and he did not feast his eyes upon this graceful well-rounded figure, but manifested impartial interest in all the youths and maidens of Green Spring Valley's fashionable set.

Lizbeth's father ordered paintings which would pay the visitor several thousand dollars in commissions and cover all the costs of his next tour. It didn't seem decent to bolt off with no more than a handshake after that. But Lanny had taken the precaution to say over the telephone that Robbie was waiting for the latest report on the Budd-Erlings—and that was important to Reverdy as well. Lanny made no attempt to gloss over the bad situation; he said that the British found all the American planes inferior to their own, and were holding the former as reserves, to be used only in the last extremity. Budd-Erling wouldn't stay behind very long, Reverdy might be sure; and Reverdy said that he *was* sure, having had from Robbie secrets which couldn't be entrusted to mail across enemy-infested seas.

VIII

Nothing would have been easier for Lanny than to become fond of Lizbeth Holdenhurst; indeed, nothing seemed more unkind and irrational than not to do so. She was his for the asking, and she would have made him a devoted wife; not brilliant, not intellectual, but then, you can't have everything. Lanny had ideas enough for two, liked to expound them, and needed someone who liked to listen. There could be no doubt that Lizbeth had money for two, or, for that matter, a dozen. She had a sweet expression, lovely large brown eyes, soft brown hair; she knew how to take care of these gifts, and would meet his esthetic requirements, morning, noon, and night.

It was a problem he argued out with himself each time he came here. His duties were "top secret," and he couldn't share them; his journeys were the same, and what would she make of being left alone three-quarters of the time, and for no imaginable reason? How long would it be before her smart friends began to whisper into her ears their suspicions of his habits? "The other woman is always just around the corner"—such was their idea of marital affairs. "There are no saints nowadays, at least not on the French Riviera, and not among the British aristocracy." So they would jeer. And what would Lizbeth, make of his visits to the Countess of Sandhaven, his former flame? What would she think about his visits to Wickthorpe, whose countess might or might not have a moral sense?

Should he trust her with his secret? Did he have a right to? Surely not unless he married her; and what a trick to play upon a girl, to let her think that she was marrying an ivory-tower esthete, a modern Marius the Epicurean, and then reveal himself as a political conspirator who was liable to be shot at sunrise on any part of the Continent of Europe where his activities were detected! Lizbeth wouldn't have the faintest understanding of his motivations; her father was a dyed-in-the-wool Republican, a man who was cheating the income tax as a matter of principle, holding it to be a form of robbery. If Reverdy Johnson Holdenhurst had known the real contents of Lanny Budd's mind, he would as soon have married his daughter to Mephistopheles.

So it was a kindness to say: "Robbie is waiting to hear all the things I have been telling you. I'll be coming this way again before long, and I'll drop by if I may." He bade farewell to this lotus land, and the sociable chauffeur drove him to the station, which to Baltimoreans is the "dee-po."

IX

The wonderful tube took the traveler underneath the Hudson River and delivered him at Pennsylvania Station; from there a taxi conveyed him in a few minutes to Grand Central Station, and something over an hour later he was in Newcastle, Connecticut. Here was another fine home, not so elaborate as Greenbriar, but much the same in the manners, costumes, and ideas of its occupants. It resembled Bienvenu and Sept Chênes in that there was an elderly lady who couldn't rest content until she had found a proper wife for the son of Budd-Erling—or the eldest of three sons of Budd-Erling, as Esther Remsen Budd would naturally see him. She was the great lady of her town and managed many things, and it was really hard on her not to be able to do something for this stepson.

Robbie Budd was like the man in the *Arabian Nights* who pulled the cork from the bottle and let the genie out; the most unimaginable monstrous genie, that spread out over the Connecticut countryside, on the river which flowed through it, and in the skies above it. Robbie had thought that he had vision, and he had foreseen a big business, but it had been a nice little big business, so to speak, never the big big business which was now turning him and his community upside down. Concrete floors were laid down by the acre, and ships and trains and barges came loaded with structural steel, and buildings arose with the speed of Jack's beanstalk. And the same thing was going on with the still more immense property of Budd Gunmakers, turning out machine guns, carbines, and automatic pistols. An agency took the job of inserting advertisements all over the country, and workingmen came from places you had never heard of: farm boys from Newfoundland, habitants from the Quebec wilderness, Negroes from places between Harlem and Texas: every sort of man who could be taught to weld, to rivet, or even to put in screws.

And the women, the girls! To Esther, daughter of the Puritans, it was most distressing, for she was sure they had no morals, and there was nobody to care about it. Where were they to sleep and what were they to eat? They worked in three shifts, and there were long queues of people waiting to get into Newcastle's small restaurants and inadequate grocery stores. The families came in trailers and lived in them, they put up tents, they even bought chicken coops and made them into sleeping places. The town had prayed for prosperity, but this was too much, and the Chamber of Commerce wanted to say: "Lord, can't you take a joke?"

X

Esther's two sons, now in their early thirties, were conscientious and well-trained executives, and it had been her hope that the business would settle down to a routine basis, so that Robbie could enjoy a hard-earned rest. But no; Budd-Erling was like one of its own planes caught in a hurricane, and Robbie was the pilot; he wasn't surrendering the controls. The hurricane was blowing the way he desired to travel, and he rode it with a sense of glory. He was a hearty, stoutish man, who took everything in his stride, and except for his gray hair bore few signs of his age. Budd-Erling was his life; he had planned it and now he talked it and worked at it, day and night, in the office and at home; he was no longer interested in anything else, and when he thought about politics and world affairs, it was always from the point of view: Will this increase or reduce the demand for fighter planes?

Robbie called himself, defiantly, a "merchant of death," meaning it as a jeer at persons who had been haunting his thoughts and goading him from his earliest years as salesman for Budd Gunmakers. Once he had confronted some of these people, at a congressional investigation in Washington, and he had never forgotten their severe, fanatical faces and their bitter words. They had accused him of desiring war in order that he might sell his deadly goods, or deadly evils, if you preferred. Robbie knew that that wasn't true; he knew that Europe was determined to have wars, and wherever in the business world there is a demand, there will soon be a supply. "Nobody has to buy my products," Robbie would say; "nobody has to use them. I put them in the shopwindow, and it's up to the customer." He would add: "Incidentally, my own country gets a defense factory, and some day it may happen that they'll find it useful."

In the days when Lanny had been a young Pink he had hated this philosophy and fought hard against it. But now he and his tough-minded father had been brought together in a peculiar and complicated way. The coming of Hitler had convinced Lanny that the country had to arm, and do it in a hurry; and now the submarine sinkings and the triumph of Nazi arms on the Continent had forced Robbie Budd to make terms with the hated New Deal, with "That Man in the White House" who had been for eight years the symbol of everything Robbie hated in public affairs. First, to Lanny's infinite amusement, his father had been forced to "go on the dole"; quite literally, because the Administration had wanted to arm, and a purblind Congress wouldn't vote the money, so the President had hit upon the bright idea of using relief funds, the WPA, the much ridiculed leaf-rakers, the boondogglers. Why wasn't it just as important to put unemployed airplane workers and battleship builders at work as any other sort of laborers? So the proud Robbie Budd had got contracts from the Army, and the payments had come from the despised "dole."

But now that stage was past, Lanny discovered. Congress, in a panic, was voting defense funds; first, in the spring, a billion dollars and then another billion; in midsummer five billion, and then another five; compulsory military service was being talked of—and right in the midst of a presidential campaign! So now Robbie could get respectable contracts from the Army and the Navy, contracts which he didn't have to keep secret, nor blush when his golfing friends found out about them. Also the British had come down off their high horses; the Colonel Blimps who had been so toplofty and had plagued Robbie through the years—except the years numbered 1914–1918! They came now to Newcastle and begged almost on their knees for planes and then more planes and still more planes, even while claiming that these planes weren't good enough to fight with, and demanding more changes at every stage of manufacture!

XI

Lanny's first duty was to sit down with his father and tell what he had been able to find out concerning the performance of the Budd-Erling Tycoon. In just what respects had the Spitfire managed to surpass it, and even more important, what was the Messerschmitt 109 now able to do? Robbie already had a mass of information, and drawings and plans and specifications for improvements; but he wanted the personal experiences of Alfy and his mates. Each detail threatened to knock out some process in Robbie's elaborately planned establishment; the sum total would mean chaos or near it for weeks, perhaps months.

It was going to be this way right along, only more so, and Robbie, in his middle sixties, had to keep his mind flexible and make life-and-death decisions between firepower and armor on the one hand and speed and maneuverability on the other. Upon his judgment would depend the lives of hundreds of British flyers, and perhaps of Britain itself. The president of Budd-Erling Aircraft, who had been an extreme isolationist, had been suddenly brought to face the fact that if Hitler got the British Fleet he would not merely have all Europe at his mercy but could cross to Africa, and from there with his bombers and paratroopers to Brazil; he would build his airports there, and might be at the Panama Canal before we were in position to offer him serious resistance. "What do you think, Lanny?"

The bombing attacks upon London were going on without cessation. Day and night the swarms of bombers and fighter planes came over. It was indeed the blitz; Göring *der Dicke* had been preparing it for almost eight years, and had boasted about it to both the elder and the younger Budd. Now the elder, deeply concerned, gazed at the younger, asking: "Can he get away with it?" All Lanny could say was: "It's the test of battle, and I doubt if anybody living can tell how it will turn out. Göring will send planes as long as he has any; and sooner or later one side or the other will be exhausted."

"This much I know," declared Robbie, "the British here in Newcastle are scared stiff; they aren't just play-acting."

"What will decide the issue, I am guessing, is how many planes the *Generalstab* will insist upon keeping on the eastern border. Somewhere they will have to draw the line and say: 'Not one more!' "

"You think the Russians might attack them?"

"I think either side will attack the moment it can see a certainty of victory. That is a war that has got to be fought some day."

"Well," said the father, "you know Abraham Lincoln's story of the pioneer who came home to his cabin and found his wife in hand-to-hand conflict with a bear?"

"I don't think I've heard it."

"The old fellow rested his gun against the rail fence, took a seat on the top rail, and called: 'Go it, woman; go it, bear!' "

XII

Lanny didn't tell his friends in Newcastle about having been present at the evacuation of Dunkirk, for that wasn't the sort of thing he could afford to have talked about. He could say that he had been in Paris at the time of the armistice, and that subsequently he had stayed in Vichy. This was enough to rouse the burning curiosity of everybody in town; the local newspaper wanted to interview him and the local women's club wanted to hear him talk; but in both cases he declined— he was an art expert and not competent to discuss public affairs. But privately he would answer questions for those whom his father and stepmother considered important. The town was rent with arguments between the friends of England and the friends of America, as the iso- lationists called themselves. "America First Committee" was the name chosen by a group of rich conservatives who were Fascists without knowing it; when Lanny read their full-page advertisements he called them "America First Aid to Hitler"—but of course only under his breath.

Naturally, people didn't talk about war and peace all the time. The Country Club set played tennis and golf, they danced, gave elaborate dinner parties, and gossiped freely about one another's love affairs. They did not spare this agreeable and eligible elder son of Budd-Erling; if he engaged in conversation with any debutante, or danced with her more than once, the rumor would spread that he was interested in her, and his stepmother would hear it and ask if he would like to have the young person invited to tea. Incidentally, Esther informed him that the town librarian, Miss Priscilla Hoyle, had married a teacher in the local high school, but was still continuing as librarian. "I don't know where we should have found anybody to take her place," said Esther, a member of the Library Board. Lanny had once kissed this lady in his automobile, though Esther had no idea it had gone that far. Now his reply was: "I have some data to look up in Vasari, and I'll stop in and congratulate her."

Also, there was the Holdenhurst family to be reported on. Esther would be expecting to hear something about Lizbeth, so Lanny re- marked that she was lovelier than ever, and that a flock of the Balti- more swains were mad about her. He didn't say as to himself, and his stepmother, playing a difficult role with patience and tact, went over the problem in her mind once again. "If I urge him he'll be bored. He may even take a dislike to her, and he won't come here or go there so often." She could never be sure in her mind about this strange man whom fate had deposited in her household; more and more her shrewd judgment told her that he wasn't all on the surface, and her most nat- ural thought was of some hidden woman. Esther had heard about the Countess of Sandhaven, and about Madame de Bruyne; what more likely than that there was some new one, perhaps even more highly placed and therefore more carefully protected? To this daughter of the Puritans, now gray of hair and austere of features, Europe was a poisonous place; its cruel wars shocked her no more than its lack of sexual morals, and indeed she would have named the former as a consequence of the latter.

XIII

The radio habit had become dominant in these critical days; people would sit and turn the dials; they would interrupt a card game, or a dinner conversation if there was a radio set in the dining-room. Somebody would say: "It's time for Swing," and not mean the music but the commentator; you had your favorite, according to his political tinge, from Pink to pure White, or with touches of Brown or Black. You wanted the latest news, and you got it even while it was happening. "This is London," Ed Murrow would announce—it became a sort of trademark; he would be standing on the roof of some building, describing the searchlights in the sky, the bombs bursting in air—sometimes you could actually hear them, as F.D.R. had done while talking with Churchill over the transatlantic telephone.

It was the genuine "all out." It went on for weeks, day and night. The Germans had decided to destroy London, the brain of the British Empire; they would break the nerve of its seven million inhabitants and end their will to resist. The Reichsmarschall, head of the Luftwaffe, had told Lanny Budd that Warsaw would be nothing in comparison; Warsaw had been far from Berlin, but London was close to the new bases in France and Belgium, and it would be merely a freighting proposition, a routine job. Impossible to miss the target, ten miles or more in every direction; no need to aim, you could drop the loads from twenty thousand feet, even thirty thousand, above the reach of ack-ack, and wipe out everything and everybody in the world's most populated metropolis.

And now they were doing it. An endless procession of planes, bombers, and fighters, by day and by night, and no rest for anybody down below. The newspapers were filled with the ghastly details; whole blocks of the city wrecked and burning, a pall of black smoke everywhere, hiding the sky and making it difficult to breathe. The firefighters worked without rest, but they could hardly get about through streets blocked with rubble; their hoselines were dragged here and there through the ruins. An appalling thing to see a six-story office building collapse and fall inward, all in a few seconds, and to know that scores, perhaps hundreds of people were trapped within those ruins; many would still be alive, and would hear the crackling flames and smell the acrid smoke and feel the deadly heat stealing closer.

The fires and the searchlights made night into day, and after a day's work people toiled at rescuing the wounded. Sirens screamed, and the roar of the anti-aircraft guns was one continuous sound, like the pounding of a freight train when you are "riding the rods." The air blasts deprived people of breath, and often killed them; there were whole districts of London without a window intact, and oftentimes a single giant blast would blow in every door in a city block. Yet people went on with their work, through all these horrors. They traveled to and fro between their homes and their jobs; they worked in shops and offices with the roofs or the walls missing; there were stories of men who set up their desks in the street and went on with their duties. Business as usual! Never say die! There will always be an England!

Lanny heard these stories, and read them in the papers, and it was as if it were his own home being destroyed. He had known this grimy old city since childhood, and loved it and the people in it. The poor were easy to know, and had "guts," as they called it, and a cheery courage; their "betters" were not so easy, but kindly and agreeable when you had broken the ice. Now they were all on a level—the bombs made no distinction. Buckingham Palace was hit, and the House of Commons wiped out. The West End, the fashionable district, suffered greatly; and Lanny thought of the splendid mansions, many of them historic, in which he had dined and danced, the luxury shops to which he had accompanied his mother in boyhood, the theaters in which he had seen Shakespeare played. Hermann Göring wouldn't spare Shakespeare; he wouldn't spare the hospitals filled with the wounded, nor the morgues in which the dead were piled. Make way for the *Neue Ordnung!*

5. *Sweet Land of Liberty*

I

FOR one who had just come from France and England, it was difficult indeed to realize that it was possible to have a car, and to stop at any roadside station and say: "Fill her up!"—and for no more than a couple of dollars per load. When Lanny tried it and found that it worked, he could understand why on the Continent so many of the middle-class people he met had expressed a hope of emigrating to America. "The land of unlimited possibilities," it had been dubbed, and apparently the only limit was on tickets of admission.

Robbie Budd had half a dozen cars in his garage, and one was a sport car which Lanny was privileged to take. He drove down the shore road to the home of his half-sister Bess and her husband, Hansi Robin, the violinist; both younger than himself, both his protégés, whose love affair he had guided and whose musical career he had fostered. They were a lovely couple, and, so far as the world knew, among the happiest. But Lanny had been watching the development of a rift that was now growing to the proportions of a chasm.

They were both as much interested in political affairs as in their art; they had both called themselves Communists, up to the time of the deal between the Soviet Union and Nazi Germany. Now Bess, a Party member, was following the Party line; this was a capitalist war, no different from any other capitalist war, and therefore every true Red must oppose it. But to Hansi, the Jew whose younger brother had been murdered by the Nazis, this point of view was beyond comprehension; to him the overthrow of Hitler was the first step toward sanity in the world. Even if it had to be done by Winston Churchill! They had tried to convince each other, and found that they could only quarrel. So they had made a rule and never spoke of politics in each other's presence. Not even when Lanny Budd came calling!

They talked about the family at Bienvenu, and the one at Wickthorpe; they talked about Rick and Alfy—and of course that led to the war, and how it was going, and what Lanny had seen in France. That came close to politics, so Bess exclaimed: "You must see the babies!" Two lovely little ones, half Jewish, half New England Puritan—strains which were spiritually not so far apart. The Puritan grandfather of Lanny and Bess had hammered the Old Jewish Testament into them as the authentic and imperative word of God. The lessons hadn't had much effect on Lanny, so far as he could see, but they had prepared his half-sister to receive the rigid orthodoxy of Marx-Leninism —that, too, being half Jewish, and in line with the Old Testament proletarian prophets. A curious thing to trace the currents of thought and impulse sweeping from one nation and one race to another, all over the world, generation after generation, millennium after millennium!

Near by was the home of Hansi's father, Johannes Robin, whose mansion in Berlin now belonged to Hermann Göring, and whose art works, selected by Lanny Budd, now hung on the walls of Karinhall. Johannes ran the sales department of Budd-Erling, which was in New York; since the product sold itself, he now put his shrewd mind on the study of contracts and the search for scarce materials. He met many people and picked up information which could be of value to a P.A. Lanny spent a week-end with him and his family, and ate *gefuellte Fisch* and *Blintzes* and other Jewish foods. Mama Robin was one of half a dozen old ladies who adored him and yearned to see him married and the father of many little ones, all as handsome and elegant as himself. With them lived Rahel, Freddi Robin's widow who had remarried; Mama had adopted the new husband and the new children, because she couldn't bear to be separated from Freddi's child, the little Johannes. They were a group of refugees who had been lashed by the Nazi terror, and were glad to be alive on any terms. They clung together, and shuddered when they thought of that wicked Old World overseas, now trampled under the hoofs of the dread four horses of the Apocalypse.

II

In the *Bluebook* magazine, which Lanny watched each month, he had found what he expected, a short story signed "Mary Morrow." Its title was an odd one, *The Gauleiter's Cousin*. It was little more than a sketch, showing what had come to be the manners and morals of the "New Order" which Adolf Hitler had established. It had been written with an acid pen, and obviously by someone who had lived there. The locale was a small *pension*, whose ruling spirit, the star boarder of the establishment, held this position because she was a cousin of the ruling Nazi politician of the town. A greedy and vicious-tempered woman, she queened it over the other guests, and even the couple who owned and ran the *pension*. Never did she lose an opportunity to boast of the powers of her upstart relative, and to call attention to his ability to reward those who pleased his cousin and to punish those who displeased her.

In carefully studied detail the writer showed this mean and petty spirit, flattered and fawned upon, claiming precedence everywhere and especially at the dining-table; the *pension* was a little miniature of Hitlerland, with its greeds, its sham glories, its raging jealousies and servile fears. The climax of the story had to do with a trunk belonging to the Gauleiter's cousin. The undernourished slave of the establishment who undertook to carry it up from the basement to the star boarder's room stumbled and fell, and both the trunk and the railing of the stairs were damaged. The man was damaged, too, but nobody thought about him; he was to be made to pay for both trunk and railing, and the question was which took precedence. A quarrel resulted between the landlady and her guest, but in the end the power of the Gauleiter's name swept everything before it—just as it was sweeping the Continent of Europe, with the rest of the world watching in awe.

Even if there had been no name signed to this story, Lanny would have known that only one person could have written it; that was Laurel Creston, who was Reverdy Holdenhurst's niece and Lizbeth's first cousin. She had lived in just such a *pension*, only it had been in Berlin instead of in a small provincial town. She had come to dislike the Nazis in that special way, and had brought to the study of them that shrewd observant eye and malicious humor. Lanny had read half a dozen sketches in the same vein, and his admiration for them was based upon his own knowledge of the locale.

There had been a duel going on in his mind for the past couple of years, having to do with his desire for the company of this brilliant woman writer. His conscience told him that he had no right to know her; she was an outspoken person, and bound to become conspicuous, more so with every product of her pen; the Nazi agents who swarmed in New York—never so thickly as now—were bound to seek her out and watch her, to find out where she got her information. From the point of view of a presidential agent she was poison.

But Lanny Budd was lonely. There wasn't a single person in this great city to whom he could talk frankly; indeed there was only one person in the world to whom he could speak with complete openness, and that was his Boss. With all others, even his relatives and best friends, there were shades and degrees, there were subjects he must shy away from. He had always been a ladies' man, yet most of the women he met now were in the enemy's camp. His half-sister was his only real woman friend in this country, and Rick's wife his only real woman friend in England; on the whole Continent there was only Raoul's wife, and Lanny hadn't seen her for a long time.

At first Laurel Creston had assumed him to be what he pretended to be among his mother's friends, an esthete, an ivory-tower dweller—only she had preferred to call him a troglodyte. Later she had decided that he must be a Fascist agent, and she had thought it her duty to investigate him. Only after she had got into trouble in Naziland and he had helped her to get out had she made the right conjecture about him. She had pledged her word never to mention him, and she was the sort of person to keep a promise.

Another tie, also; Laurel had discovered herself to be a medium, and she had promised to continue her experiments and report. In a decade of search Lanny had come upon only one medium whom he trusted, and here was another. He would have liked nothing better than to settle down somewhere and probe this woman's subconscious mind, which appeared to be entirely different from the personality she presented to the world and to herself. Apparently it was all mixed up with his own mind, and with Laurel's deceased grandmother's, and—oddest thing imaginable—with the mind of the late Otto H. Kahn, senior partner of Kuhn, Loeb and Company, one of the great international banking houses in New York. If Napoleon Bonaparte or the Emperor Charlemagne had turned up in Laurel Creston's subconscious mind, she could not have been more taken by surprise.

She was living in an apartment hotel and had sent Lanny her address; all he had to do was to call her on the telephone, and that appeared such a simple and harmless action. He had promised himself that he wouldn't; but that was before he came upon *The Gauleiter's Cousin*. The reading of this started him to arguing with himself once more. After all, they had got away with it right under the nose of the Gestapo; and here in New York you could come and go freely, and didn't have to register with the police or anything of the sort. So why not?

III

"This is Bienvenu," he said, and she exclaimed: "Oh, good!" He asked: "Will you have lunch with me?" and gave her the name of a little Hungarian restaurant on lower Second Avenue. They had lunched at such a place in Berlin, and it would remind them of old times.

Was that why she was wearing a blue and white print dress, similar to the one she had worn on those two occasions? It couldn't have been the same one, for she had left her trunk and everything else when she had fled from the attentions of the German police. She was a small person, quick in her motions, and he thought of her as birdlike; he knew that she was thirty-two, that revelation having come in the course of experiments with hypnotism. She had nice brown eyes and hair, and he thought she was quite pretty; but what really interested him was the alert intelligence that operated in that small head. She observed everything that was going on, and remembered it, and understood it in relation to other events; she was serious and attentive to his discourse, but then would come a flash of humor, of teasing perhaps, and he would be a bit afraid of her, as every heavy-footed man-at-arms has need to be of any quick-darting Amazon archer.

They sat opposite each other at a little table and ate golden brown veal goulash and drank red wine, and nobody knew them or paid any special attention to them. Even so, they kept off the subject of world politics. Lanny told her the news from his mother's home, where she had been a guest for quite a while; he told her about Parsifal's latest experiments, and what Madame had produced as purporting to come from Laurel's deceased grandmother. She said: "How strange! I tried an experiment with a woman friend here, and Grandmother came—at least, she said she was Grandmother—and told me she had known of my escape from Germany and congratulated me. It was embarrassing, because I didn't want this friend to know anything about my having been in trouble there. I laughed and said it was nothing, that I had lost my passport. I decided it was too dangerous to go on with those experiments; I didn't know what might come up next."

Lanny told her: "It will hurt you with the smart crowd in this town if you let them know about your mediumship. They will call it 'fooling with spooks,' and be sure you must be slightly cracked. It is so much easier to be ignorant than to go against the prejudices of your time, whatever they may be. Here you will meet intellectuals who call themselves Marxists but haven't read Marx, and others, or perhaps the same ones, who call themselves Freudians but haven't read Freud. They are quite certain that Freud discovered the subconscious mind, and they know nothing about the patient research that had been done before Freud was born. If you tell them that their master became convinced of the reality of telepathy before he died, they will look at you with incredulity."

"I don't go among them very much," declared the woman. "Tell me your own conclusions. Do you believe that my grandmother had anything to do with these communications?"

"My dear Laurel," he replied, "it is most awkward to have to say 'I don't know,' but that is the way matters stand with me. I don't know what my mind is now; I don't know how it came to be, and I can't form any idea what it may be after my body has turned to dust. You know that your own mind makes up stories, and persists in doing it even while you are asleep. That mind might be working in secret, making up an imitation grandmother, and gathering information about her from your memories, and from everything you have ever known, and possibly from other minds, living or dead. It will take the research and study of scientists, perhaps for centuries, to answer the question. I picture our minds as bubbles floating on an infinite ocean of mind-stuff, and when we break, we go back to that ocean, and we know everything, or perhaps nothing—who can guess?"

"Sometimes," said Laurel Creston, "I decide that it is an intolerable outrage that we should be put here so ignorant, and so helpless to remedy our ignorance."

"Still worse," smiled Lanny, "is to be sure that we know so much when we know so pitifully little."

IV

He took her to his car and said: "Would you enjoy a drive?" Who wouldn't on a lovely afternoon of sunshine with the first hint of autumn in the air? He took her across one of the East River bridges and through an avenue of Brooklyn, lined with shops and crowded with traffic; before long it had become a wide boulevard, leading into the farming country of Long Island.

They were free now to talk about the dreadful thing that was going on across the seas. One of the great decisions of history was being fought out, Lanny opined; but his companion said: "I cannot think about anything but the young men being killed, and the children and old people buried or burned alive."

"History is a dreadful thing, at whatever point you take it," he replied; "but some points are worse than others, and some decide for better or worse over long periods of time. The defeat of the Spanish Armada decided whether we should have Shakespeare, and freedom of conscience, and parliaments and constitutions—everything that England means to you and me. This battle will decide whether there is to be any more England, or whether its children will be taught to walk the goose-step and *heil* Hitler."

"I know. I have to fight with myself to keep that in mind. How is it going?"

"I have been making note of the reports, and have observed that the daylight raids are becoming less frequent and the night raids more so. That is an acknowledgment of failure on the Germans' part. They have lost as many as two hundred planes in a single daylight raid, and they can't keep that up."

"But night raids can destroy London!"

"They are far less effective, because it is impossible to pick the targets. It doesn't do much good to drop bombs on Hampstead Heath or in the Thames."

"But in the long run—"

"That is one of the questions to be decided—whether there will be any long run. The British will work out methods of defense against any form of attack—if they have time enough."

"What defense can there be against bombs dropped out of the darkness?"

"It is all very secret and I can only pick up hints. The German bombers start fires at strategic places by daylight, and then use them as targets by night. The British trick them by starting great bonfires just outside the city. Also, you may notice that you don't hear so much about searchlights as you did; the reason is that they betray the location of a city. I am told that the British have an electronic device which determines the altitude of planes in the darkness; so they can put up a box barrage and get many of the enemy; the greater the number that come, the more will be hit. I have heard hints that they have developed night-fighters which use the same electronic instruments. Be sure the Nazis haven't all the scientists on their side."

"Oh, God! Shall we never see the day when science will not be working at wholesale destruction?"

Such was the conversation of men and women in these days. The men for the most part had their thoughts on winning a tough fight; but the women thought about their sons and lovers, or those of other women. Lanny remarked: "I had a woman friend, a German Socialist whom the Nazis murdered. She had a phrase: 'It was a bad time to be born.'"

V

At one of the many villages they turned off toward the south shore. At a rise in the land the ocean came into view, and Lanny stopped the car. In the distance was a lovely rolling landscape with clumps of trees, and among them you could see part of a structure big enough to have been a hospital or hotel. Lanny pointed, and said: "I thought it might amuse you to see where I lived for long periods, off and on. This is the first time I have seen it in several years."

"What is it?" she asked, and he told her: "It is called Shore Acres, and I used to say it ought to be Shore Miles. It was built by the late J. Paramount Barnes, utilities king of Chicago, whom you may have heard of."

"Oh!" she said with a suggestion of apology. "I didn't take it for a private residence."

"I did," he smiled. "Later I took the palace of a *duc* in Paris, and then a villa next door to a castle in England. Then Irma took the castle —and the earl who owned it."

"It must have been an odd sort of life," she replied. Was she a little bit shocked because he had driven her here and brought up this subject? A lady from Baltimore who had been strictly reared was continually being shocked by things she encountered in New York, to say nothing of Berlin and the French Riviera. However, she told herself that she was a writer of fiction first and a practitioner of etiquette second.

Lanny, who had learned about Baltimore as a boy through old Mrs. Sally Lee Sibley, mother of Emily Chattersworth, could read her thoughts. Said he: "It is a story which might be valuable to you as local color. It is the sort of thing the public eats up."

If she had been really on the job, she would have said: "Tell me now." Instead, she remarked: "It is hard for me to imagine your being happy in that very extravagant world."

"I wasn't happy, but I've always been a pliable sort of person, and I let the ladies guide me. They told me I was the most fortunate man on earth, and I tried to believe it was so. Only four years have passed since I got out, but it seems like an age. I have a different sort of boss now— a man. I have to do what I am told, and it is impossible for me to have much life of my own."

She wondered: Was that what he had brought her out here to tell her? Subtle persons have the advantage of being able to recognize subtlety when they meet it, but they are at a disadvantage in that they sometimes suspect subtlety where it doesn't exist, or where, at any rate, it isn't operating. She didn't want to seem curious on the subject, so she inquired: "What has become of this estate?"

"It was put on the market and bought by someone whose name I haven't troubled to remember. One of the amazing things about this country of ours is the number of persons who possess great fortunes and whom no one has ever heard of. They turn up in the most unexpected places; they have five, ten, twenty, perhaps fifty million dollars; nobody knows how they got it, and often they don't care to tell. They are perfectly commonplace looking and acting, and they don't seem to have the remotest idea what to do with their wealth; they just reinvest their income and let it go on piling up. I remember somewhere hearing about a dingy couple from California wandering into the office of the president of some university, Yale, or perhaps it was Chicago. They said they had money and thought it might be a good idea to found a university, if they could find somebody to tell them how to begin. The man was a railroad man, he said, and his name was Leland Stanford. In the end he put up twenty million dollars."

VI

Lanny drove again, turning inland. It was a district of palatial estates with elaborate bronze gates, high fences with metal spikes turned outward, or walls of stone with broken glass bottles cemented into the top. Sometimes you couldn't see the houses from the road; but in one case there was a view, and Lanny stopped the car and pointed to a super-elegant mansion of brownstone with many gables, and extremely elaborate Italian gardens. Said he: "That was the home of a very dear friend of yours."

"You must be joking," she replied. "I don't have any such friend."

"It is your subconscious friend, Otto Kahn," he chuckled. "The place is said to have cost three millions, and to have been sold for about a fourth of that amount."

"It must have broken his heart," she commented, "assuming that he knows about it!"

"We'll try a séance, and tell him!"

"What a curious thing to think about, Lanny! Suppose he really does exist and that he knows what we are saying about him!"

"We must be careful, for he was a distinguished person, and accustomed to be treated with deference. He had charming and gracious manners, but he never forgot that he was a prince of the blood—or the blood money, should I say?"

They drove on. It was a pleasant way to spend an afternoon, and Lanny knew this district by heart, having raced about it with Irma and her swagger friends to dinners and dances, tennis and golf and polo parties, the race tracks and yachting regattas. This was the playground of the second and third generations of Wall Street speculators and de-partment-store magnates, newspaper publishers, bankers, landlords, every sort of big business which serves the great metropolis, or plunders it—according to one's point of view. Lanny told funny stories about events he had witnessed among them, or that he had heard. He had no doubt that in the course of a few months he would find the atmos-phere and ideas of the Long Island sporting set portrayed in one or more magazine stories. He had told her that the public would eat it up.

Twilight was falling when they came back to the great city. The bridges were quadruple strings of lights, and the city itself was a magical thing, a fairy spectacle to be compared only with the stars in the sky above. "You can't imagine how strange it seems after Lon-don," he remarked; "after having groped your way about in utter blackness, and knowing that you risked your life every time you stepped off a curb."

"We may see the same thing here before this war is over," said Laurel; and in this he concurred.

"History has always fascinated me," declared the amateur phi-losopher. "One reason is that we know all the answers; we know the things which were hidden from the people of that time. I often think how interesting it would be to bring some of them back and let them see what has come after them. For example, to put the score of Strauss's *Ein Heldenleben* in front of Beethoven, and watch his expression while he ran through it!"

"Or let him listen to one of our swing orchestras," suggested Laurel. "He would die again, I imagine."

VII

Lanny drove to her apartment house, not stopping in front of it but letting her out just around the corner. When he started to explain she said: "You don't need to say anything. I understand completely. I haven't told a soul that I have met you, and I won't mention this afternoon. I have had a delightful time, and whenever you have leisure again, do give me a ring." No lady from Baltimore could say more.

He went off thinking about her, and it was the old story, only more so. He, too, had had a good time, and would have been glad to have more of the same; he wondered about her, what was in her mind, or her heart, or whatever it is in women. He knew them well, and strongly doubted whether this serene and even-tempered lady was entirely absorbed in producing miniature masterpieces of fiction. He didn't believe she thought about nothing but the war and who was going to win it; or about her own subconscious mind, what it was and how it was and what would become of it when her visible part had turned to dust. She had met an eligible man whom she liked, and of course she was thinking about whether she loved him, or whether she would like to love him, and whether she would like him to love her.

Nature has played a trick upon man, making him complementary to woman, so that his thoughts dovetail into hers. Lanny Budd was thinking: I wonder if I love her; I wonder if I would like to love her; I wonder if she would like me to love her. He didn't mean to be condescending about the matter; it was just that he was the lord of creation, and accustomed to wander over the earth at his sweet will, picking and choosing.

There could be no doubt that he found pleasure in her company. She was a good listener, and appreciative of his intellectual gifts. She was interested in the same things as himself, and so far she had never failed to recognize his authority. But at the same time he was a little bit afraid of her mind as it had been revealed in her writings. Could it possibly be that in her secret soul she was looking at him with the same satirical questioning she had applied to the guests of the Pension Baumgartner in Berlin? And if she were ever to turn that loose on him, how would he like it?

In that *Hauptstadt* of Naziland he had saved her from what might have been an unpleasant experience, and during this process of saving she had been frightened and humble; he, knowing the situation in the country, had been the master and she had bowed to his authority. But could he expect that to continue indefinitely—a relationship so contrary to her nature, and to the matriarchal nature of American society? If he were to marry her—just supposing—she would come to know his weaknesses as well as his virtues, and some day, sooner or later, he would pick up a copy of the *Bluebook* and find in it a husband-and-wife story which he would recognize!

Lanny recalled Nietzsche's saying that when you are considering marriage, the question is whether or not you will be interested in the woman's conversation every morning at breakfast for the rest of your life. Lanny decided that he knew the answer; he would take two newspapers every morning and he would read one and Laurel the other; then, perhaps, they would exchange. It made an agreeable domestic scene, and the imagining of it warmed his heart like the cup of hot coffee he would be drinking. But then he thought: Suppose they should come to differ in their ideas about world affairs, as Hansi and Bess had done? Suppose, for example, that she wanted to read the *Daily Worker* while he was reading the *New Leader*? Suppose she couldn't even bear to see the label of his paper held up before her eyes!

The answer to all that appeared to be Lizbeth Holdenhurst. The thought of this lovely girl came like balm to his wounded spirit; she was a soft cushion upon which his thoughts could always rest. Lizbeth would never trouble him with any criticism; she would never concern herself about what he was reading, she wouldn't know where the *New Leader* was leading or what the *Daily Worker* was working at, daily including Sundays. Lizbeth would never weary of his conversation and never cease to think of him as the most wonderful man in the world.

When Lanny had these thoughts, he told himself that it was his lower nature which was tempted by this daughter of ease and luxury, this princess of parasites. He wanted his vanity flattered, his sensuality made comfortable. But no, that was only part of it; Lizbeth was kind, and as good as she knew how to be; and surely youth and beauty are not entirely superfluous in the scheme of things. Lizbeth represented the philoprogenitive instinct operating within him, so he told his learned self; she would make a perfect mother, and her children would be as lovely as herself. But didn't nature want brains as well as body? Or was it that nature didn't know anything about brains, and it was up to man to choose this higher gift, even though it was less comfortable, less safe—and less agreeable at the breakfast table?

Robbie Budd, discussing the daughter of the Holdenhursts, had said in his frank and hearty way: "If you ask me, I'd grab Lizbeth, and do all my analyzing of the situation afterwards." That was what Robbie had done in the case of Mabel Blackless, alias Beauty; and the result of his prompt efficient action had been Lanny Budd. Could it be that somewhere in the realm of the about-to-be there was a Lanny junior, clamoring to come into the world? If he came through Lizbeth he would be handsome and hearty, while if he came through Laurel he might be small but mentally active. Which would Lanny choose? These biological controversies kept bringing back to his mind the words of the old English song: "How happy could I be with either were t'other dear charmer away!"

VIII

"Back to business!" commanded the stern voice of duty. The P.A. would have liked nothing better than to take Laurel Creston for another drive and show her, say, the beautiful Berkshire country, where the hills had acquired their autumnal tints; or the valley of the Hudson, along the Palisades and up to where the Squire of Krum Elbow maintained the so-called "summer White House." But no, he had to call up a man whose very guts he hated, Forrest Quadratt, who called himself the most patriotic of Americans and was Hitler's most highly paid propagandist in the New World. All that Lanny had to do was to ring, and he would be invited to an elegant apartment on Riverside

Drive, to meet some Junker Nazi or some wealthy American who was a sucker for the job of saving the world from Bolshevism.

There had been a letter waiting for Lanny at Newcastle saying: "I want very much to see you; have something special in mind." So when he telephoned, the ex-poet exclaimed: "Oh, I'm so glad! Could you come up to dinner? I'll break another engagement."

The fashionable Lanny Budd, who was staying at the Ritzy-Waldorf, treated himself to the luxury of a walk. Really there wasn't much use in having a car in New York City, especially in the crowded hours toward evening; you got caught in the traffic of Fifth Avenue and crept along more slowly than a brisk pedestrian. The well-to-do had forgotten how to use their legs, but Lanny had walked on the shore paths of the Mediterranean, and along the lanes of England, and in the Tiergarten, and here in a park which had been miraculously preserved in the middle of Manhattan Island. It was badly needed by seven million inhabitants who were in danger of slow suffocation.

On this rocky soil had once been forests, and Indians hunting deer and wild turkeys with bows and arrows. Up this great river the tiny ship of Henry Hudson had sailed, seeking a passage to the Far East and certain that this must be it. The white men had bought the island from the Indians for twenty-four dollars' worth of goods, and had cut down the forests and blasted the rocks and covered the twelve-mile island with hundreds of long narrow canyons having walls of brownstone and granite and floors of asphalt and concrete. The inhabitants had become a new breed of troglodytes, cave-dwellers, or one might better say box-dwellers; their children hardly knew what horses and cows looked like, and assuredly had never seen a deer or a wild turkey unless it was in the Bronx Park Zoo. Literally thousands of boxes were piled together, all numbered so that you could find the one you wanted, and the canyons also numbered for the same reason. Both boxes and canyons were bright by night as well as by day, and it was a fascinating thing to walk and observe the variety of human types that had sought refuge on this small island: more Jews than in Jerusalem, more Italians than in Rome, more Greeks than in Athens, more Negroes than in many an African nation.

So Lanny strolled up Fifth Avenue with its shops exhibiting diamond tiaras and double ropes of pearls, tiny bottles of perfume for which you might pay as much as a hundred dollars, coats of sable and blue fox and chinchilla that might stand you in many thousands; every form of seduction with which a woman might tempt a man, and elegant limousines in which they might be sped away to a rendezvous. The luxury trades had gradually worked their way up Fifth Avenue, crowding the millionaires from the palaces, and even the gods from their temples. The traffic poured out gray fumes, unpleasant to the lungs, so Lanny was glad when he got into the wide spaces of Central Park, and from there to the splendid view of Riverside Drive and the sunset over the Hudson.

I X

Lanny Budd was ill-equipped for a secret agent in one respect: he found so much difficulty in believing evil of human beings. He had seen a lot of it, but that hadn't changed his nature. He would go off and think about the person he had talked with, trying to find excuses for him, to figure out what particular set of circumstances, what unhappy experiences, had made him the deformity he was. So now, confronting this German-American casuist with the pale, pasty face, the thick-lensed eyeglasses, the soft rapid voice, and the gentle, even deprecating manner—what had caused him to tie himself to the tail of the wild Nazi kite? Desire for money? But he was an able writer, and would never have had difficulty in earning his share. Vexation because he had thought himself a great poet and the critics had not given him the attention he demanded? Ambition, a craving for power? Had he made up his mind that Adolf Hitler was really going to conquer the world, and that Forrest Quadratt might become the Dr. Goebbels of the western hemisphere, or the Gauleiter of New York, or both?

This much Lanny had made sure of: this not too robust and by no means attractive-looking little man had really taken up the notion of the *Herrenrasse*, and was certain that he belonged to a superior grade of being. He was said to be an illegitimate grandson of one of the Kaisers, and perhaps that was the source of his craving to exercise authority. He was American-born, and tireless in calling himself an American and a believer in democracy, but that was pure camouflage, his stock in trade; all his ideas and tastes were those of an aristocrat, as were his habits, so far as circumstances permitted.

The dominating motive of his life, it seemed to Lanny, was hatred of the British Empire. The English aristocrats considered themselves the ruling race, and everywhere snubbed and insulted the Germans. The English had got there first and grabbed the best parts of the earth, and thought they had them forever, and by divine right. Everywhere they blocked off the Germans and surrounded them—*die Einkreisung*— and by superior cunning had been able to bamboozle the United States into fighting their wars. The ex-poet's lifeless complexion became flushed when he spoke of how his native land had intervened to snatch the prize of victory from Germany's grasp in World War I, and now he was laboring with fury to make certain that this should not happen a second time.

To that end he had written a shelfful of books under various pseudonyms. To that end he had composed speeches for congressmen and senators, had had them delivered, printed in the Congressional Record, and then mailed out under congressional frank all over the land. To that end he had collected money from wealthy Germans and Irish, from pacifists, mothers, and every sort of person who wanted to keep America out of war. He had helped in causing the White House to be picketed, Congress to be besieged, and mass meetings and parades to be organized all over the land. He was in deadly earnest about all this, but he had a cynical humor, too, and to the son of Budd-Erling, an insider, he laughed over the foibles of the people he had fooled.

Next to Britain, his special hatred was for Franklin D. Roosevelt. Lanny thought as he listened: Roosevelt is too clever for him! Roosevelt has tricks in his bag, too! In the ex-poet's view the President was carrying the country straight into war, and doing it by a series of deceptions. To beat him at the impending election was second in a German's mind only to having the Luftwaffe win the war of the skies over London. He asked Lanny's opinion as to the chances in both these conflicts, and listened with eager attention to what his visitor had seen and learned in France. An extraordinary thing that a man should have strolled out and fallen in with the German Army and had several chats with its Führer; still more that he should tell about it in offhand, casual fashion, as if it were a most ordinary thing that anybody could have done if he had been interested enough in world affairs!

X

There came to this party another guest, a shaven-headed, middle-aged gentleman introduced as Baldur Heinsch, and said to be an official of one of the German steamship lines. He was, according to Quadratt, worthy of all trust; and he must have been told the same thing about the son of Budd-Erling. He talked freely, and, after they had drunk some wine and brandy, he assured Lanny that he held him in high esteem, and that he might speak to him as a trusted friend. First, he wanted to know if Lanny knew the publisher Hearst and when Lanny said No, he countered: "The more I think about it, the more it seems to me that you are the man who might best be able to influence him."

"What do you want him to do?" inquired the false friend.

"First of all, to realize more than he does at present the desperate nature of this crisis, and to make more determined efforts to stave it off."

"I have been reading his papers, and it seems to me he is doing about everything a publisher could do to help us."

"But not as a man, Herr Budd. He has such great resources, and immense personal influence. If he wanted to, he could make all the other publishers print our side of the case—I mean, he could make news of it. But he sits off in that castle he has built in California and contents himself with sending telegrams instructing his editors about the make-up of tomorrow's front page."

"He's quite an old man, isn't he?"

"Seventy-seven; but he comes of a tough breed. Those western pioneers had to be; the weaklings were eliminated. May I speak to you in the strictest confidence, Herr Budd?"

"Always, of course."

"Do you think we have a chance to beat Roosevelt?"

"I don't know, Herr Heinsch. My job is overseas. When I come back here I can only ask other people's opinions."

"What does your father think?"

"My father and I are not on very good terms at present. He is making warplanes, and not thinking about anything else. Naturally, I find that repugnant, and I cut my visits short. Newcastle belongs to the merchants of death, and politics is out for the duration."

"There you have it! The thing is spreading like a forest fire—a fire of greed. Roosevelt has persuaded Congress to vote twelve billion dollars for war preparations, and every dollar is a bribe to some businessman to reduce his opposition to our involvement. If we get into it, it will cost us a hundred billion, two hundred, five hundred—nobody can make a guess. The last war won't be a circumstance in comparison."

"I agree with you about all that. It is a most dreadful thing."

"That's why my thoughts turn to Hearst. He is the most powerful single personality we have on our side. He has more money than all the people I know put together."

"I thought he was in serious financial straits."

"That doesn't mean anything to a man like him. Maybe he has lost ten million, twenty million; but he has hundreds of millions; he owns more New York real estate than any other one person; his income would finance a dozen crusades to save America."

"I read that he had had to sacrifice some of his papers, and that he had lost control of the whole set-up."

"The financial control, but not the editorial. A syndicate handles the business end, but he still gets his share, don't fool yourself."

"What, precisely, do you have in mind for him to do?"

"First of all, to realize the emergency we face. If Roosevelt is re-elected, it means we enter the war, as certain as anything on this earth—unless we do something revolutionary."

"Speak frankly, Herr Heinsch. You can count on me."

"We Americans have got ourselves hypnotized by the idea of elections. We think that votes settle everything, votes come from God. But Hitler and Mussolini have shown us that governments are not immutable, and that the rabble doesn't have to have its way."

Long practice had taught a P.A. never to show any surprise; and besides, he didn't feel so very much. "You'd be cheered if you knew how many people are talking about that idea, in the locker rooms of all the country clubs."

"You have heard it, then?"

"No end of it; I had in mind to ask you about it. Their favorite formula is: 'Somebody ought to shoot him!'"

"I don't mean anything so extreme. Assassination would have a bad effect and might lead to reaction. All that is necessary is for a group of determined men to lead him away and keep him in some quiet spot until the trouble is over. Somebody should state: 'You are still President, Mr. Roosevelt, but you're not working at it for a time. The country is going to be run by men who are sane, and don't intend to have their sons shot for the benefit of the British Empire and Bolshevik Russia.' The men in this plan are all Americans, Herr Budd."

"That is really interesting news, sir; and if anything of the sort is to be done, you can count upon my co-operation. You won't want to name your friends, and please note that I'm not asking. I understand how confidential such a matter has to be."

"That is fine of you, Herr Budd, and the attitude I expected you to take. The question is: Would you be willing to go and see Hearst and try to persuade him to give us real help before it is too late? Assure him that wealthy Americans alone are involved."

"But how can I sound a man out on matters like that, Herr Heinsch? He wouldn't dream of speaking openly with a stranger."

"You wouldn't go as a stranger; I would furnish you with introductions from several highly influential men who would vouch for you. You would have to take a little time, of course, and get acquainted with the old gentleman. You have special equipment for handling him, because you are an art authority and he is the world's greatest art collector; also, you are Hitler's friend, and Hearst has met the Führer, and I know how tremendously he has been impressed. There won't be anything novel in the ideas you present to him, I am certain."

XI

Lanny said that he couldn't give an offhand decision on a matter of such importance. He promised to think it over, and this promise he kept. What determined his thinking was the unceasing air war over the British Isles. There was a limit to the amount of radio listening and newspaper reading that anyone could stand. One day it was seventy-five enemy planes shot down and the next day it was only fifty; in either case it meant little, because you couldn't be sure if the figures were correct, and you didn't know how many planes either side had, or what was their replacement capacity. You read the news that this or that district of London had been hit, this or that landmark destroyed; but there was nothing you could do about it, and the agonies of your imagination wouldn't help a single one of the unfortunates "sticking it" in damp and chilly cellars and tunnels underground.

The members of Lanny's family begged him not to go back under those bombs. What could he accomplish there? When he asked himself the question, he couldn't find an answer. Adi Schicklgruber had revealed all there was to reveal; he would invade Britain when his preparations were complete. The British people knew that, and were getting ready for him to the best of their ability; meantime, all the world had to wait. The air war was part of Adi's preparation, and so long as it continued, you could be sure that *Der Tag* was not tomorrow. Until this was decided, there would be nothing important for a P.A. to do overseas.

Lanny thought: I have never seen my own country. His fortieth birthday was at hand, and he had never been farther west than Chicago. He thought: If we get into this war, it may not be so easy to travel. He found himself thinking of the great plains, the Rocky Mountains, and above all California, which has an advantage over the rest of the world in having the movie industry for its publicity department. Lanny could have flown there in a day and night, but what lured him was the thought of stepping into a car and driving for a solid week. Long-distance motoring had been one of his recreations since early manhood, and now Hitler and his war had ruined it in Europe.

Then another thought, a mousy little thought, stealing silently into his mind: How pleasant it might be to have Laurel Creston along on such a trip! How many things they would find to talk about, and how greatly his appreciation of the scenery would be enhanced by her comments! They had taken such a tour in Germany, keeping out of touch with the Gestapo; a semicircular tour of Central and Western Germany, starting in Berlin and stopping at Berchtesgaden, and then out by way of Austria and Switzerland. A tour that had surely not been forgotten by either of them!

He imagined himself calling her up and saying: "Have you ever seen your own country, and would you like to see it?" It would be a strictly proper, brother-and-sister tour, like the previous one, and he would make that plain in delicate, well-chosen words. They would stay in different hotel rooms, even in different hotels if she preferred. To be sure, none of her friends would believe it; but there was no reason why her friends should know about it. The project concerned themselves alone.

Lanny's imagination had always been active, and now, for some reason, it became even more so; it was interested in playing with this theme and in composing variations, a diversion familiar to all musicians. The same theme can be grave or gay, minor or major; it can be played with various instruments and in various tempos. Lanny's imagination decided to dispense with the separate rooms, or to make them part of one suite; he pictured himself calling up Laurel Creston and saying abruptly: "How would you like to marry me and have a honeymoon in California?" The women have a stock answer to such inquiries: "This is so sudden!" Now and then one of them may aspire to be original and say: "Well, it's about time!"

Lanny had no idea what the real Laurel Creston would respond, but his musical fancy was delighted with this theme. She said "Yes" in various modes, and they had a most enjoyable holiday. New Jersey lies just across the river, and on the route to California; Lanny had heard that you could get married there without any preliminaries, and so they did, in his imagination, and it was a heart-warming experience. But then began the old round of problems. The journey came to an end, and they were back in New York, and what was he going to do with her then? Where would he hide her, and how would she manage to publish her satirical stories without getting the Nazi agents on her trail? As ex-husband of Irma Barnes, Lanny could still get into Hitlerland, but as husband of "Mary Morrow" he would stand an excellent chance of disappearing by way of a torture chamber and an incinerator.

There were other variations on this theme; one in Vienna waltz time, and one in Harlem swing, or the new night-club style called boogie-woogie. You didn't have to stop and hunt for a preacher or a justice of the peace in Hoboken or Weehawken. You just sped on, the world forgetting, by the world forgot. You gathered your rosebuds while you might and you took no thought for the morrow, saying what should you eat and what should you drink and wherewithal should you be clothed. You knew that you would find cocktails and sizzling hot steaks in roadhouses along the way, and as for clothes, you had them in the trunk of the car, including pink silk pajamas, or maybe black with Chinese dragons in silver or gold. And did they cost money!

Such was the mood of the time, and you asked for what you wanted. The smart New Yorkers had a word for it, "propositioning," and the woman was not supposed to take offense; quite the contrary, she might be the one to speak, for wasn't it supposed to be a woman's world? Long ago, in France, Lanny had been "propositioned" by Isadora Duncan, and he might have accepted, only he happened to be in love with Madame de Bruyne at the time. Was he being puritanical now, and was Laurel pretending to be the same because she thought that was the way he wanted her to be?

Get thee behind me, Satan! Lanny told himself that this lady from Baltimore was a person of fine sensibilities, and that if she wanted anything from him it would be true and enduring affection. That, alas, he was not in a position to offer, and he told himself that he ought to be ashamed to think of her in ways that would humiliate and degrade her. Suppose that in one of her trances Grandmother Marjorie Kennan were to tell her about it! And suppose Laurel were to start wondering whether this message was a product of Lanny's subconscious mind or her own!

XII

Baldur Heinsch had said: "If you are going, you ought to see Hearst's art works in the department stores and in his storerooms up in the Bronx." Lanny decided that this was sound advice in any case, so he called up his friend and art mentor, Zoltan Kertezsi. Together they visited two great department stores which, for the first time in the history of the world, had set apart whole floors for the exhibiting and selling of old masters and museum objects.

For half of a long life a headstrong master of millions had amused himself accumulating such works from all over Europe. He had employed agents to scour the Continent, and had built a huge medieval palace on the Pacific Coast to contain them. When this and its various satellite buildings could hold no more, he had constructed first one and then another enormous storehouse in that northeastern part of Greater New York known as the Bronx. Many of these treasures the lord of San Simeon had never seen; he had bought them by cable and was content to know that they were his property, and safe from fire and thieves.

The great depression had come, affecting both circulation and advertising of newspaper chains; also the infamous New Deal had imposed huge income taxes. Hearst had had to kill some of his papers and sell others and let a trusteeship manage the rest. He had lost interest in his art treasures and decided to turn them into cash. Someone had had the bright idea of advertising and marketing them through department stores; so here you could look at rows of paintings, priced anywhere from fifty dollars to fifty thousand—and they were selling fast. Another store offered all sorts of *objets d'art*, statuary, vases, tapestries, armor, and weapons, from Venetian daggers which you could use as papercutters to huge halberds and battle-axes which only an athlete could wield. A price tag on every one, from ninety-eight cents up to ninety-eight hundred dollars!

The people of New York knew all about William Randolph Hearst, who had once run for mayor, and then for governor of the state, and had tried hard to run for President—but the people had got onto him by that time. They thought it would be fun to own something which they could say was from his collection; they were rolling in money, because ships and steel and copper and oil and food, paid for in cash, were being poured into Britain, or into the ocean on the way. And now here was Uncle Sam ordering twelve billion dollars' worth of armaments! Why not have a little fun, and incidentally a little culture? You could save the price tag and prove what you had paid, and it was as good as money in the bank!

Heinsch had added: "If you want to see the storerooms, let me know. Several of our most active workers are employed there." So Lanny called the official and was told: "I'll telephone and arrange it. Present your card and ask for Mr. Hickenlooper." So Lanny waited at the door of a warehouse which occupied a whole city block. Through a slot which might have belonged to a speakeasy he stuck in his visiting card, and a stoutish rosy German from Yorkville appeared and invited him in.

You couldn't believe it without seeing it with your own eyes. In this place was an office with cabinets containing one hundred and fifty fat books composed of loose leaves, the catalog of this warehouse. Ten or eleven clerks were needed to keep them up-to-date. There were twelve thousand objects listed, Lanny was told, and that didn't sound so formidable—until it was explained that an "object" included such things as a "complete medieval room," and there were seventy of these. Another "object" was a whole monastery from Spain; you might think that was a joke, but no, here it was, in fourteen thousand cases which had cost seventy thousand dollars just to pack. The monastery had been built in the year 1141, and Hearst had bought it without seeing it, and had ordered it taken down, stone by stone, each labeled on the boxes, so that the structure could be set up in any part of America which felt the need of either a monastery or a tourist attraction.

Many items were equally fantastic, and the figures staggering. There were eight million dollars' worth of tapestries—at least that was what had been paid for them. For a single set the dealer Duveen had received the sum of $575,000; perhaps that was the money with which this celebrated personality had been able to become First Baron of Millbank. Not much fun looking at rolled-up tapestries, and one packing box looks much like another, but Lanny let himself be escorted from floor to floor. If he was going to meet the master of San Simeon it would be something to report on.

Later he called Heinsch to say Thanks. "I have to visit clients in the Middle West," he announced, "and it may be that I'll decide to continue on to California. On second thought I believe it would be better not to use introductions from your friends, because that might make it seem a political call and put the old man on his guard. I'll get some of the movie people to take me and I'll talk about art. It may even be that I can do some business for him—find him some rich clients. He'll be much more disposed to trust me if I can be the means of paying him some millions of dollars."

He called his father, saying: "Can you spare the car for three or four weeks?" The answer was: "If I need another car, I can buy one. Go ahead and enjoy yourself." Lanny understood the thought behind these words: "Anything to keep you from under the bombs!"

6. *Westward the Star*

I

THE first stage of the journey was through the rolling farm country of Pennsylvania; woodlands, then hills, then the Allegheny Mountains, their valleys black with coal, their slopes denuded of timber. He came to the great steel city of Pittsburgh; in its Sewickley district, which claimed to be the richest borough in the United States, dwelt Lanny's old friends the Murchisons, just back from their summer camp in the Adirondacks. Lanny had sold them an especially fine Goya, "El Comendador." This Spanish grandee had got twelve bullet holes through him in the recent war, but they had been repaired so skillfully that you couldn't find them, and it was a favorite parlor game to try. Doubtless the old gentleman had been a stuffy and tiresome person in real life, but with all his gold lace, and the collar of the Spanish Order of the Golden Fleece, he made a grand figure for the head of a staircase, and all newcomers took up eagerly the challenge to say where he had been hit.

Lanny didn't say a word about art works. He told about his adventure with the Wehrmacht in Dunkirk and Paris, about Laval's ancient château, and so on. After Harry had plied him with questions about the war and how it was going to turn out, he could be sure that Adella would ask: "Have you found anything that would interest me?" Thus invited, he would open a brief case full of photographs and tell about one work after another, never overpraising them, but preserving his careful judicious manner. Adella would say: "I think that is lovely!" and he would counter: "It is a little old-fashioned, what the French call *vieux jeu*." The wife, who had once been a secretary and was now an ample and dignified matron, would reply: "We are all somewhat old-fashioned in this neck of the woods." He would tell her: "The price seems to me a trifle high. I might be able to get it reduced, but it would take time." To this the answer would be: "Harry is making so much money that it is a shame."

Harry had inherited the control of a plate-glass factory, and so much of his product was being smashed in London every night that, so he said, he was assured of a meal ticket for the rest of his days. Harry's waistline had increased by a considerable percentage since the days when he had tried to run away with Lanny's lovely mother at the outbreak of World War I. He had grown also in business importance, but he never tried to put on any "dog" with Lanny Budd. If his wife wanted a painting, or anything else in the world, she could have it; but Lanny would take the husband's side and try to restrain an amateur collector's ardor. This time he told about Hearst, holding him up as a terrible example of what this impulse could do when it was turned loose. But, even so, Adella ordered a painting; her choice was a Eugenio Lucas, an imitator of Goya, very good, and she said it would be fun to see if her friends could tell the difference.

II

Next came Cincinnati, home of another American family grown far too rich, this time out of hardware. These were Sophie Timmons's relatives, a lot of them, so that the government didn't get the whole fortune in income taxes. A company assembled to meet Lanny Budd, and several wanted to talk about paintings, having visited the Riviera and seen the half-dozen French masters in Sophie's villa. The older men took no stock in "foreign doodads" and guessed they were mostly "hooey"; but the ladies found Lanny Budd a delightful fresh breeze in their overgrown river town, and wished he would stay and marry their newest daughter just out of finishing school.

On to Detroit, where Mrs. Henry Ford and her son Edsel were making a modest collection, and where Henry was standing out stubbornly against the efforts of his government to persuade him to make war goods. Then to the small town of Reubens, Indiana, home of Ezra Hackabury, proprietor and retired manufacturer of Bluebird Soap; Ezra was eighty and his soap was over sixty, and both were still going strong. He had come to the Detaze show in Cleveland and bought several paintings which Marcel had done on Ezra's yacht, the *Bluebird*, and now he wanted to look at photographs of others. He was still meaning to donate them to his town library—just to spite his in-laws, he said with a grin.

And then Chicago, which to Lanny meant old Mrs. Fotheringay, who lived in a palace on the North Shore and collected babies; painted ones, of course. Every time Lanny went to Europe he would find her a new one; sometimes he would bring it along, but this time he had had his hands full and brought only photographs. Her "darlings," she called them, and fell in love with a very delightful Hoppner, and only wanted to be sure the child had rosy cheeks. When Lanny was able to assure her of this fact, she wrote him a check for twenty-seven thousand dollars, and didn't mind trusting him to buy the painting when he could and have it shipped to her by airmail so as to be safe from the submarines.

III

That was the end of business, and the rest was play. Westward on the Lincoln Highway; now and then it made a sharp turn to avoid somebody's barn, but most of the time it went straight ahead, and sixty miles an hour was all right outside of towns. Lanny would start early and drive until after dark, with no stops except for lunch and dinner; six hundred miles a day was a comfortable stint. Illinois, and then Iowa, where once the rolling prairie had been and the buffalo and Indians had roamed. Now it was all fenced, and there were farmhouses with immense red barns—that being the cheapest kind of paint. The corn had been shucked and the stalks dumped into the great tall silos, and droves of big hogs were rooting in the fields.

Then it was Nebraska, and the road began to climb, slowly and steadily, and with every rise the land became drier and the farms poorer. This had been grazing land, but it had been plowed for grain during the boom of the last war, and so it had become a country of dust storms, and the problem was to keep it from turning into desert. The effort was a part of the New Deal's "boondoggling," endlessly carped at by the enemies of F.D.R.

You had to see this land in order to realize the immensity of it; you had to watch it rolling by, mile after mile, with its monotony of scenery, and realize that it extended north and south many hundreds of miles. He would turn the dials of the radio in his car and get news about the air war still going on overseas; and when he stopped at filling stations, or to eat or spend the night, he would get into conversation with the people and ask what they thought about this world-shaking crisis. He discovered that to the last man and woman they had one idea, which was to keep their own country, their own sons, out of the mess. Mostly they were against Roosevelt because they suspected him of trying to get them in. Oddly enough, many were against Willkie, also, because he was beginning to talk more and more like his rival.

So came the Rockies, far ahead and high up, covered with snow; you climbed, and it was Wyoming, the great open spaces, the cattle country; the road was a tiny gray thread, and alongside it were sloping structures like well-braced fences to keep the snow from drifting over the roads. Eight thousand feet was the altitude, and the air was crisp and bracing, but there wasn't so much of it, and if you walked it had better be slowly. Then you were in the mountains, climbing, with high peaks and canyon walls on both sides, and a clear green stream below. Snow everywhere—and you had better keep going, for you wouldn't want to be caught here by a storm.

Then down into the broad fertile plateau where old Brigham Young had looked about him and struck his staff into the ground, saying: "Build here!" It was the country of the Latter-Day Saints, whose founders had followed the Old Testament and taken many wives and replenished the earth. It hadn't pleased the other Bible-reading Americans, but it had seemed to work—if the purpose of mankind was to labor from dawn to dark and produce enormous quantities of fruit and grain and sugar beets, copper and silver, lead and zinc. It looked as if the old Mormon prophet had foreseen the automobile, for every street of his city was wide enough for diagonal parking. His Temple, begun nearly a hundred years ago, had walls of granite six feet thick and had been one of the wonders of this high mountain world.

Lanny had no clients here. He drove around for a look, spent the night, and in the morning drove on. His road turned into southern Utah, a mass of tumbled mountains, containing some of the finest scenery in the world. It is wild country, much of it inaccessible; canyons, precipices, and boulder-strewn wildernesses, with old prospectors wandering among them, leading patient burros with packloads. But you didn't see them from the road! You saw vast spaces, a land without limits, the road winding through it in broad curves, a serpent without head or tail. The rocks were of every color, black, white, or gray, red, green, yellow, or mottled with all colors; they were of every shape, tall pinnacles, monuments, sculptured figures, huge masses that looked like fortresses or rows of office buildings in a city. No two views were the same, and the driver's eyes moved incessantly from the road to some freak of nature and then back to the road again.

Presently it was Nevada, according to a signpost, but there was little difference the motorist could observe; barren lands, red hills, with gray mountains in the dim distance, and the road winding where it could. Now and then you would see a long-legged chaparral cock, called a road runner because of its habit of trying to keep ahead of vehicles; but this didn't work with automobiles. Now and then you would see a buzzard or eagle wheeling in the sky; if you cared to stop you could make the acquaintance of lizards and rattlesnakes. It was Mary Austin's "land of little rain." Filling stations might be as much as twenty miles apart, and you were advised to be sure that your radiator was full, since all water had to be hauled in, and its price was high. Car trouble was serious, for many wanderers had perished here in the days of covered wagons, and one ribbon of gray concrete was the only mark of civilization.

IV

Lanny crossed the Colorado River by a long bridge, and was in the California desert, near the Death Valley region. It was having a hot spell now, and he had been advised to pass through at night. He couldn't see the landscape, but judged that it must be flat and level, for the road went straight, like a great steel tape stretched taut. The car lights shone on it, far ahead, and exercised a hypnotic effect—but it was better not to nod, bowling along at a mile a minute. A hot, almost suffocating wind blew upon him and seemed to be drying the blood in his veins; doubtless he was perspiring, but there was no trace upon him. A strange thing to drive into the little town of Baker, and discover broad paved streets, and filling stations and other places ablaze with light, and realize that human beings lived in this heat, not merely by night but by day! Lanny, a considerate person, didn't want to discourage them, and forbore to ask how they stood it.

He drove until he was in the orange country. He stopped at a town called Riverside—but its river was dry; he put up at a hotel called the Mission Inn—but there was no mission, only a museum full of California curiosities. He had a good sleep, and then drove through miles and miles of orange and lemon groves, laden with golden and yellow fruit. The towns had picturesque names: Pomona, which was Greek, Azusa, which was Indian, Monrovia and Pasadena which had come out of some realtor's dream.

So he came to Hollywood, his goal for the moment, and the dream of all movie fans from China to Peru. The town had been taken into the sprawling city of Los Angeles, most of the studios had moved into the near-by valleys, and the actors had their homes everywhere but in Hollywood; so it was no longer a geographical location but merely a trademark. The landscape and climate reminded Lanny of the Côte d'Azur; but there he had never seen "supermarkets" with all the fruits and vegetables of the world spread out, nor "drive-in eateries" nor "hotdog stands" and "orange juiceries" built in the shape of Indian tepees or Eskimo igloos or sitting white cats or other Mother

Goose or Walt Disney creations. It was, he discovered, like all California towns, built haphazard, a jumble of anybody's whims, with half its spaces empty because people were holding them, waiting for values to rise.

V

While driving, Lanny had been thinking of who in this region might serve his underground purpose. Sooner or later "everybody" came here, and many of them stayed. In the course of his life he had met journalists, writers, musicians, actors—hundreds of them in his mother's home, other hundreds while he and Irma had been playing about in café society in New York, and yet others while Irma had been playing the *salonnière* in Paris. Many he had forgotten, and many, no doubt, had forgotten him; but his memory lighted upon a couple, the De Lyle Armbrusters, who had "scads" of money and had amused themselves all over the world; he had run into them at the Savoy in London, and again at the Adlon in Berlin, and in Algiers when they had been on a yachting trip. Irma had mentioned that they had settled in Beverly Hills, and Lanny guessed that wherever they were they would know the celebrities.

He looked them up in the fat Los Angeles telephone book and there they were. He called the number, and a grave English voice answered. In smart society the only grave voice is that of the butler, so Lanny said: "Is either Mr. or Mrs. Armbruster at home?" The reply was: "Whom shall I say, sir?"—in smart society the only persons who bother with grammar are the butler and the social secretary. Lanny answered: "Tell them, please, that Mr. Lanny Budd is calling."

In half a moment more there was Genie, short for Eugenia, bubbling over with welcome. "Lanny, how perfectly ducky! Where are you?"

"I'm at the Beverly-Wilshire."

"Oh, you darling, how nice! We'll be having cocktails—won't you run over? Any time from five to seven—and stay for dinner and we'll chew the rag."

That's the way it is when you know the "right" people, you just don't have any troubles at all, unless you drink too many cocktails, or make love to your host's wife. Lanny had time to bathe and shave, and glance at an afternoon paper to see that London still survived. His clothes, freshly pressed, were brought to his door, and his car, freshly washed and serviced, was brought to the door of the hotel. The porter told him how to get to Benedict Canyon. There he found an Italian Renaissance villa of some twenty rooms, built on the side of a mountain, so that things above and below it had to be terraced and walled to keep them from sliding down. It was just like the heights above Cannes, or the place called Californie above Nice, where the

Duke and Duchess of Windsor had been staying. There was a tennis court and a swimming pool, and from the loggia you looked over the whole Los Angeles plain, the blue Pacific, and the Channel islands beyond. At night it was a vast plain, a bowl full of lights, an unequaled spectacle.

VI

Everywhere in the modern world are rich people trying to escape boredom, and willing to keep open house for anybody who can produce a novelty. If they are very rich they do it on a grand scale, and the drive in front of their home and the road outside will be lined with a double row of motorcars. Some specialize in "headliners," and go to any trouble to secure their presence. The "headliners" may be rich, too, but they have to work for their money, whereas the rich rich can make a business of hospitality. As a reward their names are always in the society columns and everybody knows who they are. De Lyle Armbruster was fiftyish and stoutish, as bland and smiling as the head-waiter in the dining-room of a "palace hotel." His wife, blond and animated, was Lanny's age, supposedly dangerous for women; she kissed him and called him "old dear," and was as glad to see him as if he had still been Mister Irma Barnes.

All proper homes now have a private bar gleaming with chromium, or maybe platinum—who can be sure? The room will be done in jazz colors, or paintings in the surrealist style; there may be photographs signed by celebrity friends, or original copies of cartoons from the great centers of politics and culture. The guests stand about, nibble tiny sausages and other delicacies stuck on toothpicks, sip drinks with torpedo and brimstone names, and chat about the price which not more than an hour ago was paid for the picture rights of the newest best-seller, scheduled for publication next week. Or perhaps it will be the seven-year contract which the speaker has just been offered but hasn't yet decided about; or the star who has been chosen to play the role of Joan of Arc or President Wilson. So you will know that you are in Hollywood.

The first person to whom Lanny Budd was introduced was Charles Laughton, whom he had previously known as King Henry the Eighth; the second was another round-faced and beaming gentleman, Charles Coburn, whom he had seen in comedies, always as a millionaire father perplexed by the insane behavior of his children. On the screen these personages were enlarged to godlike proportions and their voices filled a great theater. To meet them now, reduced to ordinary size, to shake hands with them and discover that they were made of flesh and blood, was an experience like walking into the Mermaid Tavern and being presented to Will Shakespeare and Ben Jonson. How does one address such supernal beings? What can one say, of admiration and awe, which they have not heard from a thousand autograph-hungry fans?

Lanny could say: "I saw you in Athens, and again in the town of Stubendorf, in Upper Silesia." That was slightly better. He could say to Bette Davis: "It might interest you to know that Hitler showed me *Dark Victory* in his home at Berchtesgaden." It did interest her, and she asked what the Führer had said. That was what Lanny wanted; for almost at once he became the center of a group, plying him with questions. People in Hollywood found it as extraordinary to meet someone who had been in the same room with Hitler as Lanny found it to be in the same room with Charles Laughton and Bette Davis. How did Hitler talk, and what did he eat, and what sort of table manners did he have? Was he really quite sane? And what about his love life? Above all, was he going to be able to knock out London?

VII

At one side of the ample drawing-room was a large overstuffed chair which bore a certain resemblance to a throne, and on it sat a round-faced ample lady who bore a certain resemblance to a queen in the movies. She rarely moved, but people came to her and made obeisance and paid tribute in the form of news: what they had done that day and what they were planning to do, what their friends had done—in short all the gossip of the studios they had chanced to pick up: who was now keeping company with whom, who was expecting a baby, or a divorce, or an elopement. They were all her friends, and they all called her Louella, and all she exacted in return was that they would give her an "exclusive." Woe betide them if they ever broke faith with her on this all-important point!

It was rare indeed that anybody ever "stole the show" from this queen of publicity, and she frowned as she observed the phenomenon. To the hostess she addressed the question: "Who is that fellow that is talking so much?"

The hostess was glad to explain, for it might be worth a paragraph, and the De Lyle Armbrusters might be mentioned in it. "His name is Lanny Budd. He used to be the husband of Irma Barnes, the heiress who was the glamour girl of Broadway some ten or twelve years ago."

"I read the newspapers," replied Louella coldly.

"His father is Budd-Erling Aircraft," added the other, putting first things first. "The son is a very distinguished art expert."

"Why does everybody want to hear about art all of a sudden?"

"It isn't that, Louella. It so happens he is a personal friend of Hitler. and has recently been visiting him."

"Can that really be true?"

"He knows Göring, and Hess, and all the leading Nazis. He has been Göring's art adviser for many years. He was with them in Paris when the armistice was signed."

"Well, Genie, what is the matter with you? Why haven't you introduced him to me?"

"I didn't know whether you'd be interested, Louella. His pictures aren't the kind that move."

"Good God, am I never to talk anything but shop? And besides, the man looks like a movie actor. He'd make another Ronald Colman. Somebody ought to give him a screen test!"

The hostess needed to hear no more. She went over and broke into the circle, interrupting a description of the Berghof. "I want to introduce you to somebody," she said, and of course that was a command. Lanny followed her, and the others came along; they must have been troubled by the discourtesy they were showing to their publicity queen. "Louella Parsons," said Genie, "this is Lanny Budd."

There was one chair, placed so that one person could be seated in front of the throne. Lanny was ordered to take it, and the others ranged themselves in a circle to hear what was going to be said. Even the bar was forgotten for a time.

"They tell me you are a friend of Hitler's, Mr. Budd." The voice was surprising, that of a child—a sweet little child of ten.

"Yes," replied Lanny meekly. "I have that honor."

"Tell me, does he make a practice of having American friends?"

"I think not, Miss Parsons. So far as I know I am his only American friend."

"And how did that come about?" She didn't add "my little man," but it was exactly so that Lanny had been questioned by duchesses and ambassadors' wives when he was a lad of eight or ten.

The visitor explained, respectfully: "It happened that when I was young, one of my playmates was Kurt Meissner, who grew up to become Germany's most honored *Komponist*. Another boy at Schloss Stubendorf became one of the Führer's earliest converts and visited him when he was in prison. The Führer never forgets any of those old-timers, and so it came about that I was brought into his circle."

"And tell me, what sort of man is he, really?"

So Lanny was launched upon one of his suave discourses. He put everything he had into it, for he knew that at this moment he was right where he wanted to be. It was for the Hearst newspapers that Louella Parsons wrote her famous column of movie gossip, and she was one of the publisher's intimates and a frequent guest at San Simeon. It wasn't that fate had been so especially kind to Lanny, but that he had been especially careful in figuring where and how to make his Hollywood debut.

VIII

He didn't tell about his joining the German Army in Dunkirk and being taken back to the Führer's headquarters. He knew that was too much like a Hollywood story, and would discredit the rest of his statements. What he told were the little commonplace things: the Führer's vegetable plate with a poached egg on top, his law against smoking in his home, the fact that you had to appear within two minutes of the sounding of the gong for meals; his fondness for Wagner's music, his insistence that all the women servants and secretaries had to be young Aryan blondes, so different from himself; his fondness for his old Munich companions, such as Herr Kannenberg, the fat little man who had been a *Kellner* and was now Adi's steward, and played the accordion for him in the evening, and sang *"Ach, du lieber Augustin"* and dialect songs from the Inn valley where the son of Alois Schicklgruber had been born. He explained Adi's propaganda technique of choosing a big lie and repeating it incessantly until everybody believed it; he told the story of the *Stierwäscher* of the Innthal —the peasants who had wanted to enter a white bull in a prize competition, but they had no white bull, so they took a black one and washed it every day for a month and then insisted that it was white, and so they won the prize.

And so on and on, far beyond the limits of confinement to one subject that a cocktail party ordinarily sticks to. There were two men who were on the front page almost every day, and who were very exclusive—Joseph Stalin and Adolf Hitler. There were few in Hollywood who could say they had met either, and probably not one who could say that he had met Hitler within the past half year. Lanny could say it, and prove it by going into details about the scene in the Hotel Crillon, where Hitler had made his headquarters, and the railroad car in the Compiègne forest where the armistice had been signed and Adi had done his little jig dance of triumph. To listen to all this was not merely idle curiosity on the part of Genie's guests, for one of the stock products of Hollywood had become anti-Nazi pictures, and Lanny's intimate stories would be useful to writers, producers, directors, costumers, property men, and on down the line.

IX

Presently he was telling about Karinhall, which was named after Göring's first wife and was the home of his second. Emmy Sonnemann, having been one of Germany's stage queens, was somebody this audience could understand. Now she had a baby—and that too was becoming a Hollywood custom and a matter of public excitement. Lanny told what happened when you went on a shooting trip with this old-style Teutonic robber baron at his lodge in the Silesian forest called Rominten: how you stood on a high stand while the stags were driven out in front of you, and you picked the one with the best horns and shot him, and then after eating an enormous supper of all kinds of game you put on your overcoat and went out into the moonlit forest where the stags had been laid in the snow, and listened while the trumpeters blew a sort of requiem for the stags, called a *Hallali.* Surely Hollywood ought to use that some day! And also the pig-sticking in the forests of the Obersalzberg—but those shots might be a bit difficult to get.

Lanny came to the subject of the Reichsmarschall's taste in art, which ran to gentlemen in magnificent costumes and ladies in no costumes at all. For years Lanny had helped him to get rid of paintings he didn't want and to acquire others more to his taste; in passing, the expert remarked: "Just before the war came, Hermann was arranging to purchase a set of sixteenth-century Flemish tapestries from Mr. Hearst's agents in London. He showed me the sketches of them, and told me a story about Sir Nevile Henderson, who had inspected the drawings. They were all of nude ladies representing various virtues, and the British Ambassador commented that he didn't see any representing Patience. Göring has a keen sense of humor, and when you hit it he throws his head back and bellows."

At this point the queen of publicity interposed: "Mr. Budd, have you ever met Mr. Hearst?"

"I have never had that pleasure," was the reply. "I missed him on his trip to Paris a couple of years ago."

"He was greatly impressed by both Göring and Hitler."

"So I have been told, and the feeling was reciprocated. Hermann and Adi are both remarkable men, and Mr. Hearst is one who would be able to appreciate them."

"I think he would be interested to hear your account of them."

"I should be honored to meet him, Miss Parsons—and especially if I had your recommendation."

That was all that was said, but after the party broke up the genial Genie remarked: "You made a hit with Louella—and believe me that isn't easy for anybody who monopolizes the conversation!" The hostess was bubbling with satisfaction, for her party had been a success, and she was sure it would get a fat paragraph in the morning. The game of publicity hunting is like the pinball device which you see in drugstores and poolrooms; you invest a lot of money, but it is only rarely that you hit the jackpot.

X

At ten o'clock next morning, after Lanny had finished his bath and his breakfast and his *Los Angeles Examiner*, the telephone rang in his hotel room. "Is this Mr. Lanny Budd? This is Louella Parsons."

"Oh, good morning, Miss Parsons. I have just read what you wrote about me in your column. It is very kind of you indeed."

"I write what I think. If you had been a chatterbox I would have said so—or I wouldn't have said anything."

"Thank you, Miss Parsons."

"I have just talked with Mr. Hearst. He would be pleased if you would visit him. He invites you for lunch today and to spend the week-end at San Simeon."

"But—how can I get there by lunchtime?"

"You will fly. His plane leaves the Burbank airport at eleven-thirty. There will be other passengers, so don't be late."

"I'll do my best, you may be sure."

"You won't need formal clothes; the place is called 'The Ranch.' Bear in mind that all guests are expected in the Great Hall every evening, and all are expected to witness the motion picture show with the Chief. No drinking is permitted in the private rooms."

"I do not drink, Miss Parsons, except when my host expects it."

"Mr. Hearst does not drink, either. There is one more rule that is imperative—no one ever mentions the subject of death in his presence."

"I will bear these admonitions in mind."

"If you do, you will have an enjoyable experience, and if the Chief likes you, you may stay as long as you wish."

"I am most grateful for your kindness, Miss Parsons."

"You may prove your gratitude by giving me any items that are suitable for my column. All my friends do that."

"I shall be truly glad to be enlisted among your friends."

So that was that; Lanny had accomplished his purpose in some thirty-six hours after his car had crossed the borders of the Golden State. He dressed hurriedly, packed his bags, paid his hotel bill, and obtained a map of the Los Angeles district, showing the route to the airport. Lanny was used to getting to places and it caused him no trouble.

He stored his car in a garage near the airport, and as he returned to the building he observed the arrival of a limousine, one of those elaborate custom-built jobs which mark the approach of a potentate, whether political, industrial, or theatrical. With the assistance of a uniformed footman there alighted a small lady with a large amount of blond hair elaborately curled. She wore much paint and powder, the costliest possible furs, and quite a display of jewels: in short, a *tout ensemble* of worldly grandeur. It occurred to Lanny that the lady's face was familiar, but he forbore to stare and went on to the big shiny silver-topped plane.

The lady followed, with the footman carrying her bags, and Lanny perceived that he was to have the honor of traveling with this vision of loveliness. He realized who it must be: the actress whom the lord of San Simeon had installed in his palace something more than two decades ago, and of whom he was accustomed to say that he had spent six million dollars to make her a star. He had set up a producing concern and featured her in several pictures per year, and with the appearance of each picture the Hearst newspapers scattered from Boston to Seattle and from Atlanta to Los Angeles would burst into paeans of praise. In the old days when Lanny had hobnobbed with newspapermen at international conferences, this procedure had been a theme for cynical jesting, and to a young Pink it had seemed a measure of his country's social decay.

Lanny gave his name to the pilot of the plane, who had it on a list. The lady said: "I am Marion Davies," and the guest replied: "I am indeed honored, Miss Davies; I am one of your ardent fans." This was a measure of Lanny's social decay, for his true opinion was that she couldn't act and that her efforts were pathetic.

XI

The roar of the plane made conversation difficult, so Lanny surveyed the landscape of California from the point of view of an eagle. First, masses of tumbled mountains, some bare and rocky, others with vegetation dried brown at this season of the year; then valleys with farms and orchards, and gray threads that were roads; always, off to the left, the blue Pacific, with a line of white surf, and now and then a vessel large or small. Very few towns, and rivers mostly dry beds; a land of which vast tracts were kept for grazing by wealthy owners who didn't want settlers and money so much as they wanted space and fresh air. Only a land-values tax could have reached them, and there could be no such tax because they owned the newspapers and controlled both political machines.

The trip took about an hour, which meant a couple of hundred miles. A great stretch of lonely land, and then, close to the sea, *La Cuesta Encantada*—the enchanted hill—and on it a group of elaborate buildings which might have been the summer palace of the prince of the Asturias. The plane came down to a private airport, and there was a car to take them to the houses, and a station wagon for their bags. "Are you familiar with California, Mr. Budd?" inquired the lady; her real name was Douras, and she had been born in Brooklyn, two facts to which you did not refer.

Lanny replied: "It is my first visit, and I am agape with wonder." It was the proper attitude. "I have lived most of my life abroad," he continued. He had this *grande dame* of the silver screen to himself for a few minutes, and knew that the success of his enterprise might depend upon the impression he made. "So I have got most of my knowledge of America from your pictures and others. Now, when I see these landscapes I think I am on location, and when I meet Miss Marion Davies face to face I think I am back in Little Old New York—or I am with Polly of the Circus, or Blondie of the Follies, or Peg O' My Heart."

"Dear me, you really must be one of my fans!" exclaimed the actress, who wasn't acting much nowadays, because in her forties she could no longer play juvenile parts and nobody dared to suggest any other parts.

"It must be a wonderful thing to know that you have given so much pleasure to so many millions of people, Miss Davies. Unless my memory fails me I saw *When Knighthood Was in Flower* in a tiny village called Stubendorf in Upper Silesia, and I saw *Miss Glory* in a wretched old shed called a theater in Southern Spain. I have never forgotten how the audience wept." The treacherous one made these speeches with tender feeling, and knew from the way they were received that he had made a friend at court. He had known what he was coming to California for, and he had not failed to stop in a library and look up in *Who's Who* the name of William Randolph Hearst, and that of his leading lady friend, with the list of her "starring vehicles."

7. *A Barren Scepter*

I

THE son of Budd-Erling had traveled three thousand miles, and here was his destination, the fabulous San Simeon, called "The Ranch." It was the ranch to end all ranchos, covering four hundred and twenty square miles, which meant that from the mansion you could ride some fifteen miles in any direction, except out to sea, and never leave the estate. You could ride a horse, as "Willie" had done all through his boyhood; or if your taste ran to the eccentric, you could ride a zebra, or a llama, or a giraffe, a bison or yak or elephant or kangaroo or emu or cassowary. There were herds of all these creatures on the place, and numbers of central California cowboys to take care of them, and if a guest expressed a desire to ride one, the cowboys would no doubt take it as a perfectly normal eccentricity of these Hollywood folk. There were also lions and tigers and pumas and leopards in cages, and if Lanny had announced that he was a tamer of wild beasts and wanted to practice on these, the host would no doubt have seen to arranging it.

But the P.A. was a tamer of a more dangerous kind of wild beast; those who killed not for food but for glory; who killed not merely men but nations and civilizations. He was driven to La Casa del Sol—all the elaborate guest houses had Spanish names, as did everything else on the ranch. He was escorted to an elegant suite with a bathroom whose walls and floor and sunken tub were all of marble. He took a glance into one of the ample closets, and discovered therein complete outfits of every sort—one side of the closet for men and the other for women—pajamas, dressing gowns, swimming costumes, tennis and golf and riding clothes, and evening clothes which were permissible though not required. Lanny didn't stop to find out how they would fit him; the sun was shining and it was warm, so he put on his own palm beach suit and, following orders, made his way to La Casa Grande, which is Spanish for what on Southern plantations is "the big house." It was an immense structure in the style of an old Spanish mission; underneath it, the visitor learned before long, were acres of storerooms packed with art treasures like those he had inspected in the Bronx.

Here came the master of these treasures, the creator of this *Arabian Nights'* dream of magnificence. He had been tall and large in proportion, like most men of these wide-open spaces, but now his shoulders were bowed and there were signs of a paunch. He had a long face and an especially long nose; his enemies called it a horse face and had made it familiar in cartoons. His strangest feature was a pair of small eyes, watery blue, so pale that they seemed lifeless: no feeling in them at all, and very little in the face, or in the flabby, unresponsive hand. A man withdrawn, a man who never gave himself; now a man grown old, with pouches under his eyes, sagging cheeks, and wattles under his chin. Lanny thought: a man unhappy, not pleased with the people around him, not pleased with his memories. and with no hopes for this world or the next.

It was easy to imagine things about him. Was his reason for keeping so many people around him the fact that he could avoid observing the defects of any one? There were seldom fewer than fifty guests, Lanny had been told, and this week-end he estimated there were seventy-five; he had to meet them all—there was an efficient major-domo who took him the rounds. There were faces familiar from the screen, and others whose names told him that they were top executives, producers and directors of pictures. He guessed that they were the friends of Marion Davies rather than of Hearst, who had drifted into her world, the world of make-believe, after he had failed so desolately to make a success in the world of politics and public affairs. He had tried to help the people—or so he must have told himself—but they had refused to trust him. Here was a new world, easier to live in; one made to order, and in which wealth could have its way.

The important, the big-money people of "the industry"—so it called itself—came here and made the place a sort of country club without dues. There was everything you could think of in the way of convenience; a Midas expended fifteen million dollars a year to maintain it, and granted the use of it to his courtiers and favorites. There was a bar, never closed, and you could have anything you asked for, provided you drank it in the public rooms. There was an immense medieval hall where you could play pool or billiards or pingpong, in between thousand-year-old choir stalls—incongruous, but no more so than other features of this fantastic estate. You could hunt or fish, or play tennis in courts with gold-quartz walls; you could swim in a pool of fresh cold water, or in another of salt water pumped up from the ocean and warmed.

II

After the cocktail hour, the lord of the manor took the arm of his star of the first magnitude and led a sort of grand-opera march into the dining-hall, which was in the style of a medium-sized cathedral. Everything was supposed to be different from what it was, and this apparently was a monks' refectory; there was no cloth on the long table, which was of bare heavy wood, many centuries old. Priceless old china and glassware suggested a museum, printed menus suggested a hotel dining-room, while paper napkins suggested the lunch counter of a "five and ten." The center of the table was marked by a long line of condiments and preserves, all in their original containers; all homemade, and the host was very proud of them. Like nothing else the much-traveled Lanny had seen on this earth was the entourage of Miss Marion Davies during the repast. Behind her chair stood a liveried manservant holding an embroidered silk tray with her toilet articles, and at a sign he would step forward and she would make use of them. The chair beside her was occupied by an elderly dog whose name was Gandhi—even though he was not a vegetarian; as each course of the elaborate meal was served, a special attendant brought Gandhi a silver tray with slices of choice meats, which were eaten with due propriety.

After the meal came the motion-picture showing, in a projection room built for that purpose. Attendance was obligatory upon all guests, and Lanny wondered about this; he had had no such experience since he had been a pupil at St. Thomas's Academy in Connecticut and had been obliged to attend chapel every morning. Was it the host's purpose to dignify the motion-picture art by setting it on the level of a form of worship? Was it a means of doing honor to the gracious lady who deigned to occupy the "Celestial Suite" in his palace? (Mrs. William Randolph Hearst lived in a mansion in New York.) Could it possibly have happened that in times past some guest had had the atrocious taste to wish to read his evening paper while a picture of Miss Davies was being run? The lord of this manor was a person of whims and furious temper; if an employe displeased him he would kick him out without ceremony and never see him again. Lanny had never forgotten a story told to him by one of the Hearst correspondents abroad: the man had been called to a conference in the master's New York home, and they had talked until long after midnight; the host, being hungry, had taken his guest to the icebox; finding it locked, he had not let himself be balked, but had taken a red-painted fire axe from the wall and chopped his way through the door.

The "feature" for this Saturday night was one of those comedies which had come to be known as "screwball." It had not yet been released, for of course this master of infinite publicity had the right to priority, and would never risk showing his guests anything shopworn. The picture had been made for a public which found life dull and depressing, and which paid its money for one purpose, to get as far away from reality as possible. The heroine of the story was the daughter of a millionaire who lived in a house with the customary drawing-room resembling a railroad station, and the hero was a handsome male doll supposed to be a newspaper reporter, that being an occupation which made it plausible for him to encounter a millionaire's daughter. The young lady, wearing a different expensive costume in every scene, tried to run away from a traffic cop and landed in jail under an alias; the reporter tried to get her out, and there resulted a series of absurd adventures, most of which all motion-picture people had seen and helped to produce in many previous films.

In short, it was a stereotype, as much so as the faces and gestures of the leading man and lady. The reporter was supposed to be poor, but when you visited his mother's home you discovered that it had a kitchen half as big as a railroad station, and that the mother and sisters wore the smartest clothes and had their hair waved and not a single strand out of place—otherwise the scene would have been reshot. Lanny watched the episodes, some of which depended upon what Broadway called wisecracks, and others upon slapstick, people falling on their behinds or into a fishpond; the scenes whirled by at breathless pace, as if the producers were driven by fear that if they paused for a moment the public might have time to realize what vapidity was being fed to them.

Lanny couldn't make his escape; he had to stick it out. But there were no chains on his mind; he thought about these men and women, all persons of importance, of some kind of responsibility. What were *their* thoughts while they watched this entertainment? In their own word, it was "tripe," and to the last person they must have been aware of the fact. Somebody here had produced it for the purpose of making money; and the others would be thinking: How much will it gross? They would speculate: Is there anything I can learn from it, any ideas I can take over, any actors, any writers I might hire?

Lanny knew the formula by which they excused themselves: it was "what the public wants." The public, in the view of movie magnates, had no heart, no conscience, no brains; the public didn't want to learn anything, it didn't want to think, it didn't want to improve itself, or to see its children better than itself. It just wanted to be amused, on its lowest level; it wanted to see life made ridiculous by grotesque mishaps; it wanted to revel in wealth, regardless of how it was gained or how wasted; above all it wanted to watch adolescents pairing off, kissing and getting ready to get married—boy meets girl! The assumption was that they would live happy ever after, though never was it shown how that miracle would be achieved, and though the divorce rate in America was continually increasing.

This code expressed boundless cynicism concerning human nature, an unfaith become a faith. It was contempt fanned by the fires of greed; it was treason to the soul of man erected into a business system, organized, systematized, and spread into every corner of the earth. This particular "hunk of cheese"—one of the phrases Lanny had learned on the previous evening—was being offered to a world tottering upon the edge of an abyss. While it was being previewed, London Bridge might be falling down, and the British Empire crashing to its doom; before the picture had finished its run, America itself might be fighting for its life; but the mob would still guffaw at a "dame" being slapped on her "butt."

Lanny thought it was no accident that Hearst had sought refuge in this screen world; his personality and his life had been an incarnation of the same treason to the soul of man. For more than half a century his papers had been feeding scandal and murder to the American public; he had been setting psychological traps for their pennies and nickels, and because these traps succeeded, his contempt for the victims had been confirmed. By such means he had accumulated the second greatest fortune in America, and when he had got it he didn't know what to do with it, except to build this caricature of a home, this costliest junk yard on the earth. Here it was, and he had invited a swarm of courtiers and sycophants, and entertained them by presenting them with a caricature of themselves, a world as empty and false as San Simeon itself. The most incredible fact of all—so thought the presidential agent—he *made* them look at it! He rubbed their noses in their own vomit! Did he hate them that much?

III

The host had been told about his new guest, and after the showing invited him to view some of the special treasures in this home. Thus Lanny learned a new aspect of this strange individual; he really loved beautiful things. Not the men who produced them—during his stay in San Simeon Lanny didn't meet a single artist, and he saw very few *objets d'art* produced by living persons. What Hearst loved were the objects, as things to admire, to show, and above all, to possess. He unlocked a special cabinet and took out a rare vase of Venetian glass; it was something marvelous, a rich green fading into the color of milk, cloudy, translucent, and when you held it up to the light the colors wavered and pulsed as if the object were alive. "When you have something like that," remarked the Duce of San Simeon, "you have a pleasure that endures; you come to think of it as a friend."

"Ah, yes," replied the expert, who had learned something about the human heart as well as the price of paintings. "And it does not turn out to be something other than you had thought. It does not become corrupted; it does not betray you or slander you; it does not try to get anything out of you."

Was there a flash of light in those pale blank eyes, or was it just a reflection from the shiny surface of the vase? "I see you understand the meaning of art, Mr. Budd," remarked the host.

They wandered through the halls of this private museum, and Lanny hadn't needed any advance preparation. He knew these painters and their works, and could tell interesting stories about both; he could make technical comments that were right; and most important of all, he knew values. He was used to talking to men who lived by and for money, and here was one of the world's greatest money masters, a man who had bought not merely all kinds of things but men and women for a vast array of purposes. When he had come to New York, half a century ago, to shoulder his way into metropolitan journalism, he had bought most of Pulitzer's crack staff; he had even hired a room in the World Building so as to do it with speed and convenience. He had bought editors, writers, advertising and circulation men, all by the simple process of finding out what they were getting and offering them twice as much. And he had the same attitude toward paintings; when he wanted one he got it, regardless of price—but he remembered the price!

So now Lanny remarked: "I found a Goya rather like that four years ago, while I was running away from the war in Spain, and I sold it in Pittsburgh for twenty-five thousand dollars." The host replied: "I got that one for seventeen thousand, but it was a long time ago." And then Lanny: "It is a fine specimen; it might bring thirty or forty thousand now. The well-to-do have discovered that old masters are a form of sound investment, and offer the advantage that you don't have to pay duty."

Presently they were in front of a Canaletto, a glimpse of Venice, bright and clear like the tones of a small bell. Lanny remarked: "I sold one for Hermann Göring not long ago."

It was a bait, and was grabbed instantly. "Louella tells me you know Göring well, and also Hitler."

"I have had that good fortune. I have known the Führer for some thirteen years, and Hermann for half that."

"They are extraordinary men," said the host. "I should like to talk with you about them sometime while you are here."

"With pleasure, Mr. Hearst." It was a date.

IV

In the middle of Sunday morning, while the guests sallied forth to amuse themselves on the estate, or sat on the veranda in the sunshine reading copies of the *Examiner* which had been flown in by plane, the publisher invited his new friend into the study where no one came save by invitation. There Lanny spread before him a treasure of knowledge concerning Nazi-Fascism which he had been accumulating over a period of two decades. He told how he had first seen Mussolini, then a journalist, in a *trattoria* in San Remo, in a furious argument with his former Red associates; how later, in Cannes, he had interviewed him during an international conference. He told about Schloss Stubendorf, where he had visited Kurt Meissner as a boy, and about Heinrich Jung who had become one of the earliest of the Nazis, and had taken Lanny to Adi's apartment in Berlin in the days before the Führer had had that or any other title.

"I thought I was something of a Pink in those days," Lanny said, "and Hitler had a program very much like the one you had when you were young, Mr. Hearst. He was going to put an end to interest slavery, as he called it, and 'bust the trusts'; it sounded like one of Brisbane's editorials with all the important phrases in caps."

"That was a long time ago," remarked the publisher, with perhaps a trace of nostalgia. "We have all learned that the trusts can be made useful with proper regulation."

"Of course; but the program pleased the people, in Berlin and Munich as it had in New York and Chicago. It is a fact which I have pointed out to my friends in England and France, that the Nazis did not come into power as a movement to put down the Reds and to preserve large-scale business enterprise; they came as a radical movement, offering the people what they thought was a constructive program. It very much resembled the old Populist program in this country."

"You are correct," said Mr. Hearst. "But the trouble is, Roosevelt has stolen all our thunder, and what can we do?"

"Congressman Fish asked the same question when I mentioned the subject to him. I cannot answer, because my specialty is painting, not statesmanship. All I can do is to point out the facts I have observed. In countries where the people have the ballot you have to promise them something desirable, otherwise the opposition will outbid you."

"They are raising the price higher and higher, Mr. Budd. I have long been saying that if the bidding continues, it will result in the destruction of our democratic system."

"You may be right. There are many in England who observe labor's demands continually increasing, and who look with envy upon what Hitler has been able to achieve."

"But even he has to go on making promises, Mr. Budd."

"Of course; but he is able to put off the fulfillment until after victory is won. Then, in all probability, he will find it possible to keep the promises. The Germans will be a ruling race, and all others on the Continent will work for them; so it should be possible to give German workers a larger share of the product."

"You think he is certain to win?"

"How is it possible to think otherwise? He no longer has any opponent but Britain; and can Britain conquer the Continent of Europe?. Sooner or later their resources will give out, and they will have to accept the compromise which Hitler holds out to them. I can tell you about this, because I myself have been the bearer of messages from the Führer to Lord Wickthorpe, who has just resigned his post at the Foreign Office in protest against Churchill's stubbornness."

V

Naturally, the publisher of eighteen newspapers wanted to know all about this mission. He wanted to know what the proposals were and what chance there would be of modifying them. He wanted to know what terms had been offered to the French, and what secret clauses might be in the armistice agreement with France. He wanted to hear about the struggle going on between Laval and Pétain within the Vichy Government, and how that was likely to turn out. Was Hitler going to get the French Fleet, and was he strong enough to take Gibraltar? What was the actual strength of the Italian army, and would it be able to break into Egypt and close the Suez Canal? An extraordinarily complicated war, and fascinating if you could take an aloof position, and not be worried about the possibility of your own country being drawn into it!

A year or so after the Nazis had taken power, William Randolph Hearst had paid a visit to both Rome and Berlin. He had made a deal with the Nazis whereby his International News Service was to have the exclusive use of all Nazi official news—a very good thing financially. The publisher had had several confidential talks with the Führer, and told Lanny how greatly he had been impressed by this man's grasp of international affairs. "Naturally, I am sympathetic to his domestic program," he explained. "There can be no question that he has made Germany over, and that he has been a blessing to the country. But I could not continue to endorse him, because of what he has done to the Jews. You understand that—if only for business reasons."

"Certainly," replied Lanny with a smile. "New York appears to have become a Jewish city."

Six years had passed since Mr. Hearst's visit; and what had these years done to the Führer, and to his *Nummer Zwei* and his *Nummer Drei?* The host plied his guest with questions, and the guest answered frankly, telling many stories about the Führer's home life, both at Berchtesgaden and Berlin; about Göring's hunting lodge in the Schorfheide, which had been the property of the Prussian State, but Göring had calmly taken it over and built it into a palace, much on the order of San Simeon, though Lanny forbore to mention that. He talked about Hess's interest in astrologers and spirit mediums, that being no secret in regard to the head of the Nazi Party. He told of confidential talks with these men, and explained how it was possible for them to accept an American art expert as a friend and even an adviser. There had to be somebody to take messages to other countries and bring replies, and official personalities were often unsatisfactory because they had become involved in factional strife and intrigues at home.

"Göring hates Ribbentrop like poison, and so does Hess," Lanny explained, "and all three of them hate Goebbels. The Führer uses them all, and plays one against another; he never trusts anyone completely, except possibly Hess, and when I come along he may be relieved to meet somebody who is untouched by this steam of jealousy and suspicion. He feels that he has known me from boyhood, because of my intimacy with Kurt Meissner and Heinrich Jung, two men who have been his loyal followers from the beginning and who have never once asked a favor of him. Then, too, both the Führer and Göring have more than once offered me money, and I have refused it, which impresses them greatly."

"They wanted you in their service?"

"Yes; but I explained to them that if I incurred such obligations I should part with my sense of freedom; I should begin to worry about whether or not I was earning my keep, and they would begin to think I was an idler, and would start making demands upon me."

A smile came upon the long face of this man of so many millions. "Are you telling me this so that I won't make you a proposal, Mr. Budd?"

"No, it hadn't occurred to me that you might wish to."

"You are a modest man, indeed. What you have been telling me is of importance to one who is getting on in years and inclined to stay in his own chimney corner. Firsthand information is not easy to come by, and I would be very pleased to pay for it, and would promise never to put the least pressure upon you. If you would come to see me now and then and let me pump your mind as I have just been doing, it would be worth, say, fifty thousand dollars a year to me—or more, if that would help."

"I have always heard that you were munificent, Mr. Hearst, and now you are proving it. I would be glad to be numbered among your friends, and now and then to run out and see you; but I would rather do it as I do for other friends, because of the pleasure I get from being helpful. My profession of art expert provides for my needs, and I am one of those fortunate persons whose work is play."

"You are able to earn so much?"

"I don't need so much, because I am a guest wherever I go—at my father's home in Connecticut, at my mother's home on the Riviera, at my former wife's home in England. It sounds odd, so I must explain that Lord Wickthorpe married Irma Barnes, and we have managed to remain friends. I have a little daughter who lives at Wickthorpe Castle, and I go there to stay with her. It is a box seat from which to view the affairs of the British Empire."

The man of money was troubled by this attitude toward his own divinity, which was money. Quite possibly nothing of the sort had ever happened to him before. "You do not consider the necessity of providing for your old age?"

"There, too, I have been favored by fortune. My father has considerable money, and if I should reach old age, I have reason to expect to inherit a share of it."

That put the matter on a different basis; it established this suave gentleman among the small group of social equals. "I suppose I have to accept your decision, Mr. Budd; but bear me in mind on your travels, and any time you have information or advice which you think I ought to have, send it to me by cable, and if you will let me have the name of your bank in this country, I will see that the cost is deposited to your account."

"As you know, Mr. Hearst, the British government makes cabling a dubious matter in wartime. But when I am in this country I can telegraph you—and it does sometimes happen that I have a suggestion that might be of interest."

"Dictate it to a stenographer and send it collect," commanded the Duce of San Simeon. "Don't worry about the length—you have carte blanche from this time forth."

VI

Louella Parsons had told Lanny that he might be invited to stay as long as he pleased, and so it turned out. He accepted, because he was curious about this man of vast power whom he regarded as one of the fountainheads of American Fascism; also about the guests who came and went so freely at this free country club. They were the rulers of California; the officials, the judges, the newspaper managers and editors, the big businessmen; but above all the motion-picture colony in its higher departments, the masters of super-publicity.

The oddest business in the world, it seemed to the son of Budd-Erling; the providing of dreams to all the peoples of the earth. "The industry" was about as old as Lanny himself, and the men in it had grown up with it, and didn't find it so strange. Its big businessmen were very little different from those who provided clothing in New York and other cities; there, too, the fashions had to be studied; elegance was another kind of dream, and the public's whims could make or break you. The men who manufactured and marketed entertainment bought the services of other men and women, just as a newspaper publisher did, and they estimated the value of these persons by what could be made out of their talents.

If a man wrote a best-selling novel they would hire him to write for them at several thousand dollars a week, and would install him in a cubicle with a typewriter and a secretary; if they had nothing for him to do at the moment they would expect him to wait, and they might forget him for six months, but they saw no reason why he should object, so long as he was receiving his salary check. His best-seller might have had to do with, say, the sufferings of the sharecroppers of Louisiana, and they would put him to work on a script having to do with a murder mystery in Hawaii. You might hear half a dozen anecdotes similar to this in a morning's chat at San Simeon, but you weren't supposed to laugh—a polite little smile would answer all purposes.

Just now the presidential campaign was at its climax, and much of the conversation of the guests had to do with this subject. "That Man in the White House" was trying to grab off a third term, and most of the top men in "the industry," like the top men in all the other industries, considered that the salvation of the country depended upon the rebuking of this insolent ambition. Every morning the *Examiner* came, and every afternoon the *Herald-Express*, Hearst papers filled with editorials and columns and doctored news, all in a frenzied effort to discredit the Administration. The guests read these papers, and talked in the same vein. Lanny heard nobody dissenting; the nearest any came to it were two or three who suggested mildly that the affairs of the country would go on much the same whether it was Willkie or Roosevelt. These men were looked upon as in very bad taste, and Lanny kept carefully away from them.

VII

Every day at San Simeon there arrived by airmail copies of eighteen Hearst newspapers from all over America. Presumably one man couldn't read them all, but he could glance over them with a pair of eyes practiced for more than half a century; then he would dictate a telegram to the managing editor of each paper, saying what was wrong, and the telegrams were famous for their vigorous language. This had been the practice ever since 1887, when Willie Hearst had taken over his daddy's newspaper, the *San Francisco Examiner*—soon after being expelled from Harvard University for the offense of sending to each of his professors an elegant *pot de chambre* with the professor's name inscribed in gold letters on the inside.

Now and then this grown-up playboy would retire from the company of his guests and seat himself in a corner of the Great Hall, and resting a pad of paper on the arm of his chair would start writing with a lead pencil. Nobody disturbed him at such times, for they knew that he was writing a directive which would change the policy of his papers, or perhaps an editorial which would change the policy of the United States government. Sometimes these editorials would be signed with their author's name, and in that case they would appear double-column in large type; or they might be published as run-of-the-mine editorials, always in all the papers on the same day.

It was quite a pulpit, and if you knew the text you could pretty well write the sermon yourself. Willie Hearst had hated the British Empire ever since he had shot off his first firecracker on the Fourth of July. He had hated France ever since the year 1930, when he had been ordered out of that country after having brought all the guests of San Simeon for a tour of Europe on a whim. He hated the Reds and the Pinks, every variety of them, ever since they had undertaken to carry out the program which Willie had been advocating when he hoped to become the people's candidate. He hated F.D.R. for having succeeded where Willie had failed—and especially for having promoted an income tax which had made it necessary for Willie to part with his art treasures and with the financial management of his chain of publications.

Lanny watched closely, day by day, and was quite sure that he recognized where some of his host's editorials had come from. For a secret agent not merely had to listen, he had to voice ideas, and be sure that the ideas were those his listener wanted to hear. Afterwards he winced when he discovered these ideas being circulated to the extent of five million copies, sometimes in the very words he had used. This new Willie-Lanny team told the American people: "If the American people want war, they should surely re-elect Mr. Roosevelt. Whether they want it or not, they will surely get it by electing him."

And again: "Congress, in the gravest hour in the history of the Republic, has ceased to function constitutionally. It is not asked whether it wants war or peace. The people, the ultimate power in our democracy, are treated and shushed away from official doors in Washington —doors behind which we are being sold down the river to war and economic slavery."

And yet again: "By its pernicious system of political bounties and pillage of the public treasury, and by its vicious appeals to class-consciousness—which inevitably begets class hatred—the New Deal has actually labored to make America mob-minded, and neither law nor democracy can survive in a mob-minded country."

VIII

Election day, November 5, 1940, arrived, and there were few guests at San Simeon, because they considered it their duty to scatter to their homes and record their votes against the great American Dictator. But after voting they came by planeload and by motorcar to play tennis and ride horseback and swim until it was time to turn on the radio in the Great Hall and listen to the returns. California, being three hours behind the East, gets the early returns in the latter part of the afternoon; by five o'clock they were coming in a flood, and by dinnertime it was all over, and everybody knew that the Third Term had swept the country. Willkie was going to carry only ten states—and you could get what comfort there was in the fact that it was a gain of eight over what the Republican candidate of four years ago had managed to obtain.

Lanny could not recall when he had ever seen so large a collection of unhappy human beings; certainly not since he had been in the old gray smoke-stained building in Downing Street, the home of the British Foreign Office, on the night or rather the early morning when Hitler had begun his raid on Poland. Conversation in the San Simeon refectory was in low tones, and not much of it. Lanny wondered: Was this Hollywood play-acting, carried on for the benefit of the host, or had they actually come to believe their own propaganda? Anyhow, it was like a funeral repast, and to have laughed would have been a shocking breach of taste.

Later in the evening, in the host's very private study, the P.A. had the serious talk for which he had journeyed across a continent. "We have met with a grave disappointment, Mr. Hearst," began the guest, "and before I take my leave, I should like to know what you think about it, and what I should advise my friends abroad."

What Mr. Hearst thought was that the country was in one hell of a mess, but there was nothing that he or anybody else could do about it. The American people had made their bed and would have to lie in it; they had lighted a hot fire under themselves and would now stew in their own juice. The vexed old man predicted a series of calamities, to which getting into the war was but the vestibule. The public debt would pile up and there would be no way out but to declare national bankruptcy; the industry of the country would be converted to war purposes, and likewise its labor, and when the horror was over, whichever side won would be the loser. There would be such an unemployment problem as had never been dreamed of in the world; there would be strikes, riots, and insurrections. Worst of all, there would be the Red Dictator sitting in the Kremlin, chortling with glee; he would be piling up his military equipment, and at the end he would be the only power left in Europe; he wouldn't even have to take possession by force of arms, his Communist agents would do it by propaganda, and bankrupt countries would tumble into his lap like so many ripe peaches.

Lanny waited until this Book of Lamentations had arrived at a chapter end, and then he said: "I agree with every word you have spoken, Mr. Hearst. My father has been saying the same things ever since Munich. I think the greater number of our responsible businessmen realize the dangers, and there are some I have talked with who aren't disposed to sit by and let fate have its way."

"But what can they do?"

"We Americans have hypnotized ourselves with the idea of the sovereignty of the ballot; and that is a great convenience to our opponents, who have the mob on their side. As you well know, it is the property owners who are going to have to pay when this débacle comes, because they are the only ones who have anything to pay with."

"No doubt about that, Budd." Lanny was being promoted by the dropping of the "Mister."

"Well, Hitler showed the industrialists of Germany that they didn't have to lie down and submit to having their pockets emptied; and it seems to some men I know that they have the same elemental right of self-defense."

"You mean they are proposing to turn Roosevelt out? That would mean a civil war. I couldn't face it!"

"It might mean a small-sized one, but surely it would be cheaper than the one we are being betrayed into. Just think of it, we are being invited to conquer the Continent of Europe! We are being put into the position where we shall be obliged to do it, for Germany will not submit forever to the treacherous underground war that Roosevelt is conducting. Also, Japan will not sit by in idleness, and we shall find that we have undertaken to conquer Asia too."

"All that is beyond dispute, Budd. But, good God, we haven't the means for overthrowing the Administration!"

"There are some who think we can get the means; and it is a matter of no little importance to them to know what your attitude will be."

The Duce of San Simeon did not exclaim: "Get out of my house, you scoundrel!" Instead he remarked, rather sadly: "I am an old man, and such adventures must be left to younger spirits."

"Old men for counsel, young men for war, the proverb says. The question is, what counsel you have to give. Surely this cannot be the first time you have heard the idea!"

"I have heard it talked about a lot, naturally. But if any group is contemplating action, I have not been informed of it."

"If tonight's news does not bring them to the point of action, then they might as well stop talking. Roosevelt is going to take this election as a complete endorsement, and will go ahead with his plans more recklessly than ever."

"That we can be sure of, Budd."

"If there are men who mean to act, they will want support, financial as well as moral. Understand, please, I wouldn't touch any money myself; but I might put them in contact with you if you would permit it."

The Duce of San Simeon looked worried; as much so as he had looked in a photograph which Lanny had seen of him when his newspapers had charged four senators with having accepted bribes, and then, summoned before an investigating committee, he had watched the documents in the case proved to be forgeries. Said W.R.H.: "This is a matter in which one could not afford even to be named without careful consideration. I shall have to ask that you do not mention me to anyone without first telling me who the person is and giving me an opportunity to consent or refuse. Count me out of it!"

"That is a proper request, Mr. Hearst, and I assure you that you may rely absolutely upon my discretion."

"It is a matter that I cannot leave to anyone's discretion. You must agree positively not to mention me in connection with this matter. *It is far too serious.*"

"You have that word. But let me urge this upon you in the meantime: Do not weaken in your opposition to Roosevelt and his war policies."

"That you may count upon, on my word. The Hearst papers will stand like a rock in the midst of a raging torrent."

So they left the matter. It wasn't until next morning that Lanny discovered how this man of much forethought had prepared in advance and sent to his newspapers an editorial to be published in the event that his long-maintained verbal war upon the Presidential Dictatorship should turn out to be unsuccessful. Said the *Los Angeles Examiner*, on the morning after the election: "The Hearst newspapers have never questioned the right of the American people to give Mr. Roosevelt a third term, or any number of terms he may seek and they see fit to grant."

IX

When Lanny decided that he had learned enough about the ideas and purposes of William Randolph Hearst, he announced his departure and expressed his thanks, and then went to his suite in the Casa del Sol to pack his suitcases. He did this in an unusual way, putting some sheets of writing paper on top of his clothing in one suitcase, and contriving it so that one sheet was slightly displaced and was caught by the lid when it was closed—but not enough to show. With his other suitcase he did the same thing with the tail of one of the shirts, folded not quite regularly, and with one edge caught by the lid—but not showing. He did not lock the suitcases, but left them in the middle of the floor to be carried down by one of the servants.

The reason for this was a chat Lanny had had with a prominent motion-picture director who was among the guests. Lanny had remarked that everything in his suite was "period," even to the toilet articles; and the director, an Irishman with a sense of humor, had replied: "Don't try to carry any of it off. Your baggage will be searched before you leave." To Lanny's exclamation of incredulity the other had offered a wager; and though Lanny hadn't accepted, he was making a test, just out of idle curiosity. He judged that anybody making a search would be in a hurry and would fail to note the significance of a bit of paper or a shirt tail caught under the lid of a suitcase.

And so it proved. When the guest was deposited at the Burbank airport he carried his bags to the car which he had stored, and there he carefully opened one after the other. Sure enough, the single piece of paper was inside with the other sheets; also the bit of shirt had been pushed back and was no longer caught by the lid. Both bags had been opened!

Lanny reflected on this episode, then and later, and realized that there was something to be said for a man who conducted a free country club for the Hollywood elite. It was a common practice of hotel guests to carry off spoons as souvenirs, and doubtless the lord of San Simeon had sustained many losses. Lanny decided that he was glad he didn't own so many things that the rest of the world wanted. "Lay not up for yourselves treasures upon earth, where moth and rust doth corrupt, and where thieves break through and steal"!

8. My Dancing Days Are Done

I

BACK in Hollywood again, Lanny attended some more parties, and cultivated the acquaintances he had made. Those he had met at San Simeon represented the rightwing of the industry; there was a leftwing, also, smaller but vociferous. The Rightists called themselves America Firsters, and their opponents called them Fascists; the Leftists called themselves Liberals, and their opponents called them Reds. Each side tried to slip something of its "ideology" into the productions with which it had to do, and then watched eagerly to see its judgment vindicated in the box-office returns, the Hollywood equivalent of ballots.

A presidential agent, of course, couldn't afford to be seen drinking cocktails with anybody from the Left. He cultivated Cecil de Mille, and Major Rupert Hughes, also Victor McLaglen, who had organized a cavalry troop of simon-pure patriots for the purpose of keeping the labor unions in their places. Lanny wanted to know how these cinema troopers were taking their recent licking at the polls, also who was putting up the money for the men who were dropping showers of leaflets from the rooftops of office buildings in Los Angeles, calling for a Nazi-style revolution in the sweet land of liberty.

This wasn't the job which had been assigned to P.A. 103, so after a while he took the precaution to get Baker on the long distance telephone. He was told that his Chief was leaving in one week for a vacation in the Caribbean. Lanny, troubled in conscience, replied: "I'll be there in six days, possibly five," and packed his bags and set out within an hour.

He took the southern route, partly to avoid the snow in the Rockies, and partly in order to see more of the land of his fathers. He drove back through the orange groves, but instead of turning north he continued eastward through the date country, and past the mountains called "Chocolate," looking very tasty from a distance but hot and deadly dry. He crossed the Colorado River by another long bridge, and it was Arizona, land of the Apaches, long since tamed and mostly departed. Here were more masses of tumbled mountains, and rocks of every color, from the size of a pebble to the size of a city, painted every hue and sculptured to every shape. The road wound through passes and climbed high ranges, and came down into broad irrigated valleys and through towns which had been desert only a generation ago.

Lanny had undertaken to drive three thousand miles in five or six days, so he would have to stick at it all the time except for eating or sleeping. He would have a sharp pain in the back of his neck, due to the strain of balancing his head against the motion of the car; but he would get over it, as he had done many times before. Landscapes gliding by seldom failed to entertain him, and when he tired, there was the verbal panorama of present-day history. At no place was he out of range of some radio station which would give him reports from the great air blitz. London was still holding out, and the R.A.F. miraculously continuing to give more than it took. The Germans had not sailed against England.

Toward midnight, emerging from a mountain pass upon a high plateau, he saw the gleam of many lights, as if it were a miniature of the Great White Way. It was an auto camp, a development of the motor age in this far western country; "motels," some of them were called, for the people here were as bold with the language as with the landscape. A row of brightly painted cabins were set back from the highway, so spaced that between each cabin and the next was a covered shelter for a car. Inside the cabin was a bedroom with twin beds, and sometimes a couch for a child; also a bathroom and a tiny kitchenette. Everything would be spic and span, and you would pay your two or three dollars and have the use of this retreat until noon of the next day.

In the morning you would find a filling station, a grocery store, and a lunch counter where you might have your orange juice or coffee and your toast and eggs. Lanny had never seen anything like this in benighted Europe, nor even in the self-satisfied eastern states; he decided that when the horror of Nazi-Fascism had been banished from the world he would like nothing better than to spend a year driving over the national highways of the West and visiting its national parks. He drove from this "motel," pondering the question: Who would be riding by his side, Lizbeth Holdenhurst or Laurel Creston? Youth or maturity, beauty or brains, philoprogenitiveness or philosophization?

II

Presently it was southern New Mexico, the same kind of country, and then Lanny's car rolled down from high gray-colored mountains into bright and shining El Paso—"the Pass." Everything had to be bright in that dry land where there were no fogs and no dust except during storms. Presently the car was speeding down the wide valley of the Rio Grande, famed in story and song. The mountains were gray and brown, and so were the adobe houses of the Mexicans; the gray concrete highway was painted with a brown stripe in the center—a harmony of colors which would have delighted Whistler, and if he had painted it he would have called it a "symphony" or an "arrangement" or something fancy like that.

Some unkind person has compared Texas to hell; but in truth Texas is a continent, and can be compared to most any place. The hills faded away, and there were barren dry plains which a stranger might have mistaken for farming country, the mesquite trees looked so much like orchards. The road went straight, mile after mile—you could drive all day at sixty miles an hour and still it would be Texas. The day was warm and the night cold, but Lanny had an overcoat and a rug. Tire trouble delayed him only half an hour to put on his spare wheel, and he had the "flat" fixed while he ate lunch. The morning and evening of the third day he rolled into the city of Dallas, where there was another auto camp in a lovely grove of trees.

Next day it was Arkansas, and then a ferry across the "Father of Waters," and he was in Memphis, where the "blues" come from, and the country which all the world knows about from *Huckleberry Finn*. Then the lovely river valleys and farms of Tennessee. It was like coming into another world, where rocks and sand have never been heard of, where rivers run all the year round, and hills and mountains are covered with hardwood trees on their lower slopes and pines higher up. Lanny's route led through the Great Smokies, the country of the moonshiners and the hillbilly songs. There was a snowstorm in the high pass, and he had to drive carefully. But he spent that night in North Carolina, and in the morning phoned to Baker and asked for an ap-

pointment in the evening. Three hours later he phoned from Lynch-
burg and had the appointment confirmed.

After that he didn't have to hurry, but could watch the Virginia
"wilderness," and learn from the tablets by the roadside that he was
passing through the battlefields of history's greatest civil war. When he
rolled into Washington at dinnertime he could say that he had really
seen his country. He had traveled from its film capital to its political
capital in five and a half days, and when he got out of the car he was a
bit stiff and shaky in the knees. But a hot bath and a good dinner fixed
him up, and then he stretched out on a bed and caught up on his newspaper reading. London was still holding out, though more than fifteen
thousand civilians had been killed or wounded by bombs during the
previous month. Ships were being sunk, several every day, and docks
bombed and burned. How long Britain could stand it was a problem
in mathematics with too many unknown factors. Lord Lothian, British
Ambassador, arrived in Washington, reporting that his country was in
a bad way and would be glad of any help we could give.

Lanny had known this suave gentleman since the days of the Peace
Conference in Paris, when he had been plain Philip Kerr, pronounced
Carr, secretary to Lloyd-George. A couple of years ago he had visited
Germany; an ardent Christian Scientist, he had believed the best even
of Hermann Wilhelm Göring—the best being a pledge of reconcilement with the British Empire on the basis of Germany being permitted
to have her way in Central Europe. Lanny had listened to his lordship
expounding this familiar cliché in Wickthorpe Castle, and had thought
of the Swedish diplomat who had advised his son to learn with how
little wisdom the world is governed.

III

At a quarter to ten Lanny was picked up at the appointed street
corner and taken to the White House in the usual way. He went up
the narrow side stairway and into the familiar high-ceilinged room,
with large sofas, overstuffed chairs, and a fireplace in front; dark blue
paper on the walls, and framed paintings of the old China Clippers
which the Chief loved. But it would be better not to mention them, for
you might get him started telling stories about his grandfather, who
captained one. "I am afraid he was an opium smuggler," the Chief
would say, with a twinkle in his blue eyes. He would talk for so long
that you might not get to transact the business for which you had
come.

There was the familiar figure in the old-fashioned mahogany bed;
there were the blue-and-white striped pajamas, the blue crew-necked
sweater, and the pile of letters and reports. There, also, the familiar

smile and the warm resonant voice. "I didn't think you'd make it, Lanny!" he exclaimed. Lanny said: "I like nothing better than motoring, and I have made the most of my chance over here. In France nowadays you don't see a car on the roads unless it is driven by a German. All French men and women have taken to bicycles."

That, too, was an unfortunate remark; for the Chief said: "In my youth I bicycled all over those roads," and he started telling about the routes, the scenery, and various adventures. Lanny was on pins and needles, for courtesy required him to listen, but he wanted so much to discuss important matters of state, and he hated to steal this busy man's sleep time. He thought: Poor fellow, he looks so tired! F.D. had stuck on his man-killing job through a long hot summer, and then had gone out and fought his foes in a bitter political campaign.

Lanny took the first chance to remark on this; and the reply was: "It was a good fight, and I enjoyed every minute of it."

The visitor told how he had heard the returns in San Simeon, and how the host and guests had taken the licking. "That old crocodile!" exclaimed F.D. "There is the man this country will have to deal with some day!" When Lanny mentioned that his bags had been searched the President found it hard to believe, and exclaimed: "You don't tell me!"—and then: "By golly!" When Lanny told of the test, he threw back his head and gave one of his hearty laughs.

After that they got down to business. "What are you planning to do?" asked the great man, and Lanny replied: "I am ready to go back to Europe and do whatever I can. Tell me what you want to know."

"I think Britain is going to hold out, and we can prepare for a long war. My military advisers tell me that Hitler cannot possibly effect a landing in winter, and by spring the British will be too strong in the air."

"I hope so, Governor. But they will need every ounce of help we can give them."

"You have read, no doubt, that I ordered the dividing of our military product, half for them and half for us. That is as far as Congress would let me go now. I have authorized Britain to contract for twelve thousand more military planes in this country; that makes more than twenty-six thousand altogether, and it ought to please your father greatly."

"It will, Governor; but the question is coming up very soon—how are they going to pay for all this? If you leave them to the mercy of the private banks, they will be plucked to the last feather; and you must realize that there is a very strong group among the British governing class who argue that if Britain has to part with her foreign holdings and become a debtor nation, they can get easier terms from Germany than from America."

"Don't think that I haven't had it pointed out to me. The big-money fellows are the same all over the world and they speak a universal language. It's a task I have to work on during this cruise, to find some way of helping our ally so that it won't be an outright gift but at the same time will give them a chance to breathe, financially speaking. I wish there was some way I could take you along on the cruise, but there inevitably would be publicity."

"Oh, of course; that would ruin me."

"What I'm going to tell our people is that when your neighbor's house is on fire, you lend him your hose to put the fire out, and you don't stop to bargain about what he is going to pay for the use of the hose."

"That's a good enough simile, Governor; but I'm afraid somebody may take it up and point out that if we really are a good neighbor we don't stop with lending the hose; we help to fight the fire."

The Chief made a wry face. "God knows, I hope it doesn't come to that! I can't imagine anything that would persuade the American people to come into this war. I would split the country in halves if I were to suggest it."

IV

They talked for a while about France. F.D. said the fear that troubled his sleep was of Hitler getting possession of the French Fleet and using it to break the British hold on the Mediterranean. "They tell me that is absolutely vital; and it's touch and go every moment."

"The miserable Mussolini"—so the President called him—hadn't been able to sit by while his partner grabbed territory. His fingers itched, and he had defied Hitler's orders and set out to grab Greece. He had thought that little country was helpless, and had rushed an army up into the mountains; but the British had furnished arms and the Greeks had used them and now the Fascist army was in rout. Also, Il Duce had an army in Africa, and was setting out to take Egypt; F.D. predicted that that army too would be soundly thrashed. But if the Germans got the French Fleet they might be able to break British sea power and take both the Suez Canal and the Strait of Gibraltar.

The President wanted information dealing with every aspect of that subject. Was Hitler going to send an army through Spain and attack Gibraltar? How was the Laval-Pétain struggle coming out, and what were our chances of dealing with General Weygand in North Africa? F.D. didn't say outright: "I want to check on our own diplomats in that field." What he said was: "Everybody has to be watched"—and Lanny grinned and replied: "Even the watchers!" He wondered if Baker had somebody watching P.A. 103.

The agent continued: "I have a contact with the underground in Vichy France, a man whom I have known for almost twenty years and who proved himself in the defense of Republican Spain. He told me he was going to Toulon, to try to build a movement among the sailors of the Fleet and the workers in the arsenal. There may be a possibility, you know, that the Fleet will some day sail out and join us. Unfortunately, the persons who work at that sort of job are always Socialists or Communists, and our State Department boys become paralyzed with horror at the thought of them."

"Well, you work on your own, Lanny, and see what you can find out. As I've told you before, if you need money, it can come out of my secret funds."

"I don't want any money for myself, Governor; but there might be a possibility of using some in the movement, and if so I'll let you know. You'll have to arrange some way for me to communicate with you without having to come to London or Paris, because getting about is a difficult business in wartime."

"I am in a position to arrange it easily. I am appointing Admiral Leahy as my personal representative to deal with Pétain. Leahy is a grand old boy, one of the officers who brought the battleship *Oregon* around the Horn during the Spanish-American War. He is a close friend of mine, and a Catholic, so he'll know how to talk to the Marshal."

"Is he another of the appeasers?"

"Quite the contrary, he's a man after your own heart; he thinks we are bound to get into the war sooner or later and it had better be at once. He won't like you in your role of Fascist sympathizer, and he's a salty old bird who says what he thinks—to Americans. I'll instruct him that he will receive letters marked 'Zaharoff,' and that he is to forward them to me unopened. Good hunting to you, Lanny!"

V

It was the time for the P.A. to offer to take his departure, and ordinarily he would have done so. But he had one other matter on his conscience and said: "May I keep you for a minute or two more, Governor?"

"Certainly. You have never worn out your welcome."

"I never mean to, if I can help it. What I want to ask is whether anybody has ever warned you that some of our near-Fascists might try to displace you."

"Oh, so you've come on that, too! It's all over the place, they tell me."

"But this is really serious, Governor."

"Well, tell me what you have heard."

The visitor told of his conversation with Baldur Heinsch, and of his trip to California, and what the Roosevelt-haters there were doing and saying. The President listened attentively, and then commented: "As to that Nazi chap, I have reason to think the F.B.I. may nail him down before long. As to the others, I will tell you that I have been informed of half a dozen such juntas within the last few months. It's amusing to note that they all propose to deal with me gently. It hasn't seemed to occur to them that I might not give up without a fight."

"Hitler didn't hesitate to murder half a dozen of the leading statesmen of Europe, Governor; and he's not through yet."

"I know it, and I'm being protected—much better than I tell about. This occurs to me, Lanny—did you ever meet Jim Stotzlmann?"

"I have heard a lot about him, but I don't think we have met."

"He's been playing around in your parts of the world most of his life. I tell him that I'm his oldest friend—I was present at his christening. You might be interested to meet him and hear what he has to reveal about our homemade insurrectionists."

"How should I meet him, Governor?"

"First you have to find him. He's a grasshopper, even more so than yourself. The rest will be easy, because he's a warm-hearted fellow and easy to know. Don't say what you're doing for me, and don't ask what he's doing—you understand, that isn't talked about."

"Surely not."

"Talk about mutual friends, of whom you must have a hundred. He knows everybody."

"But how about my supposedly being a near-Fascist?"

"He is one man who is worthy of your confidence. Pledge him not to mention your name to anybody, and you'll find his ideas and information helpful." The Chief thought for a moment, then added: "I'll give you a card. Get me one out of that desk drawer." When Lanny had complied, the other scribbled with his pencil: "Top secret! F.D.R." and said: "Show him that, and then destroy it in his presence, so that both of you will know it won't go further. After that you will be pals for life."

"It sounds exciting," remarked the son of Budd-Erling. "There are eleven persons in the world who know that I am not a Fascist sympathizer. Stotzlmann will make it an even dozen."

"Take care of yourself," said the Big Boss; and then, with a touch of concern: "Are you planning to go into Germany again?"

"I'm not sure," was the answer. "It depends on how events shape up, and whether I can get an invitation from one of the head devils. I won't take any great risk, because I want to stay alive and see you win this fight."

VI

It was the beginning of December, and the yacht *Oriole* had fled to southern waters, keeping its owner safe from throat and lung infections, or so he believed. Lanny telephoned and learned that Lizbeth had remained in Baltimore for a second winter. Did this mean she was obliging her mother and giving herself a chance to forget the unappreciative Lanny Budd? Or might it be that she was staying because she knew he was in the country, and hoped he would come again and change his mind? Lanny would have preferred not to call, but there was his duty to Robbie. It would have seemed rude indeed to pass through the city without speaking. The Holdenhursts might not learn about it, but Robbie would!

Lanny drove, and spent a day and night at Greenbriar, and told about his adventures in California, including the wonders of San Simeon. He was aware that this made him more attractive to the girl, who could have imagined nothing more exciting than to have been taken along on that trip and to have met the semi-divine figures of the screen, also the publisher of the *Baltimore American*. It was second nature to Lanny to make himself agreeable to people; and what would have been the use of coming, unless he had intended to do so?

He saw Lizbeth hanging on his words, he saw the lovelight in her eyes. She had been brought up to be proud, and to think that she was important; but she was prepared to be humble to him, and for all her life. There began that old struggle within him. The poet has testified that pity melts the mind to love; and while it is an unsatisfactory basis for marriage, it is one of the baits that nature uses in her trap. The family left the pair ostentatiously alone, and it must have been very annoying to them when they heard him playing the piano for Lizbeth. There has not as yet been any technique invented by which a man can play classical music while his two arms are where a girl wants them to be.

Lanny kept saying to himself: "She would really admire Hearst! She would admire all the people whom I despise! It would be a crazy thing to do." But at the same time his blood kept saying that it would be a very pleasant thing to put his arms around Lizbeth; that indeed it was quite cruel not to do so. The rebellious blood kept inquiring: "What the devil are you here for?"—and Lanny had no convincing answer. The ladies had a party scheduled, and Lizbeth wanted him to stay and dance with her. To his mind came words from some old English dramatist: "My dancing days are done." But he didn't speak them to the girl. He told her that he had urgent business for his father, which was her father's business too.

Next morning he stepped into his car and headed northward into a cold wind which promised more of the same. On the way he told himself that he would never again go back to Green Spring Valley; and each time his cynical blood said: "Ha, Ha!" In New York he phoned to Newcastle to report, and to make sure that the car wasn't needed. The tactful father didn't fail to inquire: "Did you stop at the Holdenhursts'?"—and to add that Reverdy had taken another good-sized block of Budd-Erling stock before sailing. So Lanny knew that both Green Spring Valley and Newcastle were in league against him!

VII

There began another duel in the heart, or mind, or soul, or whatever it is a P.A. carries. He had duties to attend to; but greater than his interest in any of them was his desire to tell Laurel Creston about his recent adventures. She was the person who really ought to hear them, and put them into little acid sketches. Not San Simeon—no, Lanny decided he would have to pledge her not to write about that; but the Hollywood stunt men and riders of the purple sage organized into a cavalry troop to put down the Jews of Boyle Heights—that would be real material for "Mary Morrow's" subtle mockery.

So Lanny called on the telephone, and took her to lunch in another obscure café, and then for a drive. He put a robe around her small person, and took her up the east side of the Hudson, viewing the Palisades, and describing the two much longer drives he had enjoyed —but not mentioning whom he had taken along in his imagination, with or without clerical blessing. He told about various Hollywood parties; about Louella Parsons trying to be at once regal and girlish; about Major Hughes, partly deaf and entirely humorless, infuriated against the Reds and equally so against the psychic researchers; to Lanny he had denied the reality even of hypnotism, and had said, somewhat rudely, that it was all pure fraud. Also at the party had been Cecil de Mille, who had managed to combine "cheesecake" with early Christian martyrs and the Ten Commandments.

Laurel was delighted, as he had foreseen. "Do you mind if I make notes?" she asked, and Lanny said: "Of course not." So she combined business with pleasure, something her escort had been doing ever since he had earned his first thousand dollars serving as secretary-translator to one of the American advisers at the Peace Conference of 1919.

They went on and on, for what were a few more miles to a man who had just driven three thousand in less than a week? They passed through the city of Poughkeepsie and presently were on a wide paved road, lined with old trees now denuded of leaves. "You are còming to Krum Elbow," Lanny said, and when she asked: "What is that?" he told her: "The summer White House of our country; but it's not occupied now."

There was a sentry box at the entrance, and two army men on duty, for it was wartime, even though not acknowledged. Lanny didn't say: "I have been in there," and Laurel didn't ask. He wondered: Had she guessed who it was that he was serving? He could hear the dogmatic Major Hughes asking: "If there is anything to your telepathy rubbish, how could you sit alongside her, bursting with that secret, and she not getting the faintest hint of it?" How, indeed!

It was dark before they returned to New York, so they stopped for dinner. When he delivered her, just around the corner from her apartment, she thanked him for a delightful time, and the P.A. went off thinking: *That's* the woman I ought to marry! *That's* the one who wouldn't bore me! And then, of course: Where on earth would I hide her? She's on the way to becoming famous, and the whole town will be after her. Answer that one, too!

VIII

A P.A.'s first duty was to report to Baldur Heinsch, and this he did next day. The steamship official was greatly excited, and invited Lanny to his apartment. "We can talk quietly here."

The guest wasn't under any obligation to report the truth to this man of no faith whatever, so he said that the Duce of San Simeon had been enormously interested in what had been proposed, and had said that he would back it, but only on condition that he was never to be named; he would deal only through Lanny, and he would first have to know the names of all the persons who were active in the proposed coup. Lanny had thought over every detail of this story, and weighed and measured every word; he made it circumstantial enough to be convincing, and thereby he was setting a trap for his pro-Nazi victim —a trap baited with a two-hundred-million-dollar fortune.

Would Heinsch step into the trap and blurt out the names of the conspirators? He was greatly delighted, and for a while Lanny thought he was going to "come clean." But then he thought it over and said that he would have to consult his friends. Lanny agreed: "Of course; that's only fair to them." Inside his mind he wondered: Was there really any conspiracy, or was it just a tale which Hitler's secret agent had made up with the idea of getting hold of Hearst? And would he now proceed to get together some conspirators to justify the carving off of some chunks from the second-greatest fortune in America? Long ago Lanny had come to realize that dealing with the Nazis you found one conspiracy inside another, like a set of those beautifully lacquered Chinese boxes that surprised and amused children. What the Chinese did with them Lanny had never learned.

Also the P.A. called on Quadratt, and remarked, casually: "I am expecting to leave for Europe any time now, and I may go in by way of Switzerland and see the Führer. Have you any message you would like me to give him?" Quadratt claimed to have met the Führer personally, but Lanny wasn't at all sure that it was true; the Herr Doktor Goebbels was the person with whom he would more naturally have dealt. Anyhow, this would be a tactful way of letting him know that Lanny Budd was an important person, and one to whom it was worthwhile telling secrets!

"A long war, I fear," said the ex-poet mournfully; "and that is the one thing the Führer was determined to avoid—so he told me."

"He told me the same," replied the son of Budd-Erling.

IX

On North Shore Drive, in what had been a remote suburb but now was Chicago, there stood a massive brownstone palace, and for three generations everybody who was anybody in the metropolis of pork packing had known that this was the home of the Stotzlmann family, descendants of the old pirate who had been the richest Middle-Westerner of his time. The building was four stories high, in imitation of a Louis Quatorze château, and the fence around the park was reported to have cost a hundred and fifty thousand dollars—people spent money for such things in those days, and their minds were a catalog of such prices. The more things had cost the better they were and the more they were talked about, which was the best of all. "Three million dollars!" people would say about the palace, and their voices would be lowered as if they were speaking of the dwelling place of deity.

Broad stairs went up to a great bronze gate and heavy double doors. It was difficult to imagine anyone being bold enough to enter through such doors, and in the times that Lanny had driven by the place he had never chanced to see them opened. But his friend and colleague Zoltan Kertezsi avowed that many years ago he had been admitted to inspect the art works inside. A family was supposed to be living there, but probably, like most rich people, they were away from home most of the time. Lanny had observed that the more money people had, the harder they found it to escape boredom.

Jim Stotzlmann was one of the heirs of this family, and evidently he had been bored in Chicago, for he was the author of several large books of travel and exploration. In *Who's Who* Lanny found his home listed as Palm Beach, Florida, and wrote duplicate letters there and to the family home. He said: "I have a card for you from a very important friend in Washington. It is marked 'top secret,' and therefore I prefer to deliver it in person. For your information, I am an American art expert and have lived most of my life in France. I am at the Ritzy-Waldorf, New York, awaiting your reply. In the event that you are away, my permanent address is in care of my father, Robert Budd, who is president of Budd-Erling Aircraft, Newcastle, Conn."

These letters were sent by airmail; and then Lanny went to a bookstore and bought all the works of Colonel James Stotzlmann that he could find. He spent the better part of the next three days and nights getting "the low-down" on this new friend who had been vouched for upon such high authority. One of the books was the writer's life story, and so Lanny could learn about him in advance.

X

Jim Stotzlmann was one of those mysteries of nature to which the biologists have given the name of "sport." For a thousand generations all flies of a certain species will have wings with gray spots; then suddenly one will appear with purple spots. And in the same way, in the palaces of privilege many generations of babies will be born who will eat what is fed to them and believe what is told to them, and grow up to be perfectly conventional members of fashionable society, wearing exactly the right clothes, thinking exactly the right thoughts, and doing exactly what all the other members of their set consider proper. But once in a blue moon will appear a freak, a black sheep, a crackpot —there will be many names for him—a child who will insist upon asking questions, and trying to make sure the answers are right; who will think for himself, and not as all the others think; who will not be sure that God in His Infinite Wisdom has entrusted to him the care of the property interests of the country. (Such were the public words of a great coal magnate during the childhood of Jim Stotzlmann and Lanny Budd.)

Jim and his sisters had been born and raised in that great brownstone palace looking out over Lake Michigan, and had been bored to death in two "ideally equipped" schoolrooms in its uppermost floor.

They had been taught exactly how to behave at receptions and teas, and how to grade their conversation and tone of voice according to the social importance of the ladies and gentlemen to whom they were introduced. Among these was the then President, Theodore Roosevelt, who sent the ten-year-old boy a formal invitation to have lunch at the White House, and there delivered to him a thirty-minute lecture on the life and ideals of Abraham Lincoln. That was the experience which really impressed the lad, and not the fact that by the time he was sixteen he had lunched and dined with every major crowned head of Europe.

Jim enlisted in the ranks and contributed his share to the blood and sweat of the war to make the world safe for democracy. When he came home he was not happy with the dancing wastrels of the North Shore and Lake Geneva smart set—any more than Lanny had been with those of Paris and the Côte d'Azur. He wanted to become a writer, and had gone out and got a newspaper job, with the idea that that was the way to learn. Soon afterwards the paper was bought by Frank Munsey, who had made forty million dollars out of the publishing business and told Jim it was just luck. When Jim went to beg him not to dismiss the newspaper staff, the publisher told him to get out and mind his own damn business.

After that Jim wanted a paper of his own—a penny paper, to defend the rights of the common man. Chicago was the place for it, he decided, and since his family wouldn't help him, he took the advice of Lord Northcliffe and sold stock to the public. Then he found that it would take a long time to get a press. Being only twenty-five, and naïve and idealistic, he went to call on William Randolph Hearst at San Simeon, to ask permission to use his Chicago presses during the interim. The interview took place at the Ambassador Hotel, and Lanny, needless to say, was interested in the scene with that royal personality.

What he had said was: "There is no room in Chicago for another newspaper. I am just buying a newspaper in Dallas, Texas, and you may become the editor. You are a novice at the game, but you have a name that is worth money. Thirty thousand a year will do for a start. Go at once to Dallas by plane and report to the managing editor of my paper there. I will send you instructions from time to time. Good morning."

When Lanny Budd read that story he thought: My nameless services are worth nearly twice as much as the Stotzlmann name! But then he reflected that this had been seventeen years ago, while America was still on the gold standard, and the value of money greater. He could just about regard himself as Jim's social equal!

XI

Several days passed, and Lanny had barely opened his eyes in the morning when the phone rang and a gentle voice said: "Is this Mr. Lanny Budd? This is Jim Stotzlmann." Lanny said: "Oh, good! I was afraid you might be in Florida." Said the voice: "When can I come to see you?" Lanny thought it was up to him to call, but the other insisted: "I am only a couple of blocks away."

The son of Budd-Erling understood this form of self-protection. If a man calls on you it may be hard to get rid of him, but if you call on him, you can leave when you please. So he asked: "Would an hour from now be agreeable?" The answer was: "Fine!"

This "sport" of the Chicago orchid greenhouse proved to be a large fellow, as tall as Lanny and heavier. He had the face of an idealist who had been made to suffer in a cruel and ugly world. His smile was warm, his manner deprecating and shy; his voice low, a little like a woman's. A generous and trusting person, not in the least suggestive of a secret agent, which Lanny had guessed from F.D.'s words that he really was. But then it was something Lanny had learned long ago, that spies do not look or act like spies—at least not if they are good ones, as Lanny himself tried to be.

Lanny presented his card, and the other took one glance at it. His face lighted up, and he exclaimed: "I guessed that was it. I am always happy to meet a friend of F.D.'s."

"The same to you, Mr. Stotzlmann."

"Honestly, I have a crush on that man like a schoolgirl. I would die for him a hundred times, if such a thing were possible."

"Then we shall understand each other. I think the American people are lucky to have such a President in this crisis."

"I wish they realized how lucky they are, Mr. Budd."

"Indeed you are right; and I am terribly afraid they may desert him before long. That is what I went to him about, and why he wanted me to meet you."

"Tell me about it, by all means."

Lanny explained how as an art expert he had met Baldur Heinsch, and had thought it the part of wisdom to pretend sympathy with this Nazi agent's point of view, so as to discover what he was up to. He told about California and the Roosevelt-haters there, and what they were talking and planning. The scion of North Shore Drive listened with attention, never once interrupting, but keeping his eyes on the speaker's face as if he were trying to read his inmost soul.

When Lanny finished, the other said: "The thing is all over the country, Mr. Budd, and you don't exaggerate the danger in the slightest degree. F.D.'s enemies hate him with such fury that they don't keep silence even in my presence, though most of them know exactly how I feel. I have heard them calling for somebody to shoot him—and not merely in New York and Washington, but in country clubs and nightspots all over. You know I get about a lot—"

"F.D. told me you were a grasshopper," smiled Lanny.

"Mostly it is shellshock from the last war; I have never got over it, and can't bear to stay in one place very long. Also, I suppose it was my upbringing; I got my education on the run."

"I spent most of the last three days reading your books."

"Oh, how kind! Then you know exactly how I feel about our roistering rich. And you won't need any assurance that I agree with you about Hearst. He is one of the most unscrupulous and most dangerous men in America. He stops at nothing to get his way. And there are many like him. I could compile quite a list from my personal experience."

XII

"I suppose," said the old pirate's descendant, "that F.D. intends for me to give you the real dope. You must understand that what I am going to say is the very last word in secrecy."

"You may count upon me absolutely, Mr. Stotzlmann."

"To begin with, let's not stand on ceremony. You can understand that I don't enjoy my family name very much; it's a sort of gold mace studded with diamonds, and when it's waved in front of people's eyes they become dizzy, and I become bored. Call me Jim and let me call you Lanny."

"Fine!" said the other. "As F.D. likes to say: Shoot!"

"Well, the contacts you have made in Hollywood may be the edges of the same conspiracy, but the center of it, and the really dangerous part, is in New York and Chicago, and in Washington. It is spreading through several government organizations, and at the heart of it are three of our top-ranking personalities."

"Good God, Jim!"

"You understand, I am in touch with many of our top-notchers. I play around a lot; I like people, and if I stay alone I get to worrying about the world. I've lived with the super-rich since I first opened my eyes, and there are few whom I haven't met in the course of years. They all know I'm a maverick, and quarrel with me, but they're not very good at keeping secrets. You know their attitude: 'What the hell?' "

"I have met a lot of them," Lanny mentioned.

"My knowledge of this conspiracy began last summer, through a fellow I know in the advertising game—which is a small-sized gold mine. He got into a jam about his income taxes—they are complicated, you know, and maybe it wasn't his fault; anyhow, he had come to Washington and he was damning That Man and his sheeny gang; he was half drunk, and he said, by God he and his friends were going to can the whole lousy lot. I pretended not to believe him, and so he got mad and spilled the story. 'Go and talk to Harrison Dengue,' he said. 'Tell him I sent you and he'll tell you about it.' Do you know Dengue?"

"Only by hearing my father speak of him."

"Well, he's a typical big-money autocrat. They are gods, and they don't let any stockholders or boards of directors check them."

"Only Congress?" put in Lanny.

"They hate the New Deal congressmen reformers like snakes, and they hold F.D. responsible because he's one who knows how to get the votes and keep the congressmen in power. They have an utter contempt for the democratic process and for everybody who professes it. Dengue is a man whose favorite diversion is seducing the wives of his fellow-officials—especially those who can't do anything about it because he is in a position to break them. He looks like a bull and acts like one."

"I know the type; and they are not confined to any special group. The big-business world is full of them."

"What the American people do not realize is that officialdom today is big business. The higher men associate exclusively with the plush-lined set. Imagine any one of them putting his feet under the dinner table of a poor man! They come to my mother's parties, half a dozen at a time, and believe me, the secretary has to know about precedence. When they open their mouths, it might be Hearst or our own Colonel McCormick."

"Don't forget, Jim, my father sold munitions, and my grandfather and his father made them."

"Of course, you know it all. Well, Dengue has tremendous power in the parts of the country where it will be needed. And then there's Poultiss, and there's Harrigues—these three are the dynamos, and will be the triumvirate."

"What exactly are they planning to do?"

"They are waiting for some public emergency, riots, or a big strike —there's a coal strike coming, I believe. They will send a bunch of their men to take charge of the district which includes Hyde Park; they will cut the telephone wires to the place and seize the President. They will use the radio stations to tell the public that there was a plot against the President's safety and that they are protecting him; they will issue orders in his name."

"But, do they imagine Roosevelt will submit?"

"What can he do, Lanny, a crippled man who can hardly get about? They will make sure that nobody gets near him but their crowd."

"They think the country will be fooled by such a trick?"

"What can the country do? This crowd have the guns—believe me, they have plenty—riot guns, tommy-guns, tear-gas guns, sawed-off shot-guns, and poison gas if needed. They know all the strategic spots in the country, and will occupy them."

"But will their forces obey them?"

"Orders will be issued to the army in the President's name. Some of the officers may suspect that the orders are phony, but how can they be sure? By the time they wake up to what is happening they will be in custody, and somebody will be keeping them quiet."

"But the army rank and file, Jim!"

"The rank and file will obey orders—what's an army for? There will be attempts at resistance, of course, but the junta will put them down. I'm not saying they can do it, mind you; I'm saying they believe they can, and they mean to try."

"You are sure it's a real thing, and not just gossip?"

"As certain of it as a man can be of anything human. I am not at liberty to go into details; but telephone wires have been tapped and people have been followed and conversations recorded over a period of several months."

"You have reported this to F.D.?"

"I have reported to him, and to the persons he has ordered me to."

"And what is he doing about it?"

"He doesn't tell me, except in hints. He refuses to worry about it —he's not the worrying kind, you know. He insists that he can deal with the gang in an inconspicuous way, without a scandal that would injure the national morale. He will send the suspected men to some district a long way off."

"But somebody ought to point out to F.D. that it doesn't take a plane very long to fly from any part of the country. The Republican Government of Spain tried that same device with General Franco some five years ago. They exiled him to the Canary Islands, but it didn't keep him from continuing with his conspiracy, and when the time came, he was on deck."

"Quite so," agreed Jim, "and be sure I have talked to the Chief about it. He says that he has his plans, and naturally I can't ask him too many questions. When I get information, I take it to him."

XIII

Lanny sat for a while in silence, then he said: "This thing takes my breath away."

"It has me worried sick," replied Jim. "Since F.D. refuses to worry, I've taken the job on."

"What strikes me especially is the resemblance to what I saw in France shortly before the war broke out. Do you know about the Cagoulard conspiracy?"

"Only what I read in our papers."

"It happened that I was close to it. The de Bruyne family, old friends of mine, were among its backers. It was a conspiracy to overthrow the Third Republic and jail its leading officials. Only this summer Admiral Darlan told me with his own lips that he had planned to put the Leftists among the French naval officers on board the antiquated battleship *Jean Bart* and take her out to sea and sink her."

"The men I have named to you would hardly have that much imagination," remarked the serious-minded Jim.

"I was struck by your statement that F.D. doesn't want a scandal because of the bad effect on morale. That's exactly why the Cagoule was never purged in France; there were more than five hundred army officers involved in the plot, and the Cabinet voted against Léon Blum and Marx Dormoy, who wanted to root them out. The result was, they stayed in the army and went on making appeasement propaganda, even in the midst of war."

"The propaganda of this bunch is anti-Jew, anti-Russian, and to some extent anti-British. It is closely tied up with the Catholic hierarchy—the Papal Knights and the Papal Delegates and our millionaires who back them."

"There you have it! Franco Spain, and the intrigues of the Nazis in South America—these are all parts of the same world conspiracy!"

"I see you know the game," said Jim. "It happens that Harrison Dengue's present mistress is a Nazi countess whose brother is one of the leading Nazi agents in Buenos Aires."

"Does that happen to be the Gräfin Schönen?"

"Dora Schönen, the same!"

"But she was the mistress of Otto Abetz, Nazi Governor of Paris."

"Well, maybe he got tired of her; or maybe the Nazis sent her here, to build up the American Cagoule. They don't let love—or passion, or whatever you choose to call it—stand in the way of politics. That would be weakness."

"I met that lovely lady; and unless I am mistaken, she has some of the evil Jewish blood."

"Quite possibly, she may be an honorary Aryan. That's another detail in which the gang over here is following the Nazis. There are wealthy Jews in the group. Dengue's finger man here in New York is a Jew who changed his name; he is a crafty anti-Democrat, who despises Roosevelt. The gang has a code name for Jews; they are 'Number Threes.' You understand, our officialdom is not supposed to discriminate against them."

"But the country clubs do, and the dinner parties!"

"You can bet on that," remarked the man from North Shore Drive. "Believe me, I have helped to make out the lists for hundreds of smart affairs."

XIV

These two who had become fast friends upon one glimpse of a visiting card behaved as if they would never stop talking. Lanny had read Jim's books, but Jim had many stories that were not in the books, and Lanny wanted to hear them all. Jim wanted to know about Lanny, where and how he lived and what he was doing. Lanny explained that in his youth he had become a Pink, but in recent years he had begun to change his coloration, as a means of getting information for friends abroad, and later for some in America. That was as near as he would come to saying the letters "P.A."; but that was near enough. He added: "If you ever speak of me to anyone except F.D., remember that I'm a near-Fascist and friend of all the top Nazis. Don't say anything good about me!"

"It will be better not to know you, and that we meet privately. You could be tremendously useful to me in running down the members of this gang."

"I would be glad to do it, but at the moment I have another commission, and must return to France. I come here every few months, and then I'll look up your three top conspirators and give them the latest news from their friends in Vichy France and Spain."

"I had better give you the code name for this group; among themselves they are 'SG's.' I have never been able to find out what that stands for, but their purpose is to 'save America,' they tell themselves. There are sincere fanatics among them, but others are self-seekers, impatient men, and arrogant—the type of Aaron Burr, if you remember the details of his conspiracy. There are several senators and congressmen in their confidence, men who are highly placed in the committees, and very powerful. It is a movement that is steadily expanding and solidifying itself. The further F.D. goes in carrying out his policies, the more his enemies are automatically driven together. That is something he himself is reluctant to face, but his friends keep pounding at him and he's beginning to wake up."

"I believe I may have helped a little," said Lanny. "Coming to him independently of you and all the others, my statements should have carried weight."

"What I want most to do," continued the other, "is to persuade him to take Hyde Park out of the New York Military District and put it under the direct control of Washington. If the Chief hadn't gone off on this cruise, I would urge you to go back and press that idea upon him."

Lanny couldn't say: "He has ordered me abroad." His answer was: "I hope to God there aren't any admirals among your SG's!"

BOOK THREE

He That Diggeth a Pit

———————————— o ————————————

9. Set Thine House in Order

I

LANNY drove back to Newcastle to return the borrowed car and say his farewells. Budd-Erling had got its share of those twenty-six thousand planes which F.D. had permitted the British to order, and now the President of Budd-Erling was under pressure from the brass hats to expand some more. His son compared him to an infant who has reached out for a nipple and got the nozzle of a hose. Everybody in the town was under the pressure of that hose, it appeared; the old-timers complained that social life was at an end and there was no room to get around on the streets. Robbie no longer came home to lunch, but ate a sandwich and a glass of milk in his office. The two sturdy sons of Robbie and Esther were like a pair of faithful drayhorses pulling in harness, and with new loads being piled onto the dray.

At Lanny's request the father put in an application for Lanny's passport to Europe. The arrangement with President Roosevelt had been that Robbie was to apply to a certain official in the War Department, on the ground that Lanny was traveling on Budd-Erling business. "War" would make the arrangements with "State," and thus there would be no ground for suspicion that Lanny was anything other than the son of Budd-Erling. The passport was to be for Portugal, Spain, Vichy France, Switzerland, Germany, and Britain. There were many persons in New York and Washington who, for reasons of their own, would have paid large sums of money for such a document, but couldn't get it because of the government's stern policy of restricting travel in the war zones.

Lanny waited; and meantime, there was private business in New-castle. Christmas was coming, and it was too bad to leave just before that! One of Esther's nieces was coming home from the Harvard School of Art, and her aunt was giving her a party. Couldn't Lanny be tempted to stay over for that? Lanny's stepmother, the subtlest of psychological manipulators, didn't drop any hints concerning love and marriage; what she said was that the family saw so little of Lanny, and enjoyed his conversation so much; also, that the dangers in Europe, both on land and sea, were so frightful in these times, and what was there in the business of old masters or in that of military planes that made it worth while for him to risk his life?

Margaret Remsen was the girl's name, and they called her Peggy. Lanny hadn't seen her for a couple of years, and what a change that time can make in a young woman's mind! She was a proper young lady of New England, conscientious and studious as anyone in Esther's family was bound to be; also she was extraordinarily eager and alert to what was going on about her. Had her aunt by any chance prompted her? She knew all about Lanny's art experting, and also his political experting. She wanted to hear about the extraordinary people he had met, and listened with attention to every word that fell from his lips. Nothing could be more acceptable to the male ego.

Lanny went off and thought it over. Here was one more temptation, one more emotional disturbance. Peggy was related to him only by her aunt's marriage and not by blood; he was perfectly eligible on that score. Manifestly, she liked him, and manifestly he had seen more of the great world than anybody she was likely to meet in an overgrown river port on Long Island Sound. Lanny wondered if she was going to take the place of Lizbeth in his imagination—or would it be the place of Laurel? She was a sort of combination of the two. She was young, and some day she would have a lot of money, for her father was president of the First National Bank of Newcastle, and her grand-father had founded that institution, which did all the business of Budd-Erling and a good part of Budd Gunmakers. Also Peggy had brains, and had read quite a number of books—something that fashionable ladies talked about more often than they did.

Lanny wondered now and then about the impact on American so-ciety of this fresh crop of young females who had got an education and were seemingly determined to think for themselves. From his point of view these young people were victims of a conspiracy of press and radio, of church and school and political platform, to per-suade them that the so-called American way of life, the "free enterprise system," was the only free system conceivable and the only one com-patible with democracy. To be sure, it meant plenty of freedom for Robbie Budd, the employer, but for the masses of workers it was the old familiar wage slavery. Now Lanny sat at his stepmother's luncheon table and heard Peggy Remsen sum up her ideas on the subject: "It seems to me it would be a lot more democratic if the workers made their own jobs, instead of having Uncle Robbie make them all." Lanny said nothing, for of course such problems lay outside the province of an art expert.

<h1 style="text-align:center">II</h1>

The passport was delayed; and Robbie phoned to "War" and was referred to "State." He phoned to "State," and was told that the matter was under consideration. That was the way with bureaucrats; they hold matters under consideration until the world comes to an end. So Lanny, who had told himself that his dancing days were done, went to the party in the Newcastle Country Club; he was one of two-score properly dressed gentlemen who danced with Peggy and paid her compliments, all of which she deserved, because she looked very lovely and behaved with gaiety and charm. Lanny had attended just such a party at the home of Lizbeth Holdenhurst, and he told himself that he had broken Lizbeth's heart, or at any rate cracked it, and now he was a philanderer, and in danger of doing the same thing to his stepmother's niece.

Finally there came a letter on elegant stationery, instructing him to call upon a representative of the State Department in New York. So he went, and met a man considerably younger than himself who looked like a college instructor, the kind that Robbie Budd especially abhorred. With the most elegant manners Mr. Titherington put Lanny Budd through an inquisition as to what he wanted to do in Europe, and why he considered himself entitled to special favors. This investigation wasn't supposed to happen at all; F.D. had given special orders to "War" that the president of Budd-Erling was to have whatever passports he requested for himself or his son. Lanny had said: "I suppose that 'State' will do whatever 'War' requests": but apparently this had been naïve. Had somebody blundered? Or were there bureaucrats so full of their own importance that they used their judgment concerning orders even from the head of the United States Government?

Lanny was treading on eggs in this office. He couldn't give the faintest hint that the President was interested in his errands abroad; he couldn't even refuse to answer questions and say that he would take the matter to higher authority, for that might affront the young man and make a malicious enemy. Lanny knew that all bureaucrats live under siege by newspapermen; some hate them and some love them, but all fear them; and suppose this Mr. Titherington were to say to a reporter friend: "Do you know anything about this chap Lanny Budd who calls himself an art expert and claims the privilege of traveling all over Europe in wartime? He is the son of Robbie Budd of Budd-Erling, and you might find it worth while to look him up and find out what he's doing." It might be that some radio newscaster would ask this question over the air, some Nazi agent would make note of it—and that would be the end of a P.A. forever!

Lanny explained with great patience and politeness that he had a mother in Juan-les-Pins, and a little daughter in England. To this the conscientious bureaucrat replied that there were many Americans in positions of the same sort, but unfortunately the State Department had had to rule against all such requests. Still patiently, Lanny explained that he had orders for several paintings in Vichy France, and must go there to attend to them. To this the polite bureaucrat replied that all commercial matters had to be attended to by mail, if at all. Pushed to the wall, Lanny became mysterious, and revealed that there were certain matters having to do with the designs of the new Budd-Erling pursuit plane; certain improvements which had been effected in recent French models and about which Lanny had been promised the blueprints. It was a matter of the greatest urgency, which was why the application had come through the War Department. The persistent bureaucrat wanted to know why the Swiss trip was necessary, and Lanny said that one of the men with whom he was dealing might be in that country.

The upshot of it all was that the application would be taken "under consideration" and that Lanny would hear from "State." Lanny realized that this Mr. Titherington was only doing what he had been told to do, and it wasn't fair to blame him for wartime restrictions. Lanny believed in the bureaucrats, as the only alternative to the business autocrats at the present stage of social development. But at the same time it was most exasperating. He couldn't phone to Baker about the matter, because Baker wasn't supposed to know his name. He thought of calling upon Professor Alston, who had introduced him to F.D., and must share in the secret, even though he had never spoken to Lanny about it. But the newspapers reported that Charles Alston, whom they referred to as "the fixer," had that day been flown by plane to join the President on his cruise.

III

So there was nothing to do but wait until F.D.'s return. Lanny decided that he wouldn't go back to Newcastle, where Esther and Peggy might be lying in wait for him. Or would they? He decided to take no chances, but to enjoy himself with his friend and art colleague, Zoltan Kertezsi, and see what new things the dealers had to offer, and what, if any, had been added to the museums. Also, he would pay another call on Baldur Heinsch and give him a chance to say whether or not the conspirators were willing to have Lanny Budd know their names and to pass them on to the Duce of San Simeon.

What the steamship official reported was that the heads of the junta hadn't been able to make up their minds; they wanted to investigate Lanny Budd, and Lanny said that was perfectly natural—unless they were fools they wouldn't risk their necks without taking every precaution. In his secret thoughts Lanny wondered whether Heinsch really knew anything, or was pretending to have information as a means of getting some. Lanny changed the subject, and after a while went to call on Forrest Quadratt, and, talking about various persons whom they both knew, he remarked: "By the way, I wonder if you know Harrison Dengue?"

"I have met him several times," replied the ex-poet casually. He was a well-trained intriguer, and if he was surprised he wouldn't show any trace of it. "Do you know him?"

"I don't think I have met him, but my father has told me about him. I should think he would be a useful man to both of us."

"That might be a good suggestion. Miss van Zandt knows him well, I believe."

Lanny didn't say: "I'd like to meet him." He seldom pushed himself; his role was that of an easy-going person, a sort of *flâneur* of the arts, and always it was Quadratt who was using him, never he who was using Quadratt. "I see that Senator Reynolds is in town," he remarked. "There is a character out of a storybook."

"I had lunch with him yesterday," responded the other. "He remembers you well and asked about you. He went to Germany, you know, and came back delighted with what he found."

"If only we could take the American people for a trip through Germany, there would be an end to the lies of the Jewish press." In this Lanny was repeating what he had read only that week in the *Deutscher Weckruf und Beobachter*, published in Yorkville, a section of New York.

Lanny said no more on this subject. He talked about his projected trip abroad, and complimented Quadratt by asking his advice as to whether the Führer would wish to meet an American under the painful circumstances existing. "I couldn't blame him if he never wished to hear of another." The Nazi agent replied that the Führer was a broad-minded man and would surely not hold an old friend responsible for the malicious intrigues of a Roosevelt. Lanny told how cordial the great leader had been in Paris, and about the genuineness of his longing for reconcilement with the British Empire; then he spoke of Lord Wickthorpe, and the significance of his resignation—Lanny exaggerated it greatly. The movement for an understanding was far more widespread than the American press allowed the public to guess.

"At any rate," said the ex-poet, "you and I can be sure that we have done everything in our power to end this madness."

I V

Jim Stotzlmann had said that Harrison Dengue was in New York at this time, so Lanny was not surprised when, on the following afternoon, there was delivered to his hotel a handwritten invitation to dine the following evening at the home of Miss Hortensia van Zandt "to meet Mr. Dengue and Senator Reynolds." Lanny had guessed that the eager agent would set to work via the telephone, and that the fanatical old lady who was one of Quadratt's financial backers would be no less prompt. In these times of blockade and censorship not many personal friends of the Führer were available in New York.

Lanny accepted by the same formal method, and at half-past six he left his hotel for a walk down Fifth Avenue. It was a crisp winter evening, and looking up through the steep canyon walls he saw bright stars, seeming very close. The time was between the rush of shopping traffic and theater traffic, but even so the great thoroughfare was crowded, and its bright lights were veiled by a gray-blue haze. Jewelry shops, fur shops, art shops, tall office buildings, and hotels lined what had once been the residential street of the "Four Hundred." The display of luxury goods was like no other in the world, for Congress had just authorized more billions for military goods. Farther down on this narrow island was the financial center through which the money must pass, and be sure that sooner or later a lot of it would find its way to these shops.

Miss van Zandt was the New York hostess of two generations ago; tall, thin, and white-haired, stubborn, stiff, and proud. Her mansion on the lower Avenue had been entirely engulfed by the clothing trade, but she refused to move; that was her manner of waging war on the Jews and the Reds, who to her mind were one and the same. She wore a long black evening gown of real silk, and a velvet collar studded with diamonds hid the tendons of her thin neck. Nowadays the *grandes dames* had imitations made of their jewels and wore these, keeping the real ones—which everybody knew they had—locked up in bank vaults. Lanny guessed that this hostess would scorn such modernisms.

The present was an intellectual occasion, and she chose to dine alone with her three important gentlemen. Forrest Quadratt didn't show up, and Lanny guessed that he himself had suggested this; the occasion would be one of simon-pure Americanism, and no one of the guests would be troubled by the idea that the Germans were responsible for it. First came "Buncombe Bob" Reynolds—by an odd quirk of fate he had been born in Buncombe County, in the state which he called No'th Ca'lina. He had once been a barker, selling patent medicines in a circus, and by lung power and genius he had risen to become Chairman of the Military Affairs Committee of the United States Senate, a position of the greatest power, which he intended with God's help to use in keeping God's country out of foreign wars, especially the wars of a power which had captured and burned the city of Washington only a hundred and twenty-seven years ago.

And then came Harrison Smithfield Dengue, a person concerning whom Lanny Budd had developed a sudden and intense curiosity. One could see at a glance that he was a man accustomed to commanding, and to being obeyed. He was a big fellow, and the swelling was in his chest and not below. He had a red complexion and wore a closely cropped gray mustache. He sat in his chair looking like a statue of capacity and determination. He didn't say much, but then nobody had to, so long as Buncombe Bob was in the company.

This Senator of the hillbillies was one of the most active and determined advocates of Fascism in the Western World; but Lanny reflected that quite possibly he didn't know it was Fascism and would have been indignant at the term. What he called it was Americanism, or plain hundred-per-cent patriotism. America was the greatest country in the world, and she was that because of her institutions under which a patent-medicine vender had risen to be a leading statesman and associate of millionaires. The Senator would have declared that any man who had ability and was willing to work hard enough could do the same. He was about to marry the daughter of a leading Washington hostess, author of a volume entitled *Father Struck It Rich*. Evalyn's father had struck a gold mine, and now Evalyn owned the Hope diamond, the biggest in the world, and wore it on her bosom at parties to which she invited swarms of people who were Fascists and didn't know it, and some who did.

V

Don't let yourself be fooled by this statesman's bland round smiling face and black hair cut long like a poet's or a pianist's. He is one of the most determined and aggressive men in the land, and if the Reds think they are going to be allowed to spread their ideas and if the Jews think they are going to be allowed to continue making all the money, the Senator is going to teach them better. He has just been to Germany and discovered that everybody there is working hard, and happy, in spite of the war which was forced upon them. He tells once more the story of what he found there, and the other three persons at the dinner table do not interrupt. The Senator has learned how the National-Socialist miracle was brought about, and he is publishing a weekly paper, the *American Vindicator*, to tell all patriotic citizens about it. Also he has founded an organization, the Vindicators, which provides its members with red, white, and blue feathers and red, white, and blue badges. There is a section for youth, called the Border Patrol, and they also wear feathers and badges, and carry banners and sing songs—in short everything the *Hitlerjugend* has, excepting only the "daggers of honor." The Senator doesn't say that the whole of the McLean fortune is behind this effort to "save America," and Lanny guesses that this is because the great man hopes to get a sizable check from his hostess when the evening is over.

When Buncombe Bob's tale is told, the hostess turns to Lanny and remarks: "I understand, Mr. Budd, that you were in Paris last summer and met the Führer and others."

So it is Lanny's turn, and he relates what he saw and heard. Mr. Dengue is interested, and asks how he managed to gain the confidence of these exalted persons. Lanny tells, for perhaps the thousandth time, how it came about, and how the Führer commissioned him to tell the French people how he, the Führer, loves the French, and to tell the British people how he loves the British, and to tell the American people how he loves the Americans. In short, Adi Schicklgruber is a man made wholly of love, and hatred has no part in his being. He goes to war because other people force him in, and never ceases to plead for the end of hostilities. Lanny can say all this with a perfectly straight face and be certain that none of his three hearers will suspect any irony.

A most unusual story, how an American art expert was commissioned to travel back and forth with secret messages from the mistress of the Premier of France to the husband of his own former wife. "It sounds melodramatic," he remarked. "It happens that we are living in melodramatic times, and the novelists and playwrights of a thousand years hence will be finding their material in the things that have been going on in Europe during the past ten." There were no novelists or playwrights at this dinner table, only the most serious-minded reformers. Mr. Dengue wanted to know how sincere the Führer was in his hatred of Red Russia, and what were the prospects of his taking that country on, if by chance the statesmen of Britain could be persuaded to agree to a settlement.

It was the red-faced gentleman's turn, and the hostess said: "Tell us what you think about the prospects for peace."

So the man of power sang for his supper. He remarked that ordinarily any nation would be well satisfied to see its leading rivals fight each other, and he would have no objection to letting the British Empire and the German Reich go to it as long as they pleased. But there was the Red Terror of the Kremlin in the background, gloating over the spectacle and ready to march into the vacuum which the war would create in Central and perhaps in Western Europe. That was something in which no sane man could take pleasure, and for that reason Mr. Dengue wanted a truce patched up as quickly as possible.

"That," remarked Lanny, "is exactly what is in the Führer's mind, as he has explained it to me scores of times." No offense was intended and none was taken, for Lanny's auditors would have no objection to agreeing with the Führer—or rather, as they would have phrased it, to having the Führer agree with them.

"The danger," continued Dengue, "is increased by the fact that our own Commander-in-Chief is so determined to bring us into the conflict. If that happens, we may no longer find ourselves with the power to deal with Russia, as some time we shall surely have to do."

Said the hostess: "Many times I find myself thinking that the destiny of our country in this crisis is in the hands of a man who is actually and literally insane."

"That would be a matter of definition," the other replied. "He is a man who is determined to have his own way, and his judgment is far from sound."

"How much does he know about the world he lives in?" broke in the Senator. "He is a millionaire, but he has never earned a dollar in his life—unless you count what he gets for his Christmas trees."

"A Christmas-tree grower for President, and an apple grower for Secretary of the Treasury!" remarked Dengue, and added: "Jew apples!"

"Perhaps these are some of them," chuckled Lanny, nodding toward the dish of fruit in the center of the table. So they all had a laugh, and felt more and more friendly as the wines were passed. When in the course of the evening Lanny revealed that he was returning to Vichy France on his father's business, and that he might go into Germany and meet Hess and perhaps Hitler, Dengue remarked: "I wish that when you come back, Mr. Budd, you would let me know what you have learned."

"Nothing would give me greater pleasure," replied the P.A.—and there was more truth in this than in other things he had said that evening.

VI

The newspapers recorded the culmination of the struggle between Laval and Pétain. The aged Marshal had deposed his faithless subordinate and placed him under arrest, and Otto Abetz, Nazi Governor of Paris, had flown to Vichy to Laval's rescue. It is at times of crisis such as this that men become excited and reveal secrets, and Lanny ought to have been there to avail himself of the opportunity. He was like a race horse champing behind a barrier, but there was nothing he could do. He tried to get Baker on the telephone, but Baker wasn't there, and Lanny couldn't find out where he was without giving his name. The President had come back from his brief cruise and was at Warm Springs, Georgia; Lanny would gladly have gone there, but he couldn't find Baker there, and he would surely not be able to get near the President without giving his name to somebody.

Two weeks after the vacation had begun, Lanny read that the Big Boss was back in the White House, and at once it was possible to get Baker. Matters would have been simplified if Lanny had been able to say: "Tell the Chief my passports have been delayed." But Baker wasn't supposed to know that Zaharoff 103 was getting any passports. All Lanny could say was: "Tell the Chief I have to see him for a minute or two about an important matter." The order came back: "Fly on the six o'clock plane and meet me at nine-forty-five tonight."

So Lanny found himself in the familiar bedroom in which many early-morning and late-evening conferences were being held during these crowded and perilous days. F.D. looked bronzed and refreshed —it was truly amazing what a few days of rest and recreation could do for this overburdened man. He had been poking about in coves and inlets which had once been the haunt of pirates and were soon going to be sites of great naval and air installations, designed to keep enemy U-boats forever away from the southern approaches to the United States and the Panama Canal.

Lanny knew what a mass of duties must be pressing upon the President now, and he wanted to come to the point and then go. "Governor, I was ready to leave for France a couple of weeks ago, but I haven't been able to get passports. 'State' has the matter under advisement, as they tell me."

"Damn!" exclaimed the "Governor" and slapped the blue-silk coverlet of his bed. "Isn't that the limit? It shows you what I am up against in trying to get things done!"

"What it seems to show," ventured the caller, "is what I've been trying to tell you for three years, that you need a housecleaning in 'State.'"

"I can't do it, Lanny. All these people are established, and all have influence. In times like these my first thought has to be to keep support in Congress. If I order the firing of a single filing clerk I earn the enmity of some congressman who got him the job."

"Well, Governor, here I sit waiting, while the filing clerk makes up his mind whether my phony excuses for wanting to get into Switzerland are good enough."

"I'll see that the passports are delivered to your father at once."

"Don't be too vehement about it," cautioned Lanny. "It might cause gossip about me."

The other broke into one of his hearty laughs. "There you have it! You don't want any publicity; multiply your problem by about a million, and you have some idea of mine!"

"I know you're crowded," said the dutiful agent, and got up to leave. But the crowded one wouldn't ever have it that way. "Tell me," he said, "did you meet Jim?"

Lanny thought: This man never forgets anything! Inside his large head was a living encyclopedia of names, places, dates, and things having to do with his job which he so loved and enjoyed, difficult and dangerous though it was. Lanny sat down again, and told about his conference with the scion of the Windy City.

"Grand fellow!" said F.D. "Nobody who knows him can fail to love him."

"His story took my breath away," replied the other. "I still can't convince myself that it's real."

This was a hint, and the President replied: "I don't think Jim overestimates the evil purposes of that bunch; but he underestimates my other sources of information, and the precautions I have taken—which naturally I can't talk about freely."

"Of course not. I think you may be interested to know that I met Harrison Dengue." Lanny told the story of the affair at Miss van Zandt's, and added: "I was careful not to hint at the conspiracy, but I got an invitation to come back to him, and when I have cultivated him a little more he may let me in on the inside. Shall I bring the facts to you or to Jim?"

"To both," was the reply. "I trust Jim's devotion completely, but of course I can't trust any man's judgment completely. If it's an important matter I have to make my own decision."

The President went on to discuss these "headstrong men," as he called them. "I didn't make the national machinery," he said; "and I have to take it as I find it. Many of its officials are conservative—they come from the conservative classes, and don't shed their ideas when they take a public job. Some of the most efficient men are the most reactionary, but I'm not asking for their ideas, only for their services, and I can't take action against them for what they say, only for what they do."

Lanny's reply was: "Léon Blum once said nearly the same words to me, referring to the Cagoulards, and his attitude has come near to costing him his life."

VII

Once more the P.A. thought that his duty was done, and he started to get up from his chair. But once more the Boss wanted to talk. "I don't see you very often," he remarked; "and I see a lot of people who know less. Tell me what you make of this blow-up in Vichy."

·So Lanny had to deliver one of his discourses, explaining the difference between the two men who had been in control of the puppet government of Unoccupied France. One was a man of no principles whatever, willing to hire himself to the Nazis as he had previously hired himself to the Comité des Forges, the organization of the French steel and munitions masters. The other was a man of the most rigid principles, a devout Catholic, doing everything in his power to save France, but meaning the ancient Catholic France, governed by a benevolent paternalism. The Marshal enjoyed the confidence of many Frenchmen, while Laval was despised even by his own gang. The Marshal was old and feeble, and had never been a man of vigor; in the old days his superior, Marshal Foch, had said of him: "When there is nothing to do, the job is Pétain's." Lanny added: "Perhaps that is the job he has now. The Nazis demand action, and this stubborn old martinet promises, and then finds excuses and delays, and nothing happens."

"What do you think the Germans will do to him?"

"I wouldn't like to guess, but it's a safe bet that they won't let him do anything to Laval; the Nazis need both of them too badly. They don't want to have to occupy the rest of France in the present state of their affairs."

"Where are they going? Into the Balkans?"

"It looks like that. If they could get Greece and Crete, they would be within bombing range of Suez, and that would make it hard for the British. They will be heading for oil, whether in Mesopotamia or the Caucasus. The fate of Europe hangs in the balance there."

The President thought for a moment, then said: "I'll tell you a secret, Lanny, something very hush-hush. It will make you happy."

"Well, Governor, frankly, I could do with a little happiness right now."

"This is something you've been begging of me for a long time. I'm going all out for aid to Britain; not military, of course, but financial, and everything we can manufacture that they need. Lothian's last report convinced me that it can't be put off any longer."

"Well, Governor, when you do it, I'll get up and dance a jig, wherever I am."

"I'm going to give a fireside chat in the next few days. I wrote my speech on the *Tuscaloosa*. Would you like to read it?"

"I'd be as proud as that dog with two tails I once told you about."

"You might have some suggestions. Take that chair over there and turn on the light beside it. Here's the script; you read it, and I'll go on with my work."

VIII

So Lanny Budd spent one of the happiest half hours of his life. It seemed to him that he saw the towers of National Socialism crumbling and a new world of peace emerging—right there before his eyes. This was the fireside chat to end all chats; it was a bugle call to America and to the world. Lanny read:

> "The Axis not merely admits but proclaims that there can be no ultimate peace between their philosophy of government and our philosophy of government. . . . There can be no appeasement with ruthlessness. There can be no reasoning with an incendiary bomb. We know now that a nation can have peace with the Nazis only at the price of total surrender. . . . The British people are conducting an active war against this unholy alliance. Our own future security is greatly dependent on the outcome of that fight. . . . Democracy's fight against world conquest is being greatly aided, and must be more greatly aided, by the rearmament of the United States and by sending every ounce and every ton of munitions and supplies that we can possibly spare to help the defenders who are in the front lines. . . . There will be no 'bottlenecks' in our determination to aid Great Britain. No dictator, no combination of dictators, will weaken that determination by threats of how they will construe that determination."

When the reading was over, the P.A. was in a glow; but he sat in silence until the Chief looked up from the documents he was signing. "Well, Lanny, how is it?"

"It's absolutely gorgeous. If you don't change your mind, Governor—"

"The time for changing minds is over; now it's time for action. Have you any suggestions?"

"I remember that early in the last war Sir Edward Grey spoke of America as 'the reserve arsenal of the Allies'—I think that was it. The circumstances are the same, and you might revive that phrase. How about saying: 'We must be the great arsenal of democracy'?"

The President thought for a moment. "That's a good sentence," he decided. "Find a place where it will fit and write it in." He went back to the signing of documents, while Lanny went over the text again. When he had inserted his little sentence he was, quite literally, as happy as that unusual English dog.

IX

Lanny went back to New York by train, and two days later he received a notice that his passport was ready. He phoned to his father, who had undertaken to get him passage on a Clipper to Lisbon. These great flying boats were hard to get into now; their spaces were taken by British officers and bureaucrats of both nations. But Robbie phoned to Juan Trippe, president of Pan American Airways; when one man is flying hundreds of planes and another is making hundreds, either is pleased to do the other a favor. Mr. Trippe said: "When does your son wish to go?" and Robbie said: "As soon as possible after Christmas." The other consulted his records and asked: "Shall we make it the last day of the year?" Robbie replied: "Thanks, I will mail you a check."

The old rascal might have obtained a date before Christmas if he had asked for it, but he wanted Lanny to spend the holiday with the family. Was he thinking about keeping him out of danger a few days longer? Or had he been talking to Esther, and been told that Peggy showed a lively interest in her cousin, and that if he stayed and attended holiday festivities, he might come to realize what a desirable young person she was? Lanny wondered if his father still had in mind "that German woman" who had been haunting Beauty's thoughts for many years. Beauty didn't know that Lanny had been married to this woman, or that the Nazis had killed her in one of their torture dungeons. Robbie might be thinking that Lanny was still tied up with her, and that if he could be got interested in the right sort of girl he might settle down in Newcastle or New York.

Anyhow, Lanny stayed since he had to, and he didn't worry too much, because it is pleasanter to oblige your friends than to affront them; he danced with Peggy Remsen because it would have been rude to evade her, and she came to lunch because Esther invited her when Lanny was there. The stepmother suggested that he take the girl for a drive through the lovely winter scenery of the Connecticut uplands, and Lanny obliged; he liked winter scenery himself. He told stories about the collecting of old masters, and about the political intrigues of old Europe—such details as were fit for a virgin's ears. When she asked if he did not think the Nazis were abominable people, he explained that there were various evil forces struggling for power in Europe, and sometimes it was hard to make a choice among them.

Meantime the dreadful bombing of Britain went on night after night. It was one city, then another, and the vast sprawling capital was seldom spared. The nights were long, and this was the time of death and destruction. One result was that telegrams and telephone calls besieged Robbie Budd, and visitors came from Washington and from overseas.

They wanted planes, more planes, still more planes. They wanted Robbie to throw away caution and go ahead and expand, and when he tried to plead the interests of his stockholders they considered him a stubborn reactionary. What value would be left in the stocks of any American plant if Britain went down?

The military men of both countries kept Robbie up late at night painting pictures of the calamities they foresaw as the result of the swift development of air war. If Hitler got Britain, he would surely get Gibraltar, and then Dakar at the western bulge of Africa. They repeated their strategical question: what was to keep him from flying an army of paratroopers from there to the eastern bulge of Brazil? And when he had an airbase there, wouldn't he have all South America at his mercy? And what could we do about it? He could fly his bombers and destroy the Panama Canal, which would be the same as cutting America in halves; we should be two nations fighting two wars, one with Germany and one with Japan.

There was a limit to the stubbornness even of Robbie Budd. The governments had the power; the British and the American governments had become for all practical purposes one, with Churchill and Roosevelt talking over the telephone every night. They could commandeer Budd-Erling if they wanted to; or they could carry out their unveiled threats to build more new plants in the Middle West and hire all Robbie's experts away from him. All right, he would put up more buildings, and start a whole new schedule; but Washington must furnish every dollar, and must agree to take the plants back at cost after the war, if Robbie so desired. "After the war?" said the bureaucrats. "Christ! Who is thinking about after the war? Our job is not to be exterminated."

They were so scared that even Robbie got scared, and said to his son: "I suppose you'd better go over there and find out what Göring is up to." An extraordinary concession.

X

Lanny went to visit Hansi and Bess. He avoided politics but listened to their music, and played duets with his half-sister while Hansi was practicing in another part of the house—something he did every day, regardless of other events. Then Lanny drove into New York and got in touch with Jim Stotzlmann. It was Sunday, the 29th of December, and they had dinner in an obscure place where nobody knew them, and then went out and sat in Lanny's car. Wearing warm overcoats and with a robe over their knees, they turned on the radio in the car to hear the scheduled fireside chat. Lanny didn't feel at liberty to say that he had already read it.

They listened with rapt attention to the warm friendly voice; and they noticed a curious phenomenon—passers-by on the street heard that voice and stopped. They stayed, regardless of a wintry wind and snow on the ground. Lanny didn't know who they were; he didn't turn to look at them, but lowered the window a crack for their benefit. More and more came and nobody went away. That was the sort of compliment the humble people paid to Franklin D. Roosevelt, all over the land; the plain people, of whom there were so many, whose names never got into the newspapers, but who discussed the country's problems among themselves, made up their minds, and managed sooner or later to let the politicians know what they wanted.

It was America burning her bridges behind her; America laying down the law that Nazi-Fascism wasn't going to be permitted to take control of the world. America was going to become the great arsenal of democracy. Lanny's phrase rang out, and his heart gave a jump when he heard it. He had promised to dance a jig, but the circumstances hardly permitted that. He and his friend patted each other on the back, and were so happy they had tears in their eyes. The impromptu audience faded away silently, as if they had been eavesdropping and were embarrassed. What they thought, Lanny would only learn in the course of years, when at the ballot box and at mass meetings and in other ways the people would register endorsement of their great President's policies.

XI

Lanny had taken Peggy Remsen to see the lovely scenery of the uplands of Connecticut in winter, and it would hardly be fair not to do the same for Laurel Creston. He discovered that he liked to tell Laurel about what had happened to him, and wished that he might be free to tell more. She enjoyed riding, and from the secure peace of New England they looked back upon perils in the land of the Hitlerites. They were veterans of a war, and could enjoy the delights of fighting their battles over again. Lanny was returning to the front, and Laurel might have liked to join him but had to stay and wage what she called her feeble little war of the pen. Lanny had to remind her that the Nazis were skilled with the pen and never made the mistake of undervaluing it.

While F.D.R. had been giving his fireside chat, the Nazis had been carrying on another mass bombing of London. This time it had been with incendiaries; and while this happy couple enjoyed the winter scenery they turned on the radio and listened to details of the dreadful conflagration blazing in the very heart of the capital, the portion known as The City. Laurel had never visited it, but Lanny had known it from childhood, because Margy Petries's husband—Lord Eversham-Watson, shortened to "Bumbles"—had been a "City man," operating busily with his wife's fortune. Now Lanny told of the sights he had then seen and which no one would ever see again.

The district was small, and crowded like an ants' nest. Nobody knows why ants run their tunnels here and not there, but presumably it is because their forefathers of generations ago started that way; and just so with London City, which had enough secret doors and hidden passages to supply the writers of murder mysteries for the rest of time. In its tangle of buildings and cellars had been developed the most modern banking technique in the world, but that had changed few of its outward forms. It was a little empire inside the great empire on which the sun never set. The sovereign was the Lord Mayor of London, and he had his own police; the army of the King of England might never enter, and the King himself might enter only after an elaborate ceremony; he was represented by a sort of ambassador with the odd title of the King's Remembrancer. The odder a title was, the more the English people cherished it.

Lanny's visit had been on St. Michael's Day, because that was the day of the Lord Mayor's procession. It had been like a fairy story to see his civilian majesty riding in a golden carriage, escorted by lackeys in wigs, and the Aldermen with caps of black velvet, and the Sheriffs, and the drummers of the City Marshal, followed by the Marshal himself in violet velvet embroidered with silver. All the different Guilds had their costumes, designed more than six hundred years ago. Each had their jealously cherished privileges—for example, the Wine Merchants' Guild were the only persons, excepting the King, who were permitted to raise swans in England!

Alongside all this ancient frippery was the Bank of England, the most powerful in the world; the Stock Exchange, and the Royal Exchange, where all the currencies of the world were sold every business day; the Clearing House, a huge establishment; the Baltic, where ships were chartered for every port known; also, the five great chain banks which ruled the land's credit. In Lanny's Pink days he would have been willing to dispense with all this, but now he would mourn for it, because these great institutions had been financing the war on Nazi-Fascism all over the earth. "Including Budd-Erling fighter planes?" suggested Laurel; and he answered: "Yes, but there weren't enough of them."

XII

Robbie's man came down from Newcastle to drive Lanny to the airport and bring the car home. Lanny's two bags and his little portable typewriter were put on board the giant flying boat, and Lanny made himself comfortable in a cushioned leather seat. When he glanced about him he observed a fellow-passenger, a slender gentleman in a rumpled gray suit; a gentleman partly bald and with a pale complexion and a worried expression suggestive of poor health. Lanny had never seen him before, but the newspapers had made his features familiar to all the world. It was the top New Dealer, the Lord High Chief Boondoggler and Grand Panjandrum of Leaf-raking, the especial pet peeve of Robbie Budd and the other economic royalists: the harness-maker's son from Iowa who had become F.D.R.'s *fidus Achates,* his Man Friday, his alter ego; the former social worker who was seeking to turn America into one gigantic poorhouse, an asylum for the lazy and incompetent—a perfectly run institution, whose floors were scrubbed every morning and whose menus were according to the latest discoveries of the dietitians. At any rate, that had been Robbie Budd's idea of the man, cherished over a period of eight or nine years, and Robbie had foamed like a soda-water siphon when anybody so much as spoke the name of Harry Hopkins.

"Harry the Hop," as his Chief called him, lost no time after taking his seat in the plane, but opened up a voluminous brief case and started studying some documents. He did that through the whole trip, and Lanny didn't interrupt him. Lanny might have got attention if he had said: "I was with the President in his bedroom just after he came back from Warm Springs." But Lanny wasn't free to say that; he couldn't even say that he was the son of Budd-Erling and was going abroad on business for his father. He would have had to say: "I am an art expert and an ivory-tower dweller," and that wouldn't have interested America's hardest-worked errand boy.

Lanny knew that Harry Hopkins was on his way to England, to help make good the promises which F.D. had just proclaimed in the most public manner possible. The documents in his brief case contained the figures as to what America was prepared to do now and over the coming months; no doubt they would be put before Churchill and his aides and compared with their schedule of what they had to have. The P.A., who would have liked nothing better than to look through those documents, consoled himself by imagining a scene that would happen some day after this grim struggle was over; he would meet the harness-maker's son in the White House bedroom, and F.D. would say: "Harry, this is my friend Lanny Budd, who has been one of my most useful agents since the days before Munich. Treat him with honor, because we couldn't have won the war without him!"

10. His Faith Unfaithful

I

THE small city of Vichy was as crowded and uncomfortable as when Lanny Budd had left it, the only difference being that the broad valley of the Allier River had been blazing hot and now it was bitterly cold. The Germans took most of the fuel of France and most of the rolling stock, and the people suffered through an unusually severe winter. It seemed to Lanny that the only times he was comfortable in Vichy France were when he was walking briskly or was in one of the hotels which had been taken over as government offices.

He didn't want to be known as a secret agent, nor yet as the son of Budd-Erling Aircraft; he wanted to be a private party, earning his living by trading in art works; so he asked no help in finding accommodations, but wandered about among lodginghouses, and got a hall bedroom by the device of paying the *propriétaire* a hundred francs extra per night to move himself into his cellar. Lanny's papers were in order, and the travel permit which Laval had got for him was still good, even though the *fripon mongol* himself was in Paris, taken there by the Germans for his safety. Lanny wandered about and looked at the sights and bought the painting for old Mrs. Fotheringay and another for Mrs. Ford, and arranged to have them shipped. He could guess that his doings were being observed and that before long the observers would decide he was harmless.

Food was fairly plentiful, since the district was productive, and the Germans, trying to make friends, were not commandeering too much. Dining in the cafés, Lanny kept a lookout for familiar faces, and presently came upon a man whom he had known in Paris: a journalist-snob by the name of Jacques Benoist-Méchin, who fancied himself a man-about-town—which meant that he spent more money than he could normally earn. Young and eager to rise, he had been one of Kurt Meissner's men in Paris, and had written a two-volume work about the Wehrmacht, so well done that the Nazis had had it translated into a number of languages. Subsequently he had been taken prisoner of war, but had been released and sent to Vichy because Otto Abetz could use him there.

Now, Lanny discovered, Benoist-Méchin had been taken into the government; quite an important post, but still he couldn't live on his salary. On the side, he considered himself an authority on antiques, and Lanny purchased a small painting from him, not haggling over the high price. So they became friends, and Lanny listened to a flood of gossip, freely poured out. He had been in many a hothouse of intrigue, but never anything to compare with half-frozen Vichy. The very impotence of the government, the impossibility of doing anything, made scheming and wire-pulling and whispering secrets the main occupations of men and women. Here were enough politicians and would-be statesmen and their wives and mistresses to have governed all Europe; but they had only the smaller and poorer half of France, and could only talk about doing things, because there were German commissions in almost every town and agents all over the place, watching, reporting, and countermanding orders when they saw fit.

It gave M. Benoist-Méchin the greatest of pleasures to tell his wealthy and generous American friend all about the quarrel between the Chief of the State and his Vice-President which had shaken the world a month ago. It appeared that Lanny's informant had unwittingly been the cause, for he had suggested to his chief that it would be a gracious gesture if the Führer were to send to Paris the mortal remains of Napoleon's unhappy son, known to the French as '*L'Aiglon*'—the eaglet— who had died a semi-prisoner in Austria. The remains had been put in a crypt in Paris with a stately ceremony, and Pétain had been invited to attend; but the old Marshal had learned, or thought he had learned, that this was a trap set by the treacherous Laval to get him in German hands and keep him there. Also, Pétain had got indubitable evidence that the *fripon* had been trying to employ units of the North African army in the interest of the Germans; so he called for the resignation of all his cabinet members, and then accepted only Laval's, and ordered him to prison.

There was melodrama for you! The blond, airy-mannered young Frenchman told with many gestures how Otto Abetz had got the news in Paris and exploded into a fury and sped to Vichy with a guard of his trusted SS men. He had ordered the instant release of Laval, but hadn't quite dared to depose Pétain; there had been several days of arguing and scolding, and Benoist-Méchin had been called into consultation, a circumstance of which he was very proud. Flandin, the new Vice-President, a tall, lean appeaser from long ago, had managed to convince Abetz that he was a man to be trusted, and so the Governor of Paris had taken Laval away, and Vichy had another lease on life, though nobody would guess for how long.

II

Who was this Admiral Leahy, who called himself a Catholic, and had been sent by the Protestant Roosevelt to undermine the political foundations of Catholic France? Was it true that Roosevelt was a Freemason, and that he was Jewish or had Jewish blood? Was it true that he was in the pay of Morgan and Morgenthau and the other Wall Street Jews? Such were the questions asked by a journalist who had been reading Nazi newspapers for a decade and helping to write them. Lanny had to say that it was difficult to be sure about such matters; however, it was true that opposition to Roosevelt's interventionist tactics was rising rapidly in America, and that from what he had heard he wouldn't be in the least surprised to pick up his morning paper and read that the President had shared the fate of Laval and been deposed.

The journalist was stirred by these tidings, and pressed Lanny to know how dependable they were. Lanny wasn't free to mention Harrison Dengue, but he felt free to tell about the Nazi agents, and about the nationalists and pacifists of Detroit and Chicago and Hollywood. Also he mentioned his visit to San Simeon, and this was received with special interest, because Jacques Benoist-Méchin had for some time been Mr. Hearst's private secretary—a fact which Lanny pretended he had not known. The Frenchman had been discharged rather suddenly, and for some reason didn't have much that was good to say about his former employer. A self-willed and violent man!

It happened just as Lanny had planned; M. Benoist-Méchin repeated Lanny's stories to his superiors, and one of them was Admiral Darlan, who promptly asked that the American be invited to call. When he asked: "Why didn't you come to me first?" Lanny replied: "I was afraid you would be too busy, *mon Amiral.*" Said the blue-eyed and weather-beaten seadog: "I never let myself get too busy to see my friends." He brought out his bottle of Pernod, and warmed himself to the task of asking questions about public sentiment in America, and the chances of Vichy's getting any food and medical supplies; also about his former friends in Britain, and what significance was to be attached to the resignation of Lord Wickthorpe, and who else had been at the castle, and had anything been said as to the likelihood of the British government standing firm on the blockade of the Mediterranean ports of France?

There was at this time a clamor being raised by Herbert Hoover and others of his way of thinking, for America to send food to the needy in Europe. This pleased the Nazis and their friends, for the more food America would send, the more Hitler would be able to draw away for his own uses. He had vowed that everybody else in Europe would starve before any German starved; but of course he didn't want anybody to starve, because if they did they could no longer work to produce the goods he needed.

As to the question of the British blockade, Vichy France wanted to bring phosphates and wheat from her North African colonies and exchange them for German coal, so that the people of the towns wouldn't have to wear their overcoats in their homes and sit wrapped up in their bedclothes. Admiral Darlan was at this moment trying to make up his mind to send his Fleet to convoy merchant ships against the British blockaders, and he would have paid a handsome price to know what the British would do about it. From Lanny Budd he was hoping to get the information for nothing; but of course he couldn't get it without revealing what was in his own thoughts. That was why Lanny distributed information freely, and most of it correct, so that his questioners would want more next time. That was why he rarely sought anybody, but waited to be sought; why he rarely asked questions, but skirted around a subject and caused his interlocutor to bring it up.

By this technique a presidential agent learned that the statesmen and officials of Unoccupied France were a badly worried lot. They had surrendered their armies and the greater part of their land in the firm certainty that Britain was done for and would have to follow suit in a very short time. But seven months had passed and Britain was still holding out; and now the President of the United States had offered to throw the wealth of that vast country behind the British effort. A few days ago the President's official emissary, Admiral Leahy, had arrived and taken up his residence a few blocks from the Hotel du Parc, where the old Marshal now had both his office and home. Leahy went almost every day to see the Chief of State and poison his mind with propaganda. As a result, the old gentleman grew more stubborn and more disobliging to the Germans, who were trying so hard to be decent and to get what they wanted without having to take it. Admiral Darlan wanted to give it to them, because his hatred of the British had become implacable since the episode of Oran, or as the French called it, Mers-el-Khébir, where the British had attacked Darlan's Fleet and put several of his best units out of action.

Lanny didn't go near the Hotel du Parc and didn't seek to meet the old Marshal again. He had been told to keep away from Admiral Leahy, and was glad to do it, for he had to send a secret report in care of this Irish-Catholic officer, and knew that he would be guessing as to the identity of the mysterious "Zaharoff." Let sleeping admirals lie! Lanny collected the information he wanted, and then, wrapping himself in his bedclothes and blowing frequently upon his fingers, he typed his report and saw it delivered by a messenger at the Admiral's residence. Then he went back to sleep in his warm tweed overcoat.

III

One of the significant aspects of the conquest of France was the economic squeeze which the Germans were applying to the country. A scientific-minded people, the Germans had experts in every field to tell them how to accomplish their purposes with the least pain and alarm to the victim. Their head financial wizard was Herr Doktor Hjalmar Horace Greeley Schacht, who shortly before the war broke out had applied to Robbie Budd in the hope that Robbie might help him get a job in America—so discouraged was he by the impending bankruptcy of his Fatherland. But the Herr Doktor was still on the Führer's job, and had devised the wondrous plan whereby the French were printing banknotes to the amount of four hundred million francs per day and turning them over to the Germans, supposedly for the upkeep of the German army of occupation; the Germans were using them to buy up the key industries of France, the steel mills, the munitions plants, the coal mines, the electrical and aluminum installations.

They had numerous commissions investigating and negotiating, and the Vichy Government had a commission in Paris to deal with them; whenever some member of this latter commission was stubborn and wouldn't do what the Germans wanted, they would have him removed and a more pliant tool appointed. This was like squeezing blood, not out of a stone, not out of a turnip, but out of a living creature, and the cries and struggles of the squeezed were pitiful. It was a part of Lanny's job to investigate these matters, and he went about in fashionable society hearing the gossip, and smiling secretly in his soul—for some of these refugees were the serene and masterful gentlemen whom he had met at the home of Schneider the armaments king. Lanny had heard them repeat the formula so popular with the "two hundred families" who ruled France: "Better Hitler than Blum!" Now they had their Hitler, and he was wringing the financial blood out of them.

Benoist-Méchin, knowing the German language well, was serving as a sort of liaison official with the Germans who came to Vichy. He knew them all, and called many his friends, and at Lanny's request he invited to lunch a certain Doktor Jaeckl, one of Schacht's leading assistants. He was one of those shaven-headed bulky Prussians with necks like their well-stuffed sausages, and Lanny had met him at the home of Doktor Goebbels, and again at Heinrich Jung's. The Prussian remembered it, for who could forget an American who was known to be a personal friend of the Führer's?

He was a jovial pirate, and Lanny imparted information concerning London and New York and Washington, and explained the excruciating embarrassment under which he suffered because his father's plant had been practically commandeered by the Roosevelt conspirators and compelled to make planes for the British. Doktor Jaeckl said it was indeed a shocking thing, the disregard for property rights that was spreading over the world; it all came from Moscow, the center of political and moral infection, and National Socialism offered humanity's only hope of immunization. Herr Benoist-Méchin could testify that the Germans were scrupulous in paying for everything they took; and Herr Benoist-Méchin spoke up promptly, like a perfect stooge. "*Ja, freilich!*"

IV

Toward the end of the *dejeuner à la fourchette* Lanny said: "I wonder if you know my old friend Kurt Meissner?" The Herr Doktor replied that of course he did; this great *Musiker* was one of the jewels in the Nazi crown. He didn't say anything about the services which Kurt had rendered as an agent of the *Generalstab*, in hiring men like Benoist-Méchin and preparing France for conquest. Lanny explained: "The last time I saw him was in Paris in June, when the Führer invited us to join him on his visit to the Invalides—you may remember that he went to inspect the tomb of Napoleon."

"I remember it very well, Herr Budd."

"I would like to get in touch with Kurt again. He goes to Stubendorf for the holidays, but it is about time he was back in Paris. I wonder if you can tell me the proper official to whom I should apply for permission to write him and let him know that I am here?"

"I shouldn't think there would be any trouble in arranging that, Herr Budd. The restrictions on mail across the border are a necessary military precaution, but they do not apply to persons such as yourself."

"What I want is to tell Kurt my address here, and that I have information which would be of importance to him. That is all I need to say, and the letter can be inspected by the proper official. You will understand that it is not a matter I should want to have generally discussed."

"*Selbsverständlich, mein Herr,*" said the Nazi, and added: "If that is all you desire, I can help you to save delay. I am flying to Paris tomorrow, and will be glad to call Kurt Meissner and give him your message."

"Thank you ever so much, Herr Doktor. It will be a great favor. You will find him at the Crillon, I believe; and if he has not yet returned to Paris, you might be so kind as to leave a memo for him."

V

So it came about that, several days later, Lanny found a note at his lodging—Kurt had been there to look for him. Kurt was at one of the hotels, for of course there were always accommodations for an important Nazi. Half an hour later Lanny was in his room and they embraced with old-time warmth. Boyhood feelings are hard to eradicate from the heart, and even though Lanny despised what Kurt was doing, he couldn't entirely forget the happy old times at Stubendorf.

A man is what his heredity and environment have made him. Kurt had been brought up under the stern Prussian system; his father had been a trusted employe of a high-up nobleman, and Kurt and his brothers had been drilled and disciplined in the sternest army regime in the world. Kurt's first wife and child had been victims of World War I, and Kurt had learned to hate the French just as the French hated him. When, after the defeat, his superiors in the Wehrmacht had ordered him to use his knowledge of France and his skill as a musician to reverse the results of Versailles, Kurt had obeyed without question.

For seven years he had been Beauty Budd's lover and Lanny's friend and almost stepfather; he had lived at Bienvenu, and had used the Budd family's social connections as a means of getting introductions and information. After Hitler had come into power he was sent back to France to use these talents and opportunities in the service of Nazism. Now, in the days of triumph, he was still obeying orders, and feeling himself completely vindicated in his life's course. "*Hitler hat immer recht!*"

It had taken Lanny a long time to wake up to the meaning of these intricate and subtle deceptions, but in the end he had come to understand clearly that you couldn't be friends with a Nazi; a Nazi was the enemy of every non-Nazi in the world. Even if you, a non-German, adopted the hateful creed, you didn't really get anywhere; the true *Herrenvolk* would use you, but in their hearts they would despise you as a traitor to your own kind and a dupe of the Nazi *Weltbetrug*. The Nazis had chosen Loki, god of lies, for their Nordic deity, and all other peoples had to learn to live under his scepter.

Lanny had heard long ago the German saying: "When you are with the wolves you must howl with them," and when he was in Naziland he howled in the most reserved and dignified manner. He made speeches about National-Socialist achievements and destiny which sounded to the Nazis almost inspired; and when he met Kurt he embraced him, and looked with utter devotion into those long and heavily lined features. He listened to Kurt's latest composition and sang its praise, he played four-hand piano compositions with an eminent virtuoso, and he poured out news about Britain and America, proclaiming how many Nazi sympathizers there were in those benighted lands, and how diligently he himself was working to spread an understanding of the great Führer and his benevolent intentions toward the world he was taking in charge.

VI

Kurt had flown from Paris because of his certainty that Lanny wouldn't bring him to Vichy for nothing. Alone in the hotel room over a dinner served at Wehrmacht expense Lanny gave first the human and personal news from Bienvenu and Wickthorpe and Newcastle. Kurt hadn't quarreled with Beauty when he had left her to marry a proper German *Mädchen*, and he always paid tribute to Beauty's kindness and generosity. He knew that Irma Barnes was a near-Fascist, and had no idea that it was this fact which had wrecked Lanny's marriage. Kurt knew Robbie Budd well and admired him; understanding Robbie's reactionary views, he was prepared to believe that Robbie was still among the Roosevelt-haters and diligently sabotaging Roosevelt efforts to force him into making fighter planes for the Royal Air Force. Had Kurt heard that the Budd-Erling had been found unsatisfactory by the British, and that their flyers refused to trust their lives to it? Yes, Kurt had heard that; it was Kurt's role to hear of everything—didn't he have at his disposal the most wonderful intelligence service in the world? Lanny could reveal just why Budd-Erling was behind and going to stay behind. That was good news indeed for the Luftwaffe, and worth a flight from Paris by one of the Wehrmacht's trusted agents.

But that was only a curtain raiser. This son of Budd-Erling, in the course of his picture-selling business—something that Kurt looked upon with concealed disdain—had been traveling all over the United States, talking with people of all classes, and had the most interesting account to give of the firmly rooted determination for peace which he had encountered everywhere, north, south, east, and west. Among influential and powerful persons there was rapidly spreading the conviction that Roosevelt was mentally irresponsible and must at all costs be prevented from carrying on his war-mongering campaign. Lanny told about the country-club conversations in Newcastle and Baltimore, and about the cowboy Rough Riders of Hollywood; also about the guests of San Simeon, and the things they had said on election night. He told about his intimate talks with Hearst, and didn't have to conform exactly to the facts; where the isolationist publisher had been reserved, Lanny could make him bold and defiant in voicing his admiration for the Führer.

As for the "junta," Lanny wasn't free to name the rebellious persons, but that was unnecessary, for this was a story which Kurt would have no difficulty in believing. Had not Hitler's own followers made plans to depose him a year or so after he took power, and had he not been obliged to slaughter some twelve hundred of them in a dreadful blood purge? A Nazi secret agent wouldn't see any reason for expecting America to be free from similar convulsions, and would be sure that persons who thought otherwise were the crudest of dupes.

VII

Lanny had put up the price; and now, would he get what he wanted? As a rule he got less from Kurt than from others, for Kurt was naturally a reticent man, and years as a secret agent had taught him distrust of nearly everyone. But he was fond of Lanny, and thought of him as a pupil; though only a year and a half older, Kurt had always taken that attitude. When Lanny said: "I am worried sick over this war; it is going to be a long one, and that is surely not what the Führer wanted," the Wehrmacht man replied: "The Führer didn't want any war; but since it was forced upon him, be sure that he isn't going to fail. Our scientists have devised weapons that will knock the British off their pins."

"New weapons take a long time to get into production, Kurt."

"Don't worry; we are further along than anybody guesses. You can take my word that I have sources of information."

"I don't doubt that. What worries me is my own country going into mass production."

"It will be all over before America can do anything much. Your productive system is a chaos, everybody going his own way and seeking his own profit. And remember, the goods have to cross the sea. Our U-boats have new devices to operate in the dark, and this winter our blockade is more complete than the world has any idea of."

Lanny wouldn't ask questions about these crucial matters; he would keep quiet and let his friend expound so long as the spirit moved him. In the old days Kurt had expounded the subtleties of Kantian metaphysics and the esoteric intricacies of Beethoven's later string quartets. Now his mind was on the maze of European diplomacy and the broad outlines of military strategy, the movements of armies and supplies, and the economic advantages to be gained in one place as compared to another. The young Kurt had been gravely concerned with moral questions, but now morals no longer had anything to do with the affairs of nations; what helped Germany was right, and what hindered her was wrong.

Whatever it was Kurt discussed, he always spoke with authority.

At the age of thirteen Lanny had been enormously impressed by this manner, and by the long abstract German words he had never heard before. Now, at the age of forty, he pretended to have the same attitude; but he could never feel entirely certain about Kurt's attitude toward him. Could it be that Kurt saw through Lanny as clearly as Lanny saw through Kurt? Was their continued intimacy due to the fact that Kurt set a higher value on what he got from Lanny than on what he gave? Hitler had used Lanny as an errand boy to take messages to the right people in Paris and London and New York, and no doubt he had taken precautions to check up and make sure that the messages were delivered properly. Kurt had no knowledge of anything else that Lanny had done, and as long as Hitler was satisfied with him, Kurt would of course play along.

Making things easier, Lanny inquired: "Do you suppose the Führer would want to see me these days?"

"Why not? He has always wanted to see you, when he wasn't too busy."

"I know he won't hold me responsible for Roosevelt's warmongering, but it seems to me it would be hard for him to endure the sight of any American."

"I don't think he has any such feeling. The Führer's doctrine is for all mankind, and any man who accepts it is his friend. The next time I see him I will mention the matter."

Lanny said: "Thank you," and at the same time made note that Kurt didn't say: "You can write him a letter and I will mail it for you in Paris." Could it be that Kurt was slightly jealous of the favor his great hero had shown to Kurt's American disciple? So many things to wonder about!

Lanny went on: "Don't think that I am trying to thrust myself forward. You know I have never asked a favor of the Führer, and I am thinking only of the cause. More than once he has told me what he wants me to say about his policies and purposes; and some of those who question me are people of great influence, as you know."

"Yes, indeed, Lanny. You can say that neither his policies nor his purposes have changed."

"That doesn't satisfy them. They say: 'Yes, but it's been seven or eight months since you saw him, and a lot of water has flowed over the dam. What does he want *now*? What are his terms?'"

"He set them forth in his great speech last month, Lanny."

"I know; but people of importance never take it for granted that a statesman means exactly what he says. They want something confidential, something personal. I have said to them: 'This is what the Führer said to me with his own lips'; and that impresses them more than I can tell you. For example, Hearst; the thing he wanted to know more than any other was whether the Führer really meant to put down Bolshevism all over Europe. Just a few days ago one of the most important persons in our United States officialdom put the point-blank question to me: 'If we succeed in getting Britain off Hitler's back, can we count upon it that he will go after Stalin?'—or words to that effect. This is one of the men who may be helping to depose Roosevelt at any time. His decision to act or not to act might depend upon what I tell him when I go back."

This was fishing in deep waters. Kurt demanded: "What can such a person expect of the Führer, more definite than he has put into his speeches, of his utter loathing for the Reds and everything they stand for? But you must remember, we have . a treaty of mutual non-aggression with Russia, and we have trade agreements also."

"My understanding is that you're not getting very much out of the trading."

"That is true, and we raise rows about it, but that is a different matter from going to war. Even if the Führer had such a purpose, his generals would hardly permit him to announce it in advance."

"Of course not, Kurt. But if he had the idea to whisper it to one discreet person, who would take it directly to one of the most influential men in London, and then to one or two in New York and Washington—that might be just enough to turn the scales in the struggles over policy now going on."

"What you say is truly important, Lanny," replied the *Komponist*. "I can't give the answer, but I'll see that the Führer has a chance to consider it."

VIII

These two cronies spent the rest of the day and evening together. Kurt had recently been in Stubendorf, where Lanny had spent half a dozen Christmases in his boyhood and youth. Kurt talked about his family, to whom the American in happier times had always sent gifts; he was "Onkel Lanny" to the children. Kurt told about the General Graf Stubendorf, who had been host to Lanny and Irma; he had been badly hurt by an artillery shell and was home at the castle. And then Kurt's older brother, General Emil Meissner, also home for the holidays; he had come through the campaign of the Argonne with flying colors and had been promoted to command an army *Korps*. Emil, Lanny knew, had been studying mass slaughter from his days in the nursery, when he had wiped out a whole *Korps* with a sweep of his tiny hand; he still did it on sheets of paper with little oblongs which he drew with colored crayons. He was considered one of the greatest authorities on logistics in the Wehrmacht, and he was known as one of the "Nazi Generals," since he shared Kurt's admiration for the greatest political genius the German race had ever produced.

Did the Führer's favorite musician, moved by all these family reminiscences, fail to realize what he was saying? Or had he thought it over and decided that Lanny was entitled to share a few of the Wehrmacht's secrets? Anyhow, Kurt told about discussions with his brother concerning the grave questions of strategy now up for decision. Kurt didn't say: "We are engaged in undermining the governments of Hungary, Rumania, and Yugoslavia, and soon we shall be able to move into those lands without serious fighting." He took this for granted, and talked about the next move, balancing various forces involved. Mussolini—"*dieser verdammte Esel*"—had got himself into a mess in Greece, and of course the Führer would have to get him out. The question was, when you had Greece, where would you go from there?

Lanny said: "You could take Crete with paratroopers, and that would put you in a position to bomb the Suez Canal full of sand. At any rate, that is what the British are expecting."

"They may get it. The question is Turkey; how much she can resist, and how much she will."

"Usually with the Turks it's a question of money, Kurt."

"Unfortunately the British have more gold than we. The main problem with us is to reach oil; and we have to decide between Mesopotamia and the Caucasus."

This was after they had had dinner, and Kurt had absorbed the greater part of a liter of Burgundy. Lanny had never seen Kurt drink too much, but he had seen him become mellow and eloquent, and this was one of the times. It is always a pleasure to talk to somebody who knows almost as much about a subject as yourself, and can appreciate every nuance of your instructed disquisitions. When Lanny exclaimed: "But you can't go into Turkey with your left flank exposed to the Russians for a thousand miles!" Kurt knew that he was talking to someone who had been looking at maps and at least hearing about the principles of the great Clausewitz.

"Don't worry too much," he answered. "I am quite sure that before this year is over you will see the Bolshevik menace eliminated from Europe."

This caused Lanny to look his friend straight in the eyes. "Listen, Kurt," he said earnestly. "I want you to get this exactly right. You know that I have never once asked you any question about confidential matters. That is true, is it not?"

"Yes, that is true."

"If you were to ask the Führer, he would tell you the same thing about me. I want to know only what he wants me to know, and what he is willing for me to pass on to others. Every time he has told me anything about his plans and purposes, he has said: 'Tell that to your friends abroad.' You have heard him say it."

"Yes, Lanny."

"All right. And make note of this: I didn't ask you anything about Russia. I wouldn't feel that, as your friend, I had a right to do so. But you have just told me something of great importance, and you haven't said: 'That is strictly between us.' What I want to make clear is, if I could say I *knew* that, if I could say I had it on the highest authority, I might be able to render a very great service to National Socialism. If I could say it to Ceddy Wickthorpe, it might be the means of over-throwing the Churchill Cabinet."

"You think Wickthorpe has such power as that?"

"Surely not, but he is one of a group that has great power—how much is something they couldn't say until they try to use it. They know that life in England is horrible, and that the people cannot stand it much longer. What Ceddy and his friends want is for Germany to fight Russia instead of Britain; they would be willing to help Germany in that, if necessary. Their political careers have been based upon such a program; and in the days before the war, as you know, I carried messages to them for both the Führer and Rudi Hess. But now my information is out-of-date. I can't say that I know what the Führer intends to do, and on my last trip to London and New York I was handicapped by that fact."

"I see your point clearly enough."

"Once more I repeat, I'm not asking you to tell me. It may be that you haven't the right to do it, and if you say so, I'll understand. All I'm explaining is what I would do with the information if I had it. The men I am in contact with in Newcastle and New York and Washington and Detroit and Chicago are making the goods which are being shipped to Britain, and they might be able to stop the procedure if they could feel certain what the consequences would be. They want the assurance that Germany will not use the breathing spell to go on arming against the West, but will carry out the program which Hess has explained to me so many times: that Germany will make a real settlement with the British Empire, and be content with what she can find to the east of her—as far as she wants to go."

IX

Kurt sat for a while in thought. It may well have been the weightiest decision he had ever been called upon to make. At last he said: "I understand your position, and I think you are right. I had a talk with the Führer in Berlin just before Christmas. I played for him a couple of hours in the New Chancellery. He did not state that what he told me was confidential, but of course he knew he didn't have to say that. I am sure that if he were here now and heard your statement, he would tell you the facts. I am sure that Rudi knows them, and he would tell you. Anyhow, it could hardly do harm from the military point of view, because the Russians are so mistrustful of everybody that they never know what to believe. I have no doubt they get a dozen rumors every day as to the Führer's intentions, and they wouldn't pay much heed to reports from American sources."

Tense as Lanny was, he permitted himself a smile. "How well you know them, Kurt!"

"Be sure that we get reports about them, also. But here is the point: the Führer told me that his mind was made up, we can no longer carry on a war while having that menace along our eastern border. He intends to eliminate it this spring, certainly not later than June, depending upon how quickly the Balkan affairs go."

"It is a colossal undertaking, Kurt."

"Our *Oberkommando* does not think so. Russia is a flat land, and we shall encounter none of the obstacles we found in the Ardennes and the Argonne. Our Panzer divisions will roll with speed that will astound you."

"But the Soviets have many fortresses, have they not?"

"We shall by-pass them. We shall roll around their armies and slaughter them like flocks of sheep. We are confident that we can finish the job in six weeks; Emil thinks even less."

"Well, Kurt, that is the most important secret I have ever been entrusted with, and I appreciate the honor you have done me."

"You understand, Lanny, I cannot afford to be named as the source of it."

"Oh, surely not! All I need to be able to say is that I have it on authority. The people I deal with are old friends, like Ceddy, and they have had time to learn that I don't indulge in idle gossip. I will put the information to work as quickly as possible." Lanny didn't say any more than that, because he never lied unnecessarily.

The two friends parted with every expression of affection and trust; and Lanny went back to his unheated room, set up his little portable, wrapped himself in the blankets, blew on his chilled fingers, and wrote:

"Hitler has decided to attack Russia this spring, not later than June. This is positive, as of this date. He expects to finish the job in six weeks."

This he double-sealed in the usual way, always using a different kind of stationery. He addressed it to Admiral Leahy, and though it was late at night he found a messenger and stood in the shadows where he could see the letter delivered to the man who answered the bell. That was all for the moment, but before the P.A. left Vichy he took the precaution to write a second note and have it delivered in the same way. Perhaps the two would go in the same diplomatic pouch and by the same plane, but F.D.R. would understand and appreciate the care being taken.

X

The visiting art expert paid another call upon Admiral Darlan, and after making himself agreeable over the Pernod, remarked: "*Mon Amiral*, I have a mother living in Juan-les-Pins whom I have not seen for a long time, and, as you know, travel is extremely difficult. I have the necessary permit, but it is a question of transportation, and it occurred to me to wonder whether your Marine might have a *camion* or other vehicle traveling to the coast on which I might stow away."

"*Sapristi!*" replied the old seadog. "We do not ship our friends as freight. We have planes flying every day, and sooner or later there will be a vacant seat. When do you wish to go?"

"The sooner the better, *mon Amiral*."

"*Bien*, I will see what can be done for you. Call my secretary in a couple of hours."

"One thing more," ventured Lanny. "As you know, my business is with paintings, and I have learned of a collection in Toulon which might be of interest to some of my American clients. Perhaps you may know the old gentleman, M. d'Avrienne." Lanny Budd had been collecting names and addresses of picture owners throughout France over a period of almost two decades, and he had a list always with him.

"I know him by reputation," replied Darlan.

The other hastened to add: "I am not seeking an introduction, only the entrée to the town. I know that in wartime a stranger does not just walk into a naval fortress."

"I will give you a letter to the commandant of the port," said the Admiral. "He will be interested in what you have to tell about both our friends and our enemies."

Yes, it was a pleasant world to live in if you had the good fortune to know the right people. It was a temptation to forget the existence of other people and enjoy the good things that were available. Lanny called the secretary and learned that he could have a seat in a plane flying to Marseille the next day; so he bade farewell to his Vichy friends, telling them, strictly *entre nous*, that he believed things were going to be better soon. Since they could not well be worse, this was possible to believe.

XI

The Massif Central of France, barren and snow-covered, unrolled like a carpet below the traveler; and then the mountains and the fertile valleys with vineyards and olive groves of the Midi. By Lanny's side rode a naval lieutenant, and they chatted freely, so that when they came down in the great Marseille airport they were friends. It developed that the young officer was proceeding to the Italian border on some official errand, and he was interested in this American gentleman who enjoyed the favor of an *amiral* and who spoke French so eloquently. Three other officers were traveling in the staff car, and it would be crowded, but they offered to squeeze Lanny in; a great favor at a time when *essence* was practically non-existent.

The guest made himself agreeable to such good effect that when they came to Cannes and learned that his home was on the Cap, they volunteered to make a slight detour. There was a tumult of welcome from the dogs, and Baby Marcel toddled out, shouting. The *officiers de marine* perceived that this was an elegant place, and when Lanny invited them in to have coffee they reasoned that it would be too late to transact any business that day, so why not?

In the well-shaded drawing-room Beauty Budd was still the most charming of hostesses; her wrinkles showed only in bright sunlight, and she never let strange gentlemen catch her there if she could help it. When she learned that they had brought her darling son all the way from Vichy she put herself out to make them feel at home; when they learned that she was the former Madame Budd of the famous Budd-Erling Aircraft and knew many distinguished persons of French social and political life, they exhibited pleasure to such effect that they were urged to stay for dinner. "*Pas de gêne*," insisted Madame; most of their food was now grown on the place, a wise precaution in wartime; the only trouble was the impossibility of getting about, so when you had company in the house you wanted to make the most of them.

There was the very kind old gentleman with snow-white hair and rosy cheeks who was Madame Budd's present husband. All Frenchmen understood that American ladies changed their husbands frequently, and they found the circumstance novel and amusing. It did not interfere with their enjoyment of a good onion soup with *croutons*, and then of a large fish called *mérou* which had come that morning out of the Golfe Juan and had been stuffed with breadcrumbs and chestnuts and slices of bacon, and baked in an oven. Yes, people know how to live on the Côte d'Azur, and there were fashion and gaiety even in the midst of war. Madame Budd told how she had had to jack her two motorcars up off the wheels, but from an old barn she had resurrected an almost-forgotten buggy and had it scrubbed and painted and the wheels greased, and now could drive herself magnificently into Cannes behind a proper middle-aged horse which she had purchased from one of the flower growers on the Cap.

XII

So Lanny was home again, amid the scenes of his childhood so dear to his heart. Here everybody knew him and loved him, here nature held out soft warm arms to him, and art invited him in the aspect of a marble Greek goddess in the court. In his study was a library, and every time he looked at the titles he was tempted to take down a book and lose himself in its pages. There were a piano and several cabinets full of music; there was the ever-fascinating subject of child study, and also the seeming-infinite field of psychic research, which drew Lanny Budd as the New World had drawn Columbus. Madame Zyszynski was waiting to try experiments with him, and indeed would have her feelings hurt if he neglected this duty. Hidden in the subconscious mind of the old Polish woman were forces which tantalized Lanny with their mystery; from her lips in trance had come words which had brought to him the feelings of that watcher of the skies in Keats's sonnet—when a new planet sweeps into his ken.

They rarely mentioned the subject of politics in the family; it had become too cruel and wicked in these times. Lanny talked about old masters, and left it to be supposed that they were his reason for traveling about over the Western World. Parsifal Dingle rested in the certainty that his duty was to set an example of loving kindness, in the certainty that men could not resist its divine force. Lanny would have liked to ask how love could make progress when all the forces of several mighty states were concentrated upon the teaching of hatred to a whole generation of childhood and youth; but that would have been a painful question, and Lanny suspected that his stepfather deliberately closed his mind to it. God was wiser than men, and God left it for men to make whatever blunders they pleased, and to learn by the hard way they seemed to prefer. In Lanny's mind was the question which no philosopher had thus far succeeded in answering: Why had God chosen to make them like that?

Lanny had to tell his mother about all the places he had been and all the people he had met, and what they were doing and what they had said. If he had failed to look up any old friend she would make gentle complaint, and when he had told her everything he could think of she would ask for more. Here she was, to all practical purposes a prisoner, cut off from communication with the outside world, and that Lanny had been able to travel to London and then to New York and back again was simply a miracle. All he could say was: "Well, you know Robbie generally manages to get what he wants; and his very survival in the business world depends upon his knowing what is going to happen in this war."

"And what *is* going to happen, Lanny?"

It was a question she had asked him on his last visit, and he gave her the answer again. "It will be a long war, old dear, and you might as well make up your mind to it."

Beauty paled, even under the *rouge vinaigre* which she skillfully applied. "As long as the last one, Lanny?"

"Certainly that long, perhaps longer."

"Oh, Lanny, I can't stand it! I shall die of the horror!"

"That won't shorten the war any. Make up your mind that you didn't start it and you can't stop it. Cultivate the ancient art of surviving." He couldn't say more than that, for she had too many friends here and they were all full of curiosity about Lanny and his doings.

XIII

Parsifal Dingle had a stack of psychic records for his stepson to examine. He rarely missed a day without a séance, and he had a mass of data concerning the monastery of Dodanduwa in Ceylon. He was firmly convinced that the voices he heard from Madame's lips were those of monks dead more than a hundred years, and he was fascinated by the idea of tracing the evolution of certain doctrines of this religion, more than five thousand years old. It was no longer possible to communicate with the living monks, but Parsifal declared that as soon as the war was over he intended to visit the place and check his findings. He had quite a library of books on New Thought and what was now called "parapsychology." Lanny, rummaging among these books and pamphlets, came upon one dealing with the Upanishads, and containing many of the doctrines in question. Parsifal declared that he hadn't read this book, and there could be no doubt that he was sincere; but Lanny speculated upon the possibility that he might have read and forgotten it, and it had stayed and worked in his subconscious mind.

Even if you supposed that, you had not solved the problem, for the words had been spoken, not by Parsifal but by Madame Zyszynski, and surely Parsifal had never expounded these doctrines to this former servant, and if he had, she wouldn't have had the remotest idea what he was talking about. Here was Lanny again, fooling with "that old telepathy"; the idea that the subconscious mind was in some way one mind, just as the ocean is one ocean. It was his favorite simile.

Lanny took the feeble old woman off to his study and seated her in the easy chair which she knew so well and which may have had some effect upon her mind, or minds. And here came Tecumseh, grumbling at a skeptical playboy as he had done for more than a decade. Presently he announced that there was the spirit of an old lady named Mary who insisted that she had met Lanny in New York; but Lanny couldn't recall her, and was bored. Then came the quavering voice of Zaharoff, greatly distressed because Lanny hadn't even tried to pay the munitions king's debt in Monte Carlo, and refusing to be satisfied with Lanny's excuses that he didn't have the money, and anyhow, nobody could get to Monte Carlo at present, it was surrounded by the Italian army, and an American would have to get permission from Washington as well as Rome. Hadn't Zaharoff heard about the war? The Knight Commander said of course he had; and then he added something that made Lanny shiver to the soles of his feet: "What do you mean by using my name the way you have been doing?"

There was only one person in the world besides Lanny who was supposed to know that Lanny was using the name of Zaharoff. That was Lanny's Boss, and he was too busy to be fooling with trance mediums or talking with spooks. But here was the former Knight Commander of the Bath and Grand Officier de la Légion d'Honneur fussing about it, and saying that his relatives on earth would sue Lanny for libel if they knew about it—and maybe he would tell them! This was something for a P.A. to think over for a long time—and to worry over. He decided that he would be careful about whom he allowed to attend séances with Madame, or for that matter with any medium!

XIV

Lanny had told his two friends of the underground, Monck in Switzerland and Palma in France, approximately when he might return to Bienvenu and be expecting a letter. He wasn't sure about letters from Switzerland to Occupied France, but presumably the underground would have ways of dealing with such a problem. However, Lanny had found no letter from either man, and he didn't like to go off on another jaunt without giving them time. It was a reason for yielding to temptation and doing what he pleased for a while. He felt very proud over what he had accomplished with Kurt, and told himself that it entitled him to a rest.

He could picture what would happen when F.D. got that note; he would instruct Sumner Welles to warn Oumansky, and that lively and genial but decidedly skeptical Soviet Ambassador would no doubt pass it on to Stalin, his personal friend. From Hitler to Kurt to F.D. to Welles to Oumansky to Stalin—that made it sixth-hand information, and no doubt it would lose most of its urgency in the journey. The P.A. could only say: "I did my best."

He read and played the piano and consulted the "spooks." Driving his mother's nag, he paid a duty call upon his near-fostermother, Emily Chattersworth. With Beauty he dined at the villa of Sophie and her husband and played a rubber of contract. He played tennis and went fishing with his old crony, Jerry Pendleton. He danced with his tiny nephew, whose mother was dancing in Berlin and couldn't visit or even write. No doubt she, like all others in Hitlerland, had been shocked by the length of the war, so contrary to promises. Lanny had to tell his mother that Berlin had been bombed by the British; not much as yet, but more was coming, because America was making big planes—the best for British purposes, since they could fly the ocean and the subs couldn't get at them.

There was domestic mail inside Vichy France, but irregular and uncertain. At last came a letter, one of that inconspicuous kind which meant so much to a secret agent. It was from Toulon, and informed M. Budd, in French, that the writer had come upon a small but very good collection of Daumier drawings which might be purchased for something like fifty thousand francs. The writer, who signed himself Bruges, said that he was employed in Armand Mercier's bookstore in Toulon, and would be happy to show the drawings at any time. Daumier being an artist of the people, a satirist of the privileged classes of his time, would have understood and loved Raoul Palma's underground friends. The sum named, worth about five hundred dollars at the moment, represented the funds Raoul wanted Lanny to bring.

So the secret agent knew that his holiday was at an end. He borrowed his mother's conveyance and drove into Cannes and drew the money from the bank; then he purchased various presents for friends and servants, as a means of getting small denomination bills. Having all his pockets stuffed with money, he went to see Jerry Pendleton at the latter's travel bureau. Lanny explained that he could buy some fine Daumier drawings in Toulon, if only he could find a way to get there. Jerry grinned and replied: "I know a nice polite pirate who will take you, and he'll agree to the price in my presence, so that he won't dare ask more than twice the amount. *C'est la guerre!*"

11. Defend Me from My Friends!

I

JERRY'S "pirate" showed up at eight o'clock in the morning with a reasonably efficient car, a tank full of *essence*, and three twenty-liter cans in the rear compartment, to complete a round trip of some two hundred miles. How he had got this he didn't say, and it would have been bad form to ask. Lanny was to have two full days in Toulon, according to the bargain, and if he stayed longer was to pay five hundred francs per day. He was to be limited to a hundred kilometers for driving about town, otherwise there wouldn't be enough fuel to bring them home. Étienne, the driver, would probably try to add other charges, Jerry warned; and Lanny said he would pay them if they were not too extreme, for he might want to take more trips in the future.

This one was without incident. Étienne was a discharged soldier and had adventures to tell. He understood that an American gentleman had nothing to do but enjoy life and did not bother himself with politics. Étienne had brought along a supply of cognac, which Lanny might have enjoyed for a price, but he didn't want any, and requested the driver to keep it corked. Also, Étienne knew a very nice girl who lived on the route, but Lanny said he had an important engagement with the commandant of the port; he didn't say anything about having his pockets stuffed with banknotes of all sizes.

Toulon is the naval base and arsenal of Mediterranean France. It is surrounded by high hills, like nearly all that shore, and every hill is fortified. Below lies a deep harbor with immense breakwaters and moles, and four great basins, called *darses*, in which lay long gray-painted battleships and cruisers and, tied up against the piers, several rows of destroyers and smaller warcraft, many of them *déclassés*. It wouldn't do to manifest too great interest in this fleet, or to ask questions; but Étienne pointed out the *Dunquerque* and the *Strasbourg*, two battleships which had got away from the British at Mers-el-Khébir. He cursed the treacherous friends who had committed that act, and the passenger made no comment.

There was a commercial harbor, and a town of some hundred thousand population, now swelled by refugees; the British blockade having cut off most of the traffic, people were having a hard time to get along. Everywhere were sailors, wearing little round caps with bright red pompons on top. Lanny went to the Grand Hotel and was told that it was crowded; he asked to see the manager and exhibited his credentials from Admiral Darlan, whereupon a room was found for him. Losing no time, he telephoned to the office of the commandant, and was received with all courtesy by a dapper old gentleman—the heads of the French Army and Navy were invariably elderly, and while they were well trained in the technicalities of their jobs they were nearly always stiffly conservative, and hadn't had a new idea since the days of the Dreyfus case.

Yes, this commandant knew the d'Avrienne family well, and was familiar with their collection of paintings, one of the cultural monuments of the city. He had no doubt that they would be pleased to have an American *connoisseur* inspect them; the officer wrote a note of introduction, and had one of his aides make out a *carte d'identification*, which would spare him formalities with the police and port authorities. Lanny went back to his hotel and telephoned to the mansion, which lay in a sheltered valley behind one of the hills of the suburbs. He was told that the master was ill, but that the paintings would be shown to him in the morning—it would be better to view them by daylight. Since the visitor didn't care to wander about a harbor town at night with all that money, he stayed in his room, wearing his overcoat in bed and reading *War and Peace*. Étienne had put his car in a garage and was sleeping in it, for fear that somebody might pour off the precious *essence* and fill the cans with something cheaper.

II

In the morning a middle-aged daughter of this ship-owning family showed M. Budd the paintings, a rather commonplace collection, mostly family portraits. Lanny admired them, as courtesy required, and made his usual tactful inquiry as to whether any of them might be for sale. Then he was driven back to town, went for a stroll, and without saying anything to anybody found the secondhand bookshop of Armand Mercier. He went in and took a quick look, but didn't see Raoul Palma. He began looking at the books, a practice which takes much longer in France than it usually does in America; you can stand and get yourself an education dipping into one old book after another, just as you can sit in a café and read a whole newspaper while you sip one cup of coffee.

There was a woman clerk, and Lanny stole glances at her. Was this a leftwing place, and were the proprietors in touch with the underground? The books were of all kinds, and the few that dealt with politics had no special character; but that meant nothing, for if a man had a stock of anti-Nazi or anti-Fascist literature, he surely wouldn't keep it in plain sight in days like these. Lanny wandered here and there, running his eyes over the shelves, and when the woman asked politely if there was any special thing he wanted, he replied that he was just browsing. What he was doing was making sure there was nobody else in the little shop. He couldn't say: "Is Raoul Palma here?" —because it might be that Raoul was going under an assumed name and that the woman did not share his secret. Certainly she must not share Lanny Budd's!

He couldn't stay forever, so he bought a paper-backed copy of *Le Lys Rouge* by Anatole France, which Beauty had read aloud to him when he was a boy, she having been an unusually frank mother, who made insufficient allowance for the difference between childhood and maturity. With the volume in an overcoat pocket—on top of a wad of money—Lanny strolled and looked at the very old city of Toulon. Like most of them along this shore, it had been conquered by Romans and Goths and Burgundians and Franks and Saracens. Here Napoleon had first made his name known by driving out the British. This he had done in the name of the republic which he destroyed a few years later; it was a melancholy story, not so different from the one that Adolf Hitler was now unfolding. Sad old Europe with her bloody soil, and her patient, toiling peoples who learned so slowly!

Lanny thought: Raoul's hours of work may be in the evening. So after dinner he went back, and the little shop was open, with a man in charge, but it wasn't the former school director. Lanny browsed again for a while, to make certain; then he bought another novel and went back to his hotel room and read. Very annoying, but there was nothing he could do but wait. Perhaps Raoul was ill; or perhaps the proprietor had sent him on some errand; or perhaps his hours were in the morning.

Early next morning the P.A. went again, and there was the same woman on duty. He looked at more books; he was pretty familiar with the contents of the shop by now, and there were many he would have been interested to read, but not standing up, and watching out for Raoul, also for pickpockets. He asked for books on art and on psychic research which he could be fairly sure the woman wouldn't have; so he struck up an acquaintance. He learned that the store had been here or some twenty years, and that rising prices were good for the trade as long as you had any books left; also that in wartime people read a great deal because they couldn't have the other amusements they were used to. But he didn't hear anything about another clerk, or any message for an American customer.

So passed the day. Lanny went to dinner in the hotel dining-room, and made up his mind that as soon as he finished he would return to the store, and whether it was the woman or the man on duty he would remark: "By the way, I was in here some time ago and was waited on by a man—I took him to be a Spaniard—a man somewhat younger than myself." Lanny would make it sound right by adding: "I asked him about a book by Professor Osty, and he promised to try to find me a copy." This could involve Raoul in no worse offense than having overlooked a duty. He might lose his job for it, but that wouldn't be so bad as losing all the money which was squeezing Lanny's elegant tweed clothing out of shape!

III

But Lanny never returned to that bookstore. In the lobby of the hotel he met a lady.

She was sitting in one of the large, overstuffed, velvet-covered chairs, just where he had to emerge from the dining-room, and when she saw him coming, she rose and stood, obviously waiting for him. So he had a good look at her, and did not find it difficult. She was young —in her mid-twenties, he would have guessed. She was tall for a Frenchwoman, slender, a brunette with very lovely dark eyes and features sensitive and refined. She was simply dressed in a tailored tweed costume, and wore a little beret of the same material. Very much the lady, he would have judged, but nothing showy, no jewels, and if there was make-up it was not conspicuous.

She came toward him and inquired: "M. Budd, I believe?" Lanny said: "Yes."

"M. Budd, I am secretary to Madame Latour, of an old family of this town, and friends of the d'Avriennes. They have told us of your visit, and that you are interested in old paintings."

"That is true, Mademoiselle."

"Those of the d'Avriennes would be difficult to purchase; but Madame Latour has sent me to tell you that she has a collection, not so large but more choice, and she would like very much to have you view it."

"I am interested, Mademoiselle. Who are the painters?"

"For one, there is a very fine Antoine le Nain."

"Indeed? Those are not so common. Are you certain it is genuine?"

"It has been viewed by many persons who understand art matters, and I have never heard of any question being raised."

"Well, that interests me greatly, Mademoiselle." Lanny didn't add that the mademoiselle interested him also; she had an unusually pleasing voice, a winning smile, a *tout ensemble* of desirability. He hadn't enjoyed the society of ladies for quite a while, except the elderly ones of his mother's set. The ladies of Vichy had impressed him as harassed and shrill; but here, apparently, was one who had not been touched by the furies of war and conquest. "When may I view these pictures?" he inquired.

"At any time convenient to you. This evening, if you wish."

"Unless the lighting is good—" he started to suggest.

"You will find the lighting adequate, I am sure."

"And where is the place?"

"It is a few miles out of town, but an easy drive. I have Madame's car, and will be happy to take you and bring you back."

"That is very kind. I am happy to accept."

Really, as a man of the world, schooled in all the rascalities of Europe, Lanny ought to have stopped to reflect for a few moments, and perhaps to make some inquiry, say of the hotel porter or clerk. There was a great scarcity of men in France, and the women were ravenous and would stop at no device. While there was no superfluity of money, it was very badly distributed, and those who lacked it were ravenous too. To go traveling with a strange lady at night, and with his pockets stuffed with money, was surely no procedure for a wise and cautious secret agent! But this lady was so exceptional, her manner so refined, her expression gentle and sweet, like the kindest of those endlessly multiplied madonnas an art expert had been viewing all over this old Continent. He forgot what had long been one of his maxims, that a spy is chosen because he or she looks as little like a spy as possible.

IV

He accompanied her to the car which was parked near by. It was a small car, and she herself was driving, a circumstance which surprised him, because in France women do not drive as freely as men, and certainly the secretary of a *grande dame* should have been brought by a chauffeur. However, he couldn't very well say: "Are you sure you know how to drive, Mademoiselle?" She was businesslike and efficient, and he got in, pulled a robe over his knees, and let himself be carried along the *route nationale*.

"M. Budd," said the lady, "what is going to become of our unhappy France?"

It was a subject Lanny was surely not going to discuss—not for an *amiral* or a *maréchal*, nor yet for the most charming secretary-chauffeur. "*Chère Mademoiselle*," he replied, "to answer that would take a learned statesman or sociologist. It can surely be no question for a mere *connoisseur d'art.*"

"We French," persisted the lady, "have the idea that you Americans are the wisest and most capable people in the world."

"*Hélas*, if there was anyone in my country who was able to foresee the calamities which have befallen Europe, I did not happen to meet him. We are successful at inventing machines, but less so at creating kindness and mercy in the world."

"My employers and all their friends are haunted by the idea that some day the hordes from Russia are going to sweep over Western Europe."

"A political lady!" thought Lanny, and he surely wasn't going to take any line until he knew her. "Many people think that," he remarked, "but such events seem to me a long way off, and one so young and charming as yourself would be wiser to enjoy the gifts which nature has showered upon her so liberally."

"*Merci, Monsieur*—you talk just like a Frenchman!" She flashed him a smile which he couldn't see in the darkness but which he could hear in her voice.

"I have lived most of my life in France," he replied. "So it has become second nature. Tell me about yourself, Mademoiselle."

She told him that her name was Marie Jeanne Richard, and that her father had been a professor in one of the near-by colleges, where she herself had studied. She had become engaged to a fellow-student who had been taken by the army and now was missing, presumably dead but possibly a prisoner of war. "It has been especially tragic to me," she said, "because I am one of those who had no heart in this war. I have been brought up to admire German culture, and to believe that friendship between Germany and France is vital to the future of both."

"It is too bad that all the nations cannot be friends," replied the cautious American. "In Europe they have acquired the bad habit of distrusting one another."

They had turned off the coast highway and were following one of the small valleys between the mountains. The lights of the car swung here and there, revealing great forests of cork oaks, and as they ascended, of pines. It seemed to Lanny that they were going a considerable distance from Toulon. The paved road came to an end, and the car bumped as it rolled on. Of course there might be some estate up here—the rich have their whims, in France as in America; but Lanny became uneasy and said: "Are you sure you are on the right road, Mademoiselle?"

"Oh, yes," she replied, "I travel it frequently. It is not much farther now."

The road had become a mere track, and the ruts were deeper. It was more like a wood-road than the entrance to a rich property. When they came to a mountain stream and had to drive through the water, Lanny said with some firmness: "If I had known it was such a journey, Mlle. Richard, I would not have consented to come at night."

"It is quite near now," she assured him; "just around this side of the mountain. You will find it an exceptionally beautiful place. Madame Latour is a nature lover and something of a recluse. People come for hundreds of miles to enjoy the view from her lookout tower; but she herself is no longer able to go there, on account of her advanced years. The moon will be up in an hour or so and you will be able to see something of the immense vistas." That sounded like a proper sort of millionaire eccentric. The more money they have, the more people try to get it away from them, and the less trust they have in the human race. Lanny knew the phenomenon well.

V

The P.A.'s personal interest in this lovely young secretary had begun to wane since she had revealed herself as among the appeasers, a *collaboratrice;* he decided that he had been neglecting his business, and began to ask questions about the paintings he was to view. The car rolled around a shoulder of the mountain, and from behind a clump of underbrush four men stepped out onto the road, men with black handkerchiefs over their faces and guns in their hands. "*Halte-là!*" they cried, and leveled the guns. There was a squealing of the car brakes, and a gasp from Marie Jeanne Richard. "*Oh, mon Dieu! Des bandits!*"

Lanny's heart gave a mighty thump, but his head still kept working, and he remembered a maxim his father had taught him early in life: "Never forget that your life is worth more to you than all the money you can carry on your person or keep in your house." He was stuffed with money like a goose with fat; but, it was only five hundred dollars, and he had earned ten times that in a single picture deal. So when the leader of the band said "*Haut les mains!*" he obeyed, and so did his companion. ("Stick 'em up!" was the American translation.) When the man said: "*Sortez!*" he clambered out, and so did his companion.

One of the men proceeded to search Lanny; and a surprising thing happened. He didn't put his hands into a single pocket, but patted all the pockets of the overcoat and then of the coat and trousers, and felt around Lanny's waist and under his armpits; he wasn't looking for money but for arms! When he had made sure, he said: "*Rien,*" and the leader gave the order to tie Lanny's hands. They had a coil of rope, long, and very strong, as the victim was to make sure before this adventure was over. The man tied it tightly about one wrist and then drew Lanny's two hands behind his back, crossed the wrists, and bound them together and made them fast; the rest of the rope was for leading. Evidently the man who did the job was familiar with it, for he worked methodically, quickly, and without a word. When he was through the result was painful to Lanny, but thoroughly satisfactory from the point of view of the others.

They searched the woman, politely and not very completely, Lanny thought. They searched the car for arms, and then one of the men turned it around—they had picked a spot where there was room for the purpose. "*Entrez,*" said the leader, addressing the woman, and opened the car door for her. "We are through with you," he said. "Go home and stay there, and don't say one word to anybody about what you have seen. We are the avengers, and our punishment is swift and sure. If you betray us, we will kidnap you and bring you up here and roast you over a slow fire We will do the same to every member of your family. *Comprenez-vous?*"

"*Oui, oui,*" was the reply, in a terrified voice, barely audible.

"*Partez,*" said the man, and the car rolled slowly down the wet and slippery track.

Lanny Budd's mind was working as hard as it knew how, for he realized that he was in serious danger. This was no question of losing fifty thousand francs; this might be a question of his life. The affair must be political, and the best guess he could make was that these were men of the underground, the movement which he had been secretly helping to build. He had not been impressed by the little drama which had been played with the woman; he took it that she was an accomplice of the band. She was one of those stern idealists who were springing up all over Europe, wherever the Panzer machine had rolled: people who would not give up their own freedom or that of their native land, people who would fight, and rouse others to fight, and keep the torch of liberty burning. Lanny had come upon another Trudi Schultz, the anti-Nazi heroine whom he had secretly married, and whom the Nazis had murdered in one of their torture camps.

The captive realized this in flashes, but he had no time to dwell on it. He realized that he was in a plight, and might have a hard time thinking and talking his way out of it. An odd quirk of fate, that this danger should come from his own crowd, the people he had been serving, openly or secretly, for a quarter of a century. His knowledge of their ways and their states of mind enabled him to realize the truly frightening nature of his situation. These people were outlaws with a price upon their heads; their lives were grim, and they had no time to waste on formalities. When they seized a wealthy and prominent foreigner, it was because they believed him to be among the most dangerous of their enemies; and having got him, they would hardly turn him loose and let him go out and reveal their secrets. "Dead men tell no tales" is a maxim known to every boy who has ever read a story of pirates, bandits, or gangsters; and all over Europe men of both sides were returning to these desperate moods.

A sudden realization swept over the son of Budd-Erling: how careless and naïve he had been! He had taken every precaution as regards the Nazi-Fascists, but he had seldom taken time to reflect how he must appear to his own friends. The idea was a painful one and he had put it out of his mind. He had gone wandering over Europe, torn by war and civil war—he bland and innocent, a child in a jungle inhabited by fierce beasts. He had not seen the looks of glowering hate, nor heard the half-repressed snarls. He had taken it for granted that everybody thought as highly of him as he thought of himself. That, alas, is something that does not happen very often in this world.

VI

With the utmost politeness he addressed the leader of the band. "Would you mind telling me what this is all about?"—"*qu'est-ce que c'est que tout cela?*" is the odd formula of the French: "what is it that it is that all that?"

"What is it that your name is?" was the counter-question.

"Lanny Budd," he replied; he could hardly expect to conceal that.

"*Bien,*" said the man. "We will tell you everything when we are ready. *Allons.*"

He led the way and Lanny followed. The rope which bound his wrists had been left long and served to keep him from trying to run away or to throw himself over a precipice. A stout fellow came behind, holding it, and the two others followed with the guns. The leader had a staff in one hand and a flashlight in the other; Lanny could see fairly well by the light, but the man behind him couldn't see so well, and every time he stumbled or delayed there was a painful jerk at the prisoner's wrists. They followed a well-trodden path, climbing through a high pass, and when they got to the top of the grade there was a freezing wind blowing. They came down along the side of a deep gorge with the sound of rushing water below. Then began another climb, and it was fortunate that Lanny had been playing some tennis and was not too soft. The penalty of lagging was what might be politely described as a push with the fist of the man behind him.

Over a saddle of mountain, by a path that hardly existed at all. There were traces of light below, and after they had descended and forced their way through a heavy thicket they came upon a tiny glade in a pine forest. There was a small campfire glowing, and two men sitting by it. The leader had already exchanged calls with them, and now the party of five came into the light. There was a log on each side of the fire, and the leader commanded his captive: "*Asseyez-vous.*"

Lanny's hands had been chilled in the high passes, and now they felt strangely numb. He said: "I am afraid my hands may be frozen." The other commanded that he be untied, and the burly fellow who had charge of the job obeyed without a word. He tied the rope around one of Lanny's ankles, and sat holding onto it, taking no chances. By the shape and color of this man's hands Lanny took him to be a peasant. Sitting on the log and gently chafing his hands and wrists, the prisoner had a good chance to study them all. Two he decided must be dockworkers or shipbuilders, men of muscle with hands calloused and scarred. The rest were more probably intellectuals or white-collar workers; one had a strong Ligurian accent, familiar to a resident of the Cap d'Antibes since childhood.

The leader was a soft-voiced but firm-willed man of thirty or so, and there was something haunting about his voice. Lanny couldn't get away from the idea that he had heard it before, but it must have been a long time ago, he decided. Lanny had been sociable, and must have met thousands of persons here in the Midi. Thinking fast, the most likely place that came to his mind was the workers' school that Raoul Palma had started, and that Lanny had helped to finance for something like a decade and a half. In the course of that time hundreds of young proletarians and some white-collar workers had sat in classes in a rickety old warehouse repaired and kept clean. They had argued and fought over doctrines and party lines, and had quarrels and splits that had driven the school director and his devoted young wife almost to distraction. Until recent years Lanny had mingled with them freely, called them all "Comrade" and tried to moderate their vehemence. A curious development, if now some zealot among them had decided to punish him for treason to the cause!

Lanny had been dealing with the underground, first in Germany, then in Spain and France; but always it had been at second hand, so to speak, through some one friend whom he trusted. This was the first time he had ever sat in at a secret session. It was more like a scene in a play or a movie than anything in anybody's real life. All six of the men wore black masks, with two holes for the eyes and a slit for the mouth; they did not remove these, and Lanny got some comfort out of the fact, taking it to mean that they hadn't definitely made up their minds to dispose of him. At least he was to have a chance to defend himself. He had been thinking as hard as he knew how, and the time had come when he had to match his one set of wits against their half-dozen associated sets.

VII

"M. Budd," said the leader without any preliminaries, "would you be so kind as to tell us what is your business in France?"

It was going to be a polite session; and politeness was Lanny Budd's specialty. "*Mais certainement, Monsieur*. I have several businesses. I am an art expert, purchasing old masters for American collections. I sometimes attend to matters for my father, who manufactures airplanes and supplied many to the French government from the outset of the war to the end. Also, you must understand that my mother has her home at Juan-les-Pins, and I have lived there most of my life, ever since I was a child in arms."

"What are your political ideas, M. Budd?"

"I used to have political ideas, Monsieur, but I discovered that I was living in a time of strife and intolerance; since I am a man of peace, I decided to confine myself to my study of paintings. I am taking part in the forming of several great collections which will find their place in museums in the United States, and which I hope will help to raise the cultural level of that country."

"You take no part in politics?"

"None whatever, Monsieur. People try to draw me into discussions, and when they do, I listen politely to what they have to say, and tell them that I have my own specialty, and leave the solution of social problems to those who are more competent to deal with them."

"You have traveled a great deal to Germany?"

"Yes, Monsieur."

"And you know Hitler personally?"

"He has been one of many clients. He purchased half a dozen of the works of Marcel Detaze, the great French painter who was my stepfather, as you may possibly know, and who died in the war to save *la patrie*."

"You have never discussed political ideas with Hitler?"

"Monsieur, one does not discuss political ideas with Herr Hitler; one listens, often for hours at a time. I listened to such good effect that he asked me to find him some good examples of Defregger, the Austrian painter who paints peasants. I could see no harm in doing that, and he paid me the customary ten per cent commission."

"You know Göring also?"

"I first met General Göring, as he was then, when he put a Jewish friend of mine in prison. I was able to persuade him to release this friend for a high price; then he became interested in my judgment as an art expert, and employed me to market some of his paintings in

New York and to purchase for him certain examples of American paintings."

"You appear to be very successful in persuading people, M. Budd." There was just a hint of sarcasm in the tone, and a suggestion: "You may not find it so easy this time!" The inquisitor continued: "You were with Hitler and Göring in Paris, were you not?"

Lanny thought: They have a good intelligence service! Ordinarily he would have been glad, but not just now. He replied: "I was invited to meet Herr Hitler at the Crillon, and I went."

"To talk to him about paintings?"

"I could not know what he wished to talk about. As a matter of fact, what he talked about was his great admiration for Napoleon Bonaparte."

"And nothing about politics whatever?"

"He talked about his plans, and I was embarrassed, because I did not want the responsibility of having such knowledge."

"Did you talk to others about them?"

"I was not told that anything was confidential, and I answered any questions that my friends asked on the subject."

"You were in Vichy not long ago, M. Budd?"

"I travel all over France. I have bought three paintings in Vichy in the past few months."

"You met Laval, did you not?"

"M. Laval owns a fine old historical painting in Châteldon, and he was courteous enough to permit me to view it."

"You called on Darlan, also. Does he own paintings?"

"Admiral Darlan was a visitor in my mother's home nearly twenty years ago. I reminded him of that, and asked him if he could do me the favor to let me travel to my mother's home in any sort of *camion*, transportation being so difficult in these times."

"And you did not have political discussions with any of these persons you know so well?"

"I did what I always do, Monsieur; I listened to what they had to tell me, and expressed no opinion, because that would have been presumption."

"And what do you do with all this confidential information that you collect?"

"None of it is confidential, Monsieur; I never permit anyone to put me in such a position. If a man says to me: 'I am going to tell you something confidential,' I reply quickly: 'Please do not, for I do not wish to carry such a responsibility. There are many chances of leakage, and I do not wish anyone to think of me as the possible source of a leak.' People of good sense respect that attitude; and people who understand what great art is appreciate that a man of art is a neutral, one whose values are permanent, and above the battle of the factions. You may recall that Romain Rolland wrote a book with that title, *Au-dessus de la mêlée.*"

VIII

This was a P.A.'s regular "spiel"; the story he told to all except the outright Nazi-Fascists on the one hand, and his few trusted friends on the other. How well it might go down with these men he could not judge, for he did not see the expressions on their faces, and they had given few hints as to what they had learned about him. Evidently somebody had been watching him for a considerable time, and had reports on him from Paris as well as Vichy.

"Search him," commanded the leader, still in the even voice. This was a moment which Lanny had been anticipating—with no pleasure. The burly fellow who was his keeper dipped a hand into the prisoner's right overcoat pocket and drew out a wad of banknotes, just about all that his large hand could encompass. "*Jésu!*" he exclaimed, and held them up; it would have been a safe guess that he had never seen that much money at any time in his life.

The leader took the wad, and the man plunged his hand into the left overcoat pocket and repeated the performance. "*Une banque ambulante!*" remarked the leader, and took off his hat to hold the treasure. The search went on, and a few banknotes came from the breast pocket of the overcoat and a huge wad from the inside breast pocket. Then came the turn of the coat, and handfuls emerged from both side pockets and the inside breast pocket; then the trousers, the side pockets, and a back pocket. Two hats were required to hold it all, and they were spilling over. "Is that all, M. Budd?" inquired the man. "Or shall we strip you?"

"You have it all," Lanny said; "*ma parole d'honneur.*" He preserved the tone of polite irony which had been set for this conference.

"May I inquire, M. Budd—you do not trust the financial institutions of l'État Français?"

"I have already explained to you, Monsieur, I am in the business of purchasing art works. I came to Toulon with the expectation of making a deal."

"You may save me time if you will give me an idea as to how much money we have here."

"Certainly, Monsieur; about fifty thousand francs."

"You would pay that much for a painting?"

"On a number of occasions I have paid several million francs, Monsieur."

"*Diable!* And you always pay in banknotes?"

"When I am dealing with strangers, yes. I find the psychological effect of the actual money is very great. I decide what I think a painting is worth, and I count that out in cash. Very few people are able to resist the sight, and when I start putting the money back into my pockets they hasten to accept my offer."

This information produced the first signs of life in this strangely silent band. They had sat perfectly motionless, letting their leader do all the talking. But now they chuckled; and Lanny thought, what a sensation he might have created by stating the fact: "All this money was intended for you." He might have brought this uncomfortable session to a sudden end if he had remarked: "Comrades, I am one of you. All you have to do is to ask Raoul Palma, whom you doubtless know. He will tell you that I have been bringing him both information and money, ever since Nazi-Fascism got its start."

But of course he couldn't say that; to do so would be to put an end to his career as presidential agent. He might have said: "Comrades, I put you on your honor to keep my secret." But suppose that some one of these six happened to be a spy of the government, watching this band and getting ready to turn them in? That was how the game was being played, plot and counterplot, spying and counter-spying, all over this wartorn old Continent. Or suppose that one of the six couldn't resist the temptation to entrust so thrilling a secret to his wife or his sweetheart? The story would spread with the speed of electricity; it would reach the authorities in Toulon, then in Vichy, then Paris, then Berlin. The son of Budd-Erling would find himself arrested again, and this time his interrogation would be far less suave.

No, he had to find some way to talk himself out of this mess. He must hold onto this secret, at least up to the moment before the last. Manifestly, he would be of no use to President Roosevelt if he were dead and buried in this rocky wilderness; so, if it came to the last extreme, he would surely confess, and go back to the land of his forefathers and marry Laurel Creston—or would it be Peggy Remsen, or Lizbeth Holdenhurst? The only trouble about this program was that these men of the underground might not take the trouble to give him formal notice of their decision; they might think it more polite for one of them to step up behind him silently and put a bullet into the base of his skull. That thought made it somewhat difficult for Lanny to concentrate on intellectual conversation.

IX

Besides paper money, the search had yielded a watch, a fountain pen, and a small pocket comb used by a gentleman with carefully trimmed wavy brown hair. Also there were documents: a passport

book, a travel permit, a *carte d'identification,* and several of those letters concerning art deals which Lanny Budd was careful never to be
without. The leader examined them—he knew English, it appeared—
and then ordered them returned to the prisoner. "Concerning the
money, we shall decide later, M. Budd. We desire you to understand
that we are not bandits, but French patriots."

"I, too, have always counted myself a French patriot," declared the
captive quickly. "I have lived in France most of my life, and have
never broken any law that I am aware of. I would take it as a courtesy
if you would give me some idea of what I am accused."

"We will tell you in good time. We are awaiting the arrival of an
investigator. In the meantime, I regret to say it will be necessary to
bind you for the night."

"I point out, Monsieur, that ropes, if they are tight, stop the circulation of the blood, and that is particularly dangerous on a cold night
like this."

"We will cause you as little trouble as possible, M. Budd."

Lanny decided that the man who tied him must be, not a peasant,
but a sailor. He made fancy knots that were not too tight about
Lanny's ankles but that wouldn't slip over his feet. He did the same
for the wrists behind Lanny's back. The others rolled the logs out of
the way, preparing to sleep close to the fire. They spread a blanket for
Lanny and covered him up with half of it. He observed that several
proposed to sleep without blankets, and he was touched by this. It was
a circumstance he had noted through all the revolutions which had
occurred on this bloodstained Continent since his childhood; the revolutionists had so often been humane toward their opponents, and sometimes had lost their cause on that account. This had been the case in
Germany, in Hungary, in Spain; and wherever the reactionaries had
come back into power, they had killed ten for every one their opponents had killed.

But that wouldn't help a P.A., if he happened to be one whom the
revolutionists thought they had to kill. He felt sure they hadn't brought
him to this rendezvous in order to lecture him or to frighten him; they
must be intending to close his mouth for keeps; and what more likely
than that they meant to do it in a painless manner while he was asleep?
So Lanny didn't go to sleep, but lay with his feet stretched out to the
warmth of the fire and thought as hard as ever he had done in his life
hitherto. They could hardly be intending to shoot him because he had
carried messages from Pétain and Madame de Portes, mistress of the
Premier of France, to Lord Wickthorpe in England; nor yet because
he had talked with Hitler and Göring, and later with Laval and Darlan.
None of these messages had been written, so what evidence could there
be concerning them?

It must be they thought he had betrayed somebody to the Nazis, or
to the *collaborateurs*. And who could it be? What trip had he taken
or what word had he spoken that could have caused blame to be fixed
upon him? Could it be that Raoul Palma had just been arrested, and
that he, Raoul's friend from old times, was under suspicion for this?
Could it be that his visits to the bookstore had been observed and mis-
interpreted? Was his visit to the commandant of the port being connected with some conspiracy against the de Gaullists? There was
bound to be a deadly war going on between the authorities here and
those who held them to be traitors to *la belle Marianne*. It would be a
war of knife and dagger, of grenades and dynamite, and it would be
growing hotter every day as pressure of the Nazis increased. Somehow
—perhaps he would never know how—a bland and elegant *étranger*
had blundered in between the firing lines of this bitter fraternal strife!

X

Lanny tried his bonds enough to make certain there was nothing he
could do except to tear the skin off his wrists. He might have chafed
the ropes against a rock, but he could only have got to a rock by
hopping, and that would surely have awakened the men. The rope
tied to Lanny's ankles was attached to the wrist of the man who was
his special keeper, and who lay flat on his back on the cold ground,
snoring loudly into one of Lanny's ears. Perhaps this crowd would
have liked nothing better than to have the prisoner attempt to escape,
so that they might apply to him what the Spaniards called *la ley de
fuga*. The fire was dying, and the cold creeping nearer, but Lanny's
trembling wasn't due to that.

He was determined not to fall asleep, because he wanted to speak one
sentence before anybody pulled the trigger of a gun. His eyes roamed
from one to another of the sleeping forms. The leader was on the other
side of the fire, wrapped in a blanket like the prisoner. Apparently
there was a distinction made in favor of the intellectuals, as being more
delicate and perishable; or perhaps it was up to each man to bring a
blanket if he wanted one. The wind had died down, and deadly cold
seemed to be settling in this little valley; he wondered, was it high
enough for snow in these mountains? They had seemed high, but perhaps that was because he was climbing them in the dark and his wrists
had hurt.

Lying on one side with your hands tied behind your back is a far
from comfortable position; especially when the fire is dying and the
cold creeping into your bones. Lanny couldn't roll over without pulling on the rope and awakening his keeper; he had the impression that
this keeper didn't like him anyway, and if the man's sleep was dis-

turbed he might cast his vote for the immediate ending of his own discomfort. Lanny remembered a long night he had spent, waiting while Monck and a locksmith were trying to rescue Trudi from the Château de Belcour; this was another night of anxious waiting, and Lanny couldn't guess the time, or how far away the dawn might be. He decided that it was the stupidest misadventure he had ever got into, and called himself a booby many times over for having gone off driving with a strange woman, no matter how well mannered. Marie Jeanne Richard—that was a *nom de ruse*, undoubtedly. Who would she be? He imagined melodramatic things about her; she was a member of the d'Avrienne family, or perhaps the mistress of the commandant of the port. She had despised Lanny as a Fascist, and had done to him what he would have liked to do to every Fascist in the world!

XI

The captive could lift his head a little, and he looked at the dying fire. The moon had come up, and was sending faint shafts of light through the pine trees. Lanny saw, or thought he saw, a movement of one of the men who lay on the opposite side of the fire. The man raised his head, and then got up on his hands and knees and began to creep backward, away from the fire. Perhaps he was going to put some more wood on, without awakening his fellows; that would be a service which Lanny would appreciate. The man got up and began to tiptoe, and Lanny watched him as far as his eyes could follow. He was the one whom Lanny had noted as having a Ligurian accent. He was coming around to Lanny's side of the circle and presently he was where Lanny couldn't see him without turning over.

The horrid idea flashed over the prisoner's mind that this might be the moment; this fellow had been ordered to put him out of his misery. Usually they did it with a shot from the rear, just at the base of the skull; that destroyed the medulla and was painless. This time, since Lanny was lying on his side, a shot in the ear would be wiser, to avoid the chance of hitting the next man. Lanny's heart was pounding wildly and he could hardly breathe; he heard the man behind him, right over him. Now, if ever, was the moment to shout: "It is all a mistake! I am one of you!"

The fellow had got down on his knees; his face came close, his warm breath in Lanny's ear. The latter checked his mad impulse, realizing that this was not the posture of an assassin. The man was about to speak to him; and the next moment Lanny heard, in the faintest imaginable whisper, four French words: "*Combien pour votre liberté?*"

How much for your freedom! So, there was a traitor among the group, just as Lanny thought likely! Or, at any rate, a man who was offering to turn traitor! That psychology which Lanny had expounded had worked right while he was speaking; this fellow had gazed, with eyes popping behind his mask, at enough banknotes to fill two hats and some spilling over, and he had decided that he was in contact with one of those most godlike of human beings, an American millionaire. Who in the world, from China to Peru, has not seen them on the cinema screen, scattering largess, commanding miracles—mountains to be removed and palaces to arise!

The man's ear was in front of Lanny's lips, almost touching them; and Lanny murmured three French syllables, slowly and distinctly, so low that it might have been a memory of speech. "*Cent—mille—francs.*"

A hundred thousand francs was less than a thousand dollars as they stood in Vichy France, and that surely wasn't high ransom for the life of a millionaire, or even a motion-picture imitation. Lanny was prepared to bid up to five hundred thousand francs, or even a million; but the next thing he knew, the man was working at the ropes which bound Lanny's hands. He must have had a sharp knife, for one or two movements cut those which bound the wrists together; he did not try to cut those which were about each wrist, for that obviously would have been difficult. With great caution he crept toward Lanny's feet, and first he cut the rope which connected him with the sleeping guard, and then he cut those which bound the two ankles together.

He moved back to Lanny's ear, and whispered: "*Venez!*"—then arose and stole back into the shadow. Lanny, with the utmost care, rolled himself over. He found that his wrists were so weak they wouldn't hold him up. He got on his knees and elbows, and thus, with agonizingly slow movements, he got away from the dim firelight. At last he got up, and found that he could stand.

His deliverer was a dim shadow, and Lanny tiptoed after him. He had no idea in what direction they were going, but the man put one arm around him to aid his tottering steps, and together they followed a path through the thicket. The man seemed to have a cat's eyes; or perhaps he had been through it so many times that he knew every dip and turn. They did not speak a word; their bargain was made, and they had only to put as much distance as possible between them and the camp.

Before long the cords around Lanny's ankles hurt so that he had to stop and ask the man to cut them. That was pretty nearly a surgical operation, and the man performed it with care and skill, working a little slack into one cord and pressing the flesh down, so that his cut would be away from the flesh and not toward it. He did the same for the wrists, and it was a blessed relief. Circulation would come back, and pretty soon Lanny would be his active self again. "What do you plan to do?" he whispered, and the man replied: "They know all the paths, and will travel faster than you can, and their bullets faster still. We must get up into the hills and hide over the day."

"Won't they be able to track us?" Lanny asked and the answer was: "Not if we get up among the rocks. The thing is to get as far as possible before dawn."

XII

The late and waning moon was hiding behind a steep escarpment. Lanny could see that it was a wild region, with piled-up rocks and cliffs, and pine and cedar trees clinging here and there. They waded a little stream, and the man said: "Get a drink, for it may be all you will have through the day." He added: "We'll have to go hungry," and Lanny replied grimly: "I can stand it." They waded downstream for a while, to conceal their tracks.

They plodded on, with brief stops for Lanny to rest, until daylight began to appear. As soon as they could see well enough, the guide picked out a spot where a dry bed of rocks made it possible to leave the path without leaving any footprints. They clambered up a steep hillside, from rock to rock, and just as Lanny was about to gasp out that he was at the limit of his tortured limbs, they came upon a sort of little niche in a cliffside; not a cave, but enough to shelter them from sight, so long as they were content to be still. Lanny was more than content; while his rescuer sat with one ear cocked, listening for sounds of pursuit, he stretched himself out and made up for lost sleep. He was quite sure that no pursuer would find them in this eagles' roost, and he decided that he would stay a couple of days and call it a fast, something he had read about and been interested in.

The name of the rescuer was Gigi; at least that was the name he gave, pronouncing it with the Italian "g," like the American "j"; he didn't say how he had got it and Lanny didn't ask. He had been conscripted into the French Army, and had decided for himself that the war was over. He had joined the rebels, not because of political convictions but because of a girl—again that was what he said. What he wanted was to get away from all fighting, and it was his plan to take his money and smuggle himself onto a ship for South America, any country that would permit a fellow to live his life in his own way. Lanny was sympathetic, and of course kept his pose as a misunderstood art expert. He gave the man his address, and assured him that the money would be forthcoming; if they became separated Gigi was to find his way to Juan-les-Pins, where Lanny would wait for him. "Take my advice," the man said, "and don't go back into Toulon, or somebody there will surely stick a knife into your back."

"And how about Juan?" Lanny asked. The answer was: "I wouldn't stay anywhere in the Midi. Things are hot as hell here, and nobody knows who can be trusted. They surely won't trust either of us again."

XIII

Gigi took off his mask and hid it under a rock; it would be no help to him now, but on the contrary a mortal danger. So when Lanny opened his eyes he had a chance to observe what his rescuer looked like: a fellow in his early twenties, swarthy and weatherbeaten but not especially sturdy. His father had been a railroad worker, his mother had come from Liguria, the westernmost province of Italy, adjoining France. He himself had been to school, and had got a job as shipping clerk; after quitting the army, he had found there were no jobs, and so he had joined the partisans.

This he narrated to Lanny in whispers, after Lanny had had his sleep. Gigi had helped to carry supplies up to the hide-out of his band; there were other bands, he said, but only the leaders knew where. The supplies had come from the hijacking of a government truck, but Gigi had had nothing to do with that, he insisted. Perhaps they hadn't trusted him enough.

He was a shifty-eyed fellow, good-looking in a crude sort of way. Lanny knew the type well. He had no politics, save that he distrusted the rich and feared the authorities; he wanted to be let alone and to enjoy himself. What troubled him more than anything at the moment was that he did not dare to smoke, lest it should give them away to a keen-eyed pursuer.

The more he thought about it, the more worried Gigi became over what he had done; the partisans would publish him among themselves as a traitor, and the first one who saw him would shoot him like a dog. They would be certain that he would give them away to the authorities, and Gigi lamented in loud whispers about this—it was most unfair, for he wouldn't do such a thing—how would it help him? He hoped Lanny wouldn't do it either, and Lanny said that under no circumstances would he get himself mixed up in any political dispute. His willingness to leave fifty thousand francs behind him without complaint, and to promise to part with twice as much—this impressed the Frenchman greatly, and doubtless in his secret heart he wished he had asked a higher price for his dangerous service.

Lanny tried to find out what was behind this strange misadventure. Why had the partisans picked on him? Gigi was vague, and apparently didn't really know. A messenger had come up from Toulon and had had a long conference with the leader; all the others had been told was that they were going to arrest an agent of the Nazis who had done great harm to the people's cause. Lanny tried to find out about Marie

Jeanne Richard, but the other insisted that he knew nothing about any such woman; certainly she wasn't his girl, who was the daughter of a shipworker in the port, a member of the syndicalist union the Vichy Government had suppressed.

Very tactfully Lanny approached the subject of the bookstore in Toulon. He had visited the city some time ago, he said, and had there met a clerk whom he took to be of Spanish nationality; a good-looking and intelligent man in his thirties who had undertaken to find some rare books for him. But this hinting did no good, for Gigi said he had seen the bookstore but had never entered it; he was not a reading man. Lanny said the clerk had given him the name of Palma, and the other replied that he had heard the name spoken, but didn't know anything about the man. If he was a member of the partisans, Gigi wouldn't necessarily know it; they were organized in small sections and the members of one section did not know those of another. This was to make things a little harder for the *flics*.

XIV

What concerned this average sensual man was how to get himself out of great danger. He wanted information and advice, and Lanny thought it the part of wisdom to give what he could, for if this fellow were to be arrested with a hundred thousand francs on him, he would have to tell how he had got them, and that would be awkward indeed for a visiting art expert. Lanny warned him to sew the bills up in the lining of his coat as soon as he got them, and that his next step should be to purchase himself an outfit such as would be worn by a gentleman of leisure. When Gigi asked, with much concern, "How can I pass for a gentleman?" Lanny replied: "Just hold yourself straight, look dignified and important, and don't say anything except when you have to."

The man's idea was to get to Marseille, where he had knowledge of a group of Americans who were assisting refugees to escape the clutches of the Gestapo. It appeared that he had been assigned to escort two leftwing writers, German Jews, and turn them over to the leader of this group, a young man named Varian Fry. Gigi didn't know the exact situation, but Lanny could explain it. Under the terms of the armistice the Vichy Government was required to "surrender on demand" any opponents of Nazism who might have sought refuge in their territories; but among the Vichyites, especially of the lower ranks, were some who had secret sympathies for the victims and were willing to wink at their escape. Gigi said this might be so, but the Americans were operating underground so far as possible; they carefully kept up the pretense that they were affording only food and medical care to the refugees, and nobody was supposed to know that they were also handing out forged visas and travel permits.

It was a worried Frenchman's idea that the news of his treason might not travel as far as Marseille, and that the Americans there would remember his previous visit and help him on his way. They had a plan by which Frenchmen and others who could pose as Frenchmen were dressed in uniforms and smuggled on board transports with troops going to North Africa, and to work on the railroad which, under Nazi direction, was being rushed through the Sahara desert to the port of Dakar. Once in Algiers, and with plenty of funds, Gigi could be fairly sure of getting on board a ship. But he was tormented by his fears, and he wanted help from Lanny which was no part of their bargain. These times were hard upon men who wanted to live their own lives.

X V

They neither saw nor heard signs of pursuit, and since hunger and thirst are sharp spurs, they crept forth from their hiding place before sunset. In this rugged country it would be dangerous to travel unknown paths in the dark. Lanny had but a vague idea where they were, but Gigi said it was somewhere between the Gapeau River and the coast, and that if they kept moving in one direction they would be bound to come upon a road. They passed through a forest of immense gnarled cork oaks, and soon they heard sounds of traffic; they hurried in that direction. When they reached the road they did not dare go out on it but hid in the underbrush, waiting for darkness. Heavy trucks passed now and then, and Lanny observed that they were red trucks, driven by red men wearing red clothes. His companion explained that they were carrying bauxite, the ore from which aluminum is made. Lanny recalled that in his boyhood he had been taken to visit these very quarries; the red-colored material had been going to Germany then, and Gigi said it was going there now. "*Les boches sont voraces!*"

They summoned their courage to walk on the road in the darkness, dodging out of sight whenever they heard a vehicle approaching. They had come to a stream, so thirst no longer troubled them; but hunger is a powerful enough urge, and when after a couple of hours a great mass of buildings loomed up in the starlighted sky they went toward them. Gigi said there was in the vicinity a very old abbey, long since abandoned; Le Thoronet was its name, and this proved to be the place. Some of the buildings were ruins, others appeared to be intact, and presently they observed a feeble light shining from a small cottage adjoining one. It was the home of a custodian, and when they told him they had lost their way he invited them in and set before them a meal of bread, onions, dried olives, and red wine. Lanny could not recall when any food had ever tasted so good.

The host, gruff in manner but kindly in soul, required only a robe and a cowl to make him a perfect monk. He informed them that he had that day celebrated the eight-hundredth anniversary of the founding of the abbey; he had had to celebrate all alone, but now that he had guests he would celebrate a second time, with a goblet of wine filled to the brim. He was there to show tourists about, and that was how he lived; it must have been a scant living, because they came only once a week on the average. Even so, on account of the anniversary he wouldn't take anything from the two wayfarers—which was fortunate, for Lanny didn't have one sou on his person. The old fellow asked no questions, but delivered free of charge his well-learned recital about the glorious old days when this monastery had been a landmark of France, and the monks had feasted on fat geese and game, fish from the sea and from the river, chestnuts and melons, "figs from Salerne and plums from Digne." These good times had been ended by the Revolution, when the monastery had been abandoned.

The old monk-at-heart offered to put them up for the night, but no, they wanted to be on their way. He gave them traveling directions and suggested that they might beg a ride on one of the bauxite trucks, which oddly enough had been brought to France by the United States Army in World War I and now were serving the Nazis. When the travelers were alone Lanny voted against getting his only suit of clothes impregnated with the red dust, for his chances of getting back to Juan without money and without identifying himself depended upon his appearance. Fortunately Gigi had a few francs on him and Lanny said that would enable them to get a shave.

They had the good fortune to encounter a truck taking a load of cork down to Toulon; the driver had stopped with tire trouble, and they helped him and got invited aboard. They didn't dare go into the city, but a few miles outside they parted from their host and took a side road to the southeast. This time they flagged a peasant cart which was taking vegetables to market. It was downhill, and the man let them climb aboard; Lanny sat in Gigi's lap, and so in the early morning they rode in state into the fashionable tourist resort of Hyeres.

XVI

Lanny got his shave and had his shoes shined and his clothes well brushed. Sleeping two nights in a brown tweed overcoat hadn't ruined it entirely, and he could still be the elegant American. He might have identified himself at a hotel or a bank, but he was afraid to do so; who could tell where he might encounter a friend of the partisans? What he wanted was to get transportation and get it quickly.

He went looking for a garage or filling station—or rather for some man who had formerly been in that business. He explained that he had urgent affairs in Cannes, and wished to be driven there this morning. The man threw up his hands. "*Impossible, Monsieur!*" But the grandson of Budd Gunmakers had been taught the power of money in childhood; he felt pretty sure there would be some gasoline hidden away in this town, and when he talked about three or four thousand francs for a two- or three-hour drive, the man said he would see what he could do. When Lanny raised the offer to five thousand, he said he could do it.

Gigi had followed behind, being afraid to let his millionaire out of his sight, but afraid to be seen with him on account of the partisans. In making his bargain Lanny said he had "*un compagnon,*" and when the car was ready the "*compagnon*" appeared and climbed in. Away they went, and got to Cannes before the close of banking hours; the car stopped in front of Lanny's bank and he went inside and wrote a counter check and had laid into his hands one hundred and ten crisp new thousand-franc notes. (The banks were stuffed with them—it was all they had.) Lanny tucked one hundred of them into an inside coat pocket, and with five in his hand he went out and paid the chauffeur.

Then he and Gigi took a walk, and when they had come to a solitary spot Lanny took out the hundred notes and counted them one by one into the hands of the pop-eyed ex-shipping clerk. "There you are," he said. "Thanks ever so much and good luck to you." They shook hands and Gigi walked down the street, looking this way and that very nervously, and so passed out of the life of Lanny Budd. Now and then the P.A. would wonder: had some woman got the money away from him the first night, or had he been impressed into those labor gangs which the Nazi-French were driving to quick death in the hot wastes of the Sahara? Now and then Lanny would shiver at the thought of one of those *râfles* which the police were conducting everywhere throughout Vichy France, rounding up all the men in some public place, a cinema or bistro or café, inspecting their papers and perhaps shipping them off to work in the Sahara. Suppose the police should find that money, and trace the bills by the serial numbers—what would Lanny tell them had been his reason for paying such a sum to an ex-shipping clerk and army deserter? For a painting, perhaps? And what painting, Monsieur?

XVII

Even more serious was his worry when he got back to Bienvenu and found there a letter from "Bruges." The postmark showed that it had arrived on the very morning that Lanny left; the postman didn't get to Bienvenu until midmorning, and Lanny had made an early start. The letter said: "I am sorry to have to tell you that the Daumier drawings of which I wrote you have been sold; all except one which is not representative of his best work. Its subject is a rather unpleasant one, of a man being tortured by bandits, and I doubt very much if it would please you, so it will not be worth while for you to come."

Obviously, Raoul was withdrawing his invitation to Toulon and warning Lanny of danger. He must have got some hint of the suspicion existing against his friend. But how had the partisans known that Lanny was coming to Toulon? Surely Raoul wouldn't have talked about it! And could it be that suspicion had now fallen upon Raoul? Did his absence from the bookstore mean that the partisans had been holding him? Or had they sent him on some errand, to get him out of the way while they dealt with Lanny? It must have been well known to them that Raoul and Lanny had been friends in the old days of the school, and Raoul could have had a hard time convincing them that those old days were no more. Would they now suspect Raoul of having plotted with Gigi to help the prisoner escape?

During the rest of his stay in Bienvenu, the P.A. didn't once dare to go out by night, and he spent a lot of time trying to think of some way to get in touch with his friend and help him if help was needed. Then one morning came the postman with one of those humble-appearing notes which said so much in so little:

"*Cher M. Budd:* Just a line to tell you how pleased I am with the little travel picture. I keep it before me always. I am well and busy. Best wishes. Bruges."

So there was one more chapter which Lanny Budd closed!

BOOK FOUR

Put It to the Touch

———————— o ————————

12. Lieb' Vaterland

I

LANNY BUDD wrote a letter, in English:

"Dear Rudi:

"I have done quite a lot of traveling since we last met in Paris. I have been all the way to California and have met a number of persons you will be interested to hear about. There is one important piece of news which can hardly have reached you and which I think you ought to have. Would it be possible for you to meet me in Switzerland? I do not suggest coming into Germany, feeling so embarrassed because of the part my country has been playing in the present struggle. It seems to me hardly possible that the German people can tolerate the presence of any American. But I know that you personally won't blame me, and your friendship is valued by me, as you no doubt know.

"Also, I have had some very interesting experiences with Madame Zyszynski. One of Tecumseh's prophecies came true in a most extraordinary way. The old lady's health has been better this winter. Conditions of travel are so hard that I wouldn't think it wise to bring her now, but when the weather moderates we might work out some way for you and your friends to see her again. I am at my mother's home in Juan-les-Pins and will wait for your reply to this letter.

"*Mit deutschem Grusse* to you and to our mutual friend,

"Your devoted Lanny."

This was addressed to Reichsminister Rudolf Hess at his Berlin residence and marked "personal." Lanny knew that mail going into Germany would be censored, but he could feel certain that no German would interfere with a letter to the Number Three Nazi. He had studied every word of it carefully; Madame Zyszynski of course was a bait, one which he had used more than once with Hess, who was as deeply interested in psychic matters as Lanny, and far more credulous. His suggestion of Switzerland was likewise a blind, for he doubted very much if Hess would leave his own country at the present time, and anyhow, it would be impossible to meet him secretly in a foreign land. Lanny wanted very much to meet Hitler, but he didn't want to ask to meet him, he wanted to be asked. "Our mutual friend" of course could mean nobody else, for the Führer was first in Rudi's thoughts and was supposed to be first in Lanny's.

In due course came the reply:

"Dear Lanny:

"I have your letter, and of course I want very much to see you, but I cannot possibly get away from my heavy duties. Do forget your idea that anybody in Germany will blame you for what has happened. We know that we have many friends in America and we appreciate them. You will be heartily welcome. I, too, have things to tell you. Assuming that you will come by way of Switzerland I am giving orders to our Consulate Generale at Berne to provide you with a visa. If there should be any hitch, put in a telephone call to me and describe it as personal.

"Our friend is well, but heavily burdened. I will tell him that you are expected.

"As ever yours,
"Rudi."

There were to be trains going up the Rhône valley, all the way to Geneva, so Jerry Pendleton had been told. Whether promises would be kept was anybody's guess, but presently Jerry phoned and reported that by the magic which he understood—a small *douceur*—he had obtained for the world-famous *connoisseur d'art* M. Budd a first-class accommodation. The train was to leave in the evening, but Jerry said: "You had better be on hand in the afternoon, and take a lunch box and a bottle of whatever you want."

Beauty Budd would see to that, of course. She was greatly disturbed by Lanny's insistence upon taking journeys in these dangerous times, but all he would say was: "Picture business." When she protested, he grinned and said: "Old darling, that's the way I earn my daily bread!" Long ago this woman of the world had learned the sad lesson that if you nag the lordly male he stops coming to you. So Bienvenu was a rendezvous and mailbox from which a P.A. could conduct his intrigues, and pending his arrival, Beauty would put his mysterious letters away in a special compartment of her escritoire. No doubt she studied their outsides carefully, and learned to know the writing, and which kind sent him to Switzerland and which to Toulon.

Had she been fooled by her son's gradual shift of political opinion? He thought it unlikely, for she was an old-time intriguer, having assisted Robbie in the handling of munitions deals to the extent of tens of millions of dollars. She knew all about how to manipulate a personality and to guide a conversation into a certain field; she had helped to teach Lanny, and when she saw him doing it, she must have understood every move and every word, and had no trouble in guessing what he was trying to find out. When he refused to take his mother into his confidence, she could be sure it was because he had given his word to somebody, and it must be somebody of importance. Through all the ages it has been the fate of women to bear sons with pain, to rear them with pains, and then see them go out into a world full of perils.

II

Lanny's journey was slow and uneventful. There was no difficulty at the border, for Swiss officials came on the train at the French border town of Annemasse, and Lanny's papers were in order. So once more he walked the streets of the very old city of watchmakers and moneylenders of which he had become fond. Geneva wasn't an exciting place from the standpoint of a world traveler; its burghers were staid and, if reports were true, rather smug concerning themselves and their town. But that didn't trouble Lanny, whose interest in night clubs and social gaieties was purely professional. The city was clean and its views fine. At Bienvenu he had left the beginnings of spring, but here it was still midwinter; snow in the streets, and nothing but snow on the mountains. He liked to walk, and found the cold bracing; the absence of almost-nude ladies on the waterfront was soothing to the senses of a gentleman whose duties compelled him to lead a celibate life.

For many years one of Lanny's pleasures in this old city had been a call upon his friend Sidney Armstrong, one of the officials of the League of Nations. Now, alas, that dream of the world's idealists was a war casualty; its beautiful white limestone palace was closed for lack of funds and Sidney had returned to the land of his fathers and was teaching a course on international affairs in what was contemptuously known as a "freshwater" college—that is to say, one which didn't happen to be Yale or Harvard or Princeton. Visiting that palace would have been like visiting the grave of his Grandfather Samuel Budd in Newcastle, a duty which Lanny had so far neglected, and for the neglect had been severely censured by the old gentleman's spirit, or whatever it was that spoke through the lips of Madame.

Always, in any part of the world, a P.A.'s first duty was to establish himself as an art expert. In this town Lanny knew an elderly lover of paintings, a merchant by the name of Fröder. He was always happy to see a visitor from overseas and to hear about events in the art worlds of Paris and London and New York. Lanny talked freely, and was rewarded with local news; the Swiss "cheese king" had recently died and left some paintings which his widow was disposed to get rid of. Lanny was pleased to be introduced to this lady and inspect her collection. He found in it two very good examples of the work of Segantini, a true genius who was claimed by both the Swiss and the Italians. He had painted in the high plateaus and had almost frozen while doing so. Lanny found it interesting to contrast him with the Dutch van Gogh, who had almost been burned while painting the dazzling sunlight of the Midi. Lanny's client, Harlan Winstead, had been wanting a Segantini for a long time. Also there were several works by Ferdinand Hodler, a Swiss painter who had been taken up by the Germans prior to World War I, and had decorated the walls of several of their universities. But he had turned against his patrons during the war, and so he was no longer their idol. Art is a weapon!

All this took time, but he was in no special hurry. The reports of what he was doing spread quickly through this small city, which was like a village—indeed, Lanny had observed that the wealthy class in every city constitute a village, and are as much interested in gossip as if they could look out of their parlor windows and see what was going on. Lanny wanted to establish himself as a person who had a right to be here, now and for the future. The Swiss, on account of their precarious position, were intensely concerned to preserve their neutrality, and to restrict the activities of the many sorts of agents who infested the country. Nazis or anti-Nazis, it was all the same to the Genevans; what they wanted was to dodge the bombs. Many of them hadn't even wanted the League of Nations in their midst.

III

An impeccably dressed American gentleman strolled along the lakefront and looked at the blue water, too deep to freeze. He looked at the monuments of Protestant reformers, as every tourist does. He stopped in at the art shops, to see if by any chance a genius had arisen in Geneva. So far they had been rather scarce. Perhaps geniuses have to break rules, and here it was hardly ever done.

A man's thoughts are his own; and always in Lanny's mind was the hope that he might run into Bernhardt Monck, and follow him at a discreet distance to some place where they could exchange a few words unobserved. Almost a year had passed since they had last met here, and Monck had told Lanny that it was the intention of the Wehrmacht to make a surprise raid upon Denmark and Norway. Since then Lanny had had only two letters from this man of the German underground, one-time sailor and Social-Democratic party official. The last letter, brief, carefully veiled, and signed with the *nom* "Brun," had informed Lanny that the writer had been ill, and that he had been unable to find any paintings which he thought worthy of an expert's distinguished attention; however, he wanted Herr Budd to know that he was not neglectful and would write as soon as he found anything good. Then silence; and of course that might mean anything in the case of one who was being ceaselessly hunted by the Gestapo.

The last rendezvous had been in the public library, which is in the University buildings. Lanny went there every day and took a look around the reading room. Failing in this, he did a little maneuvering and caused his friend Herr Fröder to mention his presence in the city to an editor of the *Journal de Genève*. There was published a brief interview in which Lanny didn't say anything about having purchased paintings for Marshal Göring and the Führer, but confined himself to mentioning important American collections to which he had been privileged to contribute. This, of course, brought letters from persons who possessed what they thought were old masters. Also, it served its secret purpose; for next afternoon, when Lanny entered the reading-room, he saw there the shaven bullet head and the broad shoulders he knew so well.

He took but one glance, then seated himself and pretended to read a book. Now and then he stole a look, and when his eyes met Monck's for a fraction of a second, he went back to his reading. When he saw that Monck had left, he got up and strolled out. Monck was going down the steps of the building, and Lanny followed across the park and into a street of shops. The man stopped in front of one of them and stood looking into the window; Lanny did the same, and heard a voice murmur: "Reformation Monument, nineteen hours." Lanny whispered: "Right," and the other strolled on.

That was the way they had made their contact a year ago, and it had served all purposes. The Reformation Monument is a long wall with statues of the Protestant reformers and heroes. At seven in the evening, in the month of March and in the shadows of high mountains, it is dark; Lanny strolled to the spot, which is in the same park as the University. He made sure there was no one following him, and when he saw his friend he followed to a spot where by a street light they could see a space all around them and at the same time be protected in the shadow of some shrubbery. There they spoke in low voices, and used no names.

"What has happened to you?" Lanny asked.

"They tried to finish me off," was the reply. "Two men slugged me on a dark street. They meant to kill me, but as it happened, a man came out of a house near by and so they ran away. I was a bit tougher than they had reckoned on. I was laid up in hospital for a spell, but I'm all right now."

"What did the authorities do?"

"It was some time before they could question me, and then I pretended to think it was an ordinary robbery. If I had admitted the truth, they would probably have ordered me out of the country, and there was no place I could go. It is a bourgeois government, you understand."

"Surely so. Did your enemies get any papers?"

"What they got gave them no information, of that you may be sure."

"You are still in danger here?"

"It is a war. I am more careful; I do not go into lonely places, and if I see anybody trying to get near me, I am not ashamed to run like the devil. Once this excited the suspicion of the police and they questioned me; I told them that I had been robbed once, and that I was afraid. They are suspicious of me and have set traps more than once, but they have never been able to get anything on me. My papers are in order and I have money in the bank; what more can you ask in the bourgeois world?"

"You haven't had any news for me of late?"

"Our group has met with a calamity, and I no longer have the sources of information that were of such benefit to us. I do not know just what happened; my key man disappeared—that is all I have heard. He may have broken under torture and revealed his own sources of information. It is a war fought in darkness and you do not see your foes."

"You attribute the attack on you to betrayal in Germany?"

"Who can say? I have always taken it for granted that the Nazis here would know me. The police of this city have made it clear that *they* suspect me, and there is apt to be a connection between them and the Nazis. Capitalist governments talk about liberty but what they mean is property. If they have to choose between a Nazi and a Red, they are for the Nazi ninety-nine times out of a hundred. If I were to meet with a police official or a consul or anybody in authority who held the balance even, I should honor him as a great man; but it has not happened to me yet."

IV

Nothing would have pleased a P.A. more than to sit down over a meal or before a warm fire and have a long talk with this one-time sailor, labor leader, and Capitán of the International Brigade in the Spanish civil war. He had been able to do it in Paris a couple of years ago, but not now in anxious and beleaguered Geneva. However, he couldn't resist the temptation to say: "I have been worried about you. Tell me something about how you live."

"I live with a Calvinist family," replied the man of the underground; "that helps to keep me respectable. I am not permitted to earn money, but I am permitted to compile data on the diplomatic history of Switzerland during the Napoleonic wars. This I do conspicuously in the library, and keep the results piled up on the desk in my room. What I do at other hours I cannot tell even to you, *lieber Genosse*."

"Surely not," agreed Lanny, who had his own secrets. "Tell me this much: you have another contact?"

"I had two, and still have one; it is not so good as the other, but I hope to improve it."

"Don't answer any question unless you think it proper. Is the underground meeting with any success in Germany?"

"I wish to God I could say yes, but I cannot. The enemy is utterly ruthless; they will kill a thousand innocent persons to get one guilty. They are extirpating us root and branch."

"I am to tell my friends outside that they are not to count upon any uprising from within?"

"They can count upon a few persons to gather information, and even that will be greatly restricted, for facts are suppressed and it is difficult to obtain them. If your friends count upon more than that, they will be disappointed. Tell them not to blame the people too severely; all those who have brains and conscience have been murdered, or else are in the concentration camps, which are a slower form of murder. This war will be fought to the end, and with a bitterness never known in modern times."

"Not in Spain?" inquired the P.A.

"The Spanish are an incompetent people; the Germans are the most competent in Europe, and perhaps in the world. If you Americans wish us to think otherwise, you will have to prove it. Tell me, what is the meaning of this 'lend lease' that I read of in the papers here?"

"It is a name which makes it possible to send help to Britain without frightening the American people too greatly." Lanny could have said more, but he was here to listen.

"Tell me this for the comfort of my soul," persisted the Capitán. "How far can America be counted upon to see it through?"

"I think you can count upon us not to let Britain go down."

"That will mean a long war. You will have to conquer half a continent."

"Our people do not realize it yet. They will move step by step, but in the end, I believe, they will do what they have to." Lanny would have liked to add: "I, too, have sources which I am not free to talk about." Instead, he continued: "I want to tell you that I got your information by mail and put it to the best use I could." This referred to the tip Monck had sent him, that the Wehrmacht was about to invade Holland and Belgium. "Not much use was made of the information, so far as I could see, but that is because statesmen are elderly and slow on the take-off."

Monck no doubt smiled in the darkness as he replied: "I belong to that class which, always and everywhere, pays for the blunders of statesmen."

V

Snow had begun to fall, which seemed to add to the feeling of inhospitality in Geneva. Both men were stamping their feet, for one does not stand still very long after dark in this high Alpine winter. "Tell me," Lanny said quickly. "Which way is the enemy going to move?"

"Everything indicates that it is to be the Balkans."

"And after that?"

"As I have told you, my source of really dependable knowledge is silent. From other sources I am led to believe it will be straight eastward."

"I too have a source of information, and am glad to have it confirmed. The campaign will begin this summer, I take it?"

"Not later than July. They expect to finish the job in a month, or two months at the utmost; but military men insist upon having a margin for error."

"One thing more: I am on my way into Germany. Do you know of any reason why I shouldn't go?"

"There is always danger, of course; but I don't know any reason having to do with *my* activities."

"Your source who has disappeared didn't have any hint concerning me?"

"Not the slightest. Of course, when we stole one of Göring's superchargers and smuggled it out of the country, you ran the risk that, if Göring missed it, he would guess you or your father must have had something to do with it. If he is keeping track of your father's doings, he may know that you have that gadget."

"My father says it has been so much improved that Göring wouldn't know his own child. I have visited the fat boy since then and he gave no sign of having any suspicion. So that is a chance I don't mind taking. But when you tell me about getting slugged, I want to be sure it wasn't on my account."

"I have not spoken or written of you to anyone. Whether anybody is shadowing us now is something about which you can guess as well as I."

"Thanks, dear comrade." Lanny held out his hand and clasped the other's. "I am doing my job and I know that you are doing yours. Let us hope that we shall live to see the day when we can sit down together and swap experiences! Meantime, *adios!*"

They parted, and walked by different routes; and be sure that Lanny kept looking in all directions, and that until he got into the frequented streets he was prepared to run fast!

VI

Lanny moved on to Bern, where he found the efficient governmental machine of the Germans all ready for him; a clerk in the Consulate Generale gave him his visa and his travel permit to Berlin. A "blue train" carried him overnight and delivered him at the Anhalter Bahnhof, bombed and now partly repaired. A taxi took him to the Adlon, where he found "business as usual"; American journalists still making its bar their "Club," and men of important affairs from all over Central Europe mixing with SS and Wehrmacht officers. The surroundings were elegant, the service perfect, and if there was a shortage of coal it was surely not felt here.

Lanny telephoned to Hess's office in the Party headquarters, and was invited to meet him that evening at Horcher's restaurant. Then he went for a stroll, to see what a year and a half of war had done to this proud cold city. He saw a few vacant places where once had been buildings; but they had been unimportant buildings, and he realized that the Nazi *Hauptstadt* had sustained little bomb damage as compared with Britain's capital. From the point of view of the bombardier Berlin was several times as far from London as London was from Berlin, the reason being that the Germans had their bases near the French and Belgian coasts, whereas the British had no place nearer to Berlin than the county of Kent. The debris was cleaned up quickly by Polish war prisoners. Everything was rationed, and the system worked perfectly, because everybody obeyed orders or went to jail. The people on the streets were well fed and clothed, and if anybody was worried because the war had lasted so long, he wasn't going to let a visiting *Ausländer* know it.

However, Lanny knew how to find out what was really going on in people's minds. He telephoned his old friend Hilde, Fürstin Donnerstein, wellspring of gossip. "Lanny Budd! *Ach, wie schön!* Come and have coffee—the last that I possess!" It was the same old Hilde, but he thought her voice sounded subdued, and when he entered her drawing-room he understood why; she was in full mourning. Her oldest son, the adored Franzi, had been killed in Poland. "The most awful thing!" she exclaimed. "A whole year after the fighting was supposed to be over, some wretched partisan hiding in a forest threw a hand grenade at him!"

Poor Hilde! The visitor had no words—none that would help her. He had met her just after the boy had gone off to the war, and had tried to cheer her with the idea that it wouldn't last long. Now he thought: She looks like an old woman—though she wasn't as old as himself. She sat with tears streaming down her cheeks, and he knew there were millions like her, in Germany and France and Britain, Poland and Czechoslovakia, Holland and Belgium and Denmark and Norway—and now all the way down into the Balkans. He had no words for any of them.

Presently she got herself together. Weep and you weep alone! Hilde was an extrovert, and very, very extro, all the way to the great capitals of the fashionable world. How was Irma, and was she really getting along in her new marriage? How was Beauty, and what a strange marriage that had been! How did matters stand with Sophie, Baroness de la Tourette, and with Margy, Dowager Lady Eversham-Watson? In happier days all these ladies had visited Berlin, and Hilde had visited the Riviera and Paris and London. Now it was all over, and what a cruel and stupid thing had taken its place! The Four Horsemen riding!

This wife of a retired Prussian diplomat, now assisting in the airraid protection of Berlin, repeated her usual performance of making certain that no servant was listening at the doors of her drawing-room, and then putting the tea-cosy over the telephone because of the generally prevalent idea that the Gestapo had some way of hearing, even while the receiver was on the hook. She sat close to Lanny and poured out her feelings, which exactly corresponded to those of the Countess of Wickthorpe—so he was able to tell her. She hated this war and all the people who were waging it. She didn't think it made any difference who won, the members of her class would lose, and the only ones who would gain were the Bolsheviks, those wolves who were lurking in Russia and in the slums of all Europe's great cities.

It was the suicide of *der Adel, le gratin*, the upper crust—this high-strung lady spoke an international language, made up of all the smart words of half a dozen languages, including Stork Club and Algonquin Hotel. If she liked something it was *très rigolo*, and if she didn't like it the thing was either lousy or putrid, depending upon whether it was American or English. Nothing pleased her more than to have Lanny repeat the latest *Witz*, *bon mot*, or wisecrack that he had picked up among the *elegantissimi* of his acquaintance. That bright world of dining and drinking and setting off verbal fireworks was gone forever, and it seemed to Lanny that the princess was in mourning for it as much as for her son. (She could only wear this costume in the house, she told him; outside it was *verboten* as being bad for morale.)

For Lanny this conversation wasn't just gossip. The Donnerstein palace was a center of hospitality for important people, the military, the industrialists, the diplomatic world, and Hilde knew not merely jests but also state secrets. Where the son of Budd-Erling was concerned she had no particle of discretion, for he was one of the "right" people, who were entitled to know what was going on and would repeat it only to others of the same sort. She had admired him, and after her friend Irma had discarded him she had gently and tactfully "propositioned" him—to employ the American slang which she found entertaining. That had been some four years ago, which made it ancient history according to modern ideas; but the ashes still smouldered, and it wouldn't have taken much breath from Lanny to have fanned them into life again. A P.A. has to use every arrow in his quiver, so he put a lot of warmth into his conversation with the Fürstin Donnerstein, even while telling her what part America was going to play in the war, and hearing her tell the details of Nazi intrigues in Hungary, Rumania, Bulgaria, Yugoslavia, Greece, and Turkey.

Lanny mentioned that he had an appointment with Hess for that evening. He made a *moue*, to show that he didn't expect to enjoy the occasion, and this served to start Hilde on a train of delightful revelations. Had he observed the glum looks, the brooding stares, which the subordinates of the beetle-browed *Nummer Drei* had learned so to dread? Lanny had been in that strange household, and had a chance to observe the tall, severe-looking lady whom the Deputy had taken to wife—or who had been assigned to him by his *Nummer Eins*. Had Hilde ever told him the rumor, which was whispered among some insiders in the regime, that the little son whom the pair called "Buz," and of whom they pretended to be so fond, was not really the Deputy's son, but was the progeny of a too-friendly doctor at Hildelang? The Deputy himself was impotent, like his Chief, and their monstrous efforts at dominance and glory were meant to compensate them in their own hearts for a shame which tormented them.

Lanny said: "A strange and terrible world!" His friend replied: "We are on our way to some dreadful catastrophe, and we are all helpless."

VII

Horcher's restaurant was a rendezvous for the powerful and wealthy Nazis, and it was a compliment for a foreigner to be invited there. Hess had engaged a private room, which meant not merely that he wanted to talk confidentially with his friend from overseas but that he himself was a man who did not care to show off or be stared at. He wore his simple Brownshirt uniform, with no decorations but the swastika. He was a man of about Lanny's age, vigorous and athletic in appearance. He had been born in Alexandria, the son of a wealthy merchant, and had been given an English education; his manners were reserved and quiet, and Lanny had to keep reminding himself that he was a killer; that he had taken part in all the Nazi brawls from the early days, and bore a scar on the side of his head where he had been hit with a beer mug. He had helped to build the Party, and had run it ever since the Blood Purge, for which he had his full share of responsibility.

Rudolf Walter Richard Hess was a fanatic who meant to make the world over in the image of his Führer, and who stopped at no means that would contribute to this end. He had a strange grim face, a mouth that made a straight line across it and heavy black eyebrows that made another line—continuous, with no break over the nose. His eyes were a grayish-green, and when he was angry with a Party delinquent he didn't have to say a word, he just glared out of those eyes and the victim wilted and his knees began to tremble. Unfortunately for the Party, but fortunately for the rest of the world, his forehead was rather low and his intelligence limited; he had begun as Adi's secretary, and he remained that in spirit even when he became a Reichsminister.

For a friend whom he trusted, this man of many cruelties would put on a genial smile and play the perfect host. To him Lanny Budd was a gentleman of high position who was heart and soul with the National-Socialist cause; who had been offered money more than once, but had turned the offers down and came freely to give such advice as he could. During the meal Lanny talked about psychic wonders, which he felt free to invent ad lib. Looking into a crystal ball he had seen an auto wreck, and a week later had come upon exactly that scene on the famed Harrisburg-Pittsburgh pike. With Madame he had had a marvelous séance, at which the spirit of Hindenburg had appeared; *der alte Herr* had been in his most sublime mood, and had dictated messages prophesying mastery of all the eastern half of Europe for his successor whom he had once insulted by calling him "the Bohemian corporal." All this the Deputy swallowed along with his broiled venison and hothouse asparagus dipped in mayonnaise.

Lanny told about London, Paris, Vichy, and then New York, Detroit, and Hollywood. After the meal had been eaten and the waiters had retired and the doors were shut, he went into really confidential matters: the significance of Lord Wickthorpe's resignation, and the strength of the movement he represented; the motives of the two bitter rivals, Laval and Darlan, and the probable consequences of the latter's recent advancement; and then, most important of all, the possibility of the removal from power of That Man in the White House who had become of his own evil choice a menace to the German cause.

Hess hadn't heard about the conspiracy against Roosevelt, except in vague rumors: "Somebody ought to shoot him!" Now he plied his guest with questions: Who was in the cabal and how far had it gone and was likely to go? Lanny said: "I gave my word of honor not to name the persons, and it wouldn't do any good for me to do so, because you cannot work with them; it would be fatal to their plans for any of them to be seen with your agents. The movement has to be simon-pure American, and it is necessary for those who take part in it to deny that they have any sympathy with Nazism. It may even be better that they believe this—as many of them do. You know how it was with your own movement, what harm it would have done if anybody had been able to show that you had been getting funds or even ideas from Russia or Britain or France."

"Of course," admitted the other. "But there may be ways we can help in strict secrecy."

"Your agents have their hands full defending your own cause. Some of them are quite influential and worth at least part of what they charge you. Forrest Quadratt, for example." *

"You don't think him trustworthy?"

"I wouldn't say that. He is skillful in promoting his private interests, but at the same time there can be no doubt that he believes in National Socialism. He has hitched his wagon to your star."

VIII

The Deputy Führer was fascinated by Lanny's account of life at San Simeon. When he heard that Marion Davies slept in Cardinal Richelieu's bed and that her apartment was known as "the Celestial Suite," Rudi made a wry face and remarked that it sounded like Karinhall. Lanny smiled, and didn't need to say anything, because he had been Göring's guest, and knew all about the fantastic extravagance there; also how the ascetic Hess despised those members of the Party who used their positions to enrich and glorify themselves.

Lanny told everything that Hearst had said, and didn't mind adding a number of things he hadn't said but might have. Rudi discussed Hearst and praised him highly; he said that was the true type of American, the men of the Far West who had conquered savages and subdued a wilderness. Such men knew how to rule and they didn't shrink at the thought of what you had to do in order to command a world full of fools and rascals. Lanny said that his grandfather had been such a man, but that he himself was too soft, he feared; he would never do for a man of action. That was the line he had taken all his life with Kurt Meissner, and apparently it went equally well with Rudolf Hess, who said with a friendly smile that he could soon make a man of action out of Lanny, but that he preferred him as a man of information.

A friendly compliment, this gave Lanny an opportunity. "I am afraid I won't be of much use to you for a while," he remarked. "You appear to be headed for the Balkans, where I have never been and have no friends."

"Don't worry," was the prompt reply. "We shan't delay long in that quarter."

"It may take longer than your leaders expect, Rudi. Are you sure the Yugoslavs won't resist?"

"Resist the Wehrmacht, Lanny? You must be joking."

"Don't forget, they have a lot of mountains."

"And we have mountain divisions. We can cut their armies to pieces in a couple of weeks."

"Well, I don't pose as a strategist, but it's obvious that you are operating on a very close timetable. Your move on Russia cannot be delayed longer than July."

The Deputy looked startled. "Who told you we are going into Russia?"

"I have a lot of friends, Rudi." The P.A. smiled gently. "Also, I have a normal amount of common sense. You have to have oil; and it is obvious that you wouldn't dare leave a left flank of a thousand miles exposed to the Red hordes."

This remark had the Deputy Führer rather stumped. He looked at his guest and remarked: "These matters are supposed to be top secret, Lanny."

"Naturally, Rudi. And please get it clear that I am not asking any questions, or even hinting for confidences. I am an art expert, and I find that I can earn a very good living, even in wartime. But I don't want to see the Reds sweep over Europe, for then I wouldn't be able to earn anything, and wouldn't want to. We'd probably both be liquidated together. You know that."

"Yes, of course."

"Well, I meet some influential man in London or New York, and he says: 'What in God's name can we do about the labor unions and the Reds?' I answer: 'It seems to me Hitler is the fellow who has the answer.' He says: 'Yes, I know that,' and I say: 'Well, then, why don't you make a deal with him, instead of helping to wipe him out? Let him be the one to put the Reds down for you.' To that there is always one objection: 'Can we trust him to do it?' Believe me, Rudi, that's the way it goes, all the way from London to Hollywood—everybody asks the same questions and raises the same objections."

"But what can *we* do, Lanny? The Führer has made his attitude plain, over and over again. To him Bolshevism is the devil incarnate."

"I know it, else I wouldn't be here and I wouldn't be your friend. I couldn't be, unless I believed in your integrity. But the problem is to convince other people. They say: 'Hitler has made a deal with the Reds.'"

"But that is obviously only a temporary matter, Lanny. Britain and France drove us to it; the French had an alliance, and the British were threatening to make one."

"The average man forgets all that—even the average big business-man in America. I have to say: 'I know. I have talked with the Führer, and with his Deputy. The goal of all their efforts is to end that horrid menace on their eastern border. As for Britain, they desire nothing so much as an understanding, a settlement that will give Germany her outlet to the east.'"

"Absolutely, Lanny!"

"The trouble was, I hadn't seen you for the greater part of a year. I suppose twenty times someone said to me: 'Yes, but that was more than half a year ago, and maybe they've changed their program—how can you be sure?' So finally I said to myself: 'I'm out-of-date. I'll go back into Germany, and sell a couple of paintings for Hermann to provide an excuse. I'll see Rudi and maybe the Führer, and hear what they have to say now—if they care to talk to me.'"

"*I* certainly care to, Lanny. There has been no change—quite the contrary. It is literally an agony to me to see Germany and Britain destroying each other. I don't want to bomb London, and neither does Hermann—he will tell you that. I give you my word, I valued the Guildhall as much as I do the New Chancellery, and I value what each stands for. I want a truce, and a deal that will last. I want an end to this madness, and I have heard the Führer say the same thing a thousand times. He doesn't even ask that Britain shall help us against the Reds. We can do it alone, and we ask only that Britain give up her insane rage against us."

"I don't say that it can be done, Rudi; I would be a fool to say that.

But I promise to do my best. If the Führer will say that to me with his own lips, I'll go out and repeat it, word for word, as faithfully as a phonograph, to a dozen key men in London and the States. There's just a possibility that Churchill might be overthrown, as well as Roosevelt, and this fratricide might be brought to a halt overnight."

"I assure you, Lanny, I'd give my life to bring that about. I mean it literally—for I have fought in the trenches and know what it means to be ready to die."

"I have never fought, Rudi, but I know I'd be willing to, in this cause. Let's try it together, and see what we can work out." It was on that bargain that they shook hands.

IX

Lanny telephoned to the official *Residenz* of Hermann Wilhelm Göring, Reichsmarschall, Reichsminister, and bearer of so many other titles that his own staff couldn't remember them all. The caller asked for Oberst Furtwaengler, who had been his friend for a matter of seven years; Lanny learned that he had just been promoted to Generalmajor. "*Herrlich, Herr Budd!*" exclaimed the SS officer, who, unlike most of them, aspired to be taken as a man of European culture. "I heard that you were in town and meant to call you." They exchanged compliments, and Lanny asked after the Generalmajor's charming wife and his children—there was a new one. Only after he had shown the proper amount of interest in a staff officer did he venture to inquire: "Is Seine Exzellenz visible these days?"

"*Leider,* I am not permitted to say where he is at the moment. But I can reach him."

"Tell him that I really ought to see him before I leave. Since we last met I have been in Vichy France twice, and in Britain, and in America all the way to California. I have some important messages for him. Also, I have news about paintings, though I don't suppose he has much time to think of that subject now."

"Don't mistake him, Herr Budd—nothing will ever be permitted to diminish his interest in paintings. I will get in touch with him and call you."

So Lanny settled down to study the four pages which now comprised the *Völkischer Beobachter,* from which one could learn much about conditions in Berlin. It was before the time that death notices were prohibited, and very nearly a page of the paper was given up to advertisements, paid for by relatives according to the German custom: each a tiny oblong enclosed in a black border, and each reverential in tone. "Fallen on the field of battle, in the twenty-second year of his dutiful life," or something like that, and always a pious phrase, with

Adolf Hitler substituted for Deity: "In the service of the Führer," or "gladly, for the Führer"—all morale-building phrases.

All the war news was favorable; the German people were not told the details of how the British had swept the Italians almost all the way out of Libya; they were told about the achievements of the German air corps which was stationed in Sicily and was closing the Eastern Mediterranean to the British and making Malta all but untenable to the foe. They were told that pro-Nazi governments were now firmly established in the Balkan states and that a pact had just been signed with Yugoslavia; they were not told that the people of Yugoslavia were in revolt against this deal—something which Lanny had learned from the newspapers of Switzerland. In every line of the *Völkischer*, one could see the fine Rhenish hand of the crooked-limbed and crooked-souled little Reichsminister, "*Unser Doktor*," who decided each day what the German people were to believe about their world.

X

The Generalmajor phoned. His great Chief would be very happy to meet Herr Budd, but it would be necessary to fly. Lanny said: "I don't mind flying—especially when I have one of the Reichsmarschall's pilots." The staff officer replied: "*Aber, es ist Krieg.*" Lanny said: "I'll take my chances."

One other detail, rather embarrassing, explained the officer; it would be necessary for the guest to be blindfolded. To this regulation there was no exception for *Ausländer*, even the most distinguished. Lanny laughed and said: "I would be willing to be blindfolded for a week if I were sure of seeing Seine Exzellenz on Saturday night." A Nazi who aspired to be taken for a good European found this delightfully clever.

A staff car would call for him at ten o'clock next morning; meantime Lanny went shopping in Berlin. He wanted to write a letter asking a price for a certain painting which he had viewed on his last trip; and apparently somebody had been too greatly tempted by the folder with a few sheets of carbon paper which he kept in his suitcase. Anyhow, it couldn't be found, and Lanny wanted one sheet—just one sheet of carbon paper! He wandered from shop to shop, and everywhere he saw a generous stock of all kinds of goods in the windows, but when he went inside he found that the shelves were bare. "*Leider, mein Herr,*" they would say. "*Wir hoffen,*" but never, "*wir haben!*"

When he mentioned that this or that was in the windows, the answer was: "But those are not for sale." When a perverse foreigner persisted: "Why do you keep them there?" one clerk replied: "*Polizeilich empfohlen*"—which fell rather oddly upon foreign ears, meaning in literal translation: "Policely recommended." That struck Lanny as a characteristic Nazi phenomenon; the police didn't have to order, it was sufficient if they "recommended" that the show windows should be kept well filled. Some shopkeepers were saving trouble by setting a little sign alongside the goods: "Not for sale"!

One thing was plentiful and free, and that was music. Any day you could hear the three B's, Bach, Beethoven, and Brahms; but only one M—Mozart, never Mendelssohn, who stood for Jewish shallowness and frivolity, or Mahler, who stood for Jewish pretentiousness. Lanny went to an afternoon concert, and found it crowded with reverent people. He could have his own emotions and his own thoughts, but they couldn't be happy ones, for in his soul was infinite unending grief for a Germany that had been murdered, or was being murdered day after day; for all the monuments of the old German civilization that were being bombed out of existence, and for all the potential Mozarts and Beethovens who were being slaughtered on battlefields far from home. Most of all he mourned because he, Lanny Budd, who had so loved German culture, now had to hate it and do everything in his power to bring it to destruction. Was there anybody else in this symphony hall thinking such thoughts while the tragic funeral march of Beethoven's *Eroica* was being played? And if there was anything in the theory of telepathy, what a jangle of brainwaves this foreign visitor must have been creating!

XI

Back to the hotel, and dinner with one of Lanny's clients, an elderly merchant who loved fine paintings. Lanny guessed that he must be in need of funds; and certainly, by his appearance and behavior he was in need of a dinner. It might be possible for Lanny to take a painting out with him—he would ask Oberst Furtwaengler about a permit, and would probably get it. They agreed upon a price and Lanny saw the old gentleman out into the blackout, and then went to bed early, for an air-raid alarm was always to be expected, and resort to the shelter was *polizeilich befohlen*.

The British bombers left their homeland at about dusk. They had become wary after a year and a half of conflict with the Luftwaffe and with the anti-aircraft guns which surrounded every German target of importance. If they were bound for Central or Eastern Germany they would fly over the North Sea and come in by unexpected routes. It seemed that one of their purposes was to deprive good Germans of their sleep, for they would aim for one city and then veer off to another. They were due over Berlin shortly after midnight, but they would vary this, too. All good Berliners now slept in their underwear, and kept their shoes and trousers and overcoats close at hand. They loudly cursed the malicious foe, calling him an enemy of humanity, a throwback to barbarism, a monster out of hell. Lanny, listening, would have liked to ask: "Did you never hear of Guernica and Madrid, of Warsaw and Rotterdam, of London and Coventry?" But of course he couldn't speak such words, and indeed he avoided speaking any word of that language which unfortunately was called English and not American. He rolled his "r's" and growled his gutturals so that no shopkeeper or waiter or other humble German might report him for a spy.

Some time in the wee small hours the sirens screamed. Lanny slipped into his clothes and ran down three of the five flights of stairs in the Hotel Adlon, and one more into the basement—it was forbidden to use the elevator. There was a well-appointed room with comfortable chairs for the guests; none of the help appeared, and presumably there was a separate shelter for them. Lanny had an interesting experience, for in the seat next to him was an elderly gentleman in the uniform of a Rumanian general; he had a gray mustache and—believe it or not—rouged cheeks; his figure indicated that he was wearing corsets. He sat very stiff and stern, telling the world that he had no particle of fear, and also that he did not care to engage in promiscuous conversation.

There was something vaguely familiar about his face, and Lanny kept stealing glances at it; he had met so many officers in so many gorgeous uniforms in the course of a social career which had begun very young. Finally it came to him, and he leaned over and whispered: "Pardon me, but is this by any chance Captain Bragescu?"

"*General* Bragescu," replied the other, with heavy accent.

"You were Captain when I knew you, sir. My name is Lanny Budd, and my father is Robert Budd who was European representative of Budd Gunmakers."

"Oh!" exclaimed the other. And then: "*Oh!*" again. "You are that little boy who took me torch fishing!"

"And you speared a large green moray," supplied Lanny. "A dangerous creature. And you told me about how they catch sturgeon at the mouth of the Danube and cut out the black caviar and throw the fish back alive."

So the great man unbent and they had a jolly time, even with bombs crashing not far away, and people cringing in ill-concealed terror all about them. The Captain had visited Bienvenu to make a deal for—what was it? oh, yes, automatic pistols! And he had stayed a couple of days, and had thought Lanny's mother the loveliest woman he had ever laid eyes on. He didn't mention it now, but he had been greatly disappointed to discover that she didn't go automatically with the pistols.

He had been entertained by a lively and talkative little boy, already a man of the world prepared to deal with every social situation. More than a quarter of a century had passed, but it all came back out of the deep, deep memory ocean. And before they went back to bed, the General, who was in Berlin representing the new Fascist government of his country, was telling this sympathetic American all about how the coup d'état had been pulled off, and what territorial emoluments had been promised his native land.

13. The Least Erected Spirit

1

THE staff car took Lanny to the great Tempelhoferfeld, which now, of course, was a military port; but there was nothing secret about it, it was one of the landmarks of Berlin and could not be camouflaged. Only when the visitor was taken out into the field and placed in the co-pilot's seat of a fighter plane did the polite young flight officer put into his hands a small bandage of black silk cloth with two elastic straps in back. "*Verzeihung, Herr Budd*," he said, and Lanny replied: "*Danke schön*," and proceeded to put it over his eyes, which it covered completely. "*Richtig?*" he asked, and the other replied, American fashion: "O.K." He added: "Please, you are not to touch it under any circumstances." Lanny replied: "I understand."

The plane took off with a roar. It had been headed east, and the pressure on Lanny's body told him that it was making a half turn. Of course Göring's headquarters—*Gefechtsstand*, it was called, "combat station"—would be in the west, probably in Belgium or northeastern France. Lanny was used to planes and the difference in their sounds, and he could tell that this was one of the fastest; he guessed that he would be sitting here for an hour and a half or two hours, and he sat slumped in the seat with his arms folded and his mind on the details of what he hoped to get from the fat commander.

They were flying low—Lanny knew that because he had had no crackling in his ears. Time passed, and he was thinking that they must be going far into France, when the pilot leaned toward him—the only time he spoke during the trip—and shouted: "*Wir sind nah daran.*" The plane made a half circle, the engine slowed, and with a light bump

.

the wheels touched the ground. A voice said: "*Guten morgen, Herr Budd. Oberleutnant Förster.*" Lanny recalled one of the younger officers whom he had met at Karinhall. His hand was taken and he was helped down from the plane and from it to a car—still with the blindfold in position.

He had tried to guess what sort of place he was going to. It would be the advanced headquarters of the Luftwaffe, from which the fighting across the Channel was being directed. It would be an ultra-secret place, and necessarily large; it probably wouldn't be new, because it must have been needed in great haste. It would be some old château in a forest; it would have an airfield near, but not too near, for airfields were an invitation to bombing. The *Gefechtsstand* would be a great telephone exchange, with direct lines to every field in Germany and the conquered lands, and likewise to all the centers of government and industry. The supreme commander would have a soundproof room, and a desk with several telephones on it, and a strong and comfortable chair in which he could sit and rave and storm and curse and govern the Luftwaffe, just as Lanny had heard him doing from the *Residenz*, and from Karinhall and Rominten and the Obersalzberg and other places where Lanny had been a guest over a period of eight years.

All this fitted in with being led along a graveled walk, and ascending half a dozen deep stone steps, and passing into an interior where there was a murmur of voices and echo of footsteps in a spacious place. Then down a long corridor with many people passing, coming and going with brisk quick talk. They stopped in front of a door, the door was opened—and suddenly came a bellow: "*Jawohl! Wie geht's bei dem blinden Maulwurf!*" It pleased the old-time robber baron to command: "Stand the *Schurke* up against that wall and shoot him!" Lanny of course grinned—for he mustn't let any old robber get a "rise" out of him.

The Oberleutnant slipped the bandage off his eyes; and there stood the figure whom all good Germans loved; they called him, affectionately, "*Unser Hermann,*" a liberty such as they never took with the Führer. He was several inches shorter than Lanny but made up for it in girth; he had weighed two hundred and eighty pounds the last time he had reported to his art expert, and certainly he hadn't lost anything since then. He wore a simple blue uniform appropriate to wartime, and his only decoration was the eight-pointed gold marshal's star; but he would never be without his emerald ring, about an inch square, and a bunch of diamonds on one finger of the other hand.

He always roared when he saw visitors; a medium roar if he was glad to see them, a double roar if he was angry. He always grasped Lanny's hand with one which was full of power, and Lanny, forewarned, grasped back with determination. He looked at his host and saw that his usually florid features had paled startlingly. That was what ten months of unanticipated war had done to him; ten months of incessant worry and thwarted hopes, for the adored Luftwaffe hadn't been able to knock out the Royal Air Force, and Hermann had had to tell his *Nummer Eins* that it was impossible to invade England then, perhaps ever. No doubt he had taken many a tongue lashing for his *Dummheit*, his *Eselei*, his *Blödsinn*. Quite a change in two years, from the happy day when the Führer had given a banquet to big leading generals and imparted to them the tidings that he had decided to wipe out Poland. *Der Dicke*, according to one of his aides who had blabbed to Lanny, had been so delighted that he had leaped onto the table and danced a war dance.

The visitor had time for a glance about him and saw that he was in a high-ceilinged room with all the marks of elegance: carved paneling, a marble fireplace, and heavy tapestries on the walls. Hermann Wilhelm Göring would never fail to do himself well. It was undoubtedly a château, and he had conquered it and was making himself at home. On his desk was a tray with an emptied glass of beer and the remains of sandwiches; there were remains also in the fat man's mouth, and now and then he made an explosive sound which had caused Robbie and his son, strictly in private, to give him the code name of "Sir Toby Belch." In Lanny's world it wasn't considered good form to mention those sounds, but Hermann thought they were funny, and when he laughed, everybody laughed with him.

II

But now, to business! "*R-r-raus!*" said the commander to his subordinates, and signed his guest to a chair by the desk. "*Na, na*, Lanny, tell me where you have been and what you have seen, *und was zum Teufel treibt dieser verdammte Roosevelt?*"

Lanny began the long story which he had told so many times that he could have said it in his sleep. First Pétain and Laval and Darlan and all that Vichy crew; then London, and Wickthorpe and his friends, and the meaning of his resignation; then the land of America Firsters and isolationists, of crowds that shouted to keep out of Europe's troubles, and fellows in the country clubs who raved about "That Man" whom "somebody ought to shoot." *Der Dicke* plied his guest with questions, and it was a pretty stiff examination; he didn't want anybody feeding him any *Bonbon*, he said—it was the Berliners' word for candy; he wanted the real facts, and if they were tough, all right, he would take them.

Lanny said: "Of course, Hermann. I tell you what I have seen and heard; but you have to allow for the fact that I don't meet the war crowd; those *Hurensöhne* wouldn't associate with me, and I don't have a chance to ask them any questions."

"How do you get along with your father?" the fat commander wanted to know. He knew Robbie Budd, respected him, and had done business with him as long as he could.

"It's rather complicated," explained the son. "Robbie has the excuse that he can't help what he's doing, and he has to consider the interests of his stockholders. I just can't agree that stockholders come ahead of civilization, and I think Robbie ought to hold out and put up a harder fight against the New Dealers who have practically taken him over. I think I may have influenced him to some extent, for the government is very ill-satisfied with the quantity and quality of the Budd-Erling plane. You may have noticed that the R.A.F. isn't using it very much."

"Yes, but I understand there is a new model in production now."

"When I asked Robbie about that he chuckled a little and said: 'You wait and see.' I had to be content with that, because of course it's the most ticklish subject in the world. My guess is Robbie has tucked his best secrets away for future use; but if the government had the slightest idea of that, they would take over his plant quicker than you could bat an eyelid."

"I'm surprised they haven't done so," commented the Reichsmarschall.

"There's generally a reason for things like that. You'd be pleased to know how many people there are in the Administration who don't like its policies and do what they can to hold back. You must understand that distrust of Britain is taught to every schoolchild in America; and from the practical point of view many of our business leaders look upon the British Empire as their principal competitor. Britain is a maritime power, like America, and these businessmen think we could get along a lot better with a land power like Germany."

Der Dicke didn't want any *Bonbon*, but Lanny observed that when one was put into his mouth he swallowed. "*Ganz richtig!*" the greedy one exclaimed; and when the visitor went on to tell about the great conspiracy that was going to put an end to Jewish-plutocratic Bolshevism in America, he beamed like the cat that had swallowed the canary. He was too well informed a man to believe that Roosevelt was a Jew, but he knew that Morgenthau was, and Frankfurter, and Frank and Rosenman and Baruch and Cohen—he had them at his tongue's end, even down to David K. Niles.

The plot to get rid of them all at one fell swoop seemed to him perfectly natural and exactly in order; it was what Hermann himself had done in the summer of 1934, and if rumor could be believed he had forced the Führer's hand on that occasion. While the Führer had flown to Munich to confront his old pal Röhm, he had left Hermann in control of Berlin, and Hermann had taken the occasion to uncover a wide conspiracy and to slaughter something like a thousand persons, including General Schleicher, one of Göring's own sort, a high-up Junker Wehrmacht man. Now the *Nummer Zwei* rubbed his hands in glee as Lanny described the rapid progress the New York and Washington conspiracy was making, and the results that would flow from it, the instant cutting off of the newfangled abortion called "lend-lease," which was really a declaration of war against Germany, though Germany was unfortunately not in a position to take up the challenge at the moment!

III

This man of action wanted to get busy on the proposition without loss of time. He had his own men in New York, he said, independent of everybody else, and he wanted to give them the tip and let them help with funds, and to keep their master informed day by day. But Lanny said: "For God's sake, go slow, Hermann; you might queer the whole deal. You must understand that this is dynamite; if the least hint reached anybody that the Germans were backing it, all the important men who are in it would have to drop it like a hot poker."

"That may be true; but there are tactful ways of going about the matter."

"If it was you doing it, there might be intelligence enough; but don't you know what secret agents are, as a rule?"

"*Idioten!*" exclaimed the Air Commander. "*Scheisskerle!*" He started cursing, and Lanny perceived that a sore spot had been touched.

But Göring couldn't drop so important a subject. He so hated and feared Roosevelt, and he so dreaded a long war, the thing against which the Oberkommando had warned everybody from the beginning. Surely he ought to make some move in the case of Hearst, who published his articles and paid him sumptuous prices! Surely Hearst would receive a representative of a featured author!

Lanny said: "You must understand that Hearst has a million enemies, and he is afraid of every single one of them. He owns eighteen great newspapers and he worries about each one, and what his enemies might do to ruin it. Right now he would be afraid to be seen in the same room with any German."

"But I could send an American to him."

"How would Hearst know that he was an American, and that he wasn't a plant of the British government, or even of the F.B.I.? Take my word and let me handle this. I am going back soon, and these people have known me a long time, and they know that I don't want any of their money. Be sure they don't need yours; good God, man, they have most of the money in the world. And do you want to squander what *Valuta* you have stowed away in New York?"

That was the right way to put it. "All right, Lanny," said *Der Dicke.* "Do what you can, and come back and tell me, because I am worrying myself to a skeleton over this war that I never wanted and tried my best to prevent. You know that is true, don't you?"

"*Ja, und als ganzer Mann!* I'll give you a certificate any time you ask for it." To himself Lanny was saying: "*Du alter Windbeutel!* You told me in 1939 you had stuck out your neck in 1938 and would never do it a second time!"

IV

The Reichsmarschall bawled for his lunch; it was five minutes late, he declared, and nobody thought to mention how recently he had stuffed himself with cheese sandwiches and beer. Orderlies came running and wheeled in a table and brought trays containing *Hasenpfeffer* and a large platter of cold meats, fried potatoes, and canned peas, buttered toast, a *compote* with rich cream and cake—you would hardly have guessed that the country was at war. *Der Dicke* went at it, and bade his guest do the same. Despite the fact that he came of a good Prussian family, his table manners were hardly pleasant; he stuffed and belched and then stuffed some more; he talked with his mouth full, and still more embarrassing, laughed loudly with his mouth wide open. "I am done with this dieting business," he declared. "I am going to be as fat as nature meant me." Then: "But what do you think they have got for me here, to reduce me?" When Lanny couldn't guess, he exclaimed: "An electric horse! I am supposed to sit on it and get bumped."

"I hope it is a good strong horse," grinned Lanny.

"A dray horse, the kind that used to haul beer barrels. A Percheron, from Normandy. I pass by and look at it, and that is all I need to do. The very thought takes several pounds off me!"

The guest brought up the subject of art, and found that it was as Furtwaengler had stated. *Die Nummer Zwei* bubbled over with delight. "I am in the wholesale business!" he declared. "I have all the worthwhile paintings in Belgium and Holland and France! There has been nothing like it since art was invented."

"I have heard rumors about it," said the other, sharing the mood of opulence.

"It is like something out of the *Arabian Nights' Enchantments*. I can hardly believe it myself. I no longer have time to look at them, I can't even study the lists. I take them in the form of statistics."

"Where are you keeping them?"

"I won't tell you where—you mightn't be able to resist the temptation!" *Der Dicke's* wide mouth spread most of the way across his face, so great was his amusement.

"At least you can tell me what you plan to do with them."

"I am going to build the greatest museum the world has ever seen, a temple of the art of all nations—a separate wing for each. The world will say there never was such a collector and never will be again. I have already drawn the plans and submitted them to the Führer."

Lanny became suddenly serious. "Listen, Hermann; let me help with this."

"Would it really interest you?"

"*Herrgott!* Have you forgotten that I am supposed to be a *Kunstsachverständiger?*"

"All right, you shall be my adviser. There will be a lot of trash, naturally. I was too busy to look at them. I just said: 'Take everything, and we'll decide later.' You shall weed out the second-rate, and we'll have nothing but the best."

"I have been helping to make just such a collection for an American millionaire; but of course not on any such scale."

"There will be nothing like this in all the world. People will remember the Hermann Göring art collection when they have forgotten who built the Luftwaffe."

"I don't think the British and the French are going to forget that for quite a while, Hermann."

"Have another piece of cake," said *Der Dicke.* "You like this Château-Chalon? I got it from the cellars of the duc de Montalembert. Enough to last me fifty years."

"Are you afraid to tell me where you have *that* stored, Hermann?" So they jested, back and forth. It was American, not Prussian; the Reichsmarschall and Reichsminister wouldn't have taken it from one of his subordinates, which was why they bored him, and why he liked this visitor from overseas—a crazy country, full of eccentricities, amusing on the cinema screen and over the air, but now becoming dangerous and having to be taught a lesson in *Machtpolitik.*

Was it some such thought as this? A shadow passed across the broad fat face, and he reached for a little bottle of white pills which he kept in his pocket. It might have been some harmless stuff, say bicarbonate of soda for his belching; but there was something furtive in his action, and Lanny quickly turned his eyes to his own glass of white wine. He knew that after World War I the fugitive Captain Göring in Sweden had become a drug addict, a serious and violent case who had to be consigned to an institution. Nothing was more likely than that under the strain of disappointment and suspense he had gone back to his habit. Was that why his fat features were sallow instead of rosy, as Lanny remembered them from Paris, less than a year ago? It was a visitor's business not to know about this, and to continue his cheerful line of conversation.

V

Lanny Budd had emptied his intellectual purse; he had given his host all the information he had, and no little entertainment. Now, after the tables had been wheeled away and they were once more alone, it was the time to collect what he could. He proceeded to give the Reichsmarschall the same line of talk that had worked so well with Kurt Meissner and Rudolf Hess. Everywhere he traveled in France, Britain, and America, his appeaser friends wanted to know what the Führer's intentions were, and to what extent they could count upon him for the all-important task of putting down the Red menace. It was the art expert's hope to have a little of the Führer's time, and get this question answered at first hand, not because he had any doubts as to where the German armies were going when they had finished in the Balkans, but because the men of big industry who controlled the foreign policies of the Anglo-Saxon lands wanted this assurance as the basis of all their planning for world peace.

"When the Führer tells you," said *Der Dicke,* "I wish you would come and tell me."

Lanny grinned. "You are trying to make me believe you don't know where the Luftwaffe is going next?"

"Upon my honor, Lanny. The Führer keeps his own counsel, as he did during the Polish crisis, and before that, over Czechoslovakia."

That was disappointing. Göring was a far more intelligent man than Hess, and wasn't going to swallow Lanny's bait so quickly.

"Tell me what I am to say for you, Hermann—to Wickthorpe and his friends, and to Hearst, and to Henry Ford, who is standing out against making munitions for the British."

"My attitude has not changed a particle; and in this I know that I speak for the Führer too. This war is the greatest calamity that has ever befallen civilization; it is the suicide of the Aryan peoples—the very ones who were in position to take control of the world and keep the backward tribes in order. If I could talk to the key people of Britain and America, I would get down on my knees and beg them to stop and reconsider, before it is too late."

"That is a good line, *lieber Freund;* I shall not fail to quote it. *Aber* —you must understand, this is not Lanny Budd talking, this is the people I shall meet. They say: 'Germany has a deal with the Bolsheviks now.' "

"No man with any sense could fail to know that that is a maneuver, a temporary device. The West forced us into it—the Franco-Russian alliance, and the Franco-British mission in Moscow. Could they expect us to sit still and let them weave a spider's web all around us? Other nations can expand, but never Germany. For us—*Einkreisung!*"

"That is an old story, Hermann; it has all been in the newspapers, and in the Führer's speeches. When I take the long trip into Germany, a difficult matter in wartime, it is not to have lessons in history. My friends will expect me to bring out something new, something that meets the situation of the moment. Tell me what you want these friends to *do*."

"I want them to get off our backs while we do the real job that every civilized man knows has to be done. Look at me: I am the Chief of the Luftwaffe, and when I make my plans to protect our armies in the east, I have to keep half my forces in the west. I have to know that our blood brothers, our fellow-Aryans, will be sending their planes to bomb our cities and kill our civilian workers and their women and children. It is a crime, Lanny, a monstrosity!"

"You don't have to tell me, Hermann; I can't sleep at night for thinking about it. The question is, what is to be *done?*"

"Nothing can be done so long as those two bandits, Churchill and Roosevelt, can sit at the telephone every night and plot new destruction."

"That is elementary, and I know hundreds of people in the two countries who realize it just as clearly as you do. But the problem is, where to begin? Somebody has to trust the other. When you move against Russia, our side has to know it and be prepared to come to your defense. You must understand, I'm not hinting for information—I have it quite definitely that you are going to attack Russia not later than July. The problem is to convince the people abroad that it's no bluff, but that they're really going to get the thing they want so desperately."

"If I had charge of our foreign policy, I would say to Britain and America: you want me to pull your chestnuts out of the fire for you, but I am nobody's monkey. If you want this job done, come and help, instead of trying to destroy me."

"You mean, you would take up a defensive strategy both east and west?"

"*Gerade das!* We have conquered an empire, and who can take it from us? Let Britain and America come and try!"

"But you know that is not the Führer's temperament, and not his policy. The Wehrmacht is getting ready to overrun Russia, and the Luftwaffe must be doing the same."

"Well, Lanny, if you know that, it's all right with me; but don't ask me to talk about it. See the Führer, and if he tells you, then you will really know."

"I am embarrassed to approach him, on account of my father's posi-

THE LEAST ERECTED SPIRIT

tion, so hard for him to understand. Would you care to tell him that I have information which it is worth while for him to hear? You remember, you did that at the height of the Polish crisis. I wasn't able to do what we had hoped, but it did no harm to try."

"How long do you intend to stay?"

"I am at your service. In a crisis like this a man does not think of his private affairs. But, at the same time, if you have any painting you want taken out, I may be able to arrange it. Our State Department puts many obstacles in the way, but so far my father's influence has been able to overcome them. By the way, he asked me to be sure to give you his cordial greetings, and his assurances that he is doing as much as any one mere businessman can."

VI

Lanny Budd learned that one way to keep the favor of these great and busy persons was to offer to leave promptly. It flattered them to have the value of their time appreciated. But, as it happened, *Der Dicke* had a different kind of vanity; it pleased him to declare that he had so systematized his work that he could always take time off. "I want you to meet some of my boys," he said. "I have several decorations to confer."

It was to be a formal ceremony, and Lanny was asked to stand beside one of the windows, out of the way. Göring pressed a button and gave a command, and presently came the sound of marching in the hall. There entered the room, first, a man in the uniform of a Luftwaffe general, a man young for that high rank, with a round, rather boyish face, pink cheeks, and dark hair close cut. This was General Milch, Göring's assistant and right bower; he had been suddenly promoted from lieutenant-colonel, something deeply resented by old-line Wehrmacht officers. Milch had a Jewish father, and was one of those military men who saved their careers by having their mothers make affidavit that they had committed adultery and that the Jew was not the actual father. One look at Milch and you would know the mother's offense was perjury, not adultery; but the Nazis didn't go by looks, they went by instructions. Göring had said: "It is I who decide who is a Jew!"

Two subordinate officers followed, and behind them marched half a dozen flight officers of various ranks, all very young, all solemn and exalted. They stood in a line before their fat commander, and saw nothing grotesque about him, but on the contrary worshiped him as the second-greatest man in the world, the author of their victories, the maker of their careers. Göring, grave as a priest celebrating high mass, stood in front of the first in line, saluted and said: "Leutnant Sieghammer, the records shows that you have shot down fourteen enemy planes, that you have been twice wounded, and that when obliged to parachute to the ground you gave first aid to a wounded comrade in spite of your own wounds. I honor your heroism, and that of your comrades who are here before me. In the name of the Führer, and as a symbol of the gratitude of the German people, I present you with this Iron Cross, first class, which you will wear with pride for the rest of your days and pass on to your descendants."

The cross was about two inches each way, and without a ribbon. It was pinned onto the coat, on the left side below the chest. The young flyer's thin face was flushed with excitement; he had fair hair and sensitive features, and bore a startling resemblance to Alfred Pomeroy-Nielson, the baronet's grandson. To Lanny it was a confirmation of what the Reichsmarschall had just said, that this was a fratricidal war, that these boys who were machine-gunning one another in the air were in very truth blood brothers. Hard indeed not to want that fighting stopped!

Göring repeated the procedure in front of each of the group, refreshing his memory from little cards. When the ceremony was over he ordered everybody at ease and chatted with his heroes. He brought Lanny forward and introduced him as "*ein amerikanischer Freund des National Socialismus.*" Each man bowed sharply from the waist and expressed his sense of honor. They were as much like automatons as twenty years' discipline could make them; but one was a little different, a rolypoly, somewhat the shape of his Kommandant, but with dark hair and lively dark eyes. He bore the name of Bummelhausen, which was to say the least unusual, like a burlesque name on the vaudeville stage. "*Es ist ein besonderer Vorzug, Herr Budd*"—an unusual privilege —exclaimed this youngster, and Lanny asked: "Have I not met you before, Herr Bummelhausen?"

"It is my younger brother whom you met, Herr Budd. He was one of a group of the *Jugendschaft* who were camping in the Teutoburger Wald, and you were motoring and stopped at their campfire."

"Oh, surely! I recall it very well."

"You gave them a little talk about the Führer, and then you were introduced to them, one by one. My brother was so excited over shaking a hand that had shaken the Führer's hand that he has never stopped talking about it. I suppose he has told it in my hearing two dozen times."

"Well, now," smiled Lanny, "you will be able to tell him that you have shaken the same hand—and much more important, you have shaken the hand of the Reichsmarschall, the Father of the Luftwaffe."

Little shivers were running up and down a P.A.'s spine. What a small Germany it was! In August, less than two years ago, when he had been helping Laurel Creston to get away from the Gestapo, they hadn't dared to stop at any hotel; they had come upon this youth encampment, and Lanny had had the bright thought that here was a place where they might spend the night without having to sign their names in a register. They had been introduced to a line of eager, excited boys, and one had borne the name of Bummelhausen, which had amused Lanny. He had commented on it later to Laurel, and it had become in their conversation a symbol for the robots turned out by the Hitler machine, the faithful and adoring children who would grow up to become crusading warriors, dying gladly on a hundred battlefields for the glory of their heaven-sent Leader.

"Where is your brother now, Herr Leutnant?" inquired the American friend of National Socialism.

"He is training at Kladow, Herr Budd, and hopes to get his wings next month."

Lanny said no more, for the subject was one full of danger. What if the youngster had heard of "*die Miss*," and were to ask after her? Lanny moved on to chat with the other men.

Later he discovered that he had made as deep an impression upon the elder as upon the younger Bummelhausen; for when he had bade farewell to the Reichsmarschall, and was blindfolded and driven back to the airfield and seated in the plane, he heard the familiar young voice saying: "*Gut Rutsch, Herr Budd! Gut Rutsch!*" That was the airmen's phrase for "pleasant journey." Like the British and Americans, they relieved the tedium of war by making a language of their own. Oddly enough, Lanny discovered that the civilians of Berlin were doing the same. Back in his hotel, he happened upon one of his father's business friends; they had a chat, and when they parted, this elderly steel magnate remarked: "*Bolona!*" Lanny wasn't sure that he had heard aright, and ventured to ask about the word. The other laughed and explained: "That has taken the place of '*Adieu*' with us Berliners. It is made of the syllables of '*Bombenlose Nacht.*'" Bombless night— of which Lanny saw few while he was in Berlin.

VII

In the headquarters of the Hitler Youth organization sat a patient and faithful bureaucrat who was one of Lanny's oldest friends in Germany. Heinrich Jung was only three years younger than the American, but had always looked up to him, because Lanny had been a guest at the castle of Stubendorf, where Heinrich's father had been *Oberförster*, head forester of the estate. Such class feelings were in the very bones of an honest German lad, and not even a Nazi revolution could get them out.

Always hitherto Lanny would telephone and invite his friend to have lunch at the Adlon, and Heinrich would be proud and excited to be in this fashionable expensive place, among visiting headliners and high-up SS officers. Always he would invite Lanny to his office and show him off to the rest of the staff. Once he had had Lanny for an *Abend* at his home, to meet Heinrich's Party friends, and eat *Leber-wurst* sandwiches and drink beer—the dullest imaginable occasion.

But this time it was different. Heinrich said: "Let me come to see you privately. There is a matter to be explained." Lanny said: "*Ja, gewiss*," and smiled to himself, knowing perfectly well what it was. Americans had come to be the most hated people in Berlin at this hour; not even the Jews stood so low. Heinrich Jung, in spite of his knowing the Führer personally, stood only medium high in the Party hierarchy, and he had a wife and half a dozen blue-eyed and fair-haired little Jungs to think about.

Lanny spared him the embarrassment of having to explain. "*Ich versteh', alter Kerl*," he said, and added: "I am the one to be embarrassed, because of the way my country is behaving. I only hope it isn't going to make any difference in our friendship."

"*Ach, Lanny, niemals!*" The Youth officer bubbled over with cordiality, to make up for his cowardice; and Lanny, who despised the Nazi soul, was a bit sick at heart but careful not to show it. Heinrich had been caught young, and would never grow up mentally, because he was a prisoner of the forces inside himself, the Prussian spirit which made it necessary for him to have someone to obey, even someone to tell him what to believe. Adi Schicklgruber had told him, and for the rest of his life Heinrich would be a smooth and efficient cog in the machine which the Austrian painter of picture postcards had constructed.

Heinrich hadn't seen the face of his divinity for a year or more, being afraid to trouble him in a time of stress. Lanny revealed how Hess and Göring were trying to arrange a meeting for Lanny, and promised that if it took place he would tell Heinrich, if permitted. Meantime, he recounted his visit to the Air Marshal's *Gefechtsstand*, and sang the praises of those noble boys who had deserved so much from the Fatherland, and had received it in the form of an Iron Cross measuring two inches horizontally and the same vertically. If anything was needed to re-establish the social position of an American visitor, this was it, and Heinrich began to wonder if he hadn't made a bad mistake.

VIII

The Youth official began to talk about his own work, and this was what Lanny wanted. Several times the P.A. had been able to find out what progress the underground was making in Germany by means of the documents on Heinrich's desk. Bernhardt Monck had been in despair over the situation, but would have been encouraged if he had been able to hear the report of his enemy. The Fatherland was under great strain, Heinrich explained, because the war had lasted so much longer than anyone had expected. There were many signs of discontent among the workers, signs which Heinrich blamed upon what he called *die verfluchten Kommunisten*. It was the older men, who had belonged to the Red trade unions in the old days. Never the youth— no, no, the youth were magnificent, they were the Führer's own children, those young heroes whom Lanny had seen in the *Gefechtsstand*.

But some older men resented the food rationing, and the long queues for everything they and their women tried to buy. They it was who went out at night in the Wedding area, where they lived, and in the Hasenheide section to the east, and painted Communist signs on sidewalks and the walls of buildings. "*Rotfront siegt!*"—the Red Front conquers! They it was who met in the back rooms of saloons and gave the Communist salute of the upraised fist instead of the Hitler salute of the arm and hand extended straight. Such a little thing it might seem, but what a world of difference it meant as to what was going on inside the saluter's head!

This was a terrible thing, for it was treason in the very heart of the *Neue Ordnung*, and the traitors had the cunning of Satan himself. When the Soviet Foreign Minister had come to Berlin to negotiate a trade treaty, they had bought up every red carnation which could be found in the city and had worn them openly on the streets. As you passed them you would hear humming of "The Red Flag," and there was nothing that even the Gestapo could do about it, because, as it happened, the dissidents had stolen for that revolutionary hymn the tune of an old German *Volkslied* which the National Socialists taught to all children. "You know, Lanny—'*O Tannenbaum, O Tannenbaum.*'" Lanny replied: "Yes, I know. We in America stole the same tune. At the outbreak of the Civil War the Southerners made up some verses called 'Maryland, My Maryland.' But that was eighty years ago, and it no longer does any harm."

"*Ja, freilich,*" assented the Youth leader. "But it's a different matter when working people hum a tune as they pass you on the street, and you know they are telling you: 'We'll keep the Red Flag flying here!'"

In the midst of these revelations, the telephone rang: the Führer's secretary calling; Herr Budd was invited to call upon the Führer at eleven o'clock the next morning in the New Chancellery building. It was a command, and Lanny said: "I will be on hand." To the awe-stricken Heinrich he remarked: "*Mein Alter*, it was you who took me to the Führer the first time, and I wish I could take you now." "*Um*

Himmel's Willen, nein!" exclaimed the reverent disciple. "He must have great matters of state in mind, and for me it would be a preposterous intrusion."

Lanny consoled him by becoming confidential. "What the Führer wants is to tell me what I am to say to friends of our cause in Britain and America as to the terms on which he would be willing to make peace."

To this the bureaucrat replied: "Isn't it marvelous, the progress our armies are making? Just count the countries: Austria, Czechoslovakia, Poland, Holland, Belgium, Luxemburg, France, and now Hungary, Rumania, Bulgaria. Soon we shall finish Yugoslavia and Greece! There has never been anything like it in the whole of history!"

IX

Promptly at the appointed hour the P.A. presented himself at the main entrance to the immense long building which Adi Schicklgruber, the greatest architect in the world, had designed and constructed: four stories high, rectangular and stern like a barracks, and built of gray granite, as somber as the soul of its designer. To the SS men on guard— the Führer's own *Leibstandarte*, in green uniforms—all Lanny had to do was to present his visiting card and say: "I have a personal appointment with the Führer." They had a list, and when they had checked it, one of them escorted him in.

There was a corridor half a block long, floored with red marble. The door to the Führer's offices had a great monogram in brass: AH. A secretary who knew Lanny greeted him politely, took his hat and coat, and ushered him into the huge high-ceilinged room which Adi had designed, presumably to have something bigger and more impressive than Il Duce in Rome. Once Adi had been a waif, sleeping in the shelter for bums in Vienna, and being put out of it because he wouldn't stop spouting. Now the whole world was hardly big enough for him, and when he spouted, radios carried his words from Argentina to Zanzibar.

The great man was wearing that simple soldier's uniform which he had put on at the outbreak of the war and had promised never to take off until victory was won. Of course he didn't mean that literally; he must have had at least two suits, for this one was neatly pressed and showed no traces of blood or sweat. He was always cordial to Lanny, shook hands with him and indicated a seat in front of the big fireplace with one of the Lenbach Bismarcks above it. "See what I am doing, *alter Herr*," you could imagine Adi saying, standing there and solemnly saluting the Iron Chancellor. "So much more than you were ever able to accomplish. Berlin to Bagdad!" There was a marble statue of Frederick the Great in the room; and it was no phantasy to imagine Adi communing with him. No, indeed. Adi was that theatrical kind of person, and certainly needed encouragement and counsel from some master strategist in the present days of perilous venture.

Hitler's complexion had always been pasty and his features pudgy, especially the nose. Now it appeared that he had gained in weight, and it was not healthy flesh. His expression showed heavy strain; he had always been a bad sleeper, sometimes keeping his friends and advisers up until daylight to save him from being alone with his own thoughts. Lanny wondered: was he, also, taking to the use of drugs? At any rate, he had no time for the smiles and gracious gestures with which he usually played the host. He began abruptly: "Rudi tells me you have news for me, Herr Budd. What is it?"

First it had been Number Three to hear that story, and then Number Two, and now it was Number One. This time Lanny went into even greater detail, for he knew that Adi was feminine in his attitude toward people; if he was hearing about someone, he wanted to see that person with his mind's eye and hear the tones of his voice. So Lanny took him to Admiral Darlan's office, and then to Laval's château, and then to the old Maréchal's combination home and office in the Hotel du Parc. He explained why the hero of Verdun was so generally trusted by the French, and why the butcher's son was less trusted. He described life in a fashionable springs resort where the hotels had all been turned into government offices, and wealthy and elegant people were sleeping in any corner they could find. All bread was gray and tasteless, unless you could find a breadlegger.

And then to London. The Führer went in his imagination to visit the gray smoke-stained building of the Foreign Office, and the still older residence of the Prime Minister in Downing Street, which was both short and narrow, a deadend way in which the Germans would have been ashamed to house any official. He described Churchill as he had watched him at Maxine Elliott's swimming-pool on the Riviera and in her great hall where every now and then all conversation had to stop while a train of the Mediterranean line roared by a few feet from the outside wall. He told about Lord Wickthorpe's resignation and what it meant; he took the Führer for a week-end visit to the Castle, where all the friends of his cause discussed what they were going to do about "Winnie." The Countess of Wickthorpe had once spent an evening at Berchtesgaden and listened to the Führer expound his program, and had said to him: "I wish you to know that I agree with every word you have said." That night had been the end of the marriage of Irma Barnes and Lanny Budd, but of course the ex-husband didn't mention that detail in his narrative.

The Führer held in his hands the fate of both these countries, France and Britain—or at any rate so he believed. He plied his visitor with a stream of questions: what did this mean, and that, and what would happen if he, the master of Europe, took this course or that? Lanny's purpose in giving information was to get the master to talk in return, and therefore his answers were directed to the pleasing of this genius-madman risen from the slums of Vienna. Like all conquerors through the ages, he had fallen victim to his own surroundings, and had come to the state where he could absorb an unlimited amount of flattery and could not stand any trace of opposition. So Lanny told him that the French were rapidly adjusting themselves to *l'ordre nouveau*, and that the sane conservative elements in British public life were rapidly realizing what a blunder they had made in letting themselves be persuaded to "die for Danzig." Lanny called the roll of the leading "appeasers" with whom he had talked; some of them had had to bow to the storm but now were straightening their backs and lifting their heads again.

And then America! Westward the star of Nazi propaganda was taking its way. America was a much younger country than Britain, more crude, more chaotic. America meant a swarm of profiteers, blinded by a frenzy of greed, the chance to make money by the billions where formerly they had made it by the millions. Anyone who tried to stand against this torrent was branded as a public enemy. Lanny described one by one the heroic men with whom he had discussed the situation: Senator Reynolds and Congressman Fish, Henry Ford and Father Coughlin, and above all, the publisher William Randolph Hearst, who had come to visit the Führer and had made such an excellent business deal. "There is my idea of a real American!" exclaimed the Führer, and the Führer's friend replied: *"Ja, wirklich!"* He went on to tell of the colossal influence the Hearst newspapers exerted in America—always, of course, against Roosevelt's devilish maneuvers to involve us in the war.

"Have you met That Man?" inquired the Führer, and Lanny, always cautious, replied: "Only casually. The man has wild eyes and is subject to brainstorms; the kindest thing anybody can say about him is that his judgment is as feeble as his legs."

X

That led up to the "junta" plot; and of course Lanny was under no obligation to limit himself to the exact truth about it. He made it more widespread than it was, connecting it with all the country-club gentlemen, and with the crackpots up and down the land who were raving in public meetings and organizing groups with shirts of white and silver and gold and all other colors which Nazis and Fascists and Falangists had not pre-empted.

Never in his many interviews with the Führer had Lanny brought any news which gave his host such delight. Adi began to slap his thighs, which was one of his tricks when he was aroused; than he popped up from his seat and began to pace the room and orate. *"So ist's!* What I have been predicting from the beginning! Put that scoundrel out of the way once for all!"

He came back to his chair, and leaning toward his guest demanded: "When is this going to happen, Herr Budd?"

"Leider, mein Führer, that is something I cannot guess. The men who plan such a drastic move will surely not talk about it freely. They have to wait for the psychological moment, sometime when the man has made a particularly obvious blunder."

"They should not wait too long! It is a calamity for the world that such a man is kept in power and allowed to prolong this cruel conflict. You must know that it would have been over long ago but for the encouragement your country has given the stubborn Churchill, and the planes they have sent, to be used in killing not merely our soldiers but our women and children in their beds."

"Indeed, Herr Reichskanzler, you don't have to point that out to me. I am bowed with shame, and I hesitated to enter Germany this time, to face all my old friends here."

"Listen, Herr Budd." The Führer leaned even closer, and lowered his voice, as though, like everybody else in Germany, he feared the omnipresent Gestapo. "Is there not something we can do at once, without waiting for officials and captains of industry to make up their minds?"

"What do you have in mind, *mein Führer?*"

"Could we not find some way to get rid of that malignant man ourselves? I could find ten thousand young heroes, any one qf whom would gladly give his life to save the Fatherland from the sufferings it now has to endure."

Lanny gazed into those deadly blue eyes, and he thought: "This is the real madman, and I have to be careful now." Aloud, he said: "It would be very difficult for a German to get anywhere near the White House now, Exzellenz."

"I could find one who has lived in America, one who speaks without any trace of accent."

"I doubt that very much," replied Lanny gravely. "One syllable wrong would cost him his life, and the lives of all those who helped him. But even supposing it were so, the President is very carefully guarded—that has been the task of what is called the Secret Service, and it is done with especial thoroughness now, in what they consider for all practical purposes to be wartime."

"That goes without saying," replied the Führer. "But there is always a weak spot to be found, a chink in every armor. And if we could get those two men, Roosevelt and Churchill, we should save the world from an unending horror." Lanny noted this extreme language, several times repeated, and realized that the war which Adolf Hitler had started was becoming too much for his nerves. A boob like Heinrich Jung could rejoice over a year and a half of marching and conquering, but Adi had a General Staff to warn him how dangerously he was extending his lines and exposing his flanks—one over the Balkans and the other away down in North Africa! Adi Schicklgruber was beginning to weaken!

XI

A student of National-Socialist affairs shouldn't have been too much surprised by a proposal of murder. Lanny knew that Adolf Hitler had caused the killing of whole populations which stood in his way, and that two leading statesmen had been assassinated at his orders—a King of Yugoslavia, and a Premier of Austria. Premier Barthou of France was supposed to have been killed by Mussolini's crowd, but Adi had undoubtedly sanctioned it. Even so, it was startling to have this technique of statecraft brought directly home to a peaceable art expert.

Realizing that he would have to step with caution, even as the bearer of such a secret, Lanny inquired: "Just what do you have in mind for me to do, *mein Führer?*"

"It is my idea that you might assist me, at least with information as to how such an agent should proceed. You know so many important persons in your country, surely you could get access to the White House." .

"That is a very difficult thing to do under the circumstances existing, and especially for one who is known as the son of Robert Budd."

"You mean that your father is not in favor now, in view of what he is doing for the government?"

"My father has been one of the most aggressive of old-line Republicans; he has contributed or raised millions of dollars in the effort to defeat the New Deal; and Roosevelt is known to be an extremely vindictive man—he cherishes grudges like an elephant. So far as concerns the present, the Administration sees very little to be pleased with in my father's achievements. Government agents are snooping about the plant trying to find out why the plane has given so little satisfaction to the British, and why the new model is so unaccountably delayed. I won't say that my father is deliberately 'stalling'—he wouldn't admit that even to his son; when I asked him questions his reply was: 'The time will come when this government of dreamers will be glad that we kept some of our military secrets to ourselves.' I trust that you,

Herr Reichskanzler, will consider this strictly between us, and not share it with even your most trusted advisers."

"Oh, surely, surely, Herr Budd. But it is most unfortunate that you cannot make any suggestions."

"I haven't meant to say quite that, Exzellenz. It is an extremely delicate matter, and one that I would have to think over with the utmost care."

"That is better! Will you let me have whatever ideas may occur to you?"

"That I will do. But I am afraid I should have to go to New York and Washington and sound out a number of persons. I would say that I was hoping to get some sort of government post, and wished to know what influence I could command. I should listen to a number of people talking about Roosevelt, in order to find someone who might be counted upon. It is a difficult matter getting into Germany, so I suggest that you give me some secret way of getting word to you."

That was what the duelists call a riposte. That was taking the burden that Adi had placed upon Lanny's shoulders and putting it back where it had come from. The Führer didn't dare meet his guest's eyes for fear of betraying the doubts in his soul. To cover the awkward moment, the guest went on, quickly: "Assign me a code name that I could use in case I have something important to suggest."

"Excellent idea," replied the other. "Will you choose a name?"

"It might be better if you would assign one, because you know the sort of name you employ."

"They are chosen quite at random. Who is your favorite German?" This was a point at which Lanny could venture a smile. "You know that without asking, *mein Führer.*"

The great man smiled in return—who could have helped it? "I mean, among those of the past," he said.

"I suppose I would say Wagner," replied the tactful guest—choosing Adi's favorite among music masters.

"That, unfortunately, is too common a name. I have several in my service. We might choose one of his characters. Would you care to be Siegfried?"

"I wouldn't mind slaying the dragon," replied Lanny, "but I wouldn't relish the stab in the back, or the funeral pyre." He said it with a twinkle in his eyes.

"We are going to revise that legend, Herr Budd. Our young Nordic hero has been forewarned, and this time he will keep his face to the foe."

"*Herrlich, mein Führer!* And to whom shall I send the information if I get it?"

Once more the pains of doubt and uncertainty were apparent in the Führer's face. It was one thing to listen to the gossip of a plausible playboy from an enemy country, and another to entrust to him a vitally important secret of the Liaison Staff—or would it be Personnel Department B? Of course Hitler might give the name of some agent in Portugal or Spain, where he had hundreds, and where the American government couldn't get at them; but that would mean delays, and perhaps secret censorship—the Führer knew it was not safe to assume that foreign governments were *too* stupid, and it was hard for him to believe that the Americans would permit airmail letters to go to Portugal and Spain without being examined on the way.

Nothing venture, nothing have—and Adi Schicklgruber was one of those who were determined to have. Said he: "It happens that a personal friend of mine, Herr Hans Heffelfinger, is at present connected with our Embassy in Washington, and if you have anything to write me you can send it in his care. Put it in an inside envelope, and mark the inner one 'Personal to the Führer.' That way it will come to me at once. You will remember the name?"

"It is engraved on the tablets of my memory, Exzellenz; and be sure that I will do my best, and as quickly as possible. One thing more: in case you should have a message to send me through Herr Heffelfinger, it might be well for you, too, to have a code name, so that I may be sure it is the real thing. Will you permit me to assign one to you?"

"*Mit Vergnügen, Herr Budd.*"

"Very well: you are Wotan, highest of the gods! You will remember the name?" Even in this august and irritable presence, a playboy could not entirely forget the habits of a lifetime!

XII

One other matter of importance had to be cleared up before Lanny offered to depart. He said: "*Mein Führer*, I explained to Rudi the importance of my being able to tell people your views and wishes as of the present hour. Wherever, in any land, I mention that I have talked with you, people crowd about and ask: 'What does he really mean? What does he want?'"

"I have told them with the utmost plainness in my speeches, Herr Budd."

"You have reminded me of that in the past; but in the so-called democratic world—which is really Jewish-plutocratic—nobody believes what any statesman says; they take it for granted that it is just so much hogwash. But when a man talks to a friend in private, that is a different matter. They assume that so busy a man as yourself wouldn't give time to a visiting art expert unless he was really a friend."

"In that, at least, they are correct, Herr Budd. Just what is the uncertainty that troubles their minds?"

"The question of your intentions toward their own countries. The
British statesmen are intensely concerned to know your attitude toward their Empire. As for America, I do not go so much among the
statesmen, for they are mostly low-grade politicians, or fanatics of the
Roosevelt cabal; but I meet the really important industrialists, and one
and all they ask: 'What does the Führer mean to do when he has conquered Russia?' "

"*Ach, so?* They think that I am going to conquer Russia for them?"

"To put it plainly, Exzellenz, they think you are going to conquer
Russia for oil. I have not met anyone who has doubt on that point,
and they consider me fatuous if I suggest otherwise."

"You might point out to them that I have developed several processes
for making petrol from coal."

"Yes, of course; but those plants are exposed to long-distance bombers, and you have told us in a speech what wonders you could work if
you had the oil and the minerals of the Ukraine. That is one of your
communications that nobody has forgotten."

"And they think that I can conquer Russia?"

"On that, too, there is general agreement. All the military men with
whom my father talks believe that you can achieve your purpose in
six weeks—about twice as long as it took with Poland."

"And when do they expect me to oblige them, Herr Budd?"

"They agree that you intend to move in the latter part of June or
early in July. They figure that you must allow yourself a greater
margin of safety than you did in 1939."

"It is really remarkable, Herr Budd, how precisely they have laid
out my program for me. It might occur to such shrewd gentlemen to
doubt whether I would be so eager to meet their wishes."

"Understand, *mein Führer*, I am not telling my ideas, but theirs.
Apparently their view is that the Reds are nearer to you, and therefore
a greater menace. The reports are that the Russians are doing everything in their power to thwart your wishes in Bulgaria, and now in
Yugoslavia."

"That is true enough, Herr Budd. They are vermin, the scum of
the earth; mad dogs who have been turned loose on our eastern border,
to the delight of our foes and the dismay of all decent people!"

The conversation was detoured for a time, while Adi called the
Bolsheviks all the bad names he could think of. He worried himself
into one of his furies of eloquence; he slapped his thighs, and got up
and paced the room, shouting as if he had all Germany for an audience.
He declared that the Red leaders, the brains of the conspiracy, were

Jewish swine, and he cited Marx and Lassalle and Kautsky and Lieb-
knecht and Luxemburg and Trotsky to prove it. Then he raved about
the Jews for a while: "Germany's misfortune," in the Nazi phrase.

Then, in the strange fashion which Lanny had noted on other occasions, the Führer suddenly turned off his rage as if with a spigot.
"Enough of that, Herr Budd, I must be boring you. I have to keep
myself reminded that I have other enemies besides Jewish-Bolshevism."

XIII

So then, quite calmly and cunningly, Adolf Hitler proceeded to discuss what he wanted his friend and secret agent to do. "Let us assume,
Herr Budd, that I intend to take upon myself the burden of slaying
this dragon. Are those British aristocrats and plutocrats to go on trying
to strangle and starve me, and shooting their poisoned arrows into my
back?"

"My efforts, Exzellenz, have been devoted to making them realize this.
situation, and bringing an end to this fratricidal strife. But it is impossible to bring two sides together when neither will take a step. The
British ask: 'What will the Führer do?' and the Führer asks: 'What
will the British do?' and I cannot answer either. When I left you in
Paris and resumed my travels, everybody wanted to know: 'Does he
mean to go after Russia?' and I had to reply: 'I don't know; he didn't
tell me.' Now everybody has become assured that you are going after
Russia—even the Russians know it, I am told. What people ask now—
hundreds of them, all the way from Vichy to Hollywood—is: 'When
he has got Russia, is he going to be satisfied? Or is he going to use the
resources of Russia to turn upon us?'"

"You must tell them, Herr Budd, that it depends entirely upon their
attitude toward me. If they are bombing my cities, of course I shall
bomb theirs."

"It is a deadlock—and who is going to make the first move to break
it? You and Britain are tied up in a net of mutual fears and suspicions,
and they want to get out of it just as much as you do. I, an American,
want to help, before that madman in the White House has managed to
draw us in. I expect to travel to London by way of Lisbon. I shall be
at Wickthorpe Castle for a couple of weeks because my little daughter, Irma's child, is there. I shall meet Gerald Albany and others of the
Foreign Office. There will be several of those noble lords who have
been your devoted friends. They will come, the moment the word
spreads that there is a chap who has talked with the Führer face to
face. You can't imagine what an impression that produces—people
won't let me go to bed at night; they ask to go with me even when I
take a walk. And right now is the critical time; the country is sick of

the bloodshed, the food is growing scarce, the ships are going to the bottom, several of them every night—"

"They are beginning to feel the pinch, then!"

"They are in a desperate plight; and everywhere the governing classes are asking: 'Why, *why* do we have to fight this man who ought to be our friend? Why can't we have a truce, and let him go after the real enemy of our civilization?' Honestly, I do not exaggerate when I say, it might be the turning point—it might be just enough to cause the Conservative party leaders to get together and send you a secret emissary."

"You want me to say that I'll be satisfied with what I can get in Russia, and that I have no designs upon the British Empire, now or at any time?"

"I don't *want* you to say anything, *mein Führer;* that is not the correct way to put the matter. It would be preposterous for me to make suggestions to a master of diplomacy like yourself. What I am doing as an act of friendship is to lay a set of facts before you. It is for you to examine them and make your own decision, and tell me what I am to say."

"*Ja, ja, Herr Budd.* You may quote me as having said what I have just spoken, and say that I am ready to deal with any Englishman, anywhere, on that basis."

"You won't change your mind, *lieber Freund?* I mean, when your agents in Britain report to you that I have been saying this in London drawing-rooms, you won't feel that I have been betraying a confidence or committing a presumption?"

"*Ausgeschlossen!* I am a man of my word, and what you have done here is to voice my own thoughts with competence and understanding."

"*Besten Dank, Exzellenz!* I have never had a pleasanter compliment in all my life!"

XIV

The master of Europe was so pleased with a gracious friend and unpaid messenger that he invited him to remain for lunch, and took him for a tour of this building which had been designed by the greatest architect in the world and was intended to be the dwelling place of his successors for a thousand years. The visitor was escorted to the enormous drawing-room, built upon two levels so that part could serve as a stage. As an art expert he was impressed by the ancient tapestries which covered one entire wall. He was interested also in the story of the deep and heavy carpet which covered the floor of this apartment; it had been ordered by the League of Nations, but the funds of that treacherous organization had dried up and it couldn't pay for the treasure, so the Führer had taken it over! The guest was shown the "green salon," and other great rooms of which he was not told the names. He inspected immense fireplaces, and the portraits of Prussian generals, also of Teutonic heroes who might have been brought from Bayreuth. He saw a winter garden with red lacquered furniture and tall rubber trees and other tropical plants, some of them in bloom. He was taken through the billiard room, and the lounge which was for the use of the *Leibstandarte*, those tall, green-uniformed young Nordics who swarmed over the place, and whose joy in life it was to throw up their right arms stiffly and shout: "*Heil Hitler!*" The Führer never once failed to respond, and never once did it occur to him that an American might find anything comical in this noisy sort of home life. Even in the kitchen—a magnificent apartment straight out of a Hollywood movie—the group of cooks and scullery maids in snow-white costumes flung up their arms and vociferated their greetings.

The dining-room made Lanny think of the council chamber in the *Braune Haus* of Munich—it had the same sort of red leather chairs with brass nails, a red carpet and cream-colored walls. Over the huge buffet was an appetizing subject, *The Feast of Bacchus* by Moritz von Schwindt. There were niches containing golden-bronze statues of Adam and Eve, with special lighting effects. The table seated twenty or more; the American guest was placed in the seat of honor, and at his right sat that young doctor who had gossiped with him about events at Berchtesgaden in the days of Schuschnigg and the *Anschluss*. All the Führer's staff were young, and all the female members had to be Nordic divinities. At the foot of the table sat Herr Kannenberg, the rolypoly Bavarian who ran the great man's household wherever he was. Good humor oozed from the ex-*Kellner* like sweat.

Nearly everybody at this luncheon knew the son of Budd-Erling, and excepted him from the hatred they bore for Americans. He was honored with a steaming hot plate of the inescapable noodle soup, a vegetable plate and poached egg like the Führer's, and a stein of the Führer's specially brewed near-beer. The great man was fond of sweets, and had a pot of honey which he passed to his guest but to no one else. He beamed his favor, displaying his abnormally small teeth liberally studded with gold fillings. His prominent blue eyes gleamed as he chatted about the cast of *The Merry Widow* which he had attended the previous night; then about the half-dozen Spitzwegs which he had installed in his Munich residence. Lanny wondered why a slightly satirical painter of the Bavarian middle classes should have appealed to the master of Europe; he guessed it must be part of the master's efforts to look down upon his recent past.

Lanny wondered if Herr Kannenberg would play the accordion after this vegetarian repast. It might have been intended; but as they rose from the table Hitler espied a minor *Beamter* whom he had summoned and who was waiting in an anteroom. The Führer strode toward him and burst into one of those tirades of which Lanny had several times been a reluctant witness. The wretch turned a yellowish green and his knees almost gave way beneath him as a torrent of the foulest words in the Austrian dialect poured over him—also a fine spray of saliva. The Führer's face became distorted and his nostrils flared to an extraordinary width. Strangest of all was the way the storm passed; Hitler would turn sharply on his heel, and behave like an actor who has finished a scene in rehearsal; his features became composed in an instant, and he did not consider it necessary to apologize, or to make any comment upon the startling episode.

To Lanny he held out his hand, saying: *"Leben Sie wohl, Herr Budd. I hope to hear good news from you."* The American went out from the presence, wondering with a mixture of awe and disgust if that was how Europe was destined to be governed for the next thousand years. It seemed so at this hour.

14. The Best-Laid Schemes

I

WHEN Lanny got back to his hotel he found a note from Hess, inviting him to spend the night at the latter's home in the suburbs. The guest was called for in a bullet-proof car with swastikas on the doors, and on the military chauffeur. Lanny had visited the house before, and had met Frau Hess, tall, severe-looking, deep voiced; she found no incompatibility between National-Socialist *Mystik* and that of the *Vedanta*. Lanny had won her regard by telling her about the ideas of Parsifal Dingle and his communicating with the monks of Dodanduwa, both living and dead. Now he brought his report up-to-date, and at the same time speculated about this seeming-odd marriage. Could it be true, as the gossip-princess Hilde declared, that the Führer had commanded this match as a means of putting an end to the rumors concerning improper relationship between himself and his devoted man secretary, co-author of *Mein Kampf?*

"Out there we shall be safe from the bombs," Rudi had said in his note. But there were no bombs on Berlin that night, and had not been for three or four nights. The R.A.F. was tapering off, and *Deutschland-sender*, the propaganda radio of the Nazis, exulted that the foe had found the price too high. Hess, more realistic, said that the nights were getting shorter, and the British planes could no longer come and go in complete darkness. He questioned Lanny about what the American army was managing to achieve in the technique of daylight bombing which they were practicing. Had the visitor heard of the Norden bomb sight? Lanny said that it was the most closely guarded of all secrets, and not even his father knew the principle on which it worked.

Lanny had taken it for granted that the Number Three's purpose in inviting him here was to find out what the Führer had said; but he discovered that in this he had misjudged the former secretary and most loyal of friends. What Rudi learned, he would learn from his Chief, and would never put himself in the position of trying to go behind his Chief's back. He did not mention the bright idea of having the President of the United States assassinated. His thoughts were centered upon the coming struggle with the Reds, and the urgent necessity of getting out of the war with Britain before that attack started.

Had the Führer told him that Lanny was permitted to know about the coming move? Anyhow, the Deputy no longer made any pretense that it was a secret. April had arrived, and the Wehrmacht was driving gloriously into the mountainous land of Greece, routing not merely those troops which had soundly beaten the Italians but a couple of divisions of British troops who had been sent from North Africa to their aid. "Not many of those chaps are going to get away alive," declared Hess; "and as soon as we finish that clean-up, we shall begin moving our troops to the Ukraine. The Russians will know it then if they don't know it already."

"Everybody that I talk to seems to know it," was the P.A.'s reply. "Doubtless the Reds are doing everything they can to get ready, but it won't be enough."

"They are a worse mess than the Italians," was the Reichsminister's opinion. "On that score I have no worry whatever. But I am deeply concerned about the continuing struggle with Britain, and it seems to me we should at any cost get it over before we embark on a new venture. It has been a basic principle of our strategy, never to let ourselves be involved in a two-front war."

"The consequences were convincing last time," replied Lanny.

"I am pleading with the Führer that we must not commit that blunder again. He agrees to the extent of authorizing me to do anything, absolutely anything, that will avoid the calamity."

"You have done a good job of converting him. He has asked me to talk to the top people and report if I make any headway."

"I beg you, Lanny, do not fail us. The thing has become an obsession with me; I cannot sleep for worrying about it. I get no pleasure whatever in the triumphs our airmen win over Britain. I feel as if it were my own property which is being destroyed."

"You have described my own attitude, Rudi. I go back and forth between the two countries, and they seem to me so nearly the same. They are the two peoples whom I trust. Why must they waste their energies in destroying each other?"

The Deputy Führer leaned toward his guest, his gray-green eyes seeming to shine and his bushy black eyebrows to bristle with excitement. "Lanny, we must, we *must* find a way to persuade them to be friends, and at least to get off our backs, even if they will not help us. We must not lose a day."

"I am willing to leave tomorrow," was the P.A.'s reply. "The Führer has armed me with powerful weapons, and I am eager to try them out."

II

That was all on the subject for a time. Lanny told about some psychic wonders, made up as he went along. This had the effect of putting Rudi into a warm mood, and after they had a snack before bedtime, he suddenly opened up: "Lanny, I am going to take you into my confidence about a really important matter. I had a communication this morning from one of my agents in London. You understand, we have some there."

Lanny smiled. "I have probably met some of them, but they were well camouflaged."

"I am informed that a leading English industrialist, one of their top men, has consented to meet me in Madrid and talk matters over. Unfortunately I am under pledge not to give his name."

"That's all right; I'll probably be told all about him within an hour after I reach London."

"That won't do any harm, so long as it is they who reveal it. It is an important sign, and I want to make the most of it. Tell me, how do you plan to travel?"

"I came by way of Switzerland, and I'll return there and make inquiries as to getting to Lisbon. From there it will be easy, as my father has a firm of solicitors in London who seem able to pull wires."

"All that will take some time, and it occurred to me that you might like to fly with me to Madrid, and be there to advise me about this man, and perhaps to meet him."

"That is very kind indeed, Rudi, and ordinarily I should be delighted. But it occurs to me—Spain is a land of intrigue, and everybody there is watched. If I arrived with the Führer's Deputy, it would be all over town in an hour."

"I am planning a secret trip. I expect to be smuggled out of the airport and into a palace. If there is any rumor that I am in Madrid, it will be officially denied."

"I doubt if you can manage it; and anyhow, *I* couldn't. There are a couple of newspapermen at the Adlon whom I used to know, and I have had to dodge them. I've an idea they have their eye on me and may be trying to find out what I'm here for. If they get the tip that I have flown to Madrid in a Luftwaffe plane—with or without the Führer's Deputy—they would cable it. As you know, my usefulness depends upon my being taken for an art expert and not as anybody's agent."

"What can you suggest?"

"Say that I pay my bill at the Adlon and drive off in a taxi. Then I get out and walk, and pick up another taxi to one of the lesser airfields. You have commercial planes flying to Paris, and I step aboard one of them. Paris is a disorderly place—not even your army can change that. I am a frequent visitor there, and nobody is going to be surprised to see me. If I say I'm on my way to London, it will be natural for me to take a commercial plane to Madrid. When do you expect your Englishman?"

"Not until next week."

"Very well, then, that does it. Tell me how I can get in touch with you in Madrid, and how I can write if anything turns up."

"Ask for Herr Knapp at our Embassy. The Führer has told me you are to be Siegfried and he is Wotan. Perhaps you had better give me a code name, so that if I communicate with you, you can be sure it is genuine."

The *Nummer Drei* Nazi said this without the trace of a smile; but the wicked Lanny Budd had a thought which it was hard for him to conceal. The enemies of Rudolf Hess had given him a malicious nickname, *Das Fräulein;* now Lanny thought with malice: You shall be Freya! But this was no time for joking, even in one's thoughts. The secret agent suggested: "Since we have gone Wagnerian, you may be Kurvenal. You remember, in *Tristan—der Treueste der Treuen.*" The truest of the true!

"Thank you for the compliment, Lanny. And one thing more—I know that you will be put to expense in this matter, and it's only decent that you should be reimbursed."

"No, no, Rudi, I don't want any money. I have no trouble in earning what I need—it's fun for me. If I take money from any government,

I am committing myself, and sooner or later I'm bound to get brand-marked."

"Never by me! I can put American money into your hands, and nobody but you and I will ever know it has happened."

"I take your word for it, but truly, I don't want it. Think of me as a disinterested friend of your country and mine. Some day, perhaps, Göring will make me the curator of that super-museum he plans to establish. Meantime, here is a favor you may do me. I am buying a couple of small paintings which I can conveniently carry out, and the commission on the deals will pay all my expenses. I don't know whether I need a permit to take them out, but if so you can have your office obtain it for me, along with the exit permit. And get me a permit, if any is required, to have my New York bank cable me ten thousand dollars."

"All that will be simple," declared the man of power, making a memo in a little book. "And pray understand: if you find any way by which you can use money to advance the cause we have in mind, don't hesitate to spend it and let me reimburse you. I have a secret fund, and there is nothing I'd rather use it for. As you Americans say, the sky is the limit!"

III

The American guest was landed at Le Bourget airfield, but did not let himself be driven into Paris in a German staff car; he just took his two suitcases, one in each hand, his portable typewriter under one arm and a roll of paintings under the other—a most uncomfortable load—and started to walk. He seated himself by the roadside, and presently along came a peasant cart, in which, for the sum of fifty francs, he got the privilege of riding into *"la ville sans lumière."* It took most of the day, but he didn't mind, for he had a chance to get acquainted with a French market gardener, and to ask many questions as to what the German occupation meant to the peasants. *"Pas si mal,"* was the old fellow's verdict; at least so far as concerned himself, who was over the draft age. For his two sons it was another matter, for they were prisoners in Germany, and *les boches* kept promising to release them but never did; the French were kept dangling on a string, just to shake more and more out of their pockets.

This weatherbeaten old laborer possessed a shrewd understanding of the economic situation. The peasants had the land, and the people in the cities, Germans as well as French, had to have their products. Therefore prices were high, and if you were a shrewd bargainer you could bid them still higher. It was a situation as old as Europe; in wartime the people of the cities suffered, and the country people lived on—unless, of course, they had the hard luck to live on or near a battlefield. Civilization had survived by grace of the fact that battle-fields were relatively small, and the marching hordes kept mainly to the highways.

The traveler put up at one of the smaller hotels, the larger ones being occupied by the Germans; their uniforms were a common sight, and the French had learned to get along with them, though many women ostentatiously turned their backs when the hated foe passed. By the ingenious device of paper francs the Germans had pretty well cleaned out France, both Occupied and Unoccupied, and food was now strictly rationed. The Parisians were allowed less than a pound of meat per week, and bread, their principal food, was of poor quality; the ration was being reduced almost every month. Ersatz foods, a German device, were coming in. Acorns, nettles, and other garden weeds were being chemically treated to make them edible, and you had "mink butter," made of tallow and chemicals. "Coffee" was roasted oats and barley; so no wonder the people of Paris were dropping their practice of two hours for lunch. "Back to work!" was the Nazi slogan.

IV

Lanny's first call was upon his old friend, Baron Eugène Schneider of Schneider-Creusot. He found this one-time munitions king of Europe broken in health and in spirit, and Lanny's first thought was that he was not long for this world. How futile had been all his efforts and how vain his hopes of "collaboration" to save the two hundred families of France! The sons of these families were many of them prisoners in Germany, or had fled to Vichy or North Africa. The older people for the most part had stayed, and were pathetically trying to keep up social life in spite of constantly increasing handicaps. For-eigners they saw hardly ever, so Lanny rated a dinner party of the old solemn stately sort—a very good dinner, revealing the fact that there was a black market in Paris, maintained by passing bribes to the Nazis, something by no means difficult.

Here came the masters of the Comité des Forges, of steel and coal and electrical power, the physical resources of France; masters also of that imaginary force which men had created and which they called money, without which nothing else could operate. They all knew Lanny Budd; they had questioned him concerning the German Führer and his purposes, and time and events had shown that what he told them was correct. Now they had a hundred questions, and Lanny re-peated what the Nazis One, Two, and Three had authorized him to say. The masters of France found it agreeable, for there was nothing in this world they wanted so much as the overthrow of the Red men-ace in the east. If there was a single one among them who had any doubt as to the ultimate victory of the Wehrmacht in this war, he did not raise his voice in Schneider's palace. They considered that Britain was committing suicide at Churchill's blind behest, and they talked about Roosevelt precisely as the gentlemen of the Newcastle Country Club had done in the days before the fall of Paris had scared them.

Really the gentlemen of the Comité des Forges weren't doing so badly under the occupation, and they explained it to an American visitor so that he might explain it at home. To be sure, the Germans had insisted upon having a majority interest in most of the prime industries; but then, they had paid the market prices and their checks had been good, so how could you object? Ever since Adolf Hitler's so-called Beerhall Putsch had failed so miserably, he had had a "passion for legality," and everything he had done had complied with the formalities of the capitalist system. It was a world of paper titles, and never would the "Economic Mobile Units" which had followed on the heels of the German armies take anything without giving a proper receipt and acquiring a certificate of title with engraved scrollwork and red or gold seals. Truly it was a comical thing to see the shrewd moneymasters of France hypnotized by these devices which they themselves or their forefathers had invented!

"What is it that a large employer wants?" demanded the head of the great electrical industry of France. "He wants to keep his plants busy, and to be able to sell his product at a profit which will enable him to meet his payroll at the end of every week. He wants to know that his workers will obey orders; that there will be no agitators stirring them up and plaguing him with strikes. All those things we have, M. Budd."

"Aren't you troubled with sabotage?" inquired the visitor, and the answer was: "Some; but the Germans know how to deal with it. When the war is over, and the population has reconciled itself to the new situation, I see no reason why we should not enjoy a long period of prosperity."

This gentleman volunteered to deliver Lanny to his hotel after the party broke up. He had an elegant Mercédès, and apparently enough *essence*. On the way Lanny commented upon the depressed appearance of their host, and the reply was: "I think that what has broken Eugène's spirit is the fact that the Germans told him his Creusot plant is hopelessly out-of-date!"

V

One other errand in Paris. Lanny had the address of Julie Palma, which Raoul had given him a year ago. It was in one of those factory districts which surrounded Paris with a dingy ring. Lanny had no idea whether she would still be there, but it could do no harm to try. He wrote a note on his typewriter, signing the name "Bienvenu." He suggested a rendezvous on a street corner, something he had done on previous occasions; it was comparatively safe, because it would be misunderstood by all the rest of the world.

He went walking, which he enjoyed, and which now was *de rigueur*. What was Paris like under the "occupation"? Well, for one thing, there were long queues, the same as in London and Berlin. The housewife who wanted food had to spend half her time waiting—perhaps only to learn that the day's supply had been sold out. For another, the newspapers in the kiosks were all *gleichgeschaltet;* they all sang German tunes, and so, for the most part, did performers in the music halls; "Lili Marlene" was the favorite of the moment, and, oddly enough, the British in North Africa had taken it up from their prisoners. Another detail, the streets of Paris had been made moral—at any rate in name. There was no longer a *rue Zola* or a *rue Renan*, both these men having been Freemasons, a vile thing.

At the appointed corner, there was the little Frenchwoman who was Raoul's devoted wife, and who had helped to run a workers' school through all the dissensions and "splits" which had paralleled those of the world outside. All through the Spanish war she had carried the burden alone, and now she had joined the underground, living the life of an outlaw, hiding in a crowded city instead of in a forest or a mountain cave. Just what she was doing Lanny had never asked, not even in the three Spanish years. This period, which the Nazi-Fascists had used for training in depredation, the rebel workers had used for training in silence and concealment.

Members of the underground did not walk up to one another and exchange greetings on the street. One walked and the other followed at a discreet distance; they turned several corners and watched to make sure they were not being trailed. Then, perhaps, the leader would slip into a doorway or an alley; or go out into a park, where it was possible to talk with a certainty of not being overheard. Since Lanny was not known in the working-class districts of Paris, it was all right for this pair to stroll on unfrequented streets. A well-dressed and well-fed gentleman and a poorly dressed and ill-nourished woman—that was a pattern all too familiar on the streets of the great capitals. Nobody would be curious about where they went or try to overhear their low-spoken words.

Julie said: "You caught me just in time. I have a way to get to Raoul, and I was about to leave."

Lanny didn't say: "Where is he?" That wouldn't have been playing the game. He asked: "Have you heard from him?"—and the reply was: "There was one sentence in his letter which I assume refers to you.

He said: 'If you should see our friend, tell him the money got to the right place.' Do you recognize that?"

"There is a story behind it," replied the man. "Is that all he said?"

"His notes are brief. They have to be smuggled past the border, you know."

"There is no reason why you shouldn't know what happened. Raoul probably knows it by now, and if not, you can tell him."

He recited the story of his misadventure in Toulon, and Julie listened with a look of horror on her face. "Oh, Lanny, what a dreadful thing to have happened to you! I am so sorry—and ashamed!"

"It was rather disagreeable at the time, but now when I look back on it I can see the humorous aspects. I was asking for it, you know. I'll surely be more careful in future."

"I think I know who the leader of that group was," said the woman. "It would not be proper for me to name him."

"His voice seemed familiar, but I have searched my memory in vain. I think he was probably at the school."

"If he is the man I think he is, there is a price of two hundred thousand francs on his head. He is bold, and a man of intense convictions; the last time I saw him he was a Trotskyite—he's a revolutionist who does not believe it possible to have Socialism in one country alone, or excusable to make deals with the Nazis."

"I know the type," replied Lanny, "and you have given me a clue. I'll recall the arguments I listened to at the school, and bring back to mind the different individuals who advanced them. Ten or fifteen years ago, I imagine, my captor would have been a shrill-voiced and bitter youth."

"In those days it was all talk," said the woman. "But now is the time for action—and many, *hélas*, have reconsidered and decided that it is the part of wisdom to look out for themselves."

VI

The P.A. was not free to reveal what he himself was doing, except in general terms; but Julie wanted him to know about her movement, which so needed help from outside. Defeat and humiliation had served to separate the sheep from the goats in France: those who wanted freedom and were willing to fight for it from those who thought only of comfort and the protection of their property. The forces of resistance were organizing in little groups here and there. "My chief is a man who would not dare to be seen on the street by daylight," said Julie, "but there are a hundred doors he can knock on and be safely hidden. Have you seen any of our papers?"

"No," was the reply, "I wouldn't dare ask for one."

"I didn't dare bring one. Ours is called *Libération*, and there is another called *Combat*. We tell the news we get over the British radio, and we tell the workers how to practice the slowdown, and how to sabotage. Most important of all is the keeping up of morale. The working-class districts of Paris are solidly for us, and when the British bomb our factories and sometimes hit our homes there is little complaint. '*C'est la guerre*,' they say."

"What do you need, Julie?"

"Arms, above all else. The British smuggle some across the Channel, and drop them by parachutes in the northern areas, but it is only a trickle and it should be a flood. We need money, too—French money."

"I have brought you a little." He took out a roll of miscellaneous banknotes which he had been collecting, not without difficulty. "I am relieved to know that Raoul got the fifty thousand francs I tried to take to him. It was a funny method of delivery."

"I should say that is an American way to look at it," responded the woman. "For me, it will be a cause of bad dreams for many a night."

"I will tell you something to cheer you up. Hitler is going to attack Russia in June."

"*Oh, mon Dieu!* Can that really be true?"

"Take my word for it. July is the latest date."

"And may we say that in our paper?"

"Surely, but you had better wait a week or two, so that it will not coincide with my arrival in Paris. Say that you got it from papers stolen from a German officer. Say that the Wehrmacht is now being mobilized on the eastern front, and that as soon as the conquest of Greece is completed, the troops there will be shifted to the Ukraine."

"That will mean a tremendous increase of strength to us, Lanny. The Communists were powerful in France before the war, and such an attack will set them to work like a swarm of hornets."

"If you can convince them, they can start swarming two months earlier. Tell them that the top Nazis are trying desperately to persuade the British to lay off, so that Germany may be free to attack Russia. But they will not get what they are asking for."

"Oh, I hope you are right, Lanny! And thank you as ever. When do you expect to be back in France?"

"I cannot say exactly, but I should guess about midsummer. Address me at Bienvenu, as usual; but don't ask me to come to Toulon!"

"God forbid!" exclaimed the woman of the underground.

VII

Two years had passed since the great city of Madrid had yielded to Generalissimo Franco's troops, but a visitor looked in vain for any signs of restoration. Buildings which had been wrecked remained as they were, and stucco which had been chipped by bullets was pockmarked. In the Hotel Ritz, where Lanny put up, the hot water ran lukewarm and stained with rust. In the dining-room you could have a meal of fish or meat cooked in the very best Spanish style, provided that you had twenty dollars to pay for it. Outside, in the narrow, ill-smelling streets, people were fainting from starvation, and an average of two every hour were committing suicide. Jails and concentration camps were jammed with half-starved prisoners, and the problem of food scarcity was solved by taking batches of them out every night and shooting them in the courtyards. In short, it was Spain—pious and incompetent, Catholic and cruel, medieval Spain. Its regime was hated by all the workers and most of the peasants, by the intelligentsia and the middle classes; it was imposed upon the country by the military, with the help of German Nazis, Italian Fascists, Moors, aristocracy, and Holy Mother Church.

Some four years ago Lanny had met General Aguilar in Seville, and had impressed that pious killer with his understanding of and sympathy for the "Nationalist" cause. Now the General was the military commander of the capital, and Lanny called upon him and exhibited his intellectual wares with the usual good results; the elderly aristocrat with silvery mustaches and a chest covered with medals invited him to his home and compelled him to drink a dangerous number of *copitas de manzanilla*. Word spread quickly in the right circles that there was an American gentleman, *digno de aceptación*, who had just come from Berlin, and had previously been in Vichy, London, New York, and Hollywood. The P.A. was taken up and invited about, and no longer had to buy his meals at ruinous prices.

There had always been a colony of Spaniards on the French Riviera, in exile from one regime or another. Lanny had known them as a proud and touchy people, inclined toward melancholy, even moroseness. Perhaps that was to be expected of exiles; and now it seemed that the whole of Spain was in exile at home. Nobody was happy, even when they were drunk; the most elaborate dinner party, even with music and dancing, could not produce any gaiety. And everybody was ready to tell a visiting stranger the reason for it. A few madmen in Spain wanted more war, and all the rest were afraid that the forces which were wrecking the modern world were going to drag this tortured land into their vortex.

Such was the attitude of everybody whom Lanny met, even the government people, even the military. Spain had no food, Spain had no transportation, and how could she take part in a war? Spain was dependent upon outsiders for so many things—and especially oil, without which she could not move a wheel. How then could she fight countries which were in position to blockade her ports and destroy the few ships she had left? That much even General Aguilar would say; and his daughter, wife of one of the city's leading bankers, lowered her voice and exclaimed: "We are in the hands of irresponsible elements! We are the pawns of propaganda!"

You could make sure of it by looking at the newspapers on the stands. The Germans had begun a huge campaign for Spanish participation, and Lanny had seen enough in other cities to know how they must be pouring out money. When bands of hoodlums who called themselves the Falange and presumed to run the affairs of the country were parading the streets waving banners and shouting for blood, Lanny knew that money and cigarettes and arms were being distributed for the asking. There were rumors all over town that the British were preparing for a landing, to use Spain as a base to attack Hitler, as they had done with Napoleon nearly a century and a half ago. Lanny didn't have to be told that it was agents of the Gestapo who were circulating such reports. Hilde von Donnerstein had told him how they were practicing this same technique in Berlin, where the story was that all Germans in the United States were forced to wear black swastikas on their left breasts, and that the persecution of Jews in Germany was in reprisal for the persecution of Germans by the Jew-dominated governments of New York and Washington.

VIII

It was a P.A.'s job to find out about these matters, and if and where and when the Führer expected to strike through Spain. From General Aguilar he learned that new motor highways were being built in the direction of Gibraltar, and great fortifications were under construction facing the Rock; not even the peasants were permitted to use the side roads in that district. No doubt the British knew about such activities, but F.D.R. would be interested to have the reports confirmed. Everybody seemed to agree that there could be no move until the harvests were in, and that, too, was important. Meantime, remarked the elderly General, the troops would be busy with another attempt to put down the rebels who were still hiding in the Guadarrama mountains, less than an hour's drive from the capital. Also, his secret service would be occupied in trying to nab those Communists who, incredible as it might seem, were managing to publish a weekly paper in the heart of the city.

Admiral Darlan came to Madrid at this juncture, and when he learned that Lanny had been in Berlin he invited him to lunch. Lanny told him enough of what Hitler and Göring and Hess had said to cheer the old seadog and make him certain that his Nazi friends were going to win the war; then he talked freely about the proposed seizure of Gibraltar, dreaded by him because the armies would have to move through Vichy France. Marshal Pétain had proposed to come to Madrid to consult with Franco, whom he knew well and greatly admired; but the Führer had not trusted the old gentleman and had forbidden the visit. Thereupon Madame Pétain had come, with a military staff —which was something of a joke, considering that women had never voted in France and that their part in government had been confined to the drawing-room and the bedchamber. The Admiral chuckled as he told this story, and his guest laughed as any man would.

Also, Juan March happened to be in town; he traveled freely from Spain into France and from Spain into Britain; he was the sort of person whom embassies and consulates approve. He had begun life as a tobacco smuggler, and had got the tobacco monopoly of Spain; this and other privileges had made him the richest man in the land. It was well known that he had put up the money for Franco's coup, so now he could have anything he wanted if it was Franco's to give. But, alas, there was so much that wasn't in Franco's possession! Peace, for example, and security! Señor Juan was one of those Jews from the Balearic Isles whom the Spanish call *Xuetas*, and do not think of them as Jews, precisely, but as "descendants of Jews." But now the Nazi wave was spreading into Spain, and how could an ex-smuggler be certain that they would take the same attitude? Señor Juan was well on in years and his mother was dead; he might have difficulty in proving that she had committed adultery!

Also, the Germans were bad for business, Spanish business; they wanted it all to themselves. Señor Juan had just been to London, where he had formed a company with a nominal capital of a hundred thousand pounds to promote trade between Britain and Spain; but what could you do when Hitler was taking everything out of the country? The *Xueta* had suggested to General Franco a wonderful scheme for making cheap motorcars for the people of Spain, and Franco had thought well of it, but Hitler had not; he had pointed out that as soon as the war was won, Germany would be in position to make all the cars the Spanish people might want, and Germany would be wanting oranges and olive oil, cork and copper and mercury and other Spanish products in exchange. "He wants us to be a colony," said Señor Juan. Ordinarily he was a close-mouthed man, but he had known Lanny for some time and had learned the same lesson that Lanny had learned, that if you want somebody to tell you things you must begin by telling *him* things. A heavy-set, round-faced man, his complexion was so gray that it made you think of rubber. A large and melancholy rubber doll, overinflated, and afraid that somebody might stick a pin into him!

This tobacco king knew all about the projected invasion of Russia, and didn't mind discussing it. Serrano Suñer, Franco's brother-in-law and Spain's Foreign Minister, had made a deal with the Nazis, pledging his country to raise a million volunteers to fight the Reds. "They will be the same sort of 'volunteers' as the Führer and Il Duce sent to us," remarked Señor Juan glumly, and Lanny said: "That won't be very popular with the Spanish people, will it?" The reply was: "It will start the civil war all over again." The visitor gathered that his host didn't think much of Suñer, who was the most ardent of *Falangistas* and a reckless talker.

"By the way," said the Señor, "I mentioned to the Generalissimo your point that the word ought to be *Falangita*, because the *falangista* is a small tree-climbing animal of Tasmania."

"And what did he reply, Señor?"

"He said that nobody in the Party had ever heard of Tasmania, so it wouldn't matter!"

IX

A stout middle-aged German gentleman in what they call a "tourist's" costume came to Lanny's hotel and addressed him in precise English: "I have a message for you, Mister Budd." Lanny took the note, and with an apology, opened it and read: "I want to see you. Kurvenal." Lanny said: "Thank you. How shall I go?" The answer was: "We have a car, just around the corner. Be so good as to follow me at a little distance." So Lanny strolled out, and got into the car. They didn't offer to blindfold him, but drove him to one of the great mansions near the Palacio Real and took him in by a side door.

There was Rudi, in a pepper-and-salt civilian suit, the first time the American had seen him out of uniform. He started up, exclaiming: "Hello, Lanny!" And then, abruptly: "That damned Englishman hasn't come! I've been waiting here for two days."

"Too bad," responded Lanny. "I can't say anything, not knowing who he is."

"I'll tell you, if you'll promise not to pass it on."

"Of course not, Rudi."

"Lord Beaverbrook."

"The devil you say!"

"That surprises you, no doubt."

"If he has changed his mind about Germany and the war, you have certainly made a great conquest. But how could you imagine that the Beaver could come to Madrid and have it a secret? He is a queer-looking little duck, and everybody knows him."

"He could be here but not have it known that he was meeting any Germans. The British have any number of agents here."

"What is your reason for thinking he would come?"

"I had a definite appointment; but I suppose he lost his nerve. Certainly it can be nothing that I have done."

There was a pause. Lanny waited, feeling sure that more was to come. "Sit down," said the Deputy, and drew a chair close. "Old man," he began in a low voice, "I need help badly. I am going to take you into my confidence, if you will let me."

"Surely, Rudi. Anything that I can do."

"I count upon our long friendship. This is ultra-secret; there is no telling how important it may be."

"You have my solemn word."

"I wonder if you know about 'The Link.'"

"I have a vague impression of it."

"The secret has been well kept. It is a group of Englishmen who are working for friendship with us. You probably know some of them; the Duke of Hamilton is one of the most active. I have been in correspondence with him for more than a year."

"That is indeed important. This date with the Beaver is the outcome?"

"A part of it. I wish I could tell you all. You know Kirkpatrick, who used to be chargé at the British Embassy in Berlin?"

"I have met him once or twice at social affairs. I can't say that I really know him."

"He is the one who arranged this date. His letters have been so encouraging—I really thought the deal was going through. Won't you see him in London for me and find out what the devil has gone wrong?"

"Why, of course, Rudi. But how shall I reach you?"

"I will have a man call upon you in London. He will say: 'I am from Kurvenal,' and you can give him any information you have got."

"You are asking me to take a considerable risk, but the matter is so important that I don't mind. Wouldn't it save time if I were to see the Beaver and find out just what has happened? I met him several times on the Riviera, and I'm fairly sure he'll remember me."

"That is good of you, Lanny. Damn it! I am in a state of exasperation. You know how it is when you wait and wait for something. The Führer was pretty sure I wouldn't get it."

"That makes it worse," agreed Lanny sympathetically.

"He doesn't trust the British; he doesn't trust any foreigners—excepting you, Lanny." This was an obvious afterthought, a courtesy. Lanny's feelings weren't hurt, for he had had no idea that the Führer trusted him, except when it was necessary in order to get something the Führer wanted.

The Deputy was in that position now. He wanted something quite frantically, so much so that he got up and paced the floor like a wild creature in a cage. If Lanny had been a less cautious secret agent he might have suggested that Rudi should tell him what he wanted said to the British newspaper proprietor. But Lanny was sure that if he waited, Rudi would have to tell him; and it was better never to display the least curiosity.

"The devil of it!" burst out the Nazi at last. "These fellows say they want a reconciliation, but they back and fill and you can't get anything definite out of them. What do they really want? What are they up to?"

"They're playing a pretty dangerous game, Rudi. If Churchill finds out what they're doing he'll chop off their heads—I mean, their official heads, and he might even put them in quod."

"Well, how can they expect to get anywhere with us unless they take a risk?"

"It may be they are holding back to make you state your terms."

"But damn it all, we are the men who hold all the cards!"

"I know that, and they doubtless know it too; but they don't want to admit it."

"The only sensible thing for two people who have a dispute is to sit down and talk things over, man to man."

"Yes, indeed, and I wish to heaven I could bring about such an event —I would be a proud art expert."

"Lanny, I have to take you still further into my confidence. The Führer authorized me to say that he would agree to withdraw entirely from Western Europe. That means Norway, Belgium, Holland, Denmark, and France—exclusive of Alsace-Lorraine, of course."

"That is certainly a generous offer. I don't see how the British could expect more."

"That was supposed to come as the climax of negotiations, and to settle the matter."

"Then you don't want me to hint at that to the Beaver?"

"I'm not sure about it. What do you think?"

"God forbid that I should butt in on matters of state, Rudi. If I were to make a mistake the Führer would never forgive me, and neither would you. Decisions like that are for statesmen."

"All right then, tell him that's our offer. Damn his soul! I can't forget the things he said about us in his filthy papers."

"They don't take things like that too seriously in the pluto-democratic world, Rudi. The papers are printed for money and what goes into them is what they think the rabble wants."

X

This man who was not trying to make money, but to make the world over in the image of his Führer, wanted to hear about all the people whom Lanny had met in Madrid and what they had told him. Lanny reported what General Aguilar had said about the state of Spanish nutrition and transportation, and what the General's daughter had said about the state of the Spanish soul. Hess, it appeared, had had a highly secret meeting with Franco on the previous day, and Franco had said the same things, only more of them. "He insists that Spain could not possibly take Gibraltar by herself."

Lanny smiled. "But he is willing for you to come and do it, I can guess!"

"I wouldn't say that exactly; he knows that we have the power, and the moral right—considering what we did for him, and the debts he owes us."

"You wouldn't really have much trouble with the Rock, I should guess. Warfare has changed. They have almost no room for aviation and what they have you could knock out in one night. When you got it, the Mediterranean would be your sea—that is, unless you chose to share it with Il Duce."

The Deputy made a face. "Leave him out! The Italians are a liability, except for the munitions they produce. But we have to resist the temptation to scatter our forces in too many fields. Look at what the British did in Greece—the most frightful military blunder, for which they are paying now. To have sent two whole divisions in a perfectly futile effort to save that miserable little country! As a result, they have weakened their forces in Libya, and we are driving them in rout and probably will not stop until we have taken Suez. If we do that, the Mediterranean will be ours; for what use will it be to the British if they cannot get to India by it?"

All that was high strategy, and Lanny expressed his admiration for it, and his willingness to accept the Führer's judgments. He sang the praises of this man of miracles—the sure way to warm the heart of the man's Deputy, as well as of the man himself. Rudi said: "What a difference between a commander of great vision and one of small! I argued with Franco for an hour: 'You are thinking about the safety of Spain, and of yourself; but where will Spain be, and where will you be, if the British win this war?' Franco smiled slyly and replied: 'But they're not going to win, Herr Hess; you cannot afford to let them.' You see his idea: we are to fight his war for him, while he trades with both sides, and takes care of his food supply and transportation."

"He doesn't stop to think what your attitude will be toward him when the war is over."

"Oh, he's thinking about it now, you can bet!" exclaimed the Deputy. "I put it to him straight that we should have learned who were our friends, and who were the ingrates of Europe."

"And he took that?"

"Took it? What else could he do? I gave him the dressing down of his life, the miserable, cringing little renegade."

"Well, that is good to hear. But he isn't going to take Gibraltar?"

"Not until we can spare troops enough to do the work and let him take the glory, as he did last time."

XI

For two days more the Deputy stayed in the Madrid palace, waiting for his Beaver, who showed none of the eagerness attributed to that creature. Each day Rudi sent for his friend and adviser, Lanny Budd, and each day in his impatience he revealed a few more of his secrets. He had had the extraordinary idea to send an airmail letter to the Governor of Gibraltar; he had somehow got the idea that this Lord Gort was a member of The Link, and Rudi had offered to fly to Gibraltar for a meeting. He was startled by the reply he received—to the effect that he was free to fly to Gibraltar, but that if he landed there his lordship would have him shot!

So there was nothing for the chief of the National-Socialist German Workingmen's Party to do but fly back to Berlin. He was in a fever of vexation about it; and after Lanny had said good-by to him one evening he summoned him again in the morning, and poured out his soul anew. This was the greatest disappointment of his life, and he was not a man to accept failure; he was a man who drove through failure to success. In the evening he had begged Lanny to get to work in London and produce results. An American art expert was to end the war between Britain and Germany, where all the intrigues of half a dozen Nazi secret services had failed! But now in the morning Hess had another and even more bizarre idea—one which he said had been haunting his mind for a long while, and which he had been keeping the closest of secrets.

"Matters of high policy simply cannot be discussed at long range, Lanny; they call for personal contacts, and the give and take of discussion. But Churchill will not send anybody, nor permit anybody to come. So it is my idea to fly to England."

"You mean—Churchill will receive you?"

"I mean to go unannounced; just fly in an unarmed plane and land at some carefully chosen spot."

"But, good God, Rudi! You would be shot down on the way!"

"I would take my chances. I am a pretty good pilot, you know."

"But, can you find a landing place that is without ack-ack?"

"If it came to the worst, I can parachute."

"But, then, they would shoot you for a spy!"

"I would wear my uniform, so they couldn't do that."

"But, at best, you would be a prisoner of war."

"I doubt it. They would give me diplomatic status, once they realized what I had come for. Surely it is permissible for a man to ask for peace!"

Lanny hesitated for quite a time. He knew that this was one of the critical moments in his job. "What do you say?" asked the Number Three, and Lanny replied: "You are putting a frightful responsibility upon me, Rudi. If I should guess wrong, you would never forgive me as long as you lived, and neither would the Führer."

"I do not have to tell him that I have spoken to you about it. As a matter of fact, I may not tell him if I decide to do it. He has given me a free hand to do whatever I think will help get Britain out of the war; and he might prefer to be spared the responsibility of knowing."

"Well, you can't expect me to feel any differently from the Führer, Rudi. How in the world can I guess what the British would do? If you succeeded, of course, it would be one of the greatest coups in history."

"That is the way I see it. I have reasons for believing that the British people don't like this war any better than we. My action would tell them, in striking and dramatic fashion, that the Germans want peace, and who is blocking it."

"That is undoubtedly true. But, my God, I can't tell you to go!"

"I don't ask for that. All I want is your frank opinion. What would Wickthorpe do if I landed at the Castle?"

"I can't imagine. He would be stunned, and probably wouldn't know what to do."

"Wouldn't he get his friends to meet me and talk things over?"

"He might want to try. But in the first place, Rudi, there is no airport there; and it's so close to London, a settled district—there are few big fields as you have in Germany, and if there are any, they have perhaps been cut with ditches to keep planes from landing."

"I might decide upon some remote place. Hamilton has an estate in Scotland. I could just as well fly there, coming in over Norway."

"Ceddy has a shooting box in Scotland; but nobody shoots in springtime."

"The Scotch highlands must be worth a visit at this season. Couldn't Ceddy and his wife take a trip just for pleasure? Couldn't you think up some excuse to get them there—say for the pleasure of your little daughter?"

"I don't know; they are both very busy in their own way, trying to end the war. I could suggest it, of course."

"If you could arrange it, I could find the shooting box. You wouldn't have to bother with the details—my agents would attend to it, and I'd have a good map—that part would be no trouble at all. I could be hidden at some remote place like that, and a few trusted people could come to see me, one or two at a time so as not to attract attention."

"You'd be taking a tremendous risk, Rudi."

"*Herrgott*, what does that matter? I am a soldier, trying to serve my cause. If I die, there are trained men who could take my place as head of the Party. The Führer would miss me, but he would know that I had done my best."

This proved to be a long visit. The Deputy was in deadly earnest, and he raked his friend's mind, asking a string of questions. He named persons, some of whom Lanny knew, and others who he guessed must be members of that mysterious organization, The Link. Evidently the collaborationist movement was far stronger than he had guessed. Neville Chamberlain was still alive, and his spirit was even livelier!

The P.A.'s last words were: "This would be a colossal sensation, Rudi; it would shake the world. I'll do what I can to help, but don't for one moment forget: I haven't advised it, and I don't take any responsibility."

"On that basis *auf Wiedersehen!*" said Rudolf Hess, and added, turning the verses around:

> "Oh, ye'll tak' the low road
> And I'll tak' the high road,
> And I'll be in Scotland afore ye!"

15. *Oh, to Be in England!*

I

THERE were many persons waiting in Madrid for airplane accommodations to Lisbon; but Lanny Budd did not have to wait, he merely had to mention the matter to Hess, who mentioned it to one of his agents. Arriving in the Portuguese capital, Lanny cabled to his father's

London solicitors, and then identified himself at the Bank of the Holy Ghost and took steps to draw on his London bankers. Tourists were sometimes surprised to learn that the Holy Ghost had gone into the banking business in Lisbon; also, when they went for a stroll in the city's most showy boulevard, they wondered why it was called Avenida da Liberdade—in a city and country ruled by an iron-handed dictator.

The soil of Portugal was at the mercy of the Nazi armies, and its harbors at the mercy of the British Fleet. Therefore the government was carefully and systematically neutral, and this attitude was tolerated because both warring powers found it convenient. Passenger and cargo planes flew in from all points of the compass, and military aviators from Britain and Germany drank at the same bars, eying one another but not speaking. Spies of every sort swarmed in the city; and the air or ether or whatever it is that carries radio messages in secret codes got no rest day or night. In the poverty-stricken countryside laborers toiled for fifty cents per day, but in Lisbon cafés and brothels and gambling casinos money flowed like water in the river Tejo, which the English call Tagus.

Fleuve du Tage was the name of an opera melody which Lanny at the age of five or six had had as a finger exercise on the piano. In the mountains of the interior he had once helped Alfy Pomeroy-Nielson to get across that river, escaping from Spain. There it had been clean, but it had become lazy and muddied in this busy estuary where ships gathered from all over the world. Now and then you would hear firing at sea, which meant that some ship was in trouble; but nobody bothered about it in Lisbon. So far as a tourist could see, nobody in Lisbon bothered about anything, and neither did anybody rejoice very much. The principal occupation of all appeared to be sitting still in cafés and looking dull.

If men had the price, they sipped oversweet coffee; if not, they stared at the foreign women—mostly at the legs, which were novelties in a Catholic capital where the women wore skirts down to their ankle-bones. This Portuguese habit of staring had been utilized by the Nazis for their propaganda. The newspapers were rigidly controlled and their falsehoods divided equally, so the Germans hired store windows and set up exhibits of the wonders of their New Order. They had speedily made the discovery that the Lisbonites had no interest in statistics as to the increase in German coal production, but would stand for hours gazing at photographs of sturdy blonde Aryan *Mädchen* in abbreviated or non-existent swim-suits. *Heil Hitler!*

It was the pleasantest time of the year, and Lanny, waiting for his plane ticket, found it enjoyable to ride out to Estoril, the swanky bathing beach and gambling resort, much like those on the Côte d'Azur. He knew so many people in Europe that he met one or more on every esplanade. The only trouble was that so many of these were refugees, frantic to escape from this slim edge of a Nazi continent. Many were out of funds, and he might have been glad to help one or two of them—if it could have been done secretly. As it was, he hardly dared be seen speaking to them.

Instead, he amused himself by permitting a Japanese spy to strike up an acquaintance with him. These small gentry swarmed all over the place, correctly dressed in outing flannels or white evening clothes or whatever the occasion called for; they bowed low and showed rows of yellowish teeth, and the polite art expert accepted an invitation to make a foursome at golf; when he found that he was beating them he played badly, having heard that they were not good losers. He gave them information, but it was mostly about modern painting, and what he gave about his own affairs was not correct. When this palled, he lay on the sand and watched Portuguese fishing craft with upswept prows inherited from the Egyptians and Phoenicians; or he read New York and London newspapers, which came by air and could be bought at a high price. When his hour of departure arrived and a British flying boat lifted him into the air, he decided that the white stone and stucco capital looked much more attractive from that point of view.

II

In London a P.A.'s first duty was to lock himself in his hotel room and type out what he had learned in Madrid and Lisbon. The promises of secrecy to Rudolf Hess had been made with his fingers crossed; Lanny told F.D. all about The Link and the Englishmen who reportedly belonged to it; also about the Deputy's mad scheme to fly to England—but predicting that when the Deputy got back to Berlin he would find more useful ways to serve his Führer. The really important matters were that the coming invasion of the Soviet Union was positively confirmed, and that Franco had definitely made up his mind to wait and allow Hitler to take Gibraltar for him. Spain's pitiful condition was doubtless already known to the President; but he would be interested to know how large a percentage of the imports then permitted to enter the country were being passed straight on to Germany.

Having seen this letter safely delivered to the American Embassy, Lanny was free. As usual the first thing he did was to get The Reaches on the telephone. "Hello, this is Bienvenu. Can you come to town?" It took Rick only two or three hours to get there, and then what a time they had! Lanny kept nothing from this lifelong friend, save only the name of his Chief in America. In the obscure hotel which they had chosen for their rendezvous there was no chance of dictaphones or spies, and Lanny unbosomed himself of the whole Hitler-Hess picture. "You understand," he said, "this project of flying here is absolutely top secret, and you mustn't even hint at it."

"Righto!" was Rick's reply. "If the man isn't mad, then I am."

"If he comes unarmed he can't hurt anybody, so we don't have to worry. He seems to have a lot of backing here, and that is what is serious. The business of The Link looks pretty black to me."

"I find it hard to believe, Lanny. Ivone Augustine Kirkpatrick is a career diplomatist; the Pater knows him, and if he's turned traitor I'll surely be surprised. As for the Beaver, his papers are shouting for more and harder war, and that hardly seems to fit in with secret trips to negotiate a surrender."

"Not exactly a surrender, Rick; but of course it would amount to that in the long run. Could it possibly be that a great newspaper proprietor has changed his mind but hasn't got around to telling his staff?"

"The devil only can guess what is going on in the mind of a press lord. But this occurs to me—that somebody on our side may be playing with Hess, somebody besides you. Have you thought of that?"

"I began thinking of it from the first moment I heard about this Link. Somebody may have made it up, and be sending Hess a lot of letters in the names of various Englishmen."

"It would be pretty tough on the Englishmen; but I suppose anything would be fair in a war against such rotters."

"Who would be doing it, do you suppose?"

"Probably B4. That's our last word in secrecy; we aren't supposed ever to breathe the syllables. They'd be trying to lure some top Nazi agent over here and then trail him and see whom he visits. Or maybe they just want revenge for the Venloo incident—you remember, at the outset of the war, the Nazis raided across the Dutch border and kidnaped two of our important agents."

"This is getting to be pretty hot stuff, Rick—spies and traitors, and plots inside plots."

"Be careful somebody doesn't kidnap *you*," remarked the baronet's son, and that seemed an invitation for Lanny to tell the story of his odd experience in the back country of Toulon. "My God!" exclaimed Rick. "What a life you do live! And how you do get about!"

Lanny asked: "How is Alfy?" and the reply was: "He had a crash, but got off lightly. He's in hospital with a couple of ribs and a shoulder cracked. What he's afraid of is that they'll ground him and put him to teaching."

"He has done his share," was Lanny's comment. "Give him my love. You know, of course, I can't go to see him."

"Surely not," said the father. "He wouldn't expect it."

III

Lanny went off and thought matters over. An idea occurred to him, and next morning he called the modern structure known as the "Black-glass House," the office of the *Daily Express* and the *Evening Standard.* He asked for the secretary of Lord Beaverbrook, and to this functionary he said: "This is the American art expert, Lanny Budd. Lord Beaverbrook will remember having met me at Wickthorpe Castle, also at Maxine Elliott's home in Cannes, along with Mr. Churchill. I have just returned from a visit to Berlin, and thought that he might be interested to have a report on what I found there. Explain that this is strictly personal and private, nothing to be published."

The secretary said: "One moment, please," and then reported: "His lordship wishes to know if you will lunch with him at the Carlton Club at one o'clock."

Lanny figured that it couldn't do him any harm to be seen with this noble gentleman, because Hitler and Hess believed him to be on their side, and Hess had asked for a report on him. "The Beaver," as he was called by the British masses with a sort of affectionate hatred, was a little bouncing man with a gnome's face. His name was Max Aitken and he had been a company promoter in Canada; he had come to London with a million pounds and devoted himself with infinite ardor to the vulgarization of English journalism. He was one of America's contributions of "ginger" to the motherland; Winston Churchill being another, or, to be exact, one-half of another. The Beaver had filled his papers with gossip, "spice," and reactionary opinion. Was it for such services that men were ennobled in the days of British commercialism rampant? His lordship had been pretty close to Fascism in the old Neville Chamberlain days, but had soon realized that that wasn't going to be a paying proposition. He hated the Reds so much more than he hated the Nazis that he would come back again and again to nibbling at the Hitler hook.

An aggressive ego, he ordinarily made it difficult to get a word in edgeways. But he really wanted to know how matters stood in Hitler-land, and also in the Franco jail, so he plied his guest with questions. He found it hard to believe that a man could be carrying on the business of purchasing old masters in the midst of a continental war. Lanny said, with a grin: "If you'll come to my room at the Dorchester I'll show you a couple of them." The American didn't say anything about Rudolf Hess's project of flying to Scotland, but he said in general terms that both Hitler and his Deputy were most anxious for an understanding with Britain, as a preliminary to their invasion of Russia.

"They've got to invade anyhow, haven't they?" asked the publisher, his shrewd little eyes twinkling.

"Of course, but if they have to fight Britain at the same time, they may not win. They figure you wouldn't like to have the Reds come out on top." This was a problem that worried all members of ruling classes, all privileged persons in the world. The proprietor of the *Standard* and the *Express* sat with knitted brows.

"Tell me," said the P.A. "Have you ever taken any interest in The Link?"

"The Link?" repeated the other. "What is that?" His tone appeared genuine.

"I don't know much about it, but was told it's a group of people trying to face up to this problem and to work out some basis for an understanding between the two countries."

"I did my share of trying," declared his lordship. "But those Nazis are bastards that nobody can trust. The feeling of our people is that they have to be put out of business. Nobody is ever again going to be left in a position to bomb these islands."

So that was that; and Lanny talked for a while about the state of German finances and food supply. He discussed Paris under the occupation, and what Schneider's friends had said. And then to Spain: he mentioned that Franco was standing out against the Nazi demand as to Gibraltar, and this the Beaver heard with satisfaction. In the course of the talk Lanny remarked, casually: "I was rather expecting to meet you while I was in Madrid."

"Why should you have expected that?" inquired the other.

"There was a report that you were coming. Somebody told me it was in the papers."

"Many silly rumors get started in wartime. I haven't any reason for going to Spain."

"Perhaps," remarked the P.A. with a smile, "the Nazis were trying to get hold of you, to talk peace."

"Never again!" said his lordship, and used language that would have ruined his papers.

When they parted, Lanny said: "All this is strictly off the record. You can use the facts as background, but I don't want to be interviewed or even mentioned."

"Certainly, certainly," said the Beaver somewhat testily, for a newspaperman does not like to have his valuable services spurned. "What you have told me is illuminating, Mr. Budd. I will esteem it a favor if you will call me up whenever you come to town."

Lanny went out and telephoned Rick. "You remember the man who was supposed to be going to Madrid? I just talked with him and he says it's not so. Evidently that matter isn't what it is supposed to be, but something else again."

"I get you," said Rick. Like many other Englishmen, his language had been corrupted by contact with Americans.

IV

Lanny strolled about London. The springtime air was balmy, and overhead the barrage balloons waved slowly in the breeze, looking like huge fat silver sausages. In all the parks were anti-aircraft guns. Lanny was curious to see what landmarks of the old City were gone. The shaky walls had been torn down and the rubble cleared away, and there were acres of empty space around St. Paul's. He wondered what they would put there when the war was over, if it ever was. Would they behave like the ants and the bees, and restore everything exactly as it had always been? He wondered how it was possible for the financial world to carry on its infinitely complex affairs in spite of such destruction. Rick had said they were doing it, a little here and a little there; some underground, some in the suburbs. There would always be an England!

According to his custom he telephoned to Wickthorpe. Would it be agreeable for him to pay a visit? Irma said: "Frances asks for you every day." Lanny specified the train he would take; a car would meet him at the station.

It was the end of April, the loveliest time of the year. Not many bombs had been wasted on this countryside, and fears were ended. When you came to the Castle, you discovered that the lovely green lawns which had been nibbled by so many generations of sheep had been plowed up and planted to cabbages. All save one little corner, where Ceddy played at bowls with the curate and other friends!

Lanny's little daughter came in the car to meet him, and she never let go of his hand. Somehow she had decided that he was a very wonderful father; his absence made her heart grow fonder, and now she dragged him all over the place, to show him new crops that had been planted and new creatures that had been born. The refugee children from London were at school; all scrubbed, fed on vitamins, and taught proper manners. Ceaseless pressure from both sides had broken down barriers, and Frances was allowed to take part in their games now and then, and even to let some of them ride on her pony. She had just celebrated her eleventh birthday with a big party, and they as well as the village children had all been invited; everybody had been nice to her and it was "scrumptious." Lanny was not allowed to teach her democracy, but if the war did it, he could approve.

Eight months had passed since he had seen her. He had had little

notes from her in America, carefully written—he suspected they had
been revised and recopied. Also drawings, and little paintings in water
color, submitted to him as an expert. Now there were more of these,
and he gave her advice; he watched her mind and the questions she
asked. She was becoming aware of the great world; the war was forc-
ing geography and history upon the attention of everyone. To Frances
it was thrilling and delightful—no sense of the pain, or of fear. He
marveled at life renewing itself; at eagerness, curiosity, trust in nature,
which was cruel as often as it was kind.

Frances Barnes Budd was going to be a little English girl; nothing
else was possible. She had the accent and the key phrases of the ruling
class. Also she would have the manners; she would learn to repress her
enthusiasms, to wear a mask before the world. Irma, sedate and placid,
would make her over in the mother image; it was a mother's privilege.
She would say: "Hush, dear! Not so loud." English children were becoming more free and easy in their manners, but Irma did not approve,
and Lanny said nothing. Only when they were alone he let the little
one enjoy herself; he told her about Isadora Duncan's dancing, gave
her an idea of it, then played the piano and let her try.

Lanny did not fail to pay his respects to the Honorable James Pon-
sonby Cavendish Cedric Barnes, Viscount Masterson, who was destined
to become the fifteenth Earl of Wickthorpe. He was two years of age,
toddling away whenever he was let loose, and staring at strangers out
of big blue eyes. Also, to make assurance doubly sure, there was his
younger brother, the Honorable Gerald Cedric Barnes Masterson,
born on the day that Paris fell. He was just trying to get up on his
feet, and whatever he could find on the floor he tried surreptitiously
to get into his mouth. Irma's duty to the British Empire had been done,
and she was concerned that it should not have been done in vain—in
other words, that the Reds shouldn't get it!

V

In the evening, Lanny sat with his former wife and her present husband. "Good breeding" made this possible; the most important thing
in their world. They talked freely about other personalities, but never
about themselves or their own troubles. When Irma had quarreled with
Lanny and left him, she had talked it over with her mother and made
up her mind: there must be no scandal, no recriminations. They were
different people and could not live together, but they were decent
people and could respect each other's rights.

Later, when the Earl of Wickthorpe had come wooing, the prac-
tical-minded Irma had had an understanding with him on the difficult
role of stepfather. Little Frances would be a permanent fact in their

lives. Having been celebrated in the newspapers as the twenty-three-million-dollar baby, she could not be treated as an ordinary human mite; Lanny couldn't just come and carry her off to a hotel, or to Bienvenu or Newcastle; her mother would never have a moment's rest for fear of kidnapers. No, he would have to come to the Castle to see the child. Ceddy said: "Why not?" and Irma remarked: "The village will call it a scandal." He replied: "The village belongs to me, not I to the village." It was the voice of his ancestors whose portraits hung in a long gallery, most of them with swords and several clad in mail.

The matter was made easier by the fact that Lanny and Ceddy had known each other since boyhood. They had never been intimates, but had been on coaching parties to the races, and later on to international conferences where they had drunk cocktails and discussed the strange manners and morals of continental diplomatists. They knew what to expect of each other; what was done and what wasn't. Irma's new marriage was what she wanted, and wiped the memories of old intimacies out of her mind. Neither she nor Ceddy knew that Lanny had been married again, but Lanny knew it, and that helped him. When he thought about love, it was heroism and martyrdom. The Trudi-ghost still walked with him, and supervised not merely his actions but his imaginings.

VI

They sat in the library with the doors closed, and talked about what to them were the most important subjects in the world. In eight months they had exchanged no letters, because what they wanted to say could not be trusted to the eyes of censors. So there was much to tell: Lanny's adventures in New York, Hollywood, Vichy, Berlin, Paris, Madrid, Lisbon. He appeared to be talking freely, but in reality he was holding back a lot. Nothing about the plot against Roosevelt, for that did not concern this couple; they might wonder how he had come to know so much, and might suspect that he was romancing. The same went for the misadventure in Toulon; let sleeping dogs lie. What concerned this pair was the personalities of the Vichy leaders, and the prospects regarding the French Fleet, North Africa, Syria. And then Franco and Gibraltar. Lanny told what Hitler had said on the all-important problem of an understanding with Britain; what Hess and Göring had said, and the activities of Hess in Madrid. There he stopped, and waited for his friends to comment. He said nothing about Hess's project of coming to England.

"The situation here is extremely depressing," declared the Earl of

Wickthorpe. "Did you see anything about my speech before the Lords last month?"

"I saw it mentioned in one of the papers, but very briefly."

"I will give you the text to read. I went as far as I dared, but I am afraid you won't think it was far enough. Sentiment in England has been steadily hardening, on account of the bombing of districts where there are no military objectives and where the purpose can only be that of terrorizing. Also, the torpedoings have been so merciless, and so cruel, especially in winter. I am afraid we have to concede that Churchill has the country in his hands."

"That is not quite the same as winning the war," ventured Lanny.

"No, indeed, and that is the tragedy of it. The ruinous struggle goes on, and we have to watch it helplessly."

"Tell me," put in Irma, "do you still feel that the Führer can be trusted?"

"I don't think I have ever said quite that, Irma. I think he can be trusted so far as his immediate objectives are concerned. He wants peace very much, because it is obviously to his interest. What his attitude will be later depends upon the arrangements you make with him and how matters work out."

"That uncertainty is precisely what makes our position intolerable," resumed Ceddy. "I find that our friends and sympathizers are conceding one point after another to the government. Most significant of all, they lose interest in the cause of peace; they just retire, and occupy themselves with their personal affairs."

"Like yourself," Lanny thought, but didn't say it.

"What has made it so impossible for us," declared Irma, "is this lease-lend business that Roosevelt has started. Does Robbie think that is going to continue?"

"I haven't heard from Robbie since it started. I cabled him from Lisbon and no doubt he'll write me here, but you know how the censorship delays mail for weeks; Robbie knows it, too, and never discusses public affairs. Just 'all well and busy,' or perhaps that one of the grandchildren has the mumps."

There it was, all very depressing, as Ceddy had declared. Really, only one gleam of light in the sky, for a member of the old nobility. (Ceddy didn't count the press lords and the beer barons, and found it hard to be polite to the labor peers of the Ramsay MacDonald era.) "Tell me," he said, "is Hitler really going after Russia?"

"He practically admitted it to me, and so did Hess. It seems to be generally accepted in Paris and Madrid."

"Yes, but should *we* accept it? It seems to me that if he really meant to do it, he'd be admitting something else."

"So far he hasn't worked that way. He makes a joke of it, saying that he always tells exactly what he is going to do, because then his enemies will be sure it can't be true."

"I know; but in this supremely important matter he might decide to vary his technique."

"It might be. We'll soon know, for he has finished in Greece and must show his hand."

"All our reports indicate that he is going into Crete."

"Yes, but that's a job for paratroopers, not for a large army. He's bound to be moving his Balkan troops to the eastward, and surely your Intelligence will report that to you before long."

"It seems almost too good to happen," was the wife's comment; and the pessimistic husband admitted: "I suppose that is the solution we have to accept. Let those two dictators chew each other up, and give us a chance to get some goods from America!"

VII

Lanny stayed a week-end at the Castle and met the usual distinguished company. He gave them picturesque and entertaining details concerning life among their enemies. Americans were still in that fortunate position, they could go anywhere in the world if they had the proper credentials—and nobody found it strange that the son of Budd-Erling should have obtained them. He didn't tell any crucial facts, and, above all, no hint that Rudolf Hess was contemplating a visit. In the first place, Lanny didn't think he was coming, and, in any case, the statement would have made a sensation, and would almost certainly have got into the newspapers, and brought Lanny in with it.

Enough to say that the Führer desperately wanted reconciliation with England, and that all three of the top men had begged the American to say this on every possible occasion. The company raised the same question as Ceddy: Could anybody trust him? Lanny evaded, saying that it was a question for psychologists and statesmen, not for an art expert. He would listen attentively and make note of facts that came out during the talk. Thus, from Gerald Albany of the Foreign Office he learned that the Russians were making overtures for new trade agreements with Britain; they had become much "softer" in their attitude, which meant, said the clergyman's son, that they had discovered which way the wind was blowing. They were trying to buy arms in America, and Washington was being extremely noncommittal.

Lanny went back to town, under the bombs, and wrote out a report on what he had learned. It was considered good form to ignore danger, so he attended a symphony concert, and some of the music was German. He came back to his hotel and was reading an evening paper in his room when the phone rang. "A gentleman to see you, sir; the name,

Mr. Branscome." Lanny didn't know any such gentleman, but it was the business of an art expert, and also of a secret agent, to see anybody. He went downstairs—it being easier to get rid of a bore that way.

There was a man in the lobby, middle-aged, well dressed, and speaking properly; but he had a dissipated look, or something off color— Lanny decided at a glance that it wasn't anybody he cared to cultivate. Then he got a start. The stranger said: "Mr. Budd, are you acquainted with a person named Kurvenal?"

Caution was instinctive in this matter. Lanny said: "I have heard the name."

"Would it be a woman, by chance?"

Smiling his most amiable smile, Lanny replied: "Why would you want to know?"

"I was asked to find out if you had a message for her."

"I see. And are you in a position to convey a message to her?"

"I am."

The P.A. didn't have to take time for thought, having anticipated this possibility and decided upon a reply. "Tell her I have been working busily and that the situation is favorable."

"Is that all, Mr. Budd?"

"She will understand that, and it will be all right."

"Thank you, sir, and good evening." The man turned and left the lobby quickly. Lanny went back to his room, wondering what kind of Englishman was doing dirty work like that. It was easy to understand why he had not stayed to get acquainted, for if he had been caught he would surely have been shot. "Branscome" was doubtless a name he had made up, and he would be careful to keep himself where the son of Budd-Erling would not lay eyes on him again. Talk about "a woman" was no doubt meant to prepare himself an alibi; he could say that he hadn't known what the message was about, he had been tricked into doing the errand for another man.

VIII

Lanny gave a lot of thought to that incident. He knew that he was playing a complicated and dangerous game, and he didn't want to make any slip. He reminded himself that he was not working for Rudi Hess, and owed him neither help nor truth. To the Wickthorpes he owed something, but nothing compared to what he owed to the cause of human freedom. The noble pair were beginning to hedge, but they hadn't been hedging eight months ago, when they had given Lanny every encouragement to go and see Hess and to speak for them. If now they had changed, Lanny had no way to let Hess know it. He certainly wasn't going to name any names or give any personal messages to a strange Mr. Branscome who looked like what was called a "ticket-of-leave" man.

The more Lanny thought about this episode, the more firmly he decided that "Kurvenal" should remain a woman from this time on. If B4 was setting a trap for Nazi Three, what was more likely than that they had been watching him in Madrid, and even in Berlin? If so, they knew that the son of Budd-Erling had visited Hess's home, and had been closeted with him in the Madrid palace. They might somehow have learned that the two had exchanged passwords, and in that case they would surely have made use of the words to find out what the much-traveled American was up to.

Lanny had been caught in one trap, and was firmly resolved not to let it happen again. The more he thought about the Toulon episode, the more clear it became to him that the French underground must have had a spy in Admiral Darlan's office, and received a report to the effect that the Admiral had been drinking Pernod brandy with an American pro-Nazi posing as an art expert, and had given that dangerous person a letter of introduction to the commandant of the port of Toulon. What sort of hornets' nest Lanny had there blundered into he could only guess. The partisans, hiding out in the hills and getting arms and ammunition by raiding government *camions*, would be hunted incessantly by government police and troops; spies and informers would be swarming, and doubtless there had been executions in the courtyard of the naval prison, and assassinations in reprisal. It was a civil war, everywhere the most cruel.

Whatever it was, Lanny had walked blandly into it, and he surely didn't want to repeat the error. Let B4 and *Nummer Drei* fight their secret war and leave a P.A. out of it! He would go back to Wickthorpe and play the piano for Frances and teach her to dance; he would help make up a four for contract bridge with Fanny Barnes, Irma's large worldly mother, and Fanny's poor crippled old derelict stock-gambler brother whom Lanny had been taught to call "Uncle Horace." Now and then, when he was tempted to worry, he told himself that it was all nonsense anyhow—Rudi Hess, while he was a fanatic, had some common sense, and would realize that the scheme was crazy. Or he would tell his Führer about it—and the Führer would send him to organize the National-Socialist Party of Yugoslavia or of Greece.

IX

Lanny returned to the Castle. On account of war crowding, he had to stay in the spare bedroom of the two-hundred-year-old cottage occupied by Fanny and her brother. It had been "modernized" by Irma, along with everything else on the estate, and had two tiled bathrooms, a telephone, and the proper kitchen gadgets. Lanny could shut himself up in his room and read, or come out and turn on the radio and listen to the tragic news from southeastern Europe. When Frances was through with her daily studies he would play croquet with her, or teach her tennis strokes. He could get more time with her by agreeing to speak French, for then it would be a lesson. His pleasure in her society he explained by saying that she was the only female creature he knew who did not wish either to marry him or to get him married. Even Irma had made a couple of passes at finding him the right sort of wife!

When his conscience troubled him in the midst of war he told himself that he had reported to F.D.R. everything he knew; he had got far ahead of the game, and now must wait until Hitler made another move. As for the cabal against Roosevelt, the Chief had as much as told him there was no need to bother with it; Europe was Lanny's field. And besides, you never knew who was going to turn up at Wickthorpe; a week-end here was better than sitting in at a meeting of the British Cabinet. All sorts of people came and brought all sorts of news, and a secret agent of any government in the world would have paid a high price for the privilege of being present.

So matters went, until Friday, the 9th day of May, 1941: a day when the newspapers were full of debates in the House, where "Winnie" had got a vote of confidence of 447 to 3—which seemed like a slap in the face to Wickthorpe Castle. Lanny read the news from New York and Washington, rather skimpy as a rule; the papers quoted the Secretary of War, who promised generous aid to Britain; also President Roosevelt had asked Congress for funds to build five hundred bombers. That would take two years and cost a billion dollars, the opposition objected; they called it "perfectly wicked."

Lanny's reading was interrupted by a maidservant bringing the morning mail to the cottage. There was only one letter for him, an inconspicuous envelope, addressed by an unfamiliar hand. Opening it he found a plain sheet of paper with four handwritten words which caused his heart to give a violent thump. "I am coming. Kurvenal."

The words were English, and the script also. It was not a note that Hess himself had written, but one that he had had written by one of his agents in England, perhaps "Branscome." The Deputy Führer might have ordered it by radio, or by one of those devices the Nazis were using, such as advertisements in the newspapers of Sweden, Spain, or Portugal, which came into Britain regularly; the advertisements looked innocent, but they were code. The letter had been mailed in London the previous day, but it bore no date and no one could guess how long the message had taken to reach London. For all that Lanny could tell, Hess might be flying tonight!

X

He took a walk, to think the matter over; then he went to the Castle, where he found the Earl of Wickthorpe in his study, busy with his secretary. Lanny said: "There is something urgent that I must talk to you and Irma about." Ceddy told the secretary to go and ask his wife to come down, and presently the three of them were shut up in the study: Ceddy in plus-fours and a polo shirt, Irma in a brocaded Japanese kimono, her hair in two long dark braids. She wouldn't have come that way, only her husband had commanded "at once."

Lanny wasted no words on preliminaries. "I have just received a note telling me that Rudolf Hess is coming to England."

"To England!" echoed Ceddy, dumfounded. "What for?"

"Mainly, in the hope of seeing you. He is going to fly in an unarmed plane, and land somewhere on your shooting grounds in Scotland. He wants you to be there and meet him."

"Good God!" exclaimed the noble earl.

"For the sake of peace on earth and good will toward men," countered the other. "He expects to enlist your aid in that cause."

"Is the man mad, Lanny? Or are you?"

"He may be a bit mad, as most men are who want to change the world. But he's not too mad to fly a plane, and to come down by parachute if necessary."

"Did he tell you about this in advance?"

"He broached it to me in Madrid. I did what I could to discourage him. I told him he would be a prisoner of war."

"He will be shot!"

"No, he will wear a uniform, and his plane will be unarmed."

"Why didn't you tell us about this sooner, Lanny?"

"I didn't take it seriously. I thought I had managed to dissuade him, and I was quite sure the Führer wouldn't permit it."

"Oh! The Führer knows of it, then?"

"How that stands I can't be sure. This is all I have." Lanny passed the letter to his friend and both he and Irma studied it. "Kurvenal is the code name that Rudi took, so that if he sent any message I would know it was genuine. He said he had agents in England." Lanny had decided that there was no use mentioning "Branscome."

"What precisely does the man expect me to do?" demanded Ceddy.

"He wants you and Irma to take me and Frances on a pleasure trip, and be at the shooting box to meet him when he arrives."

"And for what purpose?"

"To consult with him as to how to bring peace between his country and yours."

"He thinks I have such power?"

"He thinks you are the center of a group of men who have great influence. You understand, Ceddy, I have been feeding him this idea for several years, in order to get him to talk. I did that with your knowledge, and brought you the results and you accepted them. Of course I never foresaw the possibility of such a development as this. I couldn't believe it then and I can hardly believe it now."

"It's going to raise the very devil if it happens, Lanny. It can't possibly be kept secret and it will blacken us for life."

"I don't see why you should expect such results. You have never met Hess anywhere, have you?"

"Never in my life."

"And you don't want to go to Scotland, I take it?"

"I do not!"

"All right, then. Sit tight, and let the government deal with Rudi. Maybe he won't mention you. If he does, just say you know nothing about it. You have had no communication from him and no sympathy with his ideas. That lets me out as well as you."

"Suppose he mentions *you?*"

"I doubt if he will, for I'm an American, and no excuse for his coming to England. If he does, I have my story: I'm an art expert and I went to Germany on business; I have two paintings in the Dorchester vault to prove it."

"Unfortunately, Irma has met Hess, and that will look bad. Shall you deny that you met him, Irma?"

"I suppose I shall have to," said the wife. It was the first time she had opened her mouth. "It'll be difficult, for I've told so many friends about having visited Berchtesgaden and met the Führer. I probably mentioned that Hess was in the room."

"I don't see why you should bother to deny anything," ventured Lanny. "It was long ago, before the war. You were my wife, and I went there on business. I was trying to sell the Führer some Detaze paintings, and shortly afterwards I did so; also I purchased a couple of Defreggers for him in Vienna."

"I suppose we can get away with that," said the worried husband. "I hate like all damnation to have that old stuff raked up."

"I don't see why it should be. Just lie low and refuse to say a word to the press. See some of your friends in the government and let them present the story officially, in such a way as to protect you. They ought to be glad to do it, for the last thing in the world they want is to give the impression that there is a strong peace movement or appeasement sentiment in this country."

"I suppose that is so," assented his lordship, but without any great conviction.

"You're in position to try a little polite blackmail on them. Make them see that they're all in the same boat with you and Irma."

Said Irma: "What I hope is that Hess will fall into the Channel!"

XI

There followed for the three persons a period of suspended animation. Lanny tried hard to interest himself in a best-selling novel, but without success. His lordship would go out to inspect his plantation—the estate had become that—and after half an hour he would come back and find his wife at the radio. "No news yet," she would say. They would wait five or ten minutes, and then Ceddy would try again. It was like waiting for a thunderbolt to fall.

Their imaginations were occupied with all the possible things that might be happening to Walter Richard Rudolf Hess, on land and in the air and in the sea. These were unlimited in number. At this moment he might be leaving Germany, or trying to and failing; he might be in the act of being shot down, or floating in the sea, or parachuting to the land; he might be ordered away to Yugoslavia or Greece; he might be dead, or quietly eating breakfast, lunch, or dinner at home; he might be the center of the world's greatest sensation one minute from now, or he might never be heard of again. In short, there was nothing to do but wait until the thunderbolt had fallen, and then you would know where it had hit—unless it happened to hit you!

It would be years before the man in the street knew the whole story, but the Wickthorpes, being insiders, got it more quickly: a few shreds here and a few patches there, over a period of a week or two. When they had fitted them all together, this is what they had:

On May 9, the day Lanny received the four-word note, the Number Three Nazi had gone to Augsburg in Southern Bavaria, to deliver an address to the workers in the great Messerschmitt plane factory there. He took the occasion to inspect some improvements in the Me-110; he had taken a solo flight in this new fighter, designated "F," and was so pleased that he had decided to enjoy another flight on the next day. He spent the night with his friend Willi Messerschmitt, and on the following afternoon he appeared wearing the uniform of a captain of the Luftwaffe. He made sure that there was a tankful of gas, and that the guns of the plane were unloaded. Then he took off—and the worried Willi never saw either him or the plane again.

The adventurer must have flown northward, avoiding the Channel, which the German flyers called *Niemandswasser*—No Man's Water. He crossed the North Sea and approached Scotland from the east. Was it by accident or design that this same hour was chosen for one of the fiercest bombing attacks upon London? Some five hundred tons were unloaded, and as a result the most intense activity existed in the underground plotting room of the R.A.F. Fighter Command. New waves of bombers were being reported every few minutes, and when an isolated station on the eastern coast of Scotland announced an unidentified plane it was naturally guessed that it must be British. A few minutes later came a second report: the solitary plane had failed to identify itself, and its speed proved it to be a fighter.

That Scottish coast was a long way off, and fighter planes didn't get there—not if they were expecting to get back. In the plotting room of the Fighter Command was a large table that was a map, and when a hostile plane was detected a red pin was stuck in, with a tiny red arrow indicating the direction of the plane. For British fighters to take off in pursuit of such a plane was a matter of seconds, but in this case the defenders received an order never before and perhaps never since given in this war: "Force him down, but under no circumstances shoot at him!" Two Hurricanes were soon on the trail of the plane, and the air was full of radio: "Don't shoot him down! Don't fire a shot!" The pursuing pilots could hardly believe their ears.

The stranger got almost all the way across Scotland, to the west coast. The gas supply gave out before it quite reached its goal, and the flyer took to his parachute. Striking the ground, he wrenched one ankle, and by the time he had managed to extricate himself from the parachute cords, there was a farmer standing over him with a pitchfork, demanding to know whether he was British or enemy. His reply was that he was a "friendly German," and unarmed, so the farmer helped him to the house. He gave the name of Alfred Horn, and said that he wanted to see the Duke of Hamilton, whose great estate was near by; or if the Duke was not at the estate, he wanted to see the Earl of Wickthorpe, whose shooting box must be somewhere in this neighborhood. Home guardsmen of the neighborhood had arrived at the farmhouse, and one of them hurried to telephone the Duke of Hamilton's estate. This Duke, as it happened, was a Wing Commander of the R.A.F., and was not at home; instead, there was a group of B4 agents at the place, knowing that Hess was coming, and ready to take him in charge. It was they who had set this trap and baited it—and they had caught the biggest prize of the war!

XII

The first word that came to Wickthorpe Castle was from Gerald Albany, Ceddy's friend in the Foreign Office. It was early in the morning and Gerald was telephoning from his bedroom. "Ceddy, what is this I hear about you and Hess?"

"*Me* and Hess? What do you mean?" His lordship had had plenty of time to rehearse his role.

"Have you heard that Hess has flown to Scotland in a plane?"

"Good God, man! What are you saying?"

"Came down in a parachute. He says he was looking for you at your shooting box."

"Gerald, the man must be insane. I never saw him in my life."

"You haven't written to him, or sent him any messages?"

"Absolutely not."

"Somebody has probably told him that you favored an understanding. You are positive you haven't had anything to do with it?"

"Nothing—unless of course you count the fact that Lanny Budd has talked to him. And you must not mention that."

"There will probably be somebody out to see you about it before long. The whole thing seems very mysterious, and I suspect there's more to it than I have been told. I advise you to be extremely careful in talking about it."

"There is absolutely nothing that I can say, except what I have told you. The Red newspapers have been associating Wickthorpe along with Cliveden, as supposed-to-be appeasers, and maybe Hess's agents have swallowed that and reported to him that I would be the right person to approach. But it's the maddest thing I ever heard of in my life."

So there it was. Ceddy and his wife, who hadn't slept very much, talked it over and then called Lanny to the Castle. There was not a word over the radio or in the morning papers; obviously, security was involved, and the Government would wait until they had got all the data and prepared a story to suit them. Lanny was advised to go to his cottage and keep himself inconspicuous, which he did.

In the course of the morning came two men who identified themselves as representatives of Intelligence, and they gave his lordship a respectful but thorough grilling. When Ceddy denied that he had ever sent any messages, directly or indirectly, to Rudolf Hess, he was taking a risk, for Hess might have stated that Lanny Budd brought such messages. However, Ceddy would say that Hess was lying, and Lanny, if he was ever put on the griddle, would say that he had merely reported to Hess the opinions he had heard Ceddy expressing to guests at the Castle. Oh, what a tangled web we weave when first we practice to deceive!

This was Saturday morning, and week-end guests were coming. Lanny said: "Someone will surely have heard the rumors, and they won't want to talk about anything else. Because they know that I am Rudi's friend, they will make me a target for questions. So perhaps I had better go back to town."

Irma said: "I hate to send you back under the bombs, Lanny." But there wasn't very much grief in her tone, and Lanny knew it was an *au revoir*.

He told her: "I have business in New York. I'll wait in London just long enough so that I won't seem to be running away."

"Do, for God's sake, be careful what you say, Lanny!"

"I have got my lessons down pat," he told her. He didn't say what a skillful liar he had become, or how he hated it. What a relief when the beast of Nazi-Fascism breathed out its last poisonous breath, and a P.A. could become an honest man again, and say what he really thought! Would he have forgotten how?

XIII

He packed his belongings and went up to town. All the rest of Saturday he stayed in his hotel; he read all the Sunday papers, but still not a hint about a mysterious Alfred Horn who had landed by parachute in Scotland. Wartime secrecy was like a great blanket laid down over this sceptered isle, this precious stone set in the silver sea.

Until Sunday mid-morning. Then the telephone in the room rang, and there were two gentlemen to see Mr. Budd: Mr. Fordyce and Mr. Alderman. The operator didn't say "from B4," but many voices said it in Lanny's brain. He requested that the gentlemen should be brought up, for of course the conversation would have to be private.

Mr. Fordyce was middle-aged, somewhat rotund, well educated, and presumably a university man. Mr. Alderman was younger, and more grim; he did little talking but much watching, and Lanny guessed that he was the athletic member of the team, on chance that the suspicious person might attempt resistance or flight. But Lanny, a charmer from way back, soon convinced them that he enjoyed hearing himself talk. He had the advantage in that he knew more than they knew, or at any rate more than they knew he knew.

They informed him that they were from Intelligence and showed him their badges; he assured them he was happy to meet them, and would answer all their questions to the best of his ability. He realized, he said, that he had laid himself open to suspicion by coming from Germany. Yes, he had left there less than a month ago. He told about his business, which he had carried on for many years; he had a portfolio with correspondence about paintings he had bought for clients in the States; the paintings were in the hotel vault and he would be happy to show them—very lovely, and positively not war loot, having been in Germany for a century or two. Yes, he had met Reichskanzler Hitler; had known him for some fifteen years. Yes, he knew Reichsmarschall Göring, and also Reichsminister Hess; he had sold paintings for Göring, long before the war, and he had carried on psychic experiments with Hess.

Questioned along another line, the art expert explained that he took very little interest in the war; that was not his field. But he had met important people all over Europe. He happened to be the son of Robert Budd, of Budd-Erling, and had been his father's assistant for almost thirty years. When World War I had broken out, the father had been caught in Paris without a secretary, and the son at the age of fourteen had answered telephone calls, decoded cablegrams, received visitors, and shared all the secrets of the European representative of Budd Gunmakers. "You understand, gentlemen, my father is now working day and night fabricating fighter planes for Britain, and building immense factories in which to fabricate still more planes. If it should happen that I picked up some information on this subject in Germany and took it back to my father, that is a matter which you will surely not expect me to talk about."

XIV

This duel of wits went on for a couple of hours. B4 had done a quick job on Lanny Budd—or else they had been watching him for some time. They knew about his visits to Vichy, and to Paris and Madrid and Lisbon. Why had he stayed so long in each place, and whom had he seen there? Lanny had his story, carefully studied and many times rehearsed; but somehow it didn't altogether satisfy the suspicious Mr. Fordyce. "It would appear, Mr. Budd, that when you go to a city you are more interested to visit the political personalities than the artists and art collectors."

"I visit both," replied Lanny. "It is through my father's lifelong friendship with political personalities that I am able to get introductions and privileges of travel. When I went from Vichy to the Cap d'Antibes to see my mother, I traveled on my own and it cost me nearly ten thousand francs. But the second time, I called on Admiral Darlan, whom my mother and father have known for some twenty years, and the Admiral put me on a government plane to Marseille."

"And your interests are purely artistic and social? You don't ever by any chance carry political messages?"

"It is a question of phraseology, Mr. Fordyce. Admiral Darlan and Marshal Pétain tell me what they think; and when I come to visit my little daughter at Wickthorpe Castle, I find that visitors there are interested to learn what these important Frenchmen have told me. Naturally I do not refuse to talk. I believe in peace and mutual understanding, and say so wherever I go. If you have the idea that I am a paid agent, let me inform you that I have never received one farthing, one sou, or one pfennig, for the carrying of what you call 'political messages.' "

"But you sell art works for political personalities, and receive large fees from them?"

"I receive the customary ten per cent commission on sales, mostly from the purchaser, and never from both sides. As a rule my clients are wealthy Americans, and they pay the commission. When Herr Hitler asked me to find him a couple of Defreggers in Vienna, he paid the commission. That was prior to the war."

"You spoke of selling the paintings of Marcel Detaze."

"Marcel was my mother's second husband, and died in battle for France twenty-three years ago. He left a couple of hundred paintings, which are the joint property of my mother, of my half-sister Marceline, and of myself. I have been selling them as occasions arise."

"Our information is that Marceline Detaze is dancing in a night club in Berlin. Is that so?"

"She *was* dancing there. What she is doing at the moment I am not sure."

"Did you see her when you were in Berlin?"

"I was told that she was somewhere near the eastern front, with her friend Captain Oskar von Herzenberg. I am not pleased by that friendship and made no attempt to see her."

"But you saw her in Paris, where that friendship began?"

"Oskar is the son of Graf von Herzenberg, who was connected with the German Embassy in Paris, and whom I have known for some time."

XV

Yes, indeed, they had done a thorough job on this son of Budd-Erling, and it was evident that they were extremely suspicious of him. Lanny wondered where they had got their data. From Ceddy and Irma? From Hess? From Lord Beaverbrook? From some of the many guests at Wickthorpe over the previous week-end? It was to be assumed that at least one of them would be an informer, reporting to B4 on the doings of the appeasement clique. Also, many socially prominent persons had fled from Paris to England, and these, too, might be useful in affording information to the British authorities.

Mr. Fordyce had so far avoided showing any special interest in Lanny's dealings with Rudolf Hess. But Lanny could be sure that this was the occasion for the inquest; so he told about the Deputy Führer's interest in psychic matters, and how they had together consulted the famed Professor Pröfenik in Berlin, and how Lanny had brought the Polish medium, Madame Zyszynski, to Berchtesgaden to try some séances. That made quite a story, involving many of the departed Nazis and pre-Nazis: Bismarck and Hindenburg; Gregor Strasser, murdered in the Blood Purge; Dietrich Eckart, the Führer's old crony whose bust was in the *Braune Haus* in Munich.

"So the basis of your friendship with Hess is the spirits, Mr. Budd?" Was there a slight touch of irony in the question?

"I don't say that they are spirits, Mr. Fordyce. They call themselves spirits, but I am always careful to state that I don't know what they are. They make their appearance, and they say things that the medium cannot normally know; to me they are a psychological mystery, and I wish some scientist would find out what they are and tell me."

"You think that Hess is such a scientist?"

"Alas, no, I am afraid he is a dupe most of the time. My interest in him has been due in part to the fact that he so ardently desires an understanding with Britain. You know, doubtless, that he was born in Alexandria and received an English education."

"Yes, we have a dossier on him."

"I have no means of knowing how much you know. Hess told me that the Führer has made up his mind to attack Russia next month, and he, that is Hess, was frantic to get a settlement with England before that time. He even went so far as to say that he might fly here in an effort to contact friends who were sympathetic to his ideas."

"What did you tell him on that subject?"

"I told him that the idea was fantastic, and that I was afraid he would be shot. He answered that he would come in uniform and in an unarmed plane."

"Did you tell anybody in England about this?"

"I had been told it under a pledge of secrecy. I never took the idea seriously—I mean, I didn't think he would do it. If he was unarmed, he couldn't do any harm except to himself. I am wondering now, has he by any chance come?"

"I am not permitted to answer questions, Mr. Budd; but if you read the newspapers, you may get your answer tomorrow morning."

XVI

At the conclusion of this interview the skeptical Mr. Fordyce informed the American that unfortunately it would be necessary for him to be held under what was technically known as "house arrest." They would have to ask him to remain in this hotel room until the authorities had had time to consider Mr. Fordyce's report and decide about the case. The telephone would be removed, and Mr. Alderman or some other representative of Intelligence would remain on duty outside the door. Lanny smiled amiably and said: "What if there is an air-raid alarm?" The unsmiling answer was that Mr. Alderman would accompany him to the shelter. No visitors would be permitted and no mail coming or going; but he would be permitted to order meals to his room, and to have newspapers.

Lanny wasn't worried about the outcome, for he guessed what it was going to be. Three or four hours later the well-mannered agent returned, and informed him with sincere regrets that it was the decision of the authorities that they could no longer permit him to remain in Britain, or to return there until the war was over, and perhaps later. Politeness required Lanny to show distress, but inwardly he was amused. "How am I to see my little daughter?" he inquired, and all Mr. Fordyce could suggest was that he might take his little daughter to the States, or meet her in some other country if he wished; under no circumstances might he return to the British Isles.

"And how am I to travel?" inquired the undesirable personality.

"That is a matter for your own choice. How do you prefer?"

"I greatly prefer to fly."

"Very well, it will be arranged."

"The sooner the better, for me."

"Quite so, Mr. Budd. What route do you choose?"

"Say by Ireland and Bermuda?"

"Unfortunately, we have no control over Eire. How would Iceland and Newfoundland do?"

"Fine," said Lanny. "I had a yachting trip by that route twelve years ago." Lanny was tickled to death, for he was all ready to go and this gave him A-1 priority. Some military man or diplomat would be kicked off, and he would take the seat! And all without having to move a finger!

"You understand," said the Intelligence man, "the trip will be at your expense."

"Oh, surely. How shall I get the money from the bank and where shall I pay it?"

"You will be escorted. The plane will undoubtedly leave in the morning. I will notify you as soon as I have made arrangements."

"Thank you very much," said the P.A. "Let me add that I appreciate the courtesy you have shown in this unfortunate matter."

"Not at all, Mr. Budd."

The agent rose to leave, and Lanny couldn't resist a small bit of devilment. "Permit me to make a proposal, Mr. Fordyce. A wager."

"A wager, Mr. Budd?"

"Just a small one. If I am not in England within three months from today, I will remit you a fiver, and you can take your lady to dinner and a show. On the other hand, if I am back again you will blow me to a dinner."

The other looked at him sharply. Then, after a pause: "I suppose you are meaning to tell me that we are making a mistake in this matter."

Lanny grinned. "That is something about which I have to leave you to speculate. But how about my wager?"

"I'm afraid it wouldn't be quite what you Americans call 'protocol,' Mr. Budd; but if you do come, I hope you will not fail to let me know."

Who ever said that the English have no sense of humor?